At This Place
At This Time

Marcella Vineis

At This Place
At This Time

Published by

At This Place, At This Time

Published by: Stella Libri

Stella Libri
P.O. Box 643, Riverside, CT 06878
E: stella.libri@gmail.com

Cover Illustrations and Design: Brian G. Kammerer

Printed in the United States of America
May 2017

ISBN-13: 9780692886014
ISBN-10: 069288601X

For My Dad
You were the best father this girl could ever wish for

Acknowledgements

My DEEPEST AND heartfelt thanks to the following people, without you this journey would have been far less exciting.

Amy, you are my childhood friend and cheerleader from the very beginning. It took just one random conversation during a short road trip in the dark of night, to reinforce this lifelong goal.

Kidd, my fellow writer and Catskills enthusiast, your advice, encouragement and ease of all things publishing allowed me to appreciate this adventure even more.

Lisa, I'll always remember the phone call when I read you the first chapter. Your candid and positive reactions stayed with me along the way. Love to you always my sister-friend!

Jenene, your reassurance to keep going has been greatly appreciated. And for yours and Sid's assistance with the Spanish dialogue, *Muchas Gracias!*

Ellen, your energy and enthusiasm has always amazed me. I respected and valued your complete and very honest input. You better get going with your book.

Glenda, your own writing pursuits persuaded me to think I can really do this. And thank you for introducing me to your husband Brian.

Brian, you are a truly gifted and talented artist. Thank you for creating the view from the ridge so perfectly. It almost seemed as if you snuck into my brain one night while I was sleeping.

Brandon, when you were just a week old and I held you in my arms; I never could have predicted calling you many years later to school me in astronomy 101. *Baci e abbracci!*

Jason, I doubt you or I will ever forget the phone exchange discussing those tender sweet nothings in Spanish. And neither will the patrons sitting beside you at the hotel bar. *Besos!*

Alison, throughout this process, you endured my joys, my hopes and my anxieties. Your friendship went above and beyond.

Giuliana, fin dall'inizio, il tuo ottimismo e la passione hanno alimentato questo fuoco. Sono grato che sei un sognatore come me. Spero che un giorno questo libro verrà tradotto in Italiano per te.

[Right from the beginning, your optimism and passion fueled this fire. I'm thankful you're a dreamer like me. I hope one day this book will be translated in Italian for you.]

Joey, for being a supportive big brother as I pursued this to the very end, now it's your turn!

Mark, for my other older brother and Diane, my "sister", for your love and for sharing your two most valuable and cherished creations with me.

Gena and Julia, my two favorite chickie chicks in the whole world, the sound of your laughter always fills my heart with joy. Never stop uncovering the amusing aspects of life and always pursue your own dreams.

Mom, thank you for holding my hand on our walks to kindergarten, your constant love and your words of support. Promise me, when reading the steamy parts *remember to forget* the author is your daughter.

Thank you to the people of Venezuela, for making my visit unforgettable. I hope the turmoil in your beautiful country comes to an end, so you may begin to reform, prosper and live in peace.

My friends from Panama, memories from so long ago, with a dear friend and caring family, inspired the spirit for this delightfully imagined love story. You all have remained close in my heart.

Many thanks to Hal Leonard LLC, for the permission to use the lyrics for the songs mentioned in chapter seventeen. Receiving your letter allowing the excerpts from these songs was one of my most cherished highlights during this process.

My greatest appreciation goes to Billy Joel and Rod Stewart for writing these timeless and authentic songs.

Author's Note

At This Place, At This Time is a story I only dreamed I could ever write. But for one reason or another, I lacked the confidence and motivation to create, until now.

Many years ago, I travelled to the countries of Venezuela and Panama. My youthful and impressionable heart was immediately enchanted by the people, the cultures and the landscapes. These influences still lingered in the corners of my mind over two decades later. So when I decided to try my hand at writing a romance novel, I immediately knew these locations were my starting point. And much to my surprise, what began as a simple tender love story transformed into something even more charming.

Thank you for taking a chance on this unknown author. I hope you enjoy reading *At This Place, At This Time,* as much as I loved imagining it.

Marcella Vineis

*At This Place
At This Time*

Chapter 1

THE AFTERNOON SUN warms my skin caressed by a crisp autumn breeze. Hearing the leaves slowly build to a crescendo I close my eyes, breathe deeply and raise my arms into a letter V. Inhale and exhale, inhale and exhale, slowly opening my eyes I am invigorated to continue my journey. With each step I hear the crackling of branches and dried leaves beneath my feet. Ahead I notice a sign pointing me towards the right and I read, one more mile until my destination. Although I'm sure I've walked this trail before, today it feels like it's the first time I'm here. Now back on track, I follow the dirt path and wonder how many others have passed this way before me. With the incline growing steeper, I feel my stomach fluttering with excitement as I know the peak is just a short distance away.

I hear voices but with the wind rustling the leaves again, I am unable to sense whether the voices are ahead of me or on another path. I continue following the tree markers and pick up my pace. One more stretch of incline and the peak should be just ahead. Grabbing onto a tree limb I climb up to get better footing on some rocks. After settling on more solid ground, I turn around to see where I had just been. Looking down into the forest I see a couple of chipmunks darting around the spot I was just at a mere minute ago. Shaking my head thinking, had they raced across my path, I may have let out a yelp. I watch the chipmunks for another minute and continue towards the peak. As the sunlight is shining brighter on the path, I know I'm almost there. I begin to hear the voices again. Maybe I'll be joining other hikers at the top.

This part seems too steep for me so I take a few steps off the path to find an easier route. Just as I'm about to climb onto an entry boulder I get that feeling that someone or something is watching me. Slowly I turn to my left and I don't see anyone and now looking to my right I see something crouching down near a tree about five yards away. I try not to panic. Do I keep looking towards it to figure out exactly what it is? Or do I try to find a way to escape. I am paralyzed. Taking short quiet breaths as my heart is racing but my arms and legs have stiffened. As if instinctively my body knows not to move a muscle. Without turning my head, my eyes gradually shift towards the figure. Initially I see the fur and spots on its coat and presume it to be a mountain lion or bobcat.

The animal is looking down and licking its right paw. Maybe if I stand still, it will forget about me and go away. Or maybe it's hurt and is treating the wound with natural first aid. Or maybe it's licking its paw like when humans clean their forks in preparation to enjoy a meal.

I hear the voices again. But now it sounds like just one voice. But why don't I hear footsteps? If I can only hear footsteps maybe my feline friend will hear them too and run in the other direction. I just can't stand here all day. I try to remember what they say when you encounter an animal in the woods. I recall one should slowly back away. Don't make sudden movements and never make eye contact. The eye contact part I'm not completely sure of that, so, I'll focus on the animal's front legs. This cat has now stopped with the licking and jerks its head to the left. Maybe it's heard something.

I begin to walk backwards very slightly while the cat's attention is somewhere else. As I take my fourth step, I feel as if I can't go any further. I move my left arm behind me and sense I'm against a wall. I don't remember that being there before. As I try to assess my next move I hear a voice above me.

It's a man's voice. He whispers, "Don't be frightened, I'm here." I feel my body quiver and my mouth suddenly is dry. "Stay very still. I will tell you what to do." As I focus again on the bobcat, I see it looking directly at me. And it opens its mouth, I think it's about to growl, but it merely licks its chops. "You're doing fine. We'll get through this together. When the moment is right I will give you my hand. You will have to trust me. Do you understand? I've got you."

As I'm listening to this voice and watching the bobcat begin to move closer to me a muffled sound surrounds me. Like a distant metal drum. The first three beats are very low and then it stops.

"Just another minute and this will all be over. Leave no time to spare, do you understand? Every second counts. You will not get hurt. I promise you. I am here."

The tapping of the metal drum begins again. The beats are growing louder. The curious cat is now a few feet away from me. "Are you ready?" I lick my lips and swallow and finally have the nerve to say to my hero, "Yes, I am ready."

As the fur on the cat's spine rises up towards the sky, I hear the drums, Ping – Ping – Ping and then a shot from a gun, BOOM, and louder, PING – PING – PING and then I see the stranger's hand come down in front of me. "Take my hand!" he yells. "Take my hand!" he yells again. The cat stands frozen staring at me, but he doesn't look like he's been shot. "NOW! Take my hand!"

PING – PING – PING. I grab the hand and it shockingly lifts me up towards the boulders at the peak. While still grasping my hero's hand I look down and see the bobcat running away deep into the forest. As I begin to steady myself I look up towards the sun and am thankful my hero let the cat live.

The drumbeats are louder and faster. I want them to stop. Please make them stop. My hero's voice whispers in my ear, "I told you to trust me. You did beautifully, even better than I expected. We're the perfect team you and me."

At that exact point, I realize I know my hero. Tears begin streaming down my face, the beats continue. I wipe my eyes on my shirt and spin around to finally look at his handsome face. My eyes open to gaze upon him and I see sunlight filtering in through my bedroom curtains. I shut my eyes.

Ping – Ping – Ping. I know I can do it. In just a few seconds I can get back there. Ping – Ping – Ping. I open my eyes again and reach for my alarm clock. I press the snooze button and the drum beats stop.

Just relax, inhale and exhale. You know how to get back. Just fall asleep again. I try to return to my dream but now the clatter outside my windows invades my bitter sweet slumber. I just want to see him, it's been too long. His voice buried deep inside my heart, I hear it only when I'm dreaming.

Chapter 2

For as long as I can remember, I have deemed Fridays as the cheeriest day of the week, the day that holds the promise of possibilities. Whether I have a jam-packed weekend of fun planned or two days of spontaneity. Whatever my passion, I know the following two sunrises will be welcomed with my most tranquil and blissful breaths.

Swinging open the storm door I extend my right leg to keep the heavy door from slamming against me, as I slide the key in the lock I'm instantly comforted to be finally home. Managing inside I place the grocery bags on the kitchen floor as I flip on the light switch, tossing off my shoes while making my way back to the front door. My hands chilled from the early spring temperature I rub them together for warmth. I proceed to secure both doors and with my back pressed against the inside door I close my eyes and listen. Ah, complete silence, my favorite sound after a long work day.

It's a fine way to start the weekend, nobody asking for my fashion advice, ideas for gifts for a loved one or arranging ensembles for their vacation wardrobe. Tonight it's just me contently alone in my home. Most times than not I find solace in the silence. I break my minute of meditation to put the groceries away. All the while thinking what should I make for supper?

My stomach isn't growling yet, so I have awhile to decide. I pour a tall glass of water and gulp about three mouthfuls when I stop to catch my breath. I guess I was thirstier than I thought. Ah, another simple pleasure; clean drinking water. I never can understand people who say they don't like the taste of water or when some say, I rarely drink water. When I hear that, it first makes me feel less guilty for the eight plus glasses I have per day. And I also wonder how their bodies function without this natural resource. With another refreshing swig I walk up the stairs to my bedroom to change my clothes and adjust the thermostat along the way. It's a cool sixty degrees in here and the forecast for the evening calls for a bone chilling twenty-five.

Once in my bedroom I turn the lights on and draw the shades and curtains. I change into my house uniform and giggle at the thought. My brother Evan once said that to his wife and me while I was visiting them. But it was after he gently insulted a gift I gave him that previous Christmas. It was a teal blue cotton crewneck sweater. I told him if he didn't like it he could return it. And he simply smiled and said, "I do like it just not enough to wear it in public." Followed by, "It's soft and comfy and better to wear as my house uniform." I smirked and then shook my head. So, I thought, I shouldn't feel that insulted. He'd probably get more use from the ugly sweater than most other clothes he wears once or twice a month. And when he wears it almost every day, he'll think, "Ah, my loving sister and this hideous sweater."

Most of my house uniforms are a result of clothes that I bought and wore too much and have faded or pieces that I bought and never did quite match with other counterparts in my wardrobe. I like to call them the misfit clothes. If anyone saw me in these outfits they would highly doubt that people pay me to help dress them. Tonight's uniform is made up of grey flannel pajama pants, purple and white polka dot thermal shirt and a powder blue fleece jacket that's missing the zipper toggle and can only be zipped from the inside; and finally, the added cuteness to the ensemble, cuddly soft purple socks and wool slippers.

Washing my face I admire my hair in the mirror. I just love this season, my otherwise rebellious brown wavy hair in the humid summer months behaves in the crisp cold temperatures and my neat morning blowout stays the same all day. Pulling it up and away from neck and face with a hair tie I am all set for my relaxing Friday night at home.

Now downstairs in the living room I switch on a table lamp and wonder if it's a movie or DVR night. I turn on the TV and check what's been saved on the DVR. To my surprise I have two episodes of my favorite soap opera, a couple of sitcoms and dramedies. Now that I know my choices I will try to figure out what to eat.

I'm really not that hungry so I decide on soup and salad. I start the preparations to make my Italian grandmother's *risi e bisi* soup also known as rice and green peas. With the soup cooking on the stove I begin to clean, chop and slice some fennel, peppers and tomatoes for the salad.

While I wait for the soup I remember I haven't checked the mail. Sifting through the pile I left on the table I sort between catalogues, magazines, junk mail and real correspondence. I see a couple of bills to put aside and throw away the junk mail. And while thumbing through a clothing catalogue I hear my mobile phone ring. Now where is the phone? Oh, I haven't taken it out of my purse yet. I unzip the bag and find the phone and glance at the name of the caller.

It reads, Henry Morales mobile. I swipe the phone to answer. "Hello, *Hola* Enrique such a nice surprise to hear from you."

"Hello Emelia, thank you, I'm so glad to reach you." Henry's now Americanized subtle Panamanian accent is always a joy to my ears.

I reply, "How is everything?"

"Everything is good. I wasn't sure if I'd get you on the phone on a Friday night."

I laugh a bit and then say, "Henry, most Friday nights you will find me at home. How are your wife and the boys?" For a moment, I've forgotten his wife's name, that's right it's Olivia.

"They are very good, thank you for asking. How is your family? How is your mom?"

I smile and tell him, "My family is good too and especially my mom. Thank you."

I ask, "When are you planning a trip north? I'd like to see you and your family again."

"Well, that's why I'm calling. We mailed invitations yesterday I don't think you've received yours yet. But I wanted to call before you do." I quickly tell him I hadn't received the invite yet.

"We're planning a surprise birthday party for Frida and my family wants you there as the special guest. I know it's been a long while since you've seen my sister and we were hoping you'll be able to go. In fact we will gladly pay for your flights and hotel for the visit."

My heart flips a bit and I find myself smiling. While checking on the soup, I give it a stir and lower the heat. I take a breath and say, "Henry, I would love to see you and Frida and all your families. And it has been way too long since we've all gotten together. You have enough to deal with so if I agree to come, you won't need to pay for my travel, although I sincerely appreciate the gesture. When is the party?"

"You might remember my sister's birthday is in July, but we thought to completely surprise her, we'll have the party in May. We've arranged it for the Sunday of Memorial Day weekend. Do you have plans yet?"

I think for a moment and I tell him quickly, "No, I am free so far." I hear a voice near Henry ask him, "Can she come?" And he responds, "Yes, she's free that weekend."

I go to the stove and give the soup another stir, put a lid on the pot, turn off the flame and move it to a cold burner. I ask, "Was that Olivia?" and he says, "Yes." "Tell her I said hello. Henry, where will the party be held?"

"Oh at a club my parents belong to in Panama City." I respond, "This sounds like a big to do. How many guests have you invited?"

"Well, you only turn fifty once and we want to celebrate Frida, about seventy-five guests. We don't think all will come. Many are old and won't travel and others may have other obligations. But we know, once Frida sees you she'll want to be only with you and catch up. So, do you think you can plan to stay a few days following the party? Frida would be so sad if you left shortly after."

"Henry, I would be more than happy to spend as much time with Frida and everyone else. You and I saw each other just last year, but all the others, I haven't seen since Christmas over twenty years ago."

My eyes begin to water and I get a lump in my throat. I say, "Tell me when should I get there and when I should leave."

I hear him talking with Olivia. "Emmy, I will call my family to discuss and then get back to you. Now that we know you're coming, we will make more plans for your stay. I can't wait to tell them. Do you think you'll be able to stay in Panama for a week?"

Without giving it a second thought I said, "Yes I can stay for a week. Henry, let's just leave it now that I will arrive a day or so before the party and we'll all wait to decide when I should return home after you've talked it over with everyone. I don't want you or your family to over commit."

I hear him laugh a bit. "Emelia, you are almost like family. And since they haven't seen you in ages whatever plans we make for that week, you will join us. In fact, we're all planning to make a vacation of it. I will call you again this weekend so you can start looking into flights. I'm so excited that you'll be part of the celebration. And I know my family will be too, especially Frida."

I say even more excitedly, "Henry, your call tonight has made my day, my weekend, heck even my year! I too can't wait to be part of Frida's celebration and to visit with the family. I look forward to your call so I can finalize my flights. Have a great evening and give hugs to Olivia and the boys from me."

Henry replies, "Yes, of course, hugs back to you and I will call you on Sunday, bye."

"Bye."

Pressing end on my phone I place it down on the counter. I take a couple of steps to the kitchen table and sit on the soft chair cushion. While resting my chin on my hands I am smiling from ear to ear. I let out a giggle and with both pinkies tapping on my cheekbones I breathe in and let out a very happy breath. As I cover my eyes with my hands, thoughts jump from Frida, my dear friend Frida, birthday party, flights, vacation, hotel, birthday gift, Luca and clothes. And back to Luca. I move my hands off my face and sit straight up in my chair and exhale.

He'll certainly be there. Twenty something years has been a long time. What will I say, what will he say? Is he still married? He wasn't married when we were last together. But over the years, Henry has kept me informed of the family and told me Luca is married and has two children. And I know who he married.

My mouth all of a sudden is parched and my throat begins to tighten. I find my water glass and take a long sip. Walking towards the cabinet I remove a bowl for the soup. Ladling the steaming soup I sprinkle a generous amount of grated Asiago cheese on top and rest the bowl on the placemat on the kitchen table. The soup is too hot at this point to enjoy, so I begin to stir it a bit with a spoon.

A week, maybe I shouldn't plan for a week. Henry said the party is on Sunday. I can arrive on Friday night or Saturday. And leave on Wednesday or Thursday. I think staying there five days should be more than enough and that way I won't infringe on the Morales family's total vacation. Plus if I begin to feel awkward around Luca, which I'm sure I will, I can bear it knowing I'll be leaving soon.

Too much to think about and some of these thoughts are not worth considering. I take a spoonful of soup. Yum, now that hits the spot. As I sit alone in the kitchen enjoying the rice and the peas, the silence is overwhelming. It keeps me returning to thoughts about Luca. I must not think about Luca. I must not think about him.

Grabbing a tray I fill it with the dinner plates and go to the living room. I sit on the floor for my picnic style dinner and flip on the TV to find yesterday's soap opera on the DVR.

Ah, my guilty pleasure, my escape. At least I won't think about him while this is on. The show begins and I get lost in the lives of the residents of Port Charles.

Chapter 3

————————— ⟲⟳ —————————

I WAKE THE next morning from a restless night's sleep. Thankful it is Saturday and I have a clear agenda. After showering and eating breakfast I turn on my laptop to check prices for flights. They seem pretty reasonable and with many options. Once I hear from Henry I will make my reservations.

My next item of business is Frida's birthday gift. What do you get someone you haven't seen in over twenty years? I find myself opening the doors of my bookcase and pull out a few photo albums and journals. We met in the early 1990's through our mutual friend Phil. The first couple of albums are from the last fifteen years. Pushing other books aside I finally locate the album titled 1989-1994. As I flip quickly past the photos from 1989 I am taken back to Phil's phone call on one autumn afternoon. I close my eyes and I can almost hear his voice.

⟲⟳

I was still living at home with my family in Queens, New York. Phil and I worked together at a financial firm before I left for the fashion world. We hadn't seen each other much since I left the company. I thought maybe he was calling to make plans to meet up that week. And after that call, I so wished it was that simple.

Frida and Phil became friends a few years back when they met at college. They both studied business, but equally shared a passion for art. That summer they were working at developing their own company with another friend of theirs, Nathan. Phil and Frida had just signed a lease for a studio apartment in Manhattan. I was so thrilled for them to begin this chapter in their lives. As Phil continued to talk, I realized those plans will have to pause for a while.

Sadly, they hadn't heard from Nathan for a few days that week until Nathan's mother called Phil last night. She told Phil her son was in a car accident and died from complications due to his injuries. I didn't know what to say. And I remember it wasn't as if I had a break to ask too many questions, because Phil continued to talk to me. He said he received his papers. Immediately I knew what that meant. Early that summer he informed me that with the pending Gulf War, as a reservist he might be called to duty. He wasn't sure, but it remained in the back of his mind for the last few months as well as mine. I asked him when he was notified. He told me just that afternoon.

I closed my eyes and they filled with tears. In a matter of twenty-four hours he learns of the death of his friend and is informed he'll have to return to the military. And as if that wasn't enough to tell me on the call, he said, "This is why I'm calling you Emelia." He's such a dear friend of mine and I'd do whatever he asks of me. I remember just saying, "Phil, I am here for you, what can I do?" He starts off with saying, "I know you only met Frida a few months ago, but she considers you a close friend already. With Nathan's death and with me leaving I am worried about her. Can you check in with her while I'm gone?" I said, "Of course Phil. I would have, even if you hadn't asked me. When is your deployment?" He told me not for a few weeks and that he would be stationed stateside, much to my relief. He thinks he'll only be gone for a couple of months. We exchanged a few more thoughts and ended our call. I didn't realize from that call how much our lives would change.

I have now found some photos of Frida, Phil and me. I think these were taken before he left. And there are pictures of me and Frida at their apartment followed by some other pictures with her brother Henry when he came to visit.

A couple of weeks after Phil departed for South Carolina, Frida and I made plans to get together for dinner in Manhattan. Since I worked in the city it was easy for me to meet up afterwards. They lived in a studio apartment in Greenwich Village. Frida had insisted I stay over so that I wasn't commuting home late to Queens. When I arrived, she gave me the grand tour. The apartment was a good size for being one room. When I entered, there were a couple of closet doors on the left, the bathroom on the right, followed by the small kitchen. On the left there were bookcases near the steps that led up to the living area. This open area was a combination dining room – living room - bedroom. There was a round table with a few chairs in the left lower corner and a bed across from the table in the lower right corner. Across the room near the windows there were two comfy chairs and a futon. Frida and Phil had a platonic relationship. But the more time I spent with them, I could see that before he left, their connection was developing into something deeper.

I dropped my overnight bag near the futon and sat in one of the chairs. We made plans to eat at a Mexican restaurant nearby. It felt a bit strange to be with Frida without Phil. But when dinner was over and we walked back to the apartment I noticed our conversations continued with such ease. We changed into pajamas and made up the futon bed for me. It was fairly late in the evening and we kept laughing about how much both of us were yawning. We turned in for the night with Frida in the bed and me in the futon. As I lay there waiting to fall asleep I was surprised at how quiet it was in the city. And then Frida interrupted the silence, "Emmy, are you sleeping yet?" I giggled and said, "No Frida, not yet." She said, "Thanks for coming to visit me. It's been so mundane here without Phil. I can see why you two are such good friends. You are so easy to be with and you make me laugh. Tonight I had a chance to forget about all that's been going on. I just wanted to tell you that before you fell asleep." I lay there in the dark with a smile on my face. I said, "Frida I am so happy to be here with you. Thank you for saying those things to me. I wasn't sure at first if we could get along without Phil here. But as the hours passed this evening, I felt so comfortable being with you. As if we were friends for years. Thank you." We said our goodnights again and shortly after I fell asleep.

I'm not sure when we woke up the next day, all I remember is, we stayed in our pajamas all day. Frida cooked us breakfast and lunch. And we talked and laughed. She brought out her photo albums. It was a great way to meet her family that I heard so many stories about. She began with her father Rodrigo, nicknamed Rico, he was born in Panama and is an architect and her mother Claudia, born in Italy and later moved to Venezuela after meeting Rico at college in the U.S. She is the mother of five, a homemaker and church volunteer.

And there were her brothers all four of them. Rafael or Raffy, Luciano or Luca, Nicolás or Nicky and her baby brother, Enrique nicknamed Henry. Raffy was becoming a teacher, Luca was working in finance, Nicky was in medical school and Henry was at a college in the states.

I saw pictures from when they were babies and until present day. Smiling I think of one picture that Frida showed with her and her siblings. She remarked, "We look like we're from two different families." I looked closer and I knew what she meant. She and Raffy had dark eyes, dark straight hair and deeper skin tones, just like their dad. And Nicky, Luca and Henry resembled their mom, with their auburn brown wavy hair, bluish green eyes and lighter complexions. But when you see them all side by side their bone structures and body shapes showed they were an interesting blend of their parents.

She shared some funny stories and some touching moments. I remember this other picture, she asked me before she showed me, "Tell me the truth Emelia, do you think my brother is handsome?"

I noticed like most people, when she called me Emelia, it meant she was serious and wanted my complete attention. She began to show me a picture of Luca. I studied his picture and saw a guy maybe in his twenties with brown wavy hair, ocean blue eyes, a very nice physique and a slightly imperfect perfect nose. "Frida, why do you ask?"

She smiled, "All of my friends back home have fallen in love with him. I just wanted to see if he has the same effect on American girls."

I giggled and thought, oh he does, that he does. I tried to cover up my attraction towards this man I don't know, "Well, it's hard to tell in a photo, with it being so one dimensional. I will have to say, sorry, but without knowing him personally I don't know if he's my type. Is Luca a fighter, tell me the story behind his nose."

And then she laughed and smiled a huge smile. "Luca, a fighter, he's the nicest guy I know. My brother is a swimmer he swam before he could walk. During one of his competitions another swimmer elbowed him in the pool and blemished his almost flawless face, funny that you focused on that."

"Well, it gives him more character. I'm sure one would get very bored looking into his blue eyes."

"Emelia, you said he's not your type."

"He's not my type; a man that handsome instantly breaks hearts just when he enters a room."

After that weekend at Frida's place we became best friends and acted more like sisters. I remember one instance we were getting ready to go out and pointed to our similar features and then our not so similar features and laughed at how different we were. We both had dark brown hair and big brown eyes with vibrant smiles, that's where the similarities ended. She was petite, about five inches shorter than me and with perfectly straight hair. Our skin tones were shades apart. No matter our physical differences we connected on various levels that it felt like we were friends from the beginning of time.

We visited so many museums. With her being an art enthusiast it was like I had my own private tour guide. With her telling me stories of the artist and their works. I remember seeing Monet's Water Lilies with her. And she suggested that I stand across the room from the series and close my eyes a bit. And then she began to tell me that when Monet was painting the water lilies it was when his eyesight was deteriorating. Even now when I visit the Museum of Modern Art I make my way to Monet's Water Lilies and admire them with squinted eyes. And those special moments with Frida return.

We would walk all over Manhattan. From downtown to uptown, there were few neighborhoods we didn't explore. And at night, we would either find a new restaurant or return to a favorite. Our late night fun included bars and dance clubs. On occasion we'd include Frida's friends. One night her friend Alex and his boyfriend asked us to meet them at this club called Monster. I hadn't been to a predominately gay dance club so I was both curious and excited about going. After one night at Monster, we made this a regular spot. For two women who really just wanted to dance and not get hassled by straight guys, this was the best. And there was rarely a line for the ladies room, a total win-win.

And while our friendship was growing, we made sure to include Phil in our excursions by writing letters and calling him. Finally, twelve weeks had passed and he was coming home. I see pictures of when we met him at the airport and he was wearing his uniform and sporting a buzz cut. I remember even though his hair was short and he slimmed down a bit, his infectious smile immediately met us in baggage claim. After several hugs, kisses and happy tears we all drove to Brooklyn to have dinner with his family.

Life after that for Frida and Phil drastically changed once again. Sadly Frida's student visa was about to expire at the end of the summer. They were also trying to get their business off the ground while working with an immigration lawyer.

Frida's family was pressuring her to return home. By that July, I guess her family succeeded. Frida boarded a plane to Panama to start a new chapter in her life. We wrote letters frequently in the beginning, but then they tapered off. I would see Phil a couple of weekends each month. I think it was very hard for both of them. I sensed they had fallen in love. And although I think they would have opted for a quickie wedding. Their relationship needed more time to develop before getting married.

The letters I exchanged with Frida I thought seemed like a constant reminder to her about the life she left behind. And so like any good friend, I let our relationship get some distance so that she can build a new life there. By the next winter she called me on my birthday. I was so surprised to hear from her. And during that call she told me she was engaged to be married. She asked if I would go to her wedding. And the following months, my life was all about my trip to Venezuela.

⟶

I close the photo album and realize most of my Saturday afternoon was spent looking at pictures and reminiscing through my journals. After completing some chores and running errands I meet up with my friend Jenene for dinner.

We manage to have a great catch up on life when I finally tell her about my upcoming trip. She seems as excited as I am to have this reunion with Frida. And then we plan for us to go shopping together for outfits to take with me. She knows when it comes to my own wardrobe I am fashionably challenged, more specifically I dress too conservatively or boring as she once described. And I'm grateful for her support.

The next day I hear from Henry and we plan out my itinerary. I will arrive on the Friday before the party and leave the following Saturday. I was hesitant about committing to a full week, but Henry was hard to disappoint. He informed me we would be vacationing with the whole family so plan on a week of parties, dining, dancing and outdoor fun. And they will be taking care of my hotel arrangements. I told Henry that was not necessary and he said his family insists and it won't be for the full week because we'll be leaving the city on Monday for their vacation home.

With the trip just eight weeks away, I've got some shopping to do. I call Jenene and we are set for next Saturday for our field trip to the mall.

I go online to price the flights and settle on a nonstop flight that leaves on Friday afternoon and arrives in Panama City on Friday night, with the return flight departing Saturday morning and arriving back home that afternoon. The fare is reasonable and I process the tickets. I quickly email Henry with my flight details.

I check the hotel he mentioned. Wow, the Westin Playa Bonita is right on the water. I know what I'll be doing the day before the party, soaking in the sun at the beach. Oh no, is it really that time of year again? I wanted to drop these pesky pounds from last year and haven't. Could I possibly trim down in eight weeks? I certainly can try.

I call Jenene and postpone our shopping spree and explain I want to shed some weight before I buy new clothes. She laughed at me and understood. With all my plans in place, I call my mom and I tell her the good news.

Chapter 4

Six weeks of strict dieting and exercise and I'm ready to go shopping. Friday has arrived and the doorbell rings. Opening the door I see my tall slim ravishing crimson haired friend Jenene with an overnight bag in hand. I'm so glad, since it will take hours to sort from the clothes I have and shop for the outfits I will need.

"Hola! Qué tal?" [Hello, how are you?] I say to her, trying to get back to speaking Spanish before my trip.

Jenene laughs at me and exclaims as she walks into my home, "Hey, what a day I had, I'm hungry and I need a drink."

We order from my favorite Greek place EOS. And while we wait for dinner to be delivered, I set the table when I ask, "Jenene, what would you like to drink?"

"What are you having?"

I show her a bottle of rosé wine that was chilling and she says, "I'll take a glass too."

We discuss the past few weeks and I mention that since I bought my airplane tickets, I have been dieting and hitting the gym almost every day. She applauds my efforts. I laugh and say, "Thanks. Not everyone can have your perfect body. But some of us can strive for it."

"Oh please, mine is far from perfect."

I shake my head, "I've got eyes Jenene this is what I see, long slender legs, curves where you want them, a very cute tush and as the guys would say, a pretty nice rack."

She smirks and says, "Oh I've got eyes too my friend and when you actually show your legs, they are shapely, you too have the curves, a sweet rack and a very fine ass."

The doorbell rings, "Oh good, we can change the subject, our dinner has arrived."

We arrange all the containers on the table. "How many trips have you taken to Panama to see Frida?" Jenene asks.

"I only visited Frida in Panama once for Christmas and the year before that I went to Venezuela for her wedding."

Jenene smiles, "Ooh, a wedding. What was the wedding like in Venezuela? Was it similar to here?"

"Jenene, that's a bit of a story, let's start eating and then I'll fill you in. And after supper I can show you some pictures too."

We each take portions of salad with chunks of feta cheese and grab a couple of the spanakopita. Once I've enjoyed a few forkfuls of the delicious food I begin to describe to Jenene when I first arrived at the airport and located Frida outside customs.

⁓

It was the summer after my twenty-third birthday. This was my first trip to South America. I remember my flight arrived late at night. Once I was in the terminal I looked at the signs, most were in Spanish and some were both in Spanish and English. I was so tired that I just followed the passengers from my flight through the airport arrival checkpoints like baggage claim and customs. And after finally getting through all that, I walked out the security doors with my luggage and saw at least a hundred people waiting behind those divider barriers. Everyone was smiling and waving. Some children were even jumping up and down. And as I scanned the crowd I found Frida's little face smiling back at me and she was waving and calling my name. I walked around the groups of people to get closer to Frida and as soon as I approached her I dropped all my bags and we hugged each other immediately. I was so happy to see her. It had been over a year since she left and I was relieved to be in her good hands in this foreign country. After our emotional hellos Frida began to introduce me to a couple of the men that were standing with her. One man was tall and slim, olive toned complexion with dark wavy hair and golden brown eyes. Frida said, "Emelia, I want you to meet my fiancé Maximo."

I extended my hand to Maximo and smiled and said, "I'm so pleased to meet you Maximo." He took my hand and then pulled me into a hug. Maximo said, "I'm so happy to finally meet you. Frida has told me so much about you. Please call me Max."

The other man standing nearby was introduced as Max's friend Bruno. He wasn't as tall as Max, with an average build, lighter skin tone, straight brown hair and brown eyes. I extended my hand to Bruno and he hugged me too. I said, "Nice to meet you Bruno." They both took my bags and I walked alongside Frida as we made our way to the parking garage.

Max drove with Bruno sitting in the front passenger seat while Frida and I sat in the back. She pointed out different things and kept saying, "Tomorrow all of this will look completely different to you."

We got slightly lost in an area called Petare and in those days I recall we hoped not to be lost there for too long. Frida told me that we will be dropping off my luggage at the hotel and then walk across the street to her brother Luca's apartment. Her aunt, Tía Ada will be at the hotel too and we're sharing the room with her. And her father Rodrigo will meet us at Luca's apartment.

We arrived at the hotel. It looked like a nice place with the exception of the two security guards standing at the entrance with rifles secured across their chests. We made our way quickly up to the hotel room where Tía Ada was waiting up for us. From the moment I was introduced to her, I felt like she was my own aunt. She stood about five feet tall. I think she may have been even shorter than that. Copper colored wavy hair, brown eyes, olive skin and about sixty years old. And she wore eyeglasses. She mainly spoke Spanish to me but also said a few words in English. Tía Ada was wearing her pajamas and told us she is too tired to join us at Luca's place. I freshened up and we left a few minutes later.

We joined Max and Bruno who were waiting for us outside the hotel room and walked across the street to Luca's building. At the entrance to the building there was a panel of doorbells. Frida pressed the button for Luca's apartment. And we waited to be buzzed into the building. But nobody buzzed us in. We waited a couple of more minutes and then we saw Frida's father opening the door for us.

I remember a slim man about 5'10" with salt and pepper hair, dark brown eyes and a warm inviting smile like my own father's smile. Everyone said hello and we walked into the lobby of the building. Frida said, "Papá, let me first introduce you to Emelia."

He turned to me, "Hello Emelia." I extended my hand to him and said, "Hello Mr. Morales, it's wonderful to meet you." While taking my hand in both of his, he said, "Emelia, please call me Rodrigo or Rico. And it's a pleasure to meet you. Frida has told us so many nice things about you." I smiled at him and glanced over to Frida. She was smiling too.

We found our way to the elevator. Rico asked Max and Bruno if we encountered traffic from the airport and Max timidly told Rico we got slightly off track. Frida laughed and said, "We got a bit lost, but here we are now." We arrived on the third floor and Rico lead the way down the hall. He briefly knocked on the door and the door slowly opened. We entered into the dimly lit kitchen where Frida's brother Luca was standing waiting for us.

Immediately Luca looked at me and exclaimed, *"Bienvenidos a Venezuela Emelia."* [Welcome to Venezuela.] I smiled at Luca and said, *"Muchas gracias Luciano."* [Many thanks.]

I remember his voice was deep and calming. And when I looked in his eyes, I felt like my legs melted into the earth. He stood a bit taller than his dad, with brown wavy hair parted to the side and a nice physique with very broad shoulders. I noticed a little cleft under his endearing smile. From that first impression I knew my trip to Venezuela had made a sharp detour.

Frida interrupted my dizzy haze and said, "Luca, Emelia doesn't speak Spanish." And Luca raised his eyebrows and smiled at me and said, "Welcome to Venezuela Emelia." I replied, "Thank you Luca, but I did understand you."

Luca showed us around the apartment and suggested we wait for him on the terrace. Frida and I walked out to the terrace and we stood by the edge. She said, "Don't worry we won't stay for too long. My father and brother couldn't wait to meet you. And they begged for me to bring you over tonight." I said, "Frida, I'm fine, we can stay as long as you want. I'm in vacation mode now."

The rest of the group joined us too. Luca asked us all what we wanted to drink and Max and Frida followed him back inside to help collect the beverages. I noticed Luca stopping at his stereo and shortly after I heard the tune of a very familiar song. He returned to the terrace and said, "Emelia, I hope the music makes you feel at home. I'm playing Springsteen for you." I smiled at him and said, "Luca, I thought it was Bruce. Many thanks." He smiled and went to the kitchen. Bruno smirked at me and said, "Are you a big Springsteen fan?" I replied, "Yes, he's one of my favorites. But I like many singers and bands." Bruno added, "I wonder how Luca knew that." I replied, "Well, I think it was a lucky guess since he knows I'm a girl from the Northeast. Most of us like Bruce."

Bruno went over to talk with Rico. I took a moment alone to listen to the music and enjoy the view from the terrace. I giggled to myself thinking about Luca and how he pronounced Springsteen with his thick Panamanian accent.

I wasn't alone for too long when I heard Luca's voice nearby. "Can I interest you with a glass of rum?" I don't typically drink straight rum but I thought I might as well try. He had two rock glasses filled with dark rum and ice on a tray. I took one, he took the other and he said while raising his glass to me, "Let's celebrate your safe arrival and your first night with the Morales family."

We looked into each other's eyes, bumped our glasses together and sipped some rum. And he turned to everyone on the terrace and said, "And to my sister Frida and her future husband Maximo, let the wedding celebrations begin." We all tapped our glasses with one another. With each sip of rum I slowly began to appreciate the taste.

Luca had chairs arranged on the terrace and a hammock hanging in the far corner. Most of us sat on the chairs and Luca rocked in the hammock while chatting with his father who sat near him.

While Max and Bruno were joking around, I noticed something quickly move near our feet. I looked down and saw it was a huge water bug, aka cockroach. While I grabbed Frida's elbow to show her, the bug started crawling over Bruno's left shoe.

Frida yelped and said, "Bruno, move your foot there's a bug on it." He kicked both his feet up and we watched the bug fly into the air towards Luca and Rico. Frida and I both shouted, "No!" and started giggling.

At which point Luca jumped up and said to Frida in a stern voice, *"Que pasa?"* [What's up?] Frida had to stop laughing to answer him and finally said, *"Fue una cucaracha."* [It was a cockroach.]

Luca's expression was a mixture of both surprise and annoyance. Quickly he spotted the bug and stepped on it. We applauded his fearlessness and I whispered to Frida, *"Luciano Morales, el eliminator de cucarachas."* She screamed with laughter which caused Max to inquire about what I said and Frida told him. It wasn't too long until everyone heard my silly comment. And Luca came over to us and stood near me with his hands on his hips and looked directly at me. With a mischievous smirk, he said jokingly, "I thought you didn't speak Spanish." We all laughed again and raised our glasses to Luca our gracious host and hero.

It wasn't long after that when we decided we should go to the hotel. Frida informed us all we'd have an early start the next day. Rico was staying at Luca's home and embraced me and said, *"Buenas noches."* [Good night.] I repeated the same to him. Luca walked us to the elevator and embraced Frida and kissed her on the cheek. With the bright hallway lights I suddenly noticed Luca's slightly imperfect perfect nose. In person you wouldn't notice it unless you were looking for it. Simply the bridge of his nose had a minor curve or bump and while focusing on it I realized it just draws you to his beautiful blue eyes.

After saying goodbye to Frida he kissed me on the cheek. I said, "Buenas Noches Luca. Thank you for a fun night and it was wonderful meeting you." He smiled at me and said, "The pleasure was all mine, it was a joy to meet you Emelia. I will see you in a few days in Valencia." We boarded the elevator and waved goodbye to Luca as the doors closed.

On the ride down to the lobby I kept thinking about how he pronounced my name, "Eh-mee-lia" and the way his tongue lingered on the l.

Frida and I quietly got ready for bed so we wouldn't disturb Tía Ada. She was snoring gently and we were thankful we didn't wake her. As we climbed into bed together, we whispered goodnight to one another. Lying there, I thought about my first few hours with Frida and her family in Venezuela and smiled as I replayed the night over in my mind. And just before I fell asleep I thought about Luca. Little did I know this was the first of many nights when I would think of him before I went to sleep.

Chapter 5

JENENE SCREAMS EXCITEDLY, "Emelia, why haven't you told me about Luca before? And when do we get to the good part? Like do you and Luca hook up? And I want to see pictures."

I smile at Jenene and chuckle a bit. "I haven't told you because this happened so long ago. And although I had the time of my life it just hurts thinking about that trip and him."

I take a sip of wine and continue. "I was so young, we were so young. I shouldn't have cared about anyone else but Luca and me. I blew it by being nice and honorable. Ah well. Want dessert?"

Jenene sits there with a confused look and says, "Yes and wait. You can't just end the story there with filling me with dessert. I want to know more. I want to know everything. Let's clean up the kitchen and then tell me what happened next."

I shake my head and say, "Ok Jenene. I hope you know what you're getting yourself into. This could be a long night."

We start clearing up the dishes and put the leftovers in the fridge. I glance at the clock and it's almost nine in the evening. "Jenene, why don't we put on our pajamas, that way when you fall asleep as I reminisce, you'll already be in your pj's," I said with a sarcastic tone.

She responds, "There is no way I'm falling asleep during this story, I am eager to hear what happens next with El Señor Hottie."

After changing, I head downstairs to the living room and look for a few compact discs to play. Jenene enters the room while I'm searching through my collection and I ask, "Am I the only one that plays CDs these days?"

She laughs and says, "I managed to upload most of mine but I didn't have as nearly as many as you. Is that cabinet filled with them?"

I roll my eyes and say, "Yes and this one too. Hey, that's just how it was back then, you bought CDs. I think I've only transferred or uploaded about a quarter of my collection. Anyway, I'm looking for the music I got when I was in Venezuela. I figured it would add to the fun."

I find a few and load them in the player. Jenene asks, "Can I see the cases?" I hand them over to her. "Oh my gosh, my parents have this one, Juan Luis Guerra, Cuatro Cuarenta."

I purse my lips at her and say, "Thanks Jenene for making me feel so old around you." She laughs, "I didn't mean it that way. Well, we listened to this *Bachata Rosa* album a lot many years ago. I know most of the songs on this one."

I said, "So do I. But I need to have them translated again. When I first listened to them it was before the internet was the internet of today. So, I asked a colleague at work to translate the lyrics for me. I can't imagine if and where I kept those notes." I also grab the photo album. "Before we continue, what do you want to drink? More wine or move on to the soft stuff like coffee and tea?"

Jenene says, "More wine for me."

I dash to the kitchen and grab our glasses and fill them. With the music playing, we get comfortable on the couch and I open up the album to the photos of my trip.

I recall the next morning, Frida, Tía Ada, Max, Bruno and I set out for our day in Caracas. There aren't many pictures from that afternoon so I decide to give Jenene a brief summary about that day. "I'm not sure why I don't have lots of pictures from that day, I guess I was taken by all the sights and our activities that I just focused on what was happening."

She smiles, "Was the attractive blue eyed distraction around maybe?"

"No, he wasn't, don't you remember his parting words to me? I'll see you in Valencia." I add a bit of Luca's accent to that part for Jenene.

"Ha! Yes, that's right. You may continue."

"Thank you."

"I thought maybe we would run into him because we checked out of the hotel that morning and brought our luggage to his apartment. We saw Frida's dad, but Luca was at work."

"I bet you were disappointed."

"I was and I wasn't, I mean I only had just met him. I do remember feeling some butterflies though should we run into one another. Anyway, that day, we went to a museum, followed by lunch at an outdoor café. It reminds me of this odd memory of seeing the waiter retrieving all the meals from a dumb-waiter that opened up on the side of the building."

Jenene looks at me curiously when I ask, "You know what a dumbwaiter is, right?"

She nods, "No, what is that?"

"It's like a little elevator that transports food from one floor to another. So the waiters don't have to run up and down the steps."

"After lunch we did some shopping, of course, and then returned to Luca's to get our things, pack the car and drive to Valencia."

"Did you see Luca before you left?"

"No, I didn't see Luca again until Friday. And I believe this was Wednesday. I can't tell you much about the drive sadly, because once Max got us out of the city, I think I fell asleep. It wasn't that long of a trip and before I knew it, we arrived in Valencia at Frida's parents' home." As I continue to show Jenene pictures, she allows me to tell her more.

⸺

When we got there, I remember seeing iron gates surrounding each house. Back then, that wasn't very popular here. But over the years, I've seen that type of home security more and more. The Morales house was a brick three level building with a terrace on the second floor.

While we were making our way to the front door we heard someone shout, "Fridacita!" We all turned and saw a platinum blonde haired woman about sixty years old. Frida exclaimed, "Oh, Tía Ines!" And they kissed and embraced.

Tía Ines made her way to Tía Ada and Max. And then Frida introduced me and Bruno to Tía Ines. The front door to the house opened and Henry yelled to us, "*Hola*! I thought I heard voices out here." Henry came out to greet us and their mom Claudia followed too. It was quite a welcome.

Claudia like Frida stood about five inches shorter than me. She wore her golden brown hair in a cute bob and had blue eyes. After the kissing and the hugging we all went into the house. Claudia gave Tía Ada and me a tour of the home. The first time I looked around at the rooms I liked it. It was a combination of Italian Tuscan, Venezuelan and Panamanian. And as I recall, the longer I was there, I truly began to appreciate the beautiful treasures Claudia had accumulated over the years. If I was there longer, I would have asked her to tell me where she collected them. Every day I found something else I liked.

After our tour, Claudia showed us into the dining room. She prepared dinner for us that evening. After we ate, Frida, Max and Bruno helped me bring by bags and Tía Ada's to Tía Ines' house. She had guest rooms for me and Tía Ada during our visit to Valencia. Her house was only a few doors away. The layout was very much the same as the Morales' home with three levels and a terrace with the kitchen and common areas on the first level and the bedrooms on the second and third floors. Tía Ines showed me to my room. It was a very spacious pretty room decorated with pinks and florals with a full size bed in the middle, an armoire and night tables on both sides of the bed. Tía Ada was in the room next to mine. I was honored to have a room to myself. I quickly unpacked my clothes and we drove Bruno to his temporary home away from home. I was also thankful to be staying so close to Frida's house.

We planned a night out in Valencia. Frida, Max, Bruno and I went to a restaurant called Cuevas de Luis which means caves of Luis. It was true. When you walked in, the place looked like a brightly lit cave. I enjoyed the atmosphere and the music. We didn't stay for very long. Max was anxiously waiting his family's arrival in Valencia. The Garcia's were travelling with Frida's dad. When we got to their hotel, they hadn't yet arrived. Since the night was young we drove to the Intercontinental Hotel and took seats in the lounge overlooking the pool and listened to the music. I danced two songs with Bruno. I had no idea what we were dancing to, but we had fun. Bruno was a fairly good dancer. He had a forceful approach that lacked a smooth flow. Then again maybe I was challenging to lead. We called it a night and drove Bruno to his place. When I arrived at Tía Ines' I quietly went through my bedtime rituals and fell asleep the minute my head touched the pillow.

"Do you think Bruno liked you?" asks Jenene. I smirk at her, "I don't really know. I just saw him as Max's friend. We were pleasant to each other and the four of us had a good evening."

Jenene squints at me, "But he was no Luca." I giggle, "You are correct, he was no Luca."

Jenene stands and stretches, "Let's get to the part when Luca arrives." I roll my eyes and say, "Alright, I'll quickly tell you about the next day and then move on to Fun Luca Friday!" She claps her hands and says, "Yes! Let's go."

Thursday was a day of eating, shopping and eating some more. Claudia had both families over her house for a lunch buffet. And then Frida and I went out shopping for some things she needed for the wedding. I think it was more of a distraction to keep her busy; for when we returned, Tía Ines was having a little party, like a bridal shower at her place. So we ate more. And later that night, Frida and Max brought us all to Frida's friends' house for drinks, us being Max's siblings, Bruno and me. We didn't stay there too long, we knew we had to get up early the next day for the beach. I recall Frida telling me to be prompt, because Luca wanted to leave at nine o'clock sharp.

Either I was excited about going to the beach or I had a good night's rest, but I woke up earlier than planned. I wrote a little in my journal and then got ready for the beach. I recall that when I was getting ready, my monthly friend had arrived. Of all days, I had to start my period on the beach day. Thankfully I was prepared. Anyway, I went downstairs and all the ladies were around the table and Tía Ines insisted I have breakfast. I didn't want to be late, but I didn't want to be rude. These ladies were dressed up and wearing lipstick at breakfast and I was wearing almost no makeup, shorts, a t-shirt and my bathing suit underneath. I wondered where they were going. But my Spanish speaking skills were lacking. While I ate I figured if everyone was waiting on me at Frida's house, surely they'd send someone over to get me. So, I relaxed and enjoyed the meal.

When I finally headed over to Frida's house I didn't see anyone out front. As I approached the front door, I realized there wasn't a doorbell. So, I knocked on the door. After waiting a few minutes, I stepped away from the door and just under the terrace yelled up, "*Hola! Hola!*" I walked over to the door again hoping someone heard me and would be greeting me. Another couple of minutes passed and nobody appeared. Two things came to mind, either they are all still sleeping or they left without me. I knocked on the door again and walked towards the front gate to tap on it. And thought if anyone was watching me I would feel like such a fool. I tapped on the gate again and still no answer. And while I waited with my head down I thought what if Luca is watching me and getting a good laugh out of this American girl. I then looked up towards the terrace and found myself looking into Luca's eyes. Embarrassed, I smiled and said, "*Hola.*"

With his hands resting on the railing of the terrace he stood there like a statue and a smile appeared to greet mine. "Would you like to come in?" he asked in his very low voice. I replied, "Of course." He left the terrace and I saw Henry at the front door. Everyone was running around inside the house getting things ready to bring to the beach. I didn't see Luca again until we started packing the cars. He just appeared in front of the house in his car with the Garcia family. I was riding with Henry, Bruno and Max's brother Miguel.

We traveled about two and a half hours north of Valencia. This road trip with my fellow passengers was lots of fun and many laughs. We passed places named Las Vegas, El Palito, Moron and finally Tucacas and Henry said it meant "Your shit." Henry got us slightly misdirected. But that was fine. I had the chance to see more areas of the country. After that wrong turn we headed back on the right road. When we finally got on the last road to the dock this road was very bumpy and I could feel my insides wanting to come out. We were the last ones to arrive.

We were now at the Morrocoy National Park. We left the cars in the parking lot and there were about six boats waiting to take us to the island of our choice. Since I landed in this country as long as there were men around, I was told not to lift anything. But I tried helping anyway.

Luca spoke with the dispatcher and I believe paid for the taxi boats. I think there were about twelve of us and I was surprised we only needed two boats. I opted for the one less bumpy. I stepped onto the boat very carefully and to my surprise I did not tumble into the water. The boats were pulling away when I realized Luca was missing. I told Frida and she made them stop. I felt sorry for Luca. I hoped he didn't think we all forgot him. After all, he planned this excursion and has paid for everything so far.

We arrived on the island called Playuelita. We walked further onto the island to find our place under the coconut trees. I personally thought it was the perfect spot. Everyone dropped all their things down and started to take in the view.

Like a kid, Luca quickly removed his shorts and shirt and bolted into the water wearing only his swim trunks. He immediately immersed himself and swam away. I looked around to see if anyone else from our group was getting ready to swim. And when I turned back to check on Luca, I lost sight of him. In the distance I viewed a group of people swimming and saw a man swimming with the grace and form of a dolphin. I was mesmerized and jealous as I gazed upon this natural and confident swimmer.

I heard Henry nearby and he pointed towards my dolphin and said, "Do you see Luca out there?" I glanced at Henry and then back at the water and pointed towards the swimmer and asked, "Is that one Luca?" And Henry said, "Yes."

He swam a few more laps and returned to shore. As he walked out of the water with the sun sparkling around him, he looked at me and smiled. I heard him say, "The water is perfect. Are you going for a swim?"

While he shook out his hair I smiled back and said, "It looks inviting. I'll go soon." He said, "What are you waiting for? Just dive in."

We walked together towards the group so he could grab a towel. And while he was drying himself he looked at me, I guess waiting for a reply. Out there his eyes looked crystal blue like the color of the water and I almost forgot what we were talking about. And then I remembered and my entire body tensed for I knew I had to tell him something that would surely disappoint him. I felt like such a child.

I began with, "Well, I actually don't swim."

His happy face now looked confused. He asked, "Do you choose not to swim? Or do you not know how to swim?"

Gazing into his eyes gave me this sense that if I looked deep enough I could see into Luca's soul. I found myself obliged to tell him only the truth. I took a few shallow breaths and looked towards the water and then back at him and said, "I don't know how to swim."

"But why didn't you tell me earlier?" he asked with annoyance.

I glanced around and noticed the group was busy doing all sorts of things, unpacking, talking, drinking and resting. All the while I'm feeling embarrassed, I say, "Why would I even tell you? It's not a big deal. I've gone to beaches at home, Bermuda, Hawaii and I didn't swim there." Gosh and I never felt this awkward. I thought maybe I shouldn't have come.

Luca replied, "If you told me earlier, I could have brought something for you to float with and then you would have a fun experience."

I smiled at him trying to lighten the mood, "Oh thanks Luca but I assure you, I will have fun today. How can I not, I'm here at a beautiful beach with all of you." I was sure the expert swimmer that he was, could not believe me. And he finally dropped the topic when Frida walked over to us.

She asked, "So, what do you think of this place?" I smiled at her and said, "It's no Jones Beach, but it will do." Luca looked at both of us confused when Frida said, "Jones Beach is a place on Long Island in New York where Emelia and I have gone before." He nodded and left us to join the guys.

Frida and I walked away from everyone and spent awhile stepping in and out of the water. I wanted to say so much to her but I just couldn't get the courage. Here was someone who knew everything about me at one point in my life and I could not tell her all that was on my mind. I wanted to ask her if she was truly happy living back here and getting married. Maybe I just didn't want to know the answer or didn't want to dampen the day. Well, our talk was okay, but it was not like old times.

We spotted Max snorkeling and he swam over to us. We spoke for a little bit and then headed back to the others. I kept an eye out for the dolphin. He was nowhere in sight. I opened up my towel and sat down and spoke with Max's father for a bit. Frida's family thought of everything. I made a sandwich and sat near the water. I closed my eyes and started to relax listening to the waves nearby. Then Henry joined me. It was so good to be with him and catch up.

I finished my sandwich and got up to look for my camera. I took pictures of the view and I started looking up and noticed the coconut tree leaves. I snapped a few more shots of the trees when Luca called my name. He motioned to Bruno to take my camera to take a picture of me with him. I hesitated for a bit since I was not finished yet. So I quickly took a picture of Miguel and he said he will look like a native to all my friends. Then I positioned Bruno, Luca and Henry for a picture. Luca reached over and grabbed my camera and handed it over to Bruno. He insisted on a picture with the "foreign girl." I rolled my eyes wondering what I must look like. All of a sudden Luca grabbed my shoulder and moved me closer to him and we both smiled and heard the camera click.

As I walked to Bruno to get my camera, all the guys joked about having a picture taken with me. I laughed and said to Luca, "Now see what you started."

After the photo shoot was over, I walked away to take more pictures. And to my surprise Luca followed. I heard him ask me, "So, is this what you do instead of swimming?"

"Yes, one of many things I enjoy at the beach in place of swimming." He went on to ask me questions on photography. And I asked him about swimming. We really hadn't been alone together so it was finally nice to have a conversation just with him. Although a few minutes later it ended. He was hungry and wanted to make a sandwich. We walked and talked on our way back to the group. I joined him while he had lunch and we spoke about general things.

He asked me about photography again. And I shared with him my secret dream. "One day I'd like my photos to be recognized by others simply by my technique, form, style and subjects. So that when they see a photo, they easily will say, that's an Emelia photo. I don't want to be compared or up against other artists. Just stand out on my own. To me, I feel art is not a contest. It's not about the competition. In fact it's what I run away from. It's just about me bringing my view of the world for others to enjoy."

At the moment I mentioned the "C" word to Luca, his face lit up. I replied, "Wrong topic." He laughed at me and asked why. I smiled and said, "How can I go about explaining to you that I don't like to compete. When you seem like someone who thrives on it." He did not disagree but harped on how I know he loves competing. I told him, "I've never seen someone's face light up as yours did when I said the word competition." He laughed it off and asked, "How do you know this about me?" I giggled and said, "Oh that you like to be the winner, the best in everything, the leader? Maybe it was a lucky guess or it was so obvious to me the observer." He said, "Lucky guess." We spoke about other things but I sensed he kept his thoughts a little distant, probably fearing I would guess other traits about him and then he would go mad.

I got up and left him alone and walked along the water's edge to look for seashells and rocks. I noticed Luca also got up to take another swim and I followed him with my eyes. Bruno joined me. We walked for a bit and we turned around to walk towards our camp. I looked out to the water and saw Luca swimming in the distance. He is so easy to spot all the way out there especially when he does the butterfly stroke.

While I looked at Luca, Max called over to Bruno to play some sport with him. And Bruno left me and ran towards Max. I strolled passed the group and continued along the shoreline to hunt for shells on this end of the beach. I heard feet splashing behind me and it was Luca.

"Did you lose something?"

I smile, "I'm shopping, shopping for sea shells."

"Can I join you? And are you looking for any specific types?"

"No." And while nodding, "And yes, you can join me."

I began to feel more at ease with him. While I looked down and poked around the shells and rocks, Luca asked, "What do you do for work in New York?"

"I work as an assistant for a clothing designer."

"Do you like your job and the company?"

"Sort of and yes, I like that my job affords me the chance to have a life outside of work."

He smiled at me, "A college friend of mine lives in New York City. I haven't made the trip to see him yet, but I think maybe now I could free my schedule."

"You should have visited when Frida was living there. She had a great apartment in the Village. And then you could have had a taste of city living when staying with her." And I paused and said, "It would be great if you did plan a trip and if you want I can show you around."

"Maybe you can be my personal tour guide?"

I raised an eyebrow and said, "I think that could be possible."

We walked and talked a few more minutes and Luca said, "I'm grabbing a drink do you want me to bring one back for you?" I said, "No, but thanks for asking."

He walked away and said he'll be back. I was sort of glad; I still wanted to explore the shells. While I was in deep shell shopping mode, Bruno came from behind me and tried to scare me. I guess I'm not picking up shells today. We talked again and walked back to the others.

I sat near Henry and joined him in his "sandwich shop." He made some sandwiches and I distributed them. While he was making them, we were trying to remember funny diner sayings the staff would use when yelling their orders into the kitchen. We had everyone laughing at this point, especially when I said my orders in my overly emphasized thick Queens, New York accent.

When we were done I sat with Frida, Max, his younger sister Alicia and his mom. We spoke for a while and I was offered these great butter cookies that were rolled into cylinders and had chocolate in the center. I grabbed a couple and took them with me and found Luca relaxing on the blanket on his back. I stood near him and waved a cookie in the air and smiled. He just opened his mouth like a bird and I placed the sweet treat in his mouth. I also spotted Henry and fed him too.

Shortly thereafter it was about the time for us to leave so we all packed our things and headed towards the dock. Luca's boat was there and we waited only five minutes for our boat to arrive. I snapped some pictures of our return trip. We got back to our cars loaded them up and started the drive home. We made bets on when we would arrive in Valencia. Henry won. It was 6:30pm when we left and we arrived in Valencia at around 8pm.

We relaxed awhile when we got home. Tía Ines's daughter Gena and granddaughter Bella visited. I took their pictures. Bella wore Henry's hat in one. I called my mom and spoke with her briefly. It was weird talking to her since I really had not missed being home. I guess because I was being entertained. Henry spoke with my mom too.

After my call ended, I walked to the kitchen and found Frida and Max making their dinner. Luca told me he made our plans for the night, dinner and dancing and to be ready by nine thirty. I left immediately to shower and get dressed. I wore a light pink halter blouse with white jeans and tan sandals. When I left Tía's house everyone complimented my outfit. I was happy. I really didn't pack any party type outfits except for the dress for the wedding.

When I arrived at Frida's she and Max were eating dinner while Bruno sat with them and had a drink. They were telling jokes. I carried over a chair from the dining room and joined them. I asked Frida to help me write down some notes on my trip so far. And when we were finished Luca entered the kitchen. He asked if we were ready to leave. I think Henry was on the phone trying to get a date. But I didn't understand why. But then again I would be the only female to dance with all of them. In the end I was thankful they invited another girl out.

Luca, Henry, Bruno and I said our goodnights to Frida and Max. When we went outside Luca instructed me to sit in the front seat of the car. We drove to someone's apartment house. And before Luca got out of the car he remarked he was getting Bruno's date, Rita. Luca returned and opened the back door for Rita to join Henry and Bruno. Luca took the driver's seat and introduced all of us. He announced, "Tonight we will speak English for Emelia does not speak Spanish." Rita said, "Are you kidding me?" I guess I made her evening. I glanced over at Luca and smiled and then we were on our way to the restaurant.

We drove to El Canton restaurant, Henry's request. It was Italian food. Upon entering the restaurant Luca tells the host we have a reservation and we are lead into the dining room.

When we arrived the table was set for five with two on each side and one at the top of the table. I wasn't certain where to sit so I hesitated and Rita breezed past me and she immediately took her seat at the bottom corner. Henry said, "Luca always sits at the head." And he pointed at the seat to the right of Luca's and said, "Sit there Emmy and Bruno sit next to her." Henry sat on Luca's left and next to Rita, who was patiently waiting for us all to get settled. Luca appeared and took his seat. The arrangement was perfect. Even though the other three people were with us, there were moments I felt we were alone, Luca and me.

Luca assisted me with the menu as some items were easily understood but some I questioned. He ordered the wine for us. I wasn't hungry at all, which was strange, since it was late and I didn't eat much at the beach. We ordered appetizers and he suggested an entrée for me. Luca really gave me lots of attention. And I didn't mind at all.

When the appetizer arrived, fresh mozzarella and tomatoes I was still not hungry. I continued to sip the wine, it was very good. I talked and slowly enjoyed this first course. Taking small bites while hoping that everyone else would finish and the next course would be served. Then I noticed Luca watching me. He asked me in a whisper, "Do you not like what I ordered for you?"

I replied politely, "I do very much."

"Then why aren't you eating?"

"I am but I don't want to fill up too much before the main dish."

I saw the waiter preparing our pastas at the end of the table. I welcomed the distraction. I think Luca was trying so hard to please me he was not enjoying himself. The bus boy cleared our first course dishes. I was last to be served. The waiter presented my dish to me. Luca ordered me fettuccini with five cheeses sauce. It was a tremendous amount of food. I was sure it was going to be delicious. And I knew I would not finish it.

Henry led the conversation and while everyone dined on their meals we all laughed and talked about our day at the beach. Henry said, "Emmy, even though you don't swim, did you enjoy yourself?"

At which point Luca glared at Henry. I nodded my head at Henry and with a wide grin said humorously, "Yes Henry I had a fantastic day at the beach."

Luca said to Henry, "You really should think first before you speak." This obviously was not the right moment to bring up any swimming jokes. Then the two brothers engaged in an argument. Henry made a point about how Luca is always too serious and trying to be so right all the time. And Luca's argument was that he is Henry's older brother. And he is trying to give him advice about adult conversation. I felt sorry for Henry; I believed this was not the right occasion for such advice in front of mixed company. And I sensed Henry was embarrassed. I tried to help matters by saying something but realized I gained points with Henry which was good but lost points with Mr. Perfectionist.

After having at least ten forkfuls of pasta, I had to stop. Luca looked at me again and smiled. And while the others were talking, he disappointingly asked, "Why aren't you eating?"

I replied, "Because I am full." His plate was completely clean along with the others. I added, "If you didn't eat so fast you wouldn't be glancing over at my dish." I think he was now enjoying me or my humor at least. He had me right where he wanted under his watchful eye.

The busboy came to our table and I gestured to him to take my dish. Luca did not see me do that, so when the busboy came to take my plate Luca said I wasn't finished yet. I being the quick tongued American female said, "No, please do." And I looked at Luca and said, "I told him I was finished." Luca gave me that look again and shook his head. I can't imagine what he was thinking about me.

The waiter has now approached us about dessert. In normal circumstances I'd be the first to order dessert. But now my stomach is quite full and

I'm feeling a little uncomfortable too. Luca waved to the waiter to bring over the dessert cart for me. I thought to myself, oh no, now I must choose something. There were several decadent options.

I looked towards Luca for some support and said, "I can't have a dessert all for myself. Who is willing to share something with me?"

Henry said excitedly, "I'm not sharing my dessert tonight with any of you." We all laughed. Luca saved the day and said, "I might be willing to share with you. But only if we can agree on the same one."

With a smile and a giggle, I said, "Ok, let's see if I can figure out which one you want." With all the delicious desserts displayed so enticingly on the cart, I start my game. As I reached down to take hold of a cake server as my pointer, I asked the waiter, "May I?" And he replied, "Yes, Madam."

I first pointed at the chocolate mousse and looked to Luca and said, "Are you in the mood for chocolate mousse?" And his expression remained neutral. I took a quick look at Henry and he shook his head no.

Turning back to the cart, I pointed towards the strawberry shortcake. "This shortcake looks too rich for an Olympic swimmer type like you." Again, Luca's expression was unchanged. And Henry doesn't make a move.

I linger over the tiramisu and said, "If you didn't eat so much tonight, you would have room for this delectable delight." Finally, Luca laughed. And Henry smiled at me.

I then focused on the bowl of fresh strawberries. "Well, Rita and gentlemen, I believe I have found the winning dessert. We will take a bowl of those succulent strawberries with a spoonful of fresh cream on the side please."

At which point Luca started to clap his hands and raised his wine glass to me and said to the waiter, "Please wait, my lovely dinner guest is not completely correct nor is she wrong. Emelia, I too desire the strawberries, however, I must make a slight enhancement. Would you be open to swapping the boring cream for some rich vanilla ice cream?"

I smiled towards Luca, "For you, I think I could embrace that very rich modification."

And then Henry exclaimed, "Can we move on to our desserts now?" which was followed by a wave of laughter.

Everyone else got their own desserts while Luca and I enjoyed sharing our strawberries with vanilla ice cream. He leaned towards me and whispered, "You'll have to tell me later how you knew I very much wanted the tiramisu."

I smiled back and said, "We only just met, I'm not about to give away my secrets." And I dipped the tip of a strawberry in the ice cream and popped it into my mouth. Luca continued to gaze at me and said, "I hope everyone is up for dancing. It will give us a chance to work off this fine dinner."

After Luca paid the bill we left the restaurant and made our way to Mi Cabana. Upon entering I noticed the club had two levels. We entered on the first floor. The music immediately surged my energy. The group followed Luca along the dance floor. I almost lost sight of them while I was watching all the couples dancing. Some of them looked professional. And the ladies were wearing fabulous short dresses and high heels. So that when they spun around, the skirts lifted up a bit. It looked like so much fun.

I caught up with everyone at the base of the staircase. Luca said, "Let's go upstairs first and get drinks." So we all followed him. The second level was a balcony overlooking the dance floor. It was a great view. And there were tables also set up on this level. Some people were even dancing near their tables. It was such a party atmosphere. As I observed all around me, I wondered if I looked like a foreigner to them. I know I wasn't dressed for this type of place. I think of a few other outfits I could have worn that were all back home in New York. I convinced myself to not think about it anymore and just enjoy myself.

We stopped near some of Henry's friends. At this juncture, I decided to locate the "baño" bathroom. I asked Rita where they were and she pointed them out for me. As I got near to them one door had a letter "C" and the other a letter "D". I sort of thought I knew which one was which, but I panicked and walked back towards Rita. I asked her, "Which door is the ladies room?" She didn't understand my confusion so she walked with me to the restrooms. She opened the door marked "D". When I walked inside, I was still reluctant to believe she led me to the correct room 'cause I noticed a patron standing in front of the sink wearing a white tank top and had very short blond hair. From the back this woman looked like a man, so I thought Rita led me wrong.

Then I saw a woman exiting a stall. Once I left the stall and while washing my hands, I was thinking about what the letters meant on the door. And it occurred to me "C" was for "Caballeros" for men and "D" was for "Damas" for women.

I located Luca and he smiled at me when I walked towards him. "Do you like this place?" I nodded, "Yes very much. And the music is sensational."

A woman approached us who knew Luca. He introduced me. But she spoke only Spanish to Luca. I was more than fine with that, I wanted to watch the dancers below. From the inside, the club looked like it could be located on a ski mountain. The windows and glass ceilings were steamed up from all the body heat inside. I could almost imagine snow outside. Funny to have had that image while in Valencia.

Luca joined me again and due to the loud music he leaned close to my ear and asked, "What are you doing?"

I spoke close to his ear and said, "People watching."

"While you people watch, I'll go downstairs to get us a table. I'll wave to you when I find one, yes?" I nodded yes. And then Luca was gone in the crowd.

I spotted him again while he walked down the stairs. It was mesmerizing watching him from a distance. I wondered what it would be like if we dated. And said to myself, stop thinking those thoughts, you are here for just a few more days and then you'll be going home, far away from him. And just at that very moment he found a table and was signaling to me to join him. I waved back and started making my way towards the stairs. I'm here now and will have fun while this lasts. I felt like Cinderella wishing this night would go on forever. I passed Rita on the way and told her where I was going, she joined me.

We met Luca at the table and Bruno found us too. A new song started and Luca asked Rita to dance. Bruno and I took our seats to secure the table. We talked a bit about the club, the music and the people. And then Henry sat next to me. Luca and Rita came back to the table and Luca gestured to the waiter. After a few minutes, the waiter brought over a bottle of champagne and glasses. We raised our glasses and toasted our host Luca. And the men toasted Rita and me.

A new song was just starting, "Chica Fresa, please dance with me", Luca said shyly. I smiled while trying to figure out what he called me. I quickly took another sip of champagne and reached out to his awaiting hand. I was equally nervous and excited. I watched him dance with Rita and they both could move superbly together.

When we got to the dance floor Luca placed one hand firmly on my lower back and took my right hand in his left hand. He looked into my eyes and said, "I waited for a merengue, I thought it would be an easy dance for you to start with. Trust me Emelia, I'm a good dancer, you'll be fine."

And then he pulled me closer to him and our bodies were pressed against each other. I thought about a funny line from a movie, "And leave space for the Holy Spirit." And I knew that night there was no space for the Holy Spirit.

After a couple of knee knocking and toe stepping moments I was able to follow his lead. He wasn't just a good dancer, he was an exceptional dancer. We fit snugly together and the rhythms seemed to move us along the dance floor. He whirled me around and I could almost begin to sense his next move. This song, by Juan Luis Guerra, "A Pedir Su Mano" must have been popular, the dance floor was full. Some people bumped into us and other times, I could feel Luca steering me away from a potential collision.

The song ended and when the next one began he looked into my eyes and asked, "Good for another?"

"I'm game if you are. Before I forget, what did you call me before, Chica something?"

"Yes, Chica Fresa, you're my strawberry girl."

I giggled and said, "So, if I ordered the tiramisu I'd be Chica Tira?"

He smiled and nodded his head and whispered, "No."

While this song was playing our faces were pressed together as Luca sang the words for "Bachata Rosa" in my ear. Holding my hand in place on his chest made me remember when I danced with my dad and he would rest my hand near to his heart.

In that moment, I felt a calming current run through my veins as my heart was racing just being close to him. Right there among all those strangers I felt at home with Luca. While listening to words in another language as they're being sung in my ear, held in the arms of this charming man. We only met a few days before and yet he made me feel cared for. Reality reminded me moments like these can't go on forever. But it was certainly lovely and I made each second feel like an eternity.

When the song ended I was surprised at all the droplets of perspiration on Luca's face. As we walked away I could still feel his hand holding mine. When we arrived at the table, Luca took the champagne bottle and refilled both of our glasses. He passed me my glass and raised his glass. As Luca looked only at me he proclaimed, "You dance better than you swim Chica Fresa!" We tapped our glasses together and quickly drank the champagne. The rest of the evening was just as much fun. We stayed for another hour and decided to go home.

Luca dropped Rita home first and then Bruno. Henry and Bruno remarked how Rita appeared to be more like Luca's date instead of Bruno's. I was grateful my feelings towards Luca went unnoticed by the guys. We said our goodnights to Bruno and now only the three of us were left in the car. I was in the front seat near Luca and Henry was in the back seat.

Not before long Tía's house came into view. Luca parked the car right outside the gate. We talked a little and glanced at Henry sitting in the back seat. I wasn't sure if I should wait for Luca to get out and open my door. But I decided since it was late and we had a long day, maybe he was tired and was waiting for me to leave. After I said my goodbyes I opened the car door and walked around to the gate. I realized I left my camera under Luca's seat in the car. So quickly I turned around to go back to him.

I didn't even hear him open the car door, when all of a sudden he appeared before me. He placed one hand on my face and leaned towards me and kissed my lips. It happened so fast I wasn't even prepared.

When we separated, I looked into his eyes and smiled. I was so nervous and confused and the silence was both arousing and uncomfortable. I whispered, "I forgot my camera in your car."

Luca blinked his eyes and returned my smile and bashfully laughed. He opened the car door and located the camera and upon shutting the door I heard him tell Henry he'll be right back.

Luca took my hand in his as we approached the entry gate. He quickly turned the knob and pushed the gate open. As we walked together towards the front door, my heart was racing and I can sense my cheeks were blushing from the heat rising in my body. Thankfully in the darkness, Luca was unable to see my reaction.

We stood there across from one another and I so wanted him to kiss me again and I was also nervous if he kissed me again. His eyes were less transparent under the dimly lit doorway giving me room to be not as honest as earlier with him. So, I said, "Thank you for a lovely evening and good night."

I didn't know exactly what was going to happen next so I quickly released his hand, walked away, opened the front door and waved goodbye. He stood there with a confused look and waved back at me.

I closed the door behind me and stood there in the dark and felt my fluttering heart. And with my hand pressed against my lips I closed my eyes and heard Luca's car drive away.

That night before falling to sleep I could only think about Luca and replayed the entire evening in my mind over and over again until I drifted off.

Chapter 6

JENENE SAYS, "WOW, how was the kiss?" I nod, "It was too fast, I wasn't expecting it, so, as surprising as it was, as first kisses go it was fleeting yet exciting."

It was Saturday, the big day, Frida and Max's wedding. After having breakfast with the ladies, I joined Frida at her house. Our appointments at the hair salon were at one o'clock. I brought Frida and Max their wedding gift. From the looks on their faces they seemed to love the ceramic candleholders I gave them. I was pleased.

Then when I had a minute alone with Frida I told her a little about the previous evening.

"Emmy that's terrific, I'm glad you had fun and felt so comfortable with everyone. I was worried about leaving you on your own, but I didn't need to."

I smiled at her, "Frida, you have so much more on your mind, please don't concern yourself with me. And your family has been so gracious to me."

"Luca told me over breakfast about the evening and was quite complementary about your dancing. He was thankful he didn't lose a toe in the process."

We both laughed. "Your brother is a fine dancer and he's quite the catch. And will be the perfect husband to a lucky girl one day." She just smiled. I could not tell her I wished that girl was me.

Frida went on and on about Violeta, Luca's girlfriend. I sat there and listened and was thankful to hear he's dating someone the family likes but had hoped he was single for me. And so I just let the topic end.

Max stopped into the room, "Hello Emelia. How are you today?"

"Hi Max, I'm a little tired but very excited. It's your wedding day! How ARE you?"

"I'm good, just a bit harried trying to stick to the schedule. Frida I'm ready to drive over to the hotel to get my mom and sisters. Want me to bring Emelia with me so I can leave them all at the salon?" Frida nodded yes and after they quickly kissed we were off.

Once we arrived at the salon I looked around and saw Frida's mother Claudia in the chair having her hair styled. And glanced over and saw Frida getting a manicure. Gena was also there and came right over to us. One of the salon staff interrupted our hellos and said something in Spanish. Gena pointed to me and before I knew it, I was being ushered over to an empty chair. I looked at my reflection in the mirror and saw Gena standing behind my right shoulder and a man holding a comb standing behind my left shoulder. Gena asked, "Emelia, how do you want to look for the wedding?"

When I turned to look at Gena, Max's older sister Marisol joined us. I tried to explain to both of them how I wanted my hair styled. After a couple of minutes, I was sent downstairs to be shampooed. Once that was done I went back upstairs and took the seat where Claudia had been sitting. Gena came right over and started talking to the hairstylist. The explaining seemed to go on forever. I almost interrupted to suggest getting a magazine so I can show them a picture, but before I could, they all stopped talking and the stylist said, "*Sí, yo tengo.*" [Yes, I got it.]

He first started with the back of my head by putting a section of hair in a clip. And taking the sides and clipped them up too. But the front he left draped down on my face. Then he turned on the hairdryer and started drying the hair straight down in front of my face. I thought I resembled *Cousin Itt* from the *Addams Family*. While peering through the hair in front of my eyes I could only make out some images. Suddenly he turned off the dryer and walked away. From what I could see, it appeared he was needed on the telephone. I was sitting there thinking how long will I be waiting for him while looking like this? And grateful it was just us ladies at the salon.

I saw the front door of the salon swing open and through the spaces of hair I watched Luca and Bruno walking in. What are they doing here?

I just wanted to slide off the chair and find my way back downstairs without Luca seeing me. Maybe they won't recognize me. Where is the stylist? Please get off the phone! Oh no, what is Luca doing? He was saying hello to everyone. Why does he have to be such a nice guy? Oh good maybe Gena can keep him busy. Why is she pointing towards me? And Luca was looking my way. He looked back again at Gena. Good, maybe they are in deep conversation. Please Gena I beg you, just keep talking to him. Keep him distracted. Gosh darn it, where is the stylist?

No! Luca walked away from her and made his way directly to me. I remember feeling the heat of embarrassment warming up my cheeks. Last night ended so perfectly and awkwardly, and the first image he sees of me was like this? Strangling my stylist with his hairdryer cord came to mind.

"Hello Chica Fresa," Luca said cheerfully. "I almost didn't recognize you."

Why did he always look so good? I picked up a portion of hair so I could make eye contact and said, "I wonder why you couldn't recognize me, hi there."

I smiled nervously at him while drowning in his gorgeous blue eyes. This handsome man started chatting away as if I had nothing better to do. I, of course, tried to act naturally comfortable and couldn't even concentrate on what he was saying to me. Finally he ended his story and said goodbye.

Yet when he walked away he took a seat. Is he staying? Maybe he's getting his hair done. No way! Frida came over. I was near tears when she asked, "How is everything?"

"Well, things are going slowly and the stylist left for a phone call and hasn't returned. I was surprised to see Bruno and Luca here."

"Oh yes, they came to get my mom to bring her home. They should be leaving shortly."

The stylist returned and Frida left to do more primping. Maybe I shouldn't have wished for his return. After he was done blow drying and teasing my hair, I looked like a dancer from a 1970's disco movie. He turned my chair around and handed me a mirror and said, *"Bonita!"* [Pretty!] And I looked at the back of my hair and glanced over to Gena and Frida and they appeared stunned. I looked to the stylist and said, "Sí, bonita." Followed by, "Muchas gracias."

We shook hands and Frida looked at me and asked, "Ready to go?"

Holding back my tears I said, "Yes, please."

While walking home to Frida's house, I pulled my wild hair into a clip. Frida gasped and was starting to say, "You'll ruin it."

When I stopped her and said, "Really?" And we both began to laugh. We continued laughing on and off all the way home.

We arrived back at the house and found only Max waiting for us. He looked at me and my hair and glanced over to Frida. I quickly said, "Don't even ask. We've had a good laugh and soon I will wash away this catastrophe."

But before I could, Max reminded me I wanted to go shopping today for the gift for Tía Ines to thank her for her generous hospitality. Now Frida was left to herself to relax and get ready for the big evening.

Much to my amazement it did not take very long to pick out a gift. And Max and I picked up some food that the Morales family liked. I can't remember what it was, and unfortunately I did not try it.

When we returned I went to my home away from home to relax and get ready too. I showered again and kept hoping my hair would look just right. After my shower I was applying lotion on my body when I heard Tía calling my name. But at first, I didn't think she was calling me, I thought she was talking about me to someone. Then I heard my name again. I put on my robe and slippers and walked out to the stairway.

To my surprise Luca was standing on the first landing holding little Bella in his arms. He looked confused when he saw my hair was wet. Why was he here? Did he drop something off? Can he see through my robe? I just remembered I had nothing on underneath. I walked down the steps out of the sunlight peeking through the windows to meet him at the landing. And we both sat next to each other on the steps with Bella sitting between us.

Luca cleared his throat and said, "You smell lovely. And when I saw you earlier weren't you getting your hair styled?" Bella stood up and called out to her mother and walked downstairs to find her.

Jealously I admired Luca's brown curly hair with the sun showing off some golden strands. I giggled and then growled a bit. "Let's just say, there was some miscommunication. I should have showed him a picture. And now, I will just look like me tonight."

And I intentionally bumped my shoulder into his shoulder and we both laughed. "Why did you stop by?"

He took a deep breath and began to say, "I want to tell you I was thinking about how much fun I had with you last night and." Gena interrupted us, "Luca, your mom just called and needs you at home." "Ok, thank you Gena." She walked away.

Luca stood and extended his hand to me and I stood too. While looking into my eyes, he said, "I guess I should be going. And I'm glad you'll look just like you tonight. I hope we can dance together again at the party. See you later." I smiled and said, "Me too. See you later." And he was gone.

I walked back into my bedroom and sat on the end of the bed. Why did he stop by? No matter how brief it was, it was certainly sweet. And after feeling so self-conscious about my hair he put my mind at ease.

⌒

"Did you know Luca had a girlfriend, you know, before the kiss?" Jenene asks.

"I don't remember if I knew about her before Frida talked about Violeta with me that day. Plus, we didn't do anything it was just a quick kiss."

Jenene nods, "Yes, but he was the one with the girlfriend."

"I agree, but, we were very young, I wasn't aware of the depth of their relationship and isn't that what dating is all about? He wasn't married to her."

Jenene replies, "I know what you're saying, but he shouldn't have kissed you."

I smile, "That first kiss wasn't an issue. The ones that followed, well, we both should have known better."

Jenene's eyes light up and I say, "Let me tell you about the wedding and when I saw Violeta." While turning to the pages of the wedding photos in the album, Jenene said, "Ok, go on, I won't interrupt."

⌒

Once we were ready Tía Ada and I walked over to Frida's house to join the rest of the family. Frida's father was in the kitchen when we arrived and the rest of the family was scattered about the house. I heard Frida call down to me and I excused myself. When I approached the bottom of the stairwell I looked up and saw Frida. She was leaning over the railing of the staircase on the upper level. She was so beautiful and radiant. And her smile was filled with such joy. I quickly snapped a photo of her. I wanted to remember her that way on her special day forever.

"Emelia, can you help me with my dress?" Feeling so touched to be included in her preparations, I said, "Yes of course, I would be delighted." Gena was Frida's Matron of Honor, but I had hoped she had asked me.

When I joined her in the bedroom I had a chance to see Frida from head to toe. "You look absolutely stunning. This dress is perfect for your figure and your personality." Frida replied, "Thank you Emmy, I designed it myself."

I tried to help attach her train to the back of the dress but I could not figure it out. Finally I gave up and Frida went to find her mother. She walked to her brothers' rooms and I stayed behind.

I waited a couple of minutes and I didn't hear anything. So I went to see how everything was going. When I walked down the hallway, I spotted Henry frantically searching for something in a closet, so I snuck up behind him and whispered, "Hey handsome, did you lose something?" But when he spun around, I saw that it wasn't Henry and I gasped. At first I didn't know who this man was and then realized it was Frida's brother, Nicolás, we hadn't met yet. My heart was pounding. He replied, "Yes, I have lost something and I will take the compliment, gracias. Who are you?"

Embarrassed I extended my hand and said, "Hello, I'm Emelia, Frida's friend." He laughed, "Oh yes Emelia, hello. I am Nicky. It's nice to finally meet you." Still feeling awkward I replied, "It's nice to meet you too. Don't let me keep you from locating what you lost." He laughed as I walked away.

Further down the hall I found Frida standing in a doorway looking at me and I could see Luca kneeling behind her fastening the train. He was talking to her and she was giggling and answering him back. I knelt down quickly and focused my lens on them and took a picture.

Henry came out of his room and called out to his mother. I smiled thinking about my introduction to Nicky and went back towards Frida's room and waited for her there. She returned and we both took turns putting on her makeup. When Frida was all fixed up we stood in front of the floor length mirror. I finally got a chance to see myself all put together. With all the craziness of the day, I looked pretty good. The dress I wore was black with little white flowers on vines. It was a halter style long dress that ended at my ankles. And I wore strappy black sandals. I smiled and said, "If the guys at the Monster club could see us now."

I kissed Frida and gave her a drawn out hug. I whispered in her ear, "My friend, the sister I always longed for, my wish for you today on your wedding day, is a lifetime of happiness." I left her alone and went downstairs. Everyone was finishing with last minute touchups. All the while I paced through the house wanting to sit but did not in fear of wrinkling my dress. Most of the family came downstairs and into the dining room, with the exception of Luca. What was taking him so long?

When the photographer got there all the excitement started. The Garcia family also arrived. Wherever you looked there were people, so I opted to escape to the terrace alone. After a while I turned to walk back into the dining room. And when I reached the door, Luca appeared in front of me holding two glasses of champagne. Had I walked any faster, we might have crashed into one another.

"Where are you going, I was just coming to join you on the terrace. Here take one." He handed me one of the glasses.

We strolled together out to the railing and stood beside each other under the twilight sky. "Let's make this first toast to a life filled with love and joy." He raised his glass to me and while tapping our glasses, I smiled and added, "For the bride and groom." And Luca replied, "Ah, yes for the bride and groom, Salud!"

After we both sampled the champagne, Luca took my hand and said, "Now let me see you." And he began to spin me around.

I laughed and said, "I hope this frock looks better than the robe?"

He nodded and with a mischievous smile said, "The robe had its own memorable attributes, but yes, you look beautiful this evening."

He even reached out and pulled at a tendril of hair that was hanging loose around my temples. With a wink and a smile he added, "And your hair looks fantastic too."

I smiled and with a slight blush, looked up to the sky. "Now it's my turn to examine you." I said with a devilish snicker. "Turn for me please so I can admire the entire ensemble."

He nodded his head no and then followed my command. There he was, under the stars with his curls slightly tamed from earlier, stunningly wearing a black single breasted tuxedo, fitted perfectly for his physique, white shirt, black bowtie and smelling so aromatic. When he finished and was facing me, I tapped my glass to his and said, "To the second most attractive man of the evening."

I began to sip my champagne when he exclaimed, "Second!?" I laughed and said, "Surely you can't outshine the groom." He tapped my glass again with his and toasted, "For extraordinary encounters."

We both finished our champagne when our silent gazes were interrupted by Nicolás. "Luciano you're needed in here for pictures. Oh, Emelia, we meet again. Save me a dance later, I want to get to know you better." Nicolás winked at me before leaving the terrace. Luca asked, "What was that about?" I shook my head, "Your brother is just teasing me."

After the silly day I had at the salon and Luca's unexpected visit, sharing those special moments, just the two of us on the terrace, was a perfect way to start the evening.

Photographs were being set up and taken. Flashes were everywhere. Laughter and giggles were heard. I even managed to sneak a few pictures with my camera. As the chaos continued I found refuge again on the terrace. I was alone and enjoyed the view of the mountains while listening to the cheerful voices inside. Even though I didn't understand completely what they were saying I smiled while taking in all the gladness surrounding Frida and her family.

After getting lost in the cheer I felt someone was watching me. I looked down from the terrace and saw Luca looking up. I smiled to him. He said, "I came out here to rough up my shoes. I don't want to fall at the wedding."

"Good idea, I do the same when I'm wearing new shoes."

"See you later I'm off to get Tía Ines for family photos."

Once the pictures were taken we all left for the church. I rode with Luca. No one said who to go with except Frida put me in charge of some things to bring and when I looked for them to take she said Luca already put them in his car. So I figured I was to ride with him. Tía Ada rode along with us.

When we arrived at the church there was another wedding taking place. We must have been early. Finally we started walking into the church. I followed Tía Ada and we sat together on the right side of the church also known as the groom's side. She said it made no difference.

The procession started with Max walking down the aisle with his family and then Frida walked down part of the way with her brothers at her sides and her parents joined them along with Gena at the half way point. It was a very touching way of proceeding down the aisle. When Frida walked by with her parents I thought my little friend is getting married. All of our plans of her coming back to New York are changed. We can never repeat those fun experiences from our past. At that exact moment I realized all that I was going to miss. During the days I spent with Frida I knew how important it was to her family to have her live close to them. I mean they are her family, they know her more than me, so they've got to know what a beautiful person she is and I completely understood why she needs to live there. She is very lucky to have such a terrific and loving family. Just watching them all be together was one of the reasons I made the trip. I wanted to see Frida with her family like she had watched me with mine. And since I had arrived, every minute with them was special for me too.

The ceremony was moving, like most weddings. It was all spoken in Spanish; I wished I had a book so I could follow the responses. Then Frida and Max said their vows and were married. People started coming up to them before they even walked down the aisle. I just thought it's what they do but later Frida and Max walked out and then the church emptied.

As we entered the parking lot of the reception hall there was a car driving slowly in front of us, Luca proceeded to tell me his girlfriend Violeta was in that car. After Luca gave the valet his keys, I entered the reception hall with Tía Ada.

There was chaos everywhere and I left to find the bathroom. Once returning I found my place in the main dining room. I was joined by Bruno. Finally Henry came over with two of his friends, who had also joined us at the beach the day before. So I assumed who I was sitting with. Claudia came over to Henry and asked him to sit near to me so I would have someone to speak with. I found out the reception would last until five in the morning. So I knew I should pace myself.

I remember the early part of the evening seemed to start off slowly. The band did not arrive yet and I lost sight of Luca. I kept comparing it with the night before and told myself to not expect anything like that to happen again, at least not for tonight especially with Violeta in attendance. The band arrived. And from the first song, I was floored by the mixture of music they performed. They were very talented.

I was asked to dance by Bruno, Max and Nicolás. Finally Luca came round to ask me to dance. I was very surprised considering Violeta was there. We danced a merengue and he commented on how much more relaxed I was since our first dance the previous night. The next dance was a salsa and I was completely out of step. But Luca was a great lead and we managed to get through the song. And after a few missteps I just focused on being in Luca's arms once again and that's all that mattered.

The night ended in the wee hours of the morning. I was feeling tired and not myself. Luca drove me home with Tía Ada. We said our goodbyes and I helped Tía Ada find her bedroom in the darkness of the house.

Chapter 7

"So, what was Violeta like?" Jenene asks.

"She was striking, tall, slim, long dark straight hair, olive skin tone and green eyes. The dress she wore, her legs seemed to go on for miles. And when they danced together, they looked like they should enter those dance competitions. They were a perfect pair."

"Did you meet her?"

I nod, "Yes, just a brief introduction."

"Was it awkward?"

I close my eyes to try to remember that moment but it was so long ago. I reply, "Yes and no."

When I woke the next morning I felt ill. I thought maybe all that I drank and ate the night before was making me sick, but it didn't feel like a hangover. I showered and had the chills under the warm water. I knew I must be running a fever. I felt very weak and just putting on clothes made me tired. After getting dressed I walked over to the Morales' house.

Upon arriving I found they had a houseful of guests. I didn't want to mention that I was feeling sick since Claudia was busy with her visitors. So I asked Henry secretly to locate a thermometer. He couldn't find it. So we waited until the guests left. Luca asked how I was feeling and I told him the truth. So he involved his mother and she asked me some questions. She gave me the thermometer. When the thermometer was ready we found out I had a temperature of 104°F. I felt terrible; I didn't want anyone, especially Claudia to take care of me. They had been running around all week for the wedding. Claudia sent Henry out to get medicine. And I followed Claudia upstairs to her bedroom to find clean sheets in the linen closet. We went to one of the bedrooms and changed the bedding. She insisted I sit still and she will take care of everything.

Frida and Max came up to pack their bags for their honeymoon. Henry arrived with the medicine and immediately Claudia had me take it and then I went to bed. I felt like I was in a hospital with all the visitors that stopped by. First Nicolás, the future doctor, came into the room. He asked me a bunch of questions and assured me I'd be feeling better very soon. When he left, Henry and Rafael quickly said hello. Everyone finally left me alone to sleep and sweat out the fever.

After a few hours I was awakened by singing voices from the Morales family. They were downstairs continuing the wedding celebration. The songs sounded so lovely. As I tried getting out of bed I realized my t-shirt and shorts were drenched from sweat. I knew I didn't look so good, but I was feeling much better. I waited until they stopped singing and made my way downstairs to the kitchen to get some juice. While in the kitchen everyone asked how I felt and I told them the medicine was working. I returned upstairs to the bedroom and tried to sleep again. After a few minutes Luca came to visit.

During my trip he had seen me look my best and my worst. I could not say the same for him. He steadily always looked great. Even after a day at the beach. He didn't stay that long. I found out from Claudia that Luca would be driving me and Rafael to Caracas the next day. Earlier in the week Frida didn't think he could take the day off. So I thought I was left to spend my last evening in Valencia with Rafael. Which would have been fine, but after getting closer to Luca, I had hoped we were alone for my last night.

No sooner after Luca left me alone, Frida and Max came in to say goodbye. My last day to spend with them and I was in bed all day sleeping. Our goodbyes went better than I thought but I think it was because I didn't expect it just then. I hugged Frida and thanked her for including me in all the wedding festivities. And Max hugged me and invited me to visit their home and stay with them. I went downstairs to the terrace off the dining room. And as they loaded up Luca's car, Rico and Nicolás came to say goodbye. I couldn't believe how many people were leaving that day.

I stayed on the terrace so I could wave to them as they left. I was wondering where Luca was taking them. And I saw him watching me from the car. Finally they were all set to leave. Claudia said her final goodbyes and as Luca started to drive away I waved to them. I couldn't believe my friend Frida was leaving me again. My life will always be better for having met her and experience these short visits but I still hate all the goodbyes we have to exchange.

I can't remember what I did while Luca was dropping off everyone. But when he returned he asked me how I felt and what we should do that night. I thought we should try a movie. Claudia asked Luca to drive Bruno to the house where he was staying to pick up his luggage and then go to Henry's friend's house to get him too. She said if I wanted to take a ride the fresh air would be good for me. I went. We got all of Bruno's things and upon arriving at the other friend's house, Henry's friend was not ready to leave. So we left without him.

Once we arrived back at the house Henry had all his things ready to go. We talked about keeping in touch and I told him to call me and we exchanged numbers.

We all went outside when Bruno and Henry's ride arrived. There were two other guys travelling to Caracas with them. And once they put the luggage inside the car they were ready to go. I kissed Bruno goodbye and wished him well. Luca pulled Henry aside, probably to give him last minute advice. Then Henry came back to hug and kiss Claudia. And he turned to me. We hugged and kissed and we parted.

Luca, Claudia and I went into the house. We sat in the living room with Tía Ada. Claudia remembered I left her a gift earlier that day. She went to retrieve it from the dining room. When she sat down on the couch next to Luca she seemed like a child getting an unexpected birthday gift, except, she slowly unwrapped the box. But once she opened the box she was taking the rolled up pieces of tissue paper out and began unraveling them. I told her that was just part of the packaging. She smiled. Then she finally got to the little glass figure tucked inside. As soon as she could see what it was, she smiled again. It was a little yellow Murano glass duck. She said she loved it and placed the duck on the table. She came over to me and hugged and kissed me and complimented my taste and how much she enjoyed my company. For a few minutes we all shared funny stories about the wedding.

Luca asked what I wanted to do that night and Claudia interrupted our plans by saying I had been sick all day and I shouldn't be going out. Luca and I were like teenagers asking for her permission. And she finally gave in. But I had to promise to come back before going to bed to take my temperature and the medicine if needed.

We both parted to get ready. I desperately needed a shower. So I had to hurry. No matter how quickly I moved, Luca was ready before me. When he arrived he remained downstairs and visited with his aunt and uncle while I finished. As I entered the room he stood up immediately, smiled and said hello. I looked around the room at his Tía Ines and she was smiling back at me too. "Ready to go?" Luca asked. And I nodded yes. The way his relatives watched us I felt we were on our first date. The butterflies were fluttering around in my stomach, it felt great.

Luca held the doors open for me and I waited as he closed the doors. We walked side by side towards his car. Being with him felt so natural and I could have easily stayed there to get to know him. He opened the car door for me and when I settled inside, he firmly closed it. I reached over to his side of the car and grasped the door lever to open his door. As he was climbing into his seat, he looked at me with a smile and said, "That was thoughtful, nobody has done that for me." I replied with a quick, "Really?" and followed up with, "Maybe that's an American thing." He started the car and we were on our way.

"What is this American girl in the mood to do?"

"Tell me what Valencia has to offer this American girl."

"We have the typical offerings you will have at home; dinner, movies, dancing." He stopped talking as we drove by a festival of some sort that had amusement park rides. And he continued, "Want to go there? How do you like rollercoasters?"

At that point I felt my stomach do a summersault. "I love rollercoasters, the faster the better. But after the day I had, I'm sure your mom would agree we should be a bit low key."

"Oh, you've got a point."

"Don't get me wrong Luca, in normal circumstances I would have jumped at the chance. I hope you don't mind."

"I don't mind at all. I'm just surprised we got a chance to get out together. Uh, you know, without a car load of other people."

My heart fluttered and I looked out the window. We were awkwardly quiet. I quickly said, "So you mentioned movies, do you know what films are playing?"

"I looked at the newspaper earlier and the theatre is showing *Batman Returns* and *Rhapsody in August*. I've seen *Batman Returns* but not the other."

I said, "Yeah, me too. Is the other one with Richard Gere?"

"Yes, I think so."

Neither of us knew much about the film but both agreed if it's a Gere film, it's probably good.

We arrived at the theatre and parked nearby. Luca purchased the tickets while I looked at the movie poster trying to figure out what the film was about. My companion walked towards me and grabbed my elbow to direct me to the screening room. He said in a low voice, "I think the movie started a couple of minutes ago. Let's first find our seats."

Upon entering the room, it was very dark and the movie was playing. For a Sunday night thankfully it wasn't crowded. Luca guided me to two seats and once we settled in I started to watch the movie. The movie was more foreign than expected. On the screen there was a Japanese woman with a young girl. They were sitting at a table. The dialogue was in Japanese and the subtitles were in Spanish. I thought for sure, the film would be in English with only parts of it in Japanese and with Spanish subtitles. Luca leaned close to me and asked me in a whisper if I wanted any popcorn or something to drink. I looked into his eyes and replied in a whisper, "No thank you." He left to get something for himself.

During his absence I watched the screen closely to try to get some understanding of what was happening. But I couldn't get a grasp of the conversation.

Luca returned with chocolate covered mints and offered me some. I was hoping he would not ask what happened while he was gone. The scene changed and the people were still speaking Japanese. While I looked towards the screen, my thoughts began to wander.

Sitting this close to him our elbows shared the arm rest and our bodies were touching. I began to notice his fragrance and wondered what it would be like holding hands. And while keeping my head still, so he wouldn't see me not looking at the screen I glanced around at the audience to see if others were on a date and if they were enjoying the film. I didn't want Luca to notice I was not paying attention. But then I thought I couldn't sit there and pretend for two hours to like the movie.

Luca disrupted my thoughts and whispered closely in my ear, "What do you think of the movie?"

I couldn't lie to him even though I felt guilty that he paid for the tickets. Before answering I noticed the glow from the movie screen gleaming on his face, even with his slightly imperfect nose, I was transfixed by his profile. I couldn't let this go any longer, and whispered in his ear, "Do you think the film will only be in Japanese?"

Luca still watching the screen first nodded yes and then said, "Maybe."

I turned away and tried to pay closer attention to the subtitles and the character movements. I thought with their body language I might have a chance. After about ten minutes I had to tell him I had no idea what was going on. Maybe he could catch me up and I can piece it together going forward. Plus it would be fun to hear him narrate the movie for me. I leaned to him and whispered, "Can you tell me what is going on?"

He looked at me slightly confused and then he closed his eyes, smiled, shook his head and chuckled quietly. He whispered, "I'm so sorry, I forgot."

"No, don't apologize, I do understand some Spanish but certainly not Japanese."

"Do you want to stay?"

"As long you tell me what's happening, I'll be fine."

"We should go."

Luca stood up promptly, grabbed my hand and we rushed out. The theatre attendants asked why we were leaving so soon. Luca told them the problem. They laughed and we left. I was surprised they didn't give us a refund.

It was raining when we got outside and while still holding my hand we ran to the car. We were laughing along the way. Once we got to the car, Luca opened my door first and I dashed inside and quickly flipped his door open. When he settled into the seat he looked at me and we smiled and started laughing again.

"Soon you will be happy to be free of this American girl."

He reached out with his hand to touch my face and said, "On the contrary, I'm having a wonderful time with this American girl. I'll be sad to see you go."

And he kissed me. When we parted I could hear the sound of the rain dancing on the roof of the car. We looked into each other's eyes and began kissing again. My fingers combed through his hair and his hands were caressing my face and my neck. His mouth tasted like chocolate mints. We stayed close and Luca kissed my nose and my forehead. And then we sat back in our seats and gazed at one another.

It was still raining when Luca asked, "What else do you want to do?" I thought until the rain stops, we can stay parked and continue kissing. I said, "Maybe drive around until we find our next destination." He inhaled deeply and put the key in the ignition.

"When you were getting ready at Tía's house, the movie *The Big Blue* was on."

"I noticed it was on too. That's one of my favorites." He said, "Me too! Maybe we can watch it later when we get back home." I replied, "Yes, to make up for this one." We both laughed.

Luca drove us to a place that looked like many little castles and appeared to be a popular night spot. I wished we could have gotten out and walked around, but it was still raining. "Are you hungry?" I replied, "Yes, how about you?" He nodded yes and we went to El Toro.

After settling in at our table I began to look around. For a spontaneous dinner on a Sunday night, this place certainly was more than what I expected.

It seemed like a five star restaurant. Luca doesn't kid around when he dines out. The waiter gave us menus and asked if we wanted a drink. I heard Luca ask the waiter something about wine. Shortly thereafter, he returned with the wine list. I continued to read the menu. I was able to pick out a few dishes I wanted to try. I closed the menu and looked across at Luca. He was still reading the menu. The waiter was back at the table and he said something about the specials. Luca looked at me and then the waiter. When the waiter finished reciting the dishes, Luca began talking in Spanish. I enjoyed watching him and listening to his voice. He looked at me and I heard something about me and it sounded like he was ordering the fish dish I remember reading about on the menu. And it sounded like he ordered a steak for himself. He opened the wine book and told the waiter the name of the wine. The waiter said thank you and smiled at both of us and walked away.

"I ordered us both special Venezuelan dishes for this area and we can share them if you'd like. But if you don't want what I ordered I can tell the waiter to change your meal."

"No, please don't, I'm open to trying out something new. And I think you ordered the fish that I was planning to order. Thank you."

He smiled at me and took a sip of water. What was he thinking while sitting across from me? Did he have the same feelings I was having? Will we talk about the kisses? Will we kiss even more?

The waiter was back with the wine. After we sat through the routine of reviewing the bottle, uncorking, pouring, sampling and nodding, the waiter filled our wine glasses even more and left us alone. Luca began to raise his glass to me and I lifted mine as well.

"For an evening filled with surprise happenings and much laughter." We tapped each other's glasses and sipped the wine. I raised my glass to him and said, "And for my very patient, thoughtful and generous tour guide. You have certainly made this trip even more memorable. I never expected all of this. Thank you for being so kind to me." We tapped our glasses once again.

We were served our meal. And I remember how smoothly the conversations flowed. Even though I was a bit nervous being with him, for it felt like our first date, talking with Luca seemed as if I was talking with an old friend. We connected on so many levels. And where we didn't, I was equally intrigued as he was. Maybe because we had similar upbringings, maybe by this point we were comfortable with one another. I knew that night, that besides our initial attraction, physical attraction, he was someone I wanted to talk with and learn more about for many years to come.

We discussed a possible visit to New York in his future. And dinner was over. The waiter asked if we wanted dessert and Luca abruptly declined. It seemed like he wanted to rush home for something. I was completely awake and could not even think of going to sleep yet.

We drove around a little. We passed by a house where one of his friend's lives. We stopped in front of his old school. It wasn't raining and I thought about asking if we could get out and walk somewhere but I thought he should bring it up. He didn't, and to my dismay we were driving back home. Luca knew I was not tired. But I think he ran out of things for us to do.

Instead of leaving me at his aunt's house, we drove to his parents' home. We walked into the house and entered the living room. Claudia and Rafael must have been upstairs sleeping. Luca returned from the kitchen with the thermometer. I took my temperature. We sat across from each other in silence. He was reading a *Sports Illustrated* magazine while I sat quietly waiting for the results. I also watched his every move. I wanted to make sure that when I left for home I would always be able to remember Luca's handsome face when I thought about him.

The thermometer was ready and I had a slight temperature but nothing to worry about. He asked, "What were you looking at?" My face began to blush. I smiled and looked away from him. I took a deep breath and looked directly in his eyes and said, "You."

I guess he wasn't expecting that answer because he changed the subject. "Let's go to Tía's house and look for the movie on cable, yes?" I replied, "Sure let's give it a try."

When we arrived the house was dark and everyone seemed to be upstairs in their bedrooms. We walked into the living room and Luca flipped on the ceiling light. We proceeded to sit on the couch. It was too bright, no ambiance. He held the remote control and began changing channels. I didn't know what to do or say, so I just sat there feeling like a nervous teenager. If this was my home, I'd offer him a drink. And I'd turn off this spotlight for some softer lighting.

Neither of us spoke. We just sat there watching the television while he kept searching. Should I make the first move? What is he thinking? Why isn't he making a move? Can we just hit pause, reverse and start again at the front door?

He stood up, turned off the television and tossed the remote control on the couch. "I don't see the movie playing. And it's getting late. I should go. We have an early start tomorrow."

I stood too and we walked towards the front door in the darkened hallway. As he opened the door the light from the street lamp cascaded on his profile. I asked, "I thought we were leaving after lunch?" He turned to me and said, "I'm planning to show you and Tía Ada more of Valencia in the morning, if that's okay with you?"

I looked directly into his eyes and said, "Ah, so your services are still required tomorrow. Yes, it's okay with me. When should we be ready?"

"Is nine o'clock good? Or is that too early for you?"

"I can handle that early start, will you be ready?"

"Yes, of course, your guide is always ready."

I smiled, "Well, as of now you are off the clock. You should go and enjoy being free of me."

He looked out at the street and when I thought he was about to leave he turned around to me and said in a low voice, "I don't want to go and be free of you just yet."

All of a sudden he enfolded me in his arms bringing me closer to him and we're standing in the doorway with our bodies pressed together, silently looking at one another. It's like he was waiting for me to give him a signal. I whispered, "I don't want to be free of you either."

And with that, we began to devour the other with deep passionate kisses and our hands instantly began their exploration. While kissing we moved out of the doorway and I was rapturously pinned between the wall and Luca.

His fingers carefully opened the buttons of my blouse while his lips travelled down my neck with light gentle kisses. With my hands in his hair I felt his mouth on the tops of my breasts, he was kissing and sucking and I felt his warm wet tongue tenderly licking between my breasts, as his hands masterfully unfastened the front clasp of my lace bra. Delicately when he uncovered my breasts I heard him groan and whisper, "Mi Lia."

Between his touch and hearing him whisper "Mi Lia" my body trembled from the sensations of tingles coursing up and down my spine. My heart was pulsing and tears trickled down my face. I opened my eyes and leaned towards his forehead, while he continued grinding into me. With his mouth still concentrating on my breasts, I placed multiple little kisses along his forehead and moved my hands to the sides of his face. I deliberately tried to move his mouth to meet mine. We kissed deeply again and his hands moved down towards my bottom and our breathing picked up once again. I whispered his name between kisses. And I heard him groan once more. My hands gently explored his face with the hopes of sedating our longings. As our kisses began to slow down, he moved his hands to my face. Unexpectedly he found the path of my tears and he opened his eyes and looked into mine.

He kissed my nose, my chin and then the sides of my face where there were tears just moments earlier. In that instant I was so overjoyed by all that had happened. He began to dress me and in seconds he was buttoning my blouse.

Luca closed the front door and took my hand as we walked towards the diffused dining room. When he sat, he took my hips and motioned for me to sit on his lap. With his arms around me we sat there quietly together for a couple of minutes. He held one of my hands in his and began to caress it and raised it towards his mouth, tenderly kissed my palm and followed with kisses on each of my fingertips.

When he stopped he looked into my eyes. "Did I make you cry? I never meant to hurt you. I thought you also wanted this. I am sorry if I forced myself on you. Please forgive me."

I nodded my head and I gently kissed his temple and then his ear. Bringing my hands up to his face and turning his head towards mine, I kissed the corners of his mouth and finally his lips.

And with tears again streaming down my face I began to tell him, "Luca, you didn't hurt me. I do want this. You didn't force yourself on me. There is nothing to forgive. It's all so overwhelming for me. And my tears are for a multitude of reasons. Some that can be explained and plainly some that can't. But please know I wanted all this too." With our foreheads pressed against the other and our arms tightly around each other, we sat in silence.

"Emelia, I never expected to feel this way towards you. When you arrived at my place the other night and my sister introduced you, from that first moment, I felt like I've known you for a very long time. I've never experienced this with another woman before. Maybe because Frida always spoke so kindly about you I grew a fondness for you before we even met. But each day since then, I couldn't wait to be with you, talk with you and get to know you even more. When we kissed that night after dancing, I felt something come to life inside me. But when I went home and thought about what I did, I also felt like a selfish man. I shouldn't have pushed myself on you. I came over here the following day to tell you, but then we were interrupted. I wanted to apologize."

With my hand I started to caress his profile, jawline and then placed my hand over his heart. He continued, "And when I saw you before the wedding, you took my breath away. I wanted to grab you in my arms that night on the terrace and kiss you again. I've been overwhelmed with so many thoughts so many feelings. You are my sister's best friend, we don't live near each other and to make matters even more complicated, I'm dating someone. That before I met you, I thought I'd eventually marry her. And now, my feelings have shifted. I thought tonight, you and I were just going out to have fun and I would take you home. But when you came downstairs earlier and smiled at me, my heart soared and I knew that all I wanted to do was be as close to you as I can be tonight. I never wanted to disrespect you Emelia, please know all this. But, when we were trying to figure out what to do tonight, I just wanted to say, I'd be happy if we spend the next few hours lying in each other's arms. I don't know what tomorrow will bring. And the next day you fly home. I wish that we could just have more time alone before we have to go back to our regular lives." He leaned his head against my chest and became silent.

With my chin resting on top of his head and my hand pressed against his face, "Luca, what have we gotten ourselves into? Everything you just said sounds like all the things I've been feeling too. I tried not to like you let alone fall in love with you. I'm just visiting. You are my best friend's brother. And from the moment we said hello I felt this spark ignite between us. But all the while, I kept thinking, we don't live near each other. This can't work. And that your heart is meant for someone else. And I kept telling myself, you're just imagining all this, he can't possibly have feelings for me. He has a life with her. But like you said, each day, each moment I spent with you, my feelings kept increasing for you too. So tonight, when you came here to get me and I saw you waiting for me, my heart fluttered for you. I felt like we were going on our first date. And in the car, after we kissed, you asked me what I was in the mood for, I was thankful you couldn't read my mind."

At that point Luca looked up to me, smiled and raised his eyebrows in flirtation and asked, "Mi Lia what exactly did you have in mind?" Fortunately in the darkness he couldn't see me blush with desire. I faintly giggled and said, "Let's just say, what we did in the hallway a few minutes ago and then some." He tightened his grip around my waist and laughed into my chest, looked into my eyes with such yearning and said after licking his lips, "And then some." And his then some, lead into a deep tender kiss.

We kissed for a few minutes more and he said, "As much as I don't want to go home, we should say goodnight. And before this leads to 'then some' I will show myself out." I kissed him gently on his lips and got up.

As we walked down the hallway again towards the front door, he stopped midway and said, "Oh no you don't, you will say your goodbye here my love. After I leave, you can lock the door, sweet dreams Mi Lia."

He took my hand and kissed it and he quickly dashed out of the house. I sprinted towards the door to keep it from slamming shut. I watched Luca as he ran down the walkway towards the gate. He turned around and looked back at me, waved and kissed the palm of his hand and placed that hand over his heart. And then he was gone.

I quietly closed and locked all the doors and went into the living room, turned off the light and made my way upstairs to my bedroom. As I was about to enter my bedroom, I saw Tía Ada exiting the bathroom and she looked at me and smiled.

She whispered and winked, *"Tuviste una noche divertida con Luca?"* [Did you have a fun night with Luca?]

I smiled back at her and with a slight giggle replied, *"Sí Tía Ada, sí.* [Yes, Aunt Ada, yes.]

She walked over to me and hugged me and said, *"Buenos Sueños Emelia."* [Good dreams Emelia.]

I hugged her back and said, *"Buenas Noches Tía."* [Good night Aunt.] And then I remembered to tell her, to be ready at nine for Luca.

Chapter 8

"OH GOSH, LOOK at the hour. It's nearly midnight and you've allowed me to go on and on about my trip and my kiss fest with Luca." Jenene smiles, while I stand and stretch.

"Emelia, this is like a movie. I can't get enough. And just because it's late, you're not expecting me to go to bed without knowing the ending; although, that night with him at the aunt's house was very steamy. I don't know how either of you controlled yourselves."

She stands to stretch her legs too and we head into the kitchen. "Jenene, you have to understand we were both young, in our early twenties. I was at his aunt's house. He was dating someone. I had my period, thankfully. I was his sister's friend, just visiting. He was my friend's brother. We both needed to respect those relationships. But, I always felt, I was just there on a vacation and would leave and go back to my life in New York. And after I left, he'd forget me."

"No way Emelia, he was NOT forgetting you. You guys had chemistry, passion a mutual attraction. You haven't forgotten about him at all. That's why I know he still thinks about you."

I nod my head in agreement, "It was complicated, or trying to make it work would have been complicated. We just didn't have enough time to develop what we had into something greater. And that's what he probably had with her. He wasn't about to throw that all away for something so uncertain."

Jenene sighs with impatience, "You always do that, you think so little of what you can offer. You're a great woman every man sees that when they meet you. And I think you didn't give him the opportunity to see that he had a chance even if it was long distance."

I smirk at her and say, "Yeah, you're spot-on by saying I do lack confidence when it comes to men, but, this situation was overwhelming, confusing and truly life changing. There are moments that I look back on and acknowledge that no man has ever made me feel the way he did when we were together. And I say no man!"

Jenene approaches me, "I've seen you around other men and you were never over the moon about them as I sensed you were with Luca. By this point you spent a few days with him, tell me what was the allure? I want to know about every inch of him."

I smile at her and close my eyes as I try to remember my Luca and some special moments when he took my breath away. "Physically, WOW, he had it all. He exuded masculinity, from head to toe. His Italian and Panamanian genes were the perfect blend that provided a strong jawline, high cheek bones and rugged yet boyish features. Full lips that screamed kiss me. You know I like my men very manly. His height and strong broad shoulders gave him confidence and made me feel loved and protected when he held me. His body was lean for being a swimmer but his muscles were superbly toned. Don't laugh, but I've told you how I don't like overly man-scaped guys, especially the ones that have better shaped eyebrows than me. He had just the right amount of body hair, not too little and not too much. Normally a man that handsome would intimidate me. But his personality was even more attractive than his looks. He was a gentleman, had good manners, showed respect for women and his elders. He was smart, worked hard. Had this calmness about him, and his voice, he was very charming. Although he seemed serious, I felt this lightness in him. And when we were close and our bodies touched, I felt like someone opened a window in my heart and allowed it to love again and feel loved again."

I open my eyes and Jenene is watching me. She remarks, "You had it bad for him."

I nod, "The best part, were his eyes, sometimes when we'd look at one another it appeared as if I could see into his soul. I never said this to anyone, when we'd talk and those few days when we were thrown together, we talked a lot. He'd watch me or look at me in a way that made me feel I was the only one in that moment. And with his eyes, I felt that he was really listening to me. That night in the aunt's house, when we kissed, his eyes told me something else. He looked at me in such a way I could almost feel my clothes dissolving from the heat of my desires for him, my hunger for him, my need for him. I never felt that for anyone else but Luca. I always believed we were two souls on the verge of merging so perfectly together."

Jenene and I remain silent for a few seconds while I force myself back to reality, "Let me tell you how it all came to an end. Well, how it all ended on this trip."

Jenene's eyes lifted and her mouth popped open. "What? You saw him again? You have been holding back too many details. We better put some coffee or tea on; you're not using the tired excuse to leave me hanging. Tell me all that happened next."

After we fill our cups with some warm energy, Jenene gulping coffee and me sipping tea, we went to grab seats at the dining room table. Before I sit down I grab the photo album. "Here are some pictures from our day in Valencia with Tía Ada. It was like we had a sweet chaperone with us. After what she said to me the night before, I would have loved to know what was going on in her mind."

Chapter 9

I WAS ALL packed and dressed and ready by nine o'clock. Before leaving to find Luca I gave Tía Ines her gift. She had tears in her eyes when she was opening the present. I told her that I needed to leave for Luca was waiting to show Tía Ada and me around Valencia. And we'd be back after lunch.

When I arrived at the house, Claudia opened the door for me. She must have just woken up.

"Is something wrong? How are you feeling?"

"Claudia I'm so sorry, did I wake you? I'm fine. Luca told me to be ready at this hour."

We proceeded into the living room. Claudia handed me the thermometer. I remember feeling so thirsty. My temperature was back to normal.

"Do you want something to eat or drink?" I didn't want her to take care of me, it was early and she just woke up. "I'm not hungry. Just thirsty, but I can find something. Please Claudia, you've done so much."

But, she went into the kitchen and within minutes I hear her making fresh orange juice. She filled two glasses and gave me one and she took the other.

After taking a few gulps, "Thank you Claudia, the juice is delicious. Do whatever you were doing before I got here. I'll just wait for Luca."

She put her hand to her mouth and shook her head. "Emelia, he's still sleeping." I laughed. "I don't know what he has planned for us, but he did tell me to be here by nine."

"Will you be taking Tía Ada?"

"Yes, she's just waiting back at Tía Ines'for us."

Claudia stood and said, "I will wake him." I wanted to tell her to tell him, we can delay our start time if he wants. But she left before I had the chance.

While she was gone, I picked up the *Sports Illustrated* magazine Luca was reading last night and thumbed through it. But I couldn't really concentrate on any of the articles. So I glanced around the room and noticed his shoes under the piano bench, his jacket and his watch. He must have stayed up later after leaving me. I wonder if he was thinking about me as much as I thought about him before going to sleep.

Claudia returned, "He was showering when I got upstairs. He should be down here soon. Please make yourself comfortable."

If she wasn't in the room, I would have wrapped myself in his jacket. I just relaxed on the couch and waited for him. In a few minutes, Tía Ada arrived and we talked a little. I told her that Luca is getting ready. And suddenly he appeared. Each and every moment on this trip, he always looked attractive and that day was not an exception. I certainly wouldn't mind waking up to him every day for the rest of my life.

With an unintentional sexy voice, he said, "Good morning. I'm sorry I kept you waiting."

"Luca, please don't apologize. This week has been very busy for all of us. I'm sure you would have rather slept late today."

He grinned at me. "Do you have your camera?"

I nodded yes. He said, "Let's go then." Tía Ada, Luca and I got into the car and left. While waving to Claudia I thought about how later that day I'll have to say my final goodbye to her.

During our ride we spoke a little Spanish and a little English. I enjoyed Tía Ada's company. She was very sweet. Now that it was daylight, Luca pointed out many places of interest. We passed a soccer and baseball stadium. Then we saw a bullfight arena from a distance. We stopped at a grocery store where Luca bought some water and pretzels. Then we drove a little longer and arrived at Simón Bolívar Memorial Park. And to our surprise the park was open but the changing of the guards was scheduled for an hour later. We decided to have a look anyway. Luca helped Tía Ada out of the car and when we walked towards the entrance we each took Tía Ada's arms and walked close to her. She smiled at both of us while saying, "Gracias." We walked up as far as the main gate when Luca pointed out the rain in the distance. "I have other places to show you. Let's leave and we'll come back later when it's not raining. Stay here and I'll get the car." He hurried away to bring the car closer for Tía Ada.

Luca drove us to the bullfight arena which was closed, since it was Monday. But I got out of the car and took a couple of pictures. Then Luca brought us to the Hipódromo Nacional de Valencia racetrack. Upon entering the parking lot we saw many underfed cows grazing on the road. I couldn't believe how emaciated they looked. The racetrack was open but there weren't any races, because it was Monday. But we walked around anyway.

Luca suggested, "Let's go up to the higher levels so you can get a better view." Tía Ada insisted we go without her. We promised we won't be too long. Luca took my hand and we hurried up the ramps. The higher we got the better the view. Among the shots I took of the racetrack I asked Luca to pose for me. His expression and presence will be long remembered not only through a photograph but in my memory.

We went back to join Tía Ada. I now asked the two of them to pose for a picture. Then he smiled his warm boyish grin. In that one smile he expressed his tender childlike characteristics. Lucky Tía, she's known him since he was a baby.

We left the racetrack and went back to the memorial park. When we arrived Luca was able to leave the car where he picked us up before. We now walked all over the grounds and took many pictures. Before the changing of the guard took place Tía Ada noticed a man taking Polaroid pictures. She asked to have one taken of the three of us. That was the only picture of the three of us that day. I didn't even have a photo of me and Luca. The changing of the guard was formal and brief. Then we left.

Luca suggested we have lunch. We went to the Casa Valencia. This restaurant had a personality all of its own. I was sure it looked very romantic in the evening. We ordered our meals and while we waited for the food we watched the parrots in the cages situated behind Tía Ada and me. We ate pretty fast and didn't talk much. I looked up from my plate and Luca was staring right back at me. His eyes reflecting off his blue shirt looked as vibrant as the feathers of the parrots. He gave me a slanted smile and in those brief seconds, our silence spoke volumes. The check arrived and Tía Ada swiftly grabbed the bill and offered to pay. We headed home after that.

When we arrived we all went into Claudia's house. I heard Luca mention something about suitcases to me. But I wasn't sure what he was saying. And then he was gone. I thought he was getting a bag for himself. About ten minutes later I see him struggling up the stairs with a suitcase. I thought how strange. How could it be so heavy if there was nothing in it? It turned out he got both mine and Tía Ada's suitcases. He put mine in his car and he was carrying hers to the bedroom upstairs. He must have thought I was this princess who expected him to carry all my bags. I was so embarrassed. We decided to take a nap and meet in an hour for the drive to Caracas.

When I woke I packed the rest of my things, freshened up and gathered my bags. As I entered the room downstairs Gena and her mom told me they will say goodbye to me later. I left and brought my bags to Claudia's house. When I arrived Claudia was waiting for me. She gave me two jars of some kind of dessert topping and a unique fabric from Panama. The bright materials were all hand stitched and made a lovely piece of artwork. She had many of them hanging in her home and she was giving me one as a gift. Claudia always made me feel so welcome in her home and with her family. Rafael was gathering all his things.

I went upstairs to talk with Luca. I knocked on his bedroom door. He quickly responded with a very strong, "Sí."

I opened the door a bit and said, "Hi."

"Oh, I didn't realize it was you. Please come in."

I sat on the chair near his desk. "I'm sorry about before, with the luggage. I didn't hear you say you were going to get our bags. I thought you said you were getting YOUR luggage."

"Don't worry about it. How much did you pack?" He smirked and winked at me.

I replied with "Men! No matter what country, you are all the same."

He glanced up from packing his bags, "Did you have fun today?" I nodded yes. "Are you ready to go? Do you have more bags?"

I tilted my head and said, "Yes and can you run and get them for me?"

He started to walk out of the room and I jumped up to stop him. Reaching out for his arm, "Wait, I was joking." Standing close and looking into his eyes, I let go of his arm and he grasped my hand quickly and squeezed it. "I was getting my shaving kit." He leaned in, kissed my nose and vanished.

We loaded up the car. And I caught Luca counting all my bags. As he brushed past me, he whispered, "Women." The family is lined up near the car to say goodbye. I gave hugs and kisses to baby Bella, Gena, Tía Ada and Tía Ines. I turned to Claudia and noticed tears in her eyes. "Please know you are welcome in our home anytime. You are more than Frida's friend, you are now family." We hugged and kissed. She started to smile. "Luca told me about the foreign movie mix up. I told him you were very polite and considerate not to offend him."

I felt sad for Claudia. Only twenty-four hours ago she had her entire family together. As we pulled away I waved goodbye and then I felt the tears fill up in my eyes.

As the car got further away from the house, Luca caressed my shoulder and said, "She'll be fine. Soon Mamá will be with Papá in Panama." I took out a tissue and wiped my tears and nose. I didn't have the courage to tell him my tears were not only for his mom.

"There's a music store nearby, let's buy some CDs. Did you like the music we danced to?"

"Yes, I loved it all. That's a great idea. I just wished I knew what they were singing about. I'll have to get my Spanish dictionary out when I get home."

Rafael stayed in the car while we shopped in the music store. "Here's a club mix and Juan Luis Guerra's, *Bachata Rosa*. We heard lots of these songs the other night." Luca insisted on paying for them. After getting back in the car I noticed he only had a cassette player. I was bummed that we couldn't play these CDs on our road trip. I'll have to wait until I get home. Our long drive started out with a heavy rainfall.

On our trip to Caracas we listened to mostly Luca's music and the radio. It was about seven o'clock when we arrived in the city and very dark. While Luca navigated through the city, I was feeling tired and anxious about my trip home the next day. How could he have this effect on me? Is this just a vacation romance?

"We're here. I'll park my car and then we'll get you set up at the hotel." It was comforting knowing the hotel is just across the street from Luca. I checked in and got the key to my room. Luca and Rafael walked me to my room with my bags. They came inside and Luca looked around. "Can you be ready in an hour?" I nodded yes. Ready for what in an hour I wondered? The brothers left me alone and I locked the door. I turned looked around the room and felt a wave of sadness come over me. I told myself not to cry. I can't look a mess in an hour. But I can't help it. After a few tears trickled down I went to the bathroom and washed my face with cold water.

Chapter 10

I FINISHED GETTING ready. Not sure where we were meeting, I walked across the street to his place.

When I got upstairs, Rafael opened the door for me and said, "I'm tired and will be staying home tonight." I nodded. Without Rafael, it's just me and Luca.

"Good night, Raffy. See you in the morning." Rafael waved to us as Luca closed the apartment door. We rode down the elevator to the parking garage in silence.

Once in the car I asked Luca what are the plans. I remembered he said something about meeting up with his roommate Peter for a drink and then some dinner. I was thankful we didn't have plans with Violeta.

We arrived at a place called El Atico. After leaving the car with the valet, we went inside to look for Peter. It was fairly crowded for a Monday night. Luca didn't see him during our walk around so we got a table.

The waiter approached us and we ordered our drinks. While waiting, Luca informed me that Peter is also American and they've been friends since college. We got our drinks and I glanced around the room. Luca asked, "Are you people watching?" I smiled, "Yes, plus I like to admire what everyone is wearing." He joined in with me and we exchanged comments about the patrons near us. And when the crowd closest to us dissipated, Luca and I had a clear view of a table far across the room from us.

Suddenly I heard a man's voice, "Luciano, I've been looking for you." A tall, broad shouldered football player physique kind of guy with dark hair, light eyes and deeper skin tone is standing next to us. With Luca's attention still on that other table I replied quickly, "Hi, are you Peter?" The man turned to me and smiled, "Yes, are you Emelia?" I nodded, "Yes, please join us."

As Peter was about to take his seat, Luca stood up, murmured something to him and walked away. I looked to Peter, "Did I miss something?" Peter shrugged his shoulders, "I'm not sure what's going on. Luca asked me to keep you company." I replied while watching Luca walk across the room, "I think he might know those people over there."

The waiter stopped and took Peter's drink order. He then said, "Luca knows everybody. When I moved here it was easy to make friends. Every time we'd go out, we'd bump into someone else that he knew and soon they became my friends too." While trying to keep our conversation flowing, I kept a watch over Luca. From a distance it looked like a man and a woman sitting. Luca was blocking my view somewhat and then the woman stood up.

"Peter, can you see who Luca is talking with? She looks familiar to me." He leaned his head towards me, "Where is he?" I replied, "Over there by the window." At which point the man also got up from the table and they walked away. Luca remained at the table for a moment looking towards the exiting couple. Peter said, "I'm not a hundred percent sure, they were leaving when I looked to them, but the woman might have been Violeta and I don't recognize the man."

The waiter brought over Peter's drink and I noticed Luca coming back to our table. On his return he talked with the waiter.

I smiled to Luca and he gave me a smirk when he took his seat. He said, "My apologies for just sneaking away. I thought I saw someone I knew." Luca took a sip of his first drink and as the waiter served us another round of drinks, Luca quickly downed the first one and handed the waiter his empty glass.

I glanced to Peter and said, "Luca, I know we only just met about a week ago, but I thought for sure, you'd indulge me with a goodbye toast tonight." I smiled at Luca trying to change his mood.

Luca reached across the table and took my hand in his, "My mind was elsewhere, yes, I do owe you a toast." I placed my other hand over his, "Luca, what happened over there? Did you know those people?" He laughed and nodded his head, "I know one of them and the other I just met tonight." He gulped the second drink. "Let's get another round."

Peter said, "Luciano, I'm good for now, I haven't finished my first one yet and I'm meeting my girlfriend soon." Feeling Luca's tension I changed the subject and soon I had the roommates sharing stories with me of their escapades at college.

After we finished our drinks and said our goodbyes to Peter, Luca leaned towards me and said, "I'm sorry would you mind if we went home? I'm getting tired and we have an early start in the morning." I nodded in agreement.

While waiting for the valet to bring the car, Luca said to me, "I haven't had a chance to thank you for the invitation, but I would like to make a trip to New York. Let's plan something when you get back home." I smiled and said, "I look forward to it."

The car was now in front of us and we took our seats inside. My head was spinning from his last comment and the two pure alcohol drinks I had guzzled on an empty stomach. With just the stereo playing, we rode without talking for a while. And inexplicably he started to talk about his past girlfriends. Followed by why he doesn't handle long distance relationships well. Was that a statement about us?

Feeling uncomfortable I changed the subject and said, "Luca I should apologize to you."

"What for, what did you do?"

I looked at him while he was driving, "Tonight, when Peter came to the table he said your name differently than how I've been pronouncing it. Have I been saying your name wrong all along?"

He snickered, "The first night we met, you said my full name. But since then you've only called me Luca. Most people usually use the Spanish pronunciation for Luciano, but actually when my mother named me, she used the Italian. So, you were not wrong at all."

I giggle, "Wow, what do you know. Did you mind how I said it? Would you prefer the other way?"

He took my hand and kissed it, "Mind, no in fact, I was touched."

We arrived at his building and he parked the car in the underground garage. We boarded the elevator and I noticed Luca pushed the button for his floor not the lobby.

While looking over at him, "Did you forget I'm staying across the street?"

"No, I didn't forget, let's go to my place and talk for a while."

"Ok, that would be nice. But I thought you were tired."

"I was, tired of the situation. We should talk." He looked down at the ground as we walked to his door.

Once in his place we sat at the dining room table. "Are you hungry or thirsty? You haven't eaten since lunch."

I replied, "First, I need a big glass of water. Those drinks were strong. And yes, I am hungry, what are you offering? You better join me."

Luca quickly heated frozen lasagna in the microwave. Waiting for it to warm up, we sat at the kitchen table and looked at each other. Why were we here together alone in his home? Well, sort of alone, his brother was in the other room. And I wasn't sure if Peter returned. I started feeling butterflies in my stomach, the kind when you know something is about to happen.

After gulping down half the glass of water, I took the glass with me as I walked out of the kitchen and towards the balcony for some fresh air. I so wanted Luca to kiss me right there under the stars on my last night in Venezuela. Where it all started and where it all would end. In the distance I heard music streaming from the living room.

My kind, gentle, generous and very handsome tour guide joined me on the balcony holding a tray with two wine glasses, a plate of lasagna, two forks, napkins and a burning candle. "I hope this will do for your last evening in Venezuela." I smiled at him and moved two chairs together so we were sitting across from one another. As we took our seats, our knees touched and we balanced the tray across our laps. Before even sipping the wine, we dove into the lasagna. After my first forkful I said, "I'm glad I wasn't the only famished person here." He was enjoying his mouthful so much that he was only able to agree with a nod and murmurs of satisfaction. It just took us a minute or two to wipe the plate clean. "Where did all that food go? I might have to heat up another piece." We both laughed.

As Luca lifted the tray he signaled for me to take the wine glasses. He got up and left the tray in the living room and returned to me. I gave him his wine glass and he extended his other hand to me. We walked over to the railing and gazed up at the sky. After a minute or so of silence and a sip or two of wine, Luca began to hum along with the song playing on the stereo. "I've heard this song before, but I think the English version. Is this Jon Secada?" He nodded yes. "May I have this dance with you?"

When I said yes, Luca placed our glasses on the cabinet and took both my hands in his. This man should have been a professional dancer. He glided so naturally and led me effortlessly around the balcony. After a few spins the mood became more serious. The space between us got closer and closer. With his one hand pressed gently on my lower back and the other holding my hand in his near to his heart; I rested my head on his shoulder while nuzzling his neck and I heard him singing along in Spanish the words to the song "Angel". I could have stayed in his arms forever, I felt as if I was in heaven.

When the song ended we were still moving together in the memory of the melody. The next song began and Luca ran his hands through my hair. I raised my head and looked into his eyes. He gently touched my nose with his nose and tenderly kissed the corners of my mouth. I closed my eyes and inhaled deeply while tilting my head back. My mind and body were crashing against one another. I knew we shouldn't be doing this but my body was surging with desire. Suddenly I trembled when he traced my jaw line with kisses. He must have felt my body shiver and feared I was about to swoon, surprisingly I found myself held in his arms as he carried me over to the hammock. Before he placed me onto the hammock we started kissing. Waves of tingles travelled up and down my spine again when I felt his tongue thrusting into my mouth. I gained back some control and moved my hands to his face and began stroking his neck, his ears and his arms. We were so caught up in the moment I don't even remember how we both climbed into the hammock.

As we moved around to get comfortable he stretched over me to grab my water glass. He placed the rim of the glass on my lips and helped to quench my thirst. When I was done I took the glass and did the same for him. We continued this ritual until the glass was empty. He placed it back on the cabinet and we settled into a groove. His arms around me while I rested my head on his chest with our legs entangled.

In silence we rocked back and forth until the hammock stopped. As our breaths became synchronized I listened to the gentle rhythm of his heart while inhaling his fragrance. I wanted the clock to pause just so I could imprint that moment in my memory forever.

He kissed the top of my head and inhaled deeply. I felt him tracing my hand with his fingertips. With my ear pressed against his chest, I started to hear his voice vibrate from his body, "I don't want this magic between us to end. And I fear talking about the obvious will ruin the little time we have left. I wish we could just make this night go on forever. And let life work itself out around us. I say magic because all my life I've never felt all these emotions for someone. And like magic, you will soon disappear and I'm left wondering how this all came about and how I could let you go away."

He took a deep breath and continued, "I'm ashamed because this must be so confusing to you. You're probably wondering how I can be with you telling you all this when I'm in another relationship. Just saying that to you makes me cringe with the thought of that part of my life tainting the happiness we have found with one another. I never thought I could feel this way towards someone. Do you think it's because we know it's a fleeting romance? Forget all this, I don't even want to understand why, I just want to cherish being with you and only with you." He raised my hand to his lips and placed featherlike kisses on my palm.

I too didn't want the magic to end. But I knew I had so much to tell him. And yet I didn't know where to begin. I closed my eyes hoping the darkness would connect my thoughts and words as superbly as he expressed.

"I also fear that if I talk about how I'm feeling this magic between us will fade away. But I know that I can't get on that plane tomorrow without sharing with you all that I'm experiencing and thinking. It just wouldn't be fair to either of us."

He squeezed my hand and held it lovingly against his chest. "I am confused by so many things. How could you be interested in someone like me especially after I met your girlfriend? You seemed happy together, you seemed compatible. But the more time we spent together, the more I felt we fit well together. I haven't dated many men and my longest relationship lasted just a couple of months. And I never felt what I'm feeling for you with any of them. As you said, could this be just a fleeting romance? We don't have all the pressures of our everyday lives. And maybe if we did, this magic would cease. Should we even entertain the thought of what happens tomorrow after we say goodbye? Or will promising to keep in touch tarnish all this? For we know, reality sometimes diminishes even the most genuine connections. Maybe the beauty of what has developed should remain frozen in our memory. I can already feel myself pulling away from you, not because I don't care for you. It's to protect me from the sadness I will feel just twenty-four hours from now, when I get back to my life in New York without you."

I sighed and shifted around in the hammock looking for something to drink. Luca sensed my struggles and quickly got the wine glass for me. I sat up in the hammock and took a couple of sips to wet my parched mouth. I offered him the glass and he finished the rest and placed it back on the cabinet. I moved around to face him and we almost flipped out of the hammock.

After a round of laughs we settled into place, I took his hands in mine and looked into his eyes. "No matter what happens with you and me after tomorrow, I want you to know, I have loved every moment that we've spent together. You have given me such joy and I hope I've done the same for you. I will never forget you Luciano Morales. And you must remember you will always have a place in my heart." He took his hands from mine and wiped the tears streaming down my face and I gently wiped the tears running down his.

We quietly held one another for a few minutes and were startled when we heard, "Ahem" in the doorway. "It's so late, when are we getting up in the morning?" Rafael asked.

Luca looked at his watch and grimaced. "We should leave here about eight-thirty." He climbed out of the hammock and gave me a hand. Once I got both my feet on the ground I felt a bit light headed. But I didn't stumble. We all walked into the living room and Luca brought the tray and glasses into the kitchen. Rafael was quietly observing us. He probably realized he interrupted something. Luca looked at me from the kitchen, "I should walk you to the hotel, let's go." I nodded yes and said goodnight to Rafael.

We clasped our hands together as if holding on for those last few minutes would keep the magic intact. All the way to my room we held hands. Before I put the key in the door, Luca took hold of my hips. "Just a few nights ago I first met you and here we are tonight. Our souls will remain connected forever. I have no doubt. After tomorrow we have to figure out how to navigate our lives to bring us back together. And wherever life takes either of us, you must know you too will always have a place in my heart." We embraced for a very long time. I sensed that neither of us wanted to let go.

He took the key from my hand and opened the door. We walked into the room together and the door shut behind us. He inspected our surroundings and placed the key on the dresser. "As much as I want to make love with you tonight, I know it will complicate matters even more for both of us." I walked up to him and placed a finger on his lips and said, "I understand." I stepped away and opened the door to let him go home. He walked out and said, "Good night."

I shut the door and locked it. All I thought was, is this the end? Why did this week have to go so fast? I looked around the room and I felt so sad and alone. I got through all the bedtime practices with very little thought of my actions. My mind was crowded with thoughts of Luca and our last night. I only remembered crawling into bed and crying myself to sleep. What I did not know then, it was the first of many nights that I would cry myself to sleep missing Luca.

Chapter 11

I WOKE UP before the alarm and I was ready early. There was a knock at the door, it was Luca and he appeared to be in a daze that morning. I couldn't pick up on his mood, so I just kept the tone light. We left the room and took the elevator to the lobby. I dropped off my key, settled the hotel bill and then we were gone.

Rafael sat in the front seat and I was in the back seat behind Luca. The ride to the airport didn't take very long. Fortunately when we arrived we saw both flights were leaving from the same terminal. Luca handed us our luggage and went to park the car.

Rafael helped me check in. After Rafael's several comments during my trip about my sunglasses, I gifted them to him. I thought he would like them more than me. He was thankful.

When I was checked in Luca returned. We left Rafael to deal with his travel arrangements and told him to meet us upstairs in the cafeteria. Luca went ahead and got us breakfast while I hunted down a table. I watched him from my seat and thought about all the sweet memories from my visit. While we were eating, Luca told me what happened the previous night at the bar.

"I had this feeling she was seeing someone else, but last night confirmed it."

Shocked by what I was hearing, I asked him, "How long have you been dating?"

He looked away from me, "Officially, six months, but we've known one another for years. Her father and my father are friends and well, we've sort of grown up around one another."

"I don't know what to say Luca. I'm sure seeing her with the other man was unsettling for you."

He looked into my eyes, "At that moment, yes, but now that I've had a few hours to think about it, I'm adjusting to it. I'm free, free to be with you. I knew what I had with her was nothing compared to what we have found with one another." He took my hands in his.

"You look very sad today Emelia."

I looked away from him, "Yeah I am. I hate goodbyes." What can I say to him that either of us hasn't said already? "Words cannot express my gratitude for all you did for me during this visit. You must come to my home in New York, so I can be your personal guide." He nodded yes.

Rafael joined us and while we finished eating, Luca talked about his job and an upcoming presentation he was preparing. I asked, "Are you nervous about the meeting at work?" Luca nodded with confidence, "No, it's all prepared. That's the part of my job I like most. I'll mail you a copy of the video if you want." "Oh that would be great to see you in action." He said, "Give me your address."

We exchanged addresses. He looked over the paper I handed to him, "I don't see your phone number I told you I don't write letters, I will call you." I purposely left out my phone number to see if he would ask for it. He handed me back the paper and I quickly wrote my number on it.

The time approached for me to go to the boarding gate. Luca has carried all my bags while we walked around the airport. And as I look back he took good care of me since the moment I met him.

We rode the escalator down to the boarding gates. "You know how I said I don't like goodbyes, I was very serious. Before we get downstairs, I will say goodbye now. Thank you so much with making sure I had a wonderful trip. I will miss you and your family. And thank you for giving me a piece of your heart. I will forever cherish you and this week we spent together." The escalator ride was coming to an end.

We looked up at the signs for the gate numbers. Mine was the opposite direction of Rafael's gate. Rafael began to take my bags from Luca, "I will walk with you to your gate." "Raffy no, but thank you, you don't have to. Your gate is not even near mine." I took my bags from him.

Rafael and I smiled to each other. "Take care of yourself Rafael, I will miss our conversations and please come and visit me." We hugged and kissed.

I turned to Luca. My eyes were dry and I was very nervous. Gosh, I didn't want to do this in front of his brother. But I had no choice. I placed all my bags on the floor and looked into Luca's eyes. "My trip here was for Frida's wedding. And I leave today with memories that will last me a lifetime." My eyes began to water. "What more can I say that I haven't told you? Let's keep this simple so that I'm not a mess going through security. I hope to see you very soon."

I kissed him softly on his cheek and hugged him as if I never wanted to let him go. And when we released I picked up my things and smiled at him.

He just stood and stared and asked or remarked, "That's it?" And I said, "I told you I'm not good at goodbyes." And then I walked away. Never turning back, just moving forward. Suddenly I felt a hand gripping my wrist and I turned around and found Luca standing next to me.

"Well, I don't like saying goodbye and especially to someone who has stolen my heart. But Mi Lia I certainly will make this a better goodbye than you." He embraced me wildly and I dropped all my bags. The sounds of travelers passing us by and the overhead announcements suddenly were drowned out by our insatiable kisses. One of his hands was pressed against my back and the other behind my neck making sure I didn't have a chance to get away from him during the last few minutes afforded for his goodbye. As our kisses slowly ended, I opened my eyes and saw him looking at me.

With tears streaming down his face I hugged him tightly. I sweetly whispered, "You weren't kidding you are so much better at goodbyes than me." I heard his muffled laugh pressed into my shoulder. I kissed his ear and his cheek and when we split apart I kissed his lips gently. We wiped each other's tears. "Emelia, I promise I will call you after I simplify my life." I replied, "Let's just say until we see each other again."

One last embrace and one last kiss I walked away from him towards the passport check. Once I reached the desk I turned sideways and glanced over at the place I left Luca. He was now joined by Rafael and they were standing there together watching me. As the security clerk reviewed my travel documents I waved to both of them. The clerk said, "You may proceed. Thank you for visiting Venezuela." They waved back to me and as I turned from them one last time, I tried my hardest to hold back my tears but it was no use, it was like a waterfall of sadness.

Chapter 12

JENENE BRINGS OVER the box of tissues and we both sit at the table drying our eyes. "Emelia that must have been so difficult leaving him that day, I'm crying so I can't imagine how you felt. What happened next? Did you ever hear from him?" I rose from the table and went to refill my glass with water. "Do you want any?" Jenene nods her head. I fill our glasses and return to the table. I take a sip of water and begin walking around the dining room.

"It was so long ago. I remember after a few weeks, I called him. And the conversation was friendly but not assuring. I didn't press him about anything and just said goodbye." "But you said you went back again, for Christmas. When did that happen? And how did that come about?"

I glance over at the clock and it's almost two in the morning. "Jenene, it's very late. We'll sleep the day away tomorrow if we don't go to bed now. And we need to go shopping. I promise I'll tell you about my second trip." Her eyes looked tired and as weary as mine felt. She says, "I will hold you to that promise." I smile and nod.

Turning off the stereo and the lights downstairs we walk upstairs to the bedrooms. I stroll with Jenene towards the simply furnished guest room.

"Although the décor is sparse the bed should be very comfortable. Just remember my house is your house Jenene. If you need anything from the kitchen just help yourself. We should plan to wake up around nine o'clock."

"Thanks Emelia, don't worry, I've gotten used to your work in progress home by now. Plus I don't think I'll move from this bed all night. I'll dream about you and Luca celebrating Christmas together."

"You're crazy, you dream about your own guy. And I'll take care of my own dreams. Good night Jenene, thanks for listening to me go on and on."

"Are you kidding, don't thank me, I should be thanking you. I'm glad it doesn't just end there. Good night Emmy."

I go to my bedroom down the hall and crawl under the blankets. After all this reminiscing I only see Luca's face as I drift off to sleep.

Chapter 13

My SHOPPING SPREE with Jenene was fun, expensive and well worth it. We managed to pick out a dress for the party and three more dresses for dining and dancing and a couple of outfits for afternoon jaunts. She even convinced me to buy two sets of pajamas and one of them is family appropriate.

When we arrived home we both collapsed on the couch. "Wow, we really went to town today. I'd like to try everything back on again, but I just can't move." I hear Jenene murmuring something. We started out later than intended but even so, I think we shopped for five hours.

Exasperated Jenene says, "I'm glad you had the smart idea to pick up supper on our way home." After a giggle she adds, "I can't believe that we lasted all those hours. I didn't feel tired until we sat down. And now I don't want to leave. Do you mind if I stay another night?"

While smiling back at my tired and loyal friend I say, "No, please, I don't mind at all. You put up with me all day the least I can do is give you a good night's rest."

"Well, you do owe me the second part of the story. And if I leave now, I don't think you'll get to telling me about Christmas in Panama." I grab a pillow from the couch and put it on my face. She takes it from me. "You promised! I'm cashing it in now."

"I thought you said you were tired. You have a one track mind." In a demanding voice Jenene says, "Well, I need to know what happened. I want to make sure, what you bought today to wear on your trip will be fitting. This second part will tell me if you should be wowing Luca or making him sorry he's not with you now."

"Jenene, I told you before, whatever it was between me and Luca was innocent, sweet and complicated. And my upcoming trip is about my friendship with Frida. Too many years have stood between us and I want us to reconnect. I don't know why we haven't in all these years. But now, the time has come. And as for Luca, I understand from his brother Henry, he's still married and has a family. It will be awkward at first for me, I'm sure he's so engrossed in his own life he won't even remember our past. As long as I see he's happy, isn't that all that matters?"

"Oh Emelia, yes, I agree, this trip is all about Frida. But, you have to admit, you and Luca had some connection and no matter where he is in his life now, when he sees you he will remember. And I know you Emmy you will need to feel confident about yourself when you're with him. If you don't, you'll feel sad about seeing him in the life he has built for himself. I'm hoping these new clothes will empower you to get through those first critical moments. Do I believe the clothes will make the difference; not completely. But they certainly will provide the encouragement you'll need when you're there. When you wear them just think of me and it will be like I'm on this trip with you."

I don't know if I'm just tired or all these memories have dragged up feelings from a long time ago. But suddenly my eyes well up with tears. "I didn't mean to upset you." I get up to look for the tissue box.

"You didn't, it's just. Maybe I shouldn't even go. Part of me hopes that I only spend my visit with Frida, Max and their son. I know, initially it will be heartbreaking for me to see Luca. I don't know how I'll manage, if I have to spend the whole week with him and his perfect life. And it's just so silly, it's not like we were married, or dating we were just two people that experienced a special connection decades ago."

Jenene places her hand on my shoulder, "I understand why you feel so anxious about going, but what happened between you two on your next visit? Did you have sex with Luca? Did he make you more promises?" I close my eyes to gather my thoughts along with the memories of that Christmas.

When I open them she's watching me. I smirk at Jenene thinking how little she knows about me in my younger virtuous years. She laughs and with eyes wide open says, "You didn't?" I nod at her and say, "We didn't." Now looking disappointed she says, "Emelia, why not? You seemed to be on the edge of hooking up at the aunt's house and in the hotel. What were you waiting for? Were you still a virgin?"

I cover my eyes and say, "Jenene, no. By that time, someone had already conquered my fortress. Plus, on this next trip, I was slightly apprehensive with him." She takes my hands away from my eyes and says while glaring at me, "Emelia, I know I'm a bit younger than you, but I never heard that phrase before, where'd that come from?"

Trying to remember the saying from my youth I begin to tell her, "When I was a teenager and learning about life being a young woman, I was given this advice by someone dear to me." Let me see if I can recall her exact words, oh yes.

"My worldly friend Lisa who was a few years older than me advised; don't let just any man's love spear conquer your fortress." We both crack up and Jenene says, "Were medieval books the trend back then?" Still laughing, I say, "I have no idea, but love spear and fortress have always remained in the back of my mind."

"Love spear?" Jenene asks. I nod, "Yes, love spear." I admit, "Over the years, I've thought of other fun names, what about you; what do you call *IT*?" She replies, "I've got one or two that I think about but they're in Spanish. And they're not as funny as love spear. I want to hear about your other words."

I nod, "No, we're getting off topic." Jenene nudges me, "Come on Emelia, I have to get love spear out of my head, you better tell me the other ones. Otherwise I'll keep asking you about Luca's *lanza del amor*." [Love spear]

"Lanza Jenene, what the heck is lanza?" Happily she replies, "Spear of course. Come on!"

Begrudgingly I say, "Ok, but first I want to get some water or maybe something stronger." Jenene follows me to the kitchen. Knowing it might be a long night, I start us off with water and I begin filling each of the glasses.

"So after the love spear talk, I remember that I took Lisa's advice and waited for the right guy to enter my fortress. In my early twenties I was close friends with a guy and we made out whenever we were alone, but I never felt like he was THE one. Not that I wasn't attracted to him, but during some heated moments he would refer to his love spear as..." I stop talking and take a sip of water wondering why am I telling this to Jenene? "Emelia, you can't stop now."

I giggle nervously and continue, "Well he was one of those guys that would refer to *IT* as his junior. His name was Jack and he would say things like, Jack Jr is so excited for you. Or Jack Jr wants to feel your touch. And then he started abbreviating and would say things like, JJ just wants to be held by you or loved by you." Jenene is laughing with me and I say, "So I knew Jack and JJ were not occupying this fortress." Jenene looking confused, "So, do you call the love spear JJ now?"

"Ah! No! But good question. Well, I guess, just his. But Jack got me started on this silly word game I only played in my mind of course, until NOW!" I sneer at Jenene.

"It all began with my first conqueror, we dated for a few months and he was very sweet and romantic. During our special sleepover and my getting acquainted with his love spear, these two words popped into my head, Marvelous Treat. Thankfully he was a kind and gentle lover and made me feel sex was an indulgence. And funny enough MT are his initials. So, JJ and love spear were tossed aside and going forward, I would give each a unique name according to their initials."

With lips pursed and eyes squinting, Jenene says, "So, what are Luca's initials?"

I tilt my head to the side and say, "LM, why?"

"Well, what name would you give to Luca's lanza?"

"Jenene, I have to, you know, be in contact with it to create this personalized word pairing."

"Oh Emmy just play with me and quickly think of something for LM."

With my face blushing I say, "LM, LM." I giggle, "Remember, this is purely word play and based only on his excellent dance moves, powerful hips and with very little thought. I will say, Lanza Magnífica." Jenene screams with delight.

After Jenene's laughter calms, says, "Oh that's so hilarious. Now tell me, what other labels have you given out? And do you have a special name for your fortress?" I walk back into the living room as Jenene follows me. "Emmy,

I know you remember them, tell me." Sitting on the couch I say, "You are relentless Jenene."

She sits next to me, "After you divulge some, I'll keep quiet while you continue with the rest of the story. You have to admit this was a fun distraction. And I got you smiling again."

"For you maybe, but going down memory sex lane at my age, when I've had this long of a break, is somewhat frustrating."

She giggles, "Just tell me your top three."

Reclining back into the cushions I run my hands through my hair while I try to recall some of my past loves. Embarrassed that I even started this with Jenene, I settle on three she should find humorous. I begin, "I won't tell you their names and don't ask me for explanations or descriptions, got it?" Jenene smiles and says, "Got it."

Looking down I say, "Distinguished Dilly...Everlasting Chubby...and Mysterious Wonder."

I glance up at Jenene and she says, "What were they again?"

I shake my head, "No, I am not repeating them."

She laughs, "I think I heard, Distinguished Dilly and Everlasting Chubby, what was the last one?"

With a scowl I say, "Mysterious Wonder."

Jenene says, "I may have figured out the first two and I know I'm not supposed to ask, but, what's the story behind Mysterious Wonder?"

I should have told her another and left that one out, but I know the others would probably need further discussions as well. Trying to find the most delicate way to describe this particular man's circumstance I take a swig of water. I reply, "Well, due to this gentleman's minor offering I was often left wondering of its whereabouts."

With my arms folded across my chest and wearing a comical expression I remain quiet until Jenene understands my cryptic explanation. She smiles and with questioning eyes raises her right hand up between us and with closed fist, simply extends her pinkie finger and waves it to me. I giggle and nod yes to her. Grateful she figured out Mysterious Wonder's biggest, rather smallest challenge.

I add, "But in all honesty, Mysterious Wonder, even with his limitations, provided many unique ways for keeping The Empress very satisfied."

Jenene rolls her eyes and hurls the pillow at me while screaming, "The Empress! So perfect, now I have to think of a name for mine."

Hoping not to continue with this conversation, I interrupt her and say, "And now may I go on with my story?" Jenene settles into the cushions and says, "Yes, I'm eager to hear more about how The Empress rejects the Lanza Magnífica."

"The following year, Frida and I kept in touch with letters and some phone calls. My life here was changing. I was moving to Manhattan as my parents were selling our home. Frida knew I was sad about that and suggested I visit for Christmas. So, I jumped at Frida's invitation. And this trip would be to Panama not Venezuela. Most of the family was living there at this point."

"What did your family think? Were they disappointed you were spending the holiday away?" I reply "I'm sure they were, but they always knew when I got something in my head, there really wasn't a chance to change my mind."

"When my trip was getting closer, I recall Frida telling me she wasn't certain if all her family would be together for Christmas. So, I wasn't even sure I'd see Luca. She did say something about him going through a break up and taking it badly. And that's why he might not be with them and he didn't know if he'd get the days off from work. Part of me wondered if he was saying that to avoid seeing me. So that trip, I remember I was tackling many feelings. But knew I had to go."

"I'll just tell you about some highlights of that Christmas. I remember spending most of my visit with Frida and her husband. And the days we spent with her family celebrating Christmas, well, they were special, because of the traditions, her grandparents and Luca. But it also was very puzzling because of Luca and the year we spent out of touch. Even today I'm still not sure what happened to him."

Chapter 14

FRIDA AND MAX met me at the airport. It was such a relief to see them both once I cleared customs. I had a bag for clothes and a bag of gifts for the family. And security went through everything. So, the minute I saw the two of them, I was grateful for their help to carry some of these things. While we walked to the parking lot to find their car, I was greeted by the hot Panamanian breezes. I knew from that point, it was not going to be like any Christmas up north. We secured my things in the trunk of their jeep and made our way to the city.

We stayed at Frida and Max's home the first night. They had an apartment right in the city. After dropping off my things and freshening up, we went back out. First we stopped at the Garcia's house, you know, Max's family. It was nice to see them all again. And then we tried to visit Frida's parents. When we arrived at their apartment building we rang the bell. And after a couple of tries Luca answered the intercom. Frida spoke in Spanish to him. And she looked at both me and Max and suggested we leave.

We grabbed a quick bite and drove back to their place. Over dinner Frida said her parents weren't home and mentioned we'll see them the next day. And since we'll be leaving early tomorrow morning for the drive to her grandparents' home it was just as well.

We enjoyed dinner and caught up on life. And afterwards, they were busy making special gifts for everyone. I also was organizing and wrapping the gifts I brought and soon it was bedtime. And I remember just collapsing into bed.

The next morning we drove to Chiriqui. We stayed there with the family for Christmas. It was a long drive from the city. Max drove and Frida was his copilot and they both were my tour guides. They would tell me all about the areas we drove through while listening to music and sharing more stories about our lives that past year.

Frida and her family spent many holidays and vacations in Chiriqui. So, it was a special place for all of them. When we arrived she introduced me to her grandparents. They looked fairly young. Maybe they were in their seventies and both had white hair. Her grandfather, Abuelo Romano or Manny was slim, average height, wore dark framed glasses and had a childlike charm to him. Her grandmother, Abuela Liliana or Lily was shorter than Frida. Not even five feet tall, a sturdy lady with a sparkle in her eyes and a very warm smile. I understood immediately after meeting them, why the family had such special memories there.

The house was nicely laid out. Very open and had many bedrooms. Frida showed me to my room. I unpacked my things and freshened up.

Not long after that, Frida's parents arrived. I learned during our reunion, Nicolás was spending the holiday at his girlfriend's home in the states. But Luca and Henry should be joining us very soon. Frida's other brother Rafael, lived in town with his fiancée Teresa and her family. It seemed we'd have a full house for Christmas.

I helped Abuela unpack and put away all the groceries Claudia and Rico brought. I overheard Claudia speaking to Frida about Luca. It was in Spanish so I didn't understand much except that Frida was annoyed at him the night before when he didn't open the door for us. And Claudia said he had been sleeping and we had just woken him.

Claudia began to prepare lunch. I helped to set the table with Frida while Max found more chairs to put around the table.

I noticed everyone seemed on edge. And I wasn't sure if I should ask Frida what was going on. But since her brothers hadn't arrived and we were alone I decided to ask her anyway.

"Frida, is everything ok? It seems like there's something going on. But, if it's a family thing, I will understand if you don't want to tell me." She looked around to see where everyone was and then she moved closer to me on the couch.

"It's just Luca. He's going through a rough time. He and Violeta broke up. We don't know why they ended things. He hasn't said anything to any of us.

We weren't even sure he'd come for Christmas. But then he arrived yesterday afternoon and stayed with my parents. My mom said he didn't say much except that he was happy to be home for Christmas with the family."

Even though I was confused I tried to give her some hope. "Well, maybe that means he's coming to terms with the break up. It's a good sign that he made the trip to be with all of you." She nodded yes and then glanced over at the kitchen door, "I think I hear them now."

We went to the kitchen and I was overcome by the aroma of whatever Claudia was cooking. I proceeded to the stove, "Something smells delicious. What are you making?" Claudia lifts the lid off the big pot and showed me, "Bolognese sauce for pasta." She smiled back at me. "But we'll have to wait a couple of hours. It's not ready yet."

The kitchen door opened and I saw Henry's smiling face. "*Hola, Felice Navidad!*" We all ran to him. Relieved him of his bags and one by one he exchanged hugs and kisses with his family. Henry had been away at college and hadn't seen everyone since August. He's such a bright star in this family.

He saw me and yelled, "Emelia, come here!" We kissed and hugged each other so tightly. "Henry, it's so very good to see you! I missed you." He laughed, "When Frida said you'd be here for Christmas I was so excited to see you again." "Yes, I'm so thankful for the invite to invade your family holiday." He laughed again.

And I saw Luca walking in with his dad. They were both carrying loads of stuff. After they put their bags down, the welcoming committee started again for Luca. He looked fairly the same but he grew a beard and his hair was much longer. This wilder look on Luca was very attractive. His grandfather embraced Luca and they exchanged words. They were both smiling when they separated. And then Luca took his petite grandmother in his arms. She wiped tears from her eyes as they stood in front of one another. And Luca kissed her gently on her cheek and touched her face so tenderly.

He said his hellos to his mom, Frida and Max and then he noticed me. With a huge smile, he exclaimed, "*Bienvenido a Chiriqui Emelia!*" [Welcome to Chiriqui!] I smiled and he kissed me and held me close to him. In a whisper

I said, "Thanks Luciano, I'm happy to be here." He tightened his grip once again before letting me go.

"Do you have anything else in the car?" Rico asked Luca. "Yes, I will be quick." And he was gone.

Frida and Claudia were busy unpacking and putting away the food that Henry and Luca brought. I overheard them discussing plans. "Emelia we need to find a tree for the living room and get some decorations. So before lunch we'll go into town."

Luca replied, "Me too, I will join you."

Claudia interrupted, "No Luca, I need you with me to help with other things I must get." Henry mentioned they will look for a tree in the mountains. Frida said, "Can we do that first with you? I want Emmy to see how we get our tree."

They all laughed. I looked around, "Why are you laughing? What's so funny about getting a tree?" Frida replied, "Around here, you won't see the typical trees you use back at home. And we always encounter some problem bringing one down from the mountain."

Soon we were on our way to find this tree. Max was driving the jeep with Frida, Henry and me. Rico, Luca and Abuelo followed in Rico's car. In minutes we were driving on a dirt road and soon the road inclined. At Frida's direction, she told Max to continue driving. He kept asking her if she was sure. And Henry was giggling and added, "Yes, keep going." And we heard the car horn behind us blaring. We all turned around to look at Rico and he was waving for us to stop.

We got out of the cars and I heard him tell them his car can't drive up further or he'll get stuck. So we started walking around looking for the tree. She was right; there weren't any typical trees from back home. They all looked like these tall skinny trees with delicate willowy branches. Abuelo pointed to one and Rico started to place a rope around the tree. Everyone saw the tree Abuelo picked out and smiled. I looked around and it was just as skinny and tall as the rest. I wasn't sure why this one was special to him.

Finally all the men began to help with the ax to knock the tree down. After a few minutes, the tree toppled over and the men carried it to the cars.

After securing it on the jeep, we began our trip back down the mountain. One problem, Rico's car was not moving. Instead of just letting his car roll backwards in reverse, he had tried to turn it face forward down the mountain. So when the car was horizontal his tires kept spinning but not getting traction. The guys all got out and assisted, leaving me and Frida alone in the jeep. "I told you Emelia, there's always something when we get the tree."

I laughed after seeing the car finally begin to move backwards down the mountain. Rico wasn't taking any chances so when the car started to move, he didn't stop to get Luca. So Luca waved goodbye to his grandfather and father and got a ride with us. I sat in the backseat between the two brothers. We all laughed when Henry retold how their dad just drove away without Luca. Within a few minutes we were back at home and bringing the tree into the house.

After everyone cleaned up from that excursion, we left in two separate cars for more shopping. Max, Frida and I were in charge of decorations and flowers for the table. Luca and Claudia were buying some last minute food items.

We could have taken one car, since after we found the decorations we met Claudia and Luca in town. While securing our purchases in the trunk, Frida said we're off to pick some flowers. Luca asked where we were going and he told Frida to wait a minute for him. He and Claudia walked away and I saw them loading up the trunk. And he opened the driver's side door for her.

He quickly returned to us and hopped in the back seat next to me. We headed out of town. The music was playing, the wind from the open windows was making my hair fly all around and we were merrily making our way to get flowers.

After driving down another dirt road, Max stopped the jeep at the end of the pathway. We all got out, Luca asked, "Do you have your camera Emelia?" I nodded yes. "You will want to take pictures here."

I grabbed my camera and smiled at him. Thinking, that's nice he remembered. We walked a few minutes down a narrow dirt path. We came upon a little house when Luca grasped my arm. "Come this way." Frida and Max went towards the right and Luca and I walked towards the left.

I could not believe what was ahead of us. It looked like all these flowers were just growing wild. But they were grouped together for acres and acres and as far as the eye could see. First, there were flowers that looked like purple daisies and then another section of pink hibiscus followed by fields of calla lilies. I had never seen calla lilies like this. I usually saw them in florist shops at home. They were breathtaking. I was so taken by the abundance of beauty I hadn't realized that Luca was still holding my arm leading me into this paradise. I just wanted to capture all this grandness.

"Go, I will wait for you here." I smiled at Luca.

"Are you sure, don't you want to come with me?"

"I'll stay to make sure we won't get lost. I know you want to go."

"Thanks, I won't be too long."

He smiled and waved me away. My goodness, I've always loved the unique look of calla lilies but had never been surrounded by them is such multitudes. I didn't even know where to start. After shooting about twenty pictures, of which I knew I could never capture them in all this glory, I slowly made my way back to Luca.

"I thought I'd have to send a search party for you. At times I didn't see you."

I laughed, "Ah yes, that's when I knelt on the ground to get some close up pictures of these beauties."

He put his hand out. "I want to take your picture surrounded by the flowers." I smirked.

"Give me your camera you should see how happy you look. I want you to remember this moment."

I handed over the camera to my silly photographer. He gestured for me to walk away from him and barked his instructions as if I was at a photo shoot. "Spin, smile, arms open, spin, tilt your head, smile and now come to me." I just kept hearing the shutter clicking away while I saw Luca's smile peeking out from behind the camera.

"Ok, are we done yet?"

He lowered the camera and replied, "Yes, let's go find Frida before she worries about us."

He grabbed my hand and we ran through the field of purple daisies towards the little house. I think about what he said and I know with or without pictures, I would always remember that time in the fields with him. Why was it so easy to be with Luca?

We saw Frida and Max and they had bunches of flowers in their arms wrapped in brown paper.

"Did you see the calla lilies Emelia?"

"Yes Frida, they were spectacular."

"Ready to go home?" Max asked us. We all agreed to leave. On the drive back, I think everyone was feeling a bit tired. We just listened to the music and relaxed in our seats. I leaned back on the head rest and just enjoyed the scenic views. The ride was a bit bumpy. So, I steadied myself by holding on to the seat cushion with one hand and the other resting on the space between me and Luca. After a few more jostles of the road, I felt Luca's pinky finger interlocking with mine. Suddenly I felt the butterflies in my stomach fluttering around. I turned to look towards him but he didn't look my way. His eyes stayed affixed on the view out of his window. And then he gently enveloped my hand in his with a slight squeeze. I caressed his wrist with my thumb and looked out my window. I felt like the two of us were secretly sharing our feelings without bringing any attention to our companions in the front seats.

Soon we arrived back at the house. Upon entering we became immediately intoxicated with Claudia's cooking.

Luca exclaimed, *"Mamá, cuándo comemos, tengo mucha hambre!"* [Mom, when do we eat, I am very hungry!]

We saw Claudia walking in from the living room, "Just a few more minutes, go wash your hands. And then come into the living room, Rafael and Teresa are here."

At her orders we all went our separate ways to clean up for lunch. Luca stayed with Claudia in the kitchen. Frida and I took over one of the bathrooms. As we were washing, we laughed again about getting the tree. And I told her how much I was enjoying being there with her and her family.

Frida went to her bedroom and as I was leaving the bathroom for the hallway I saw Luca coming out of my bedroom. I first wondered what was he up to and thought maybe he put my purse and camera in the room. I remembered I had left them on a chair when we first arrived.

Sure enough, I found the purse and camera on the dresser. I also spotted a little ceramic jar on the dresser filled with some of the wild flowers Frida had earlier wrapped in paper from the fields. I touched the jar and I felt my heartbeats increase.

After my quick primping I went to join the family. I first saw Luca opening a wine bottle and he welcomed me with his gorgeous smile. I smiled back to him and joined him.

"Will you have some wine with us?"

"Yes, I think I will."

Frida was taking down the wine glasses from the cabinet. Luca informed Frida that I too will need a glass. She said, "Ok, I'll just place a few glasses on the table and whoever is drinking wine can take one."

I walked over to Claudia who was overseeing the pasta. "Can I help you at all?" She nodded, "Yes, there's a salad in the refrigerator. Take it out and I made some dressing. It's in the bowl over there. Just drizzle it over the salad and mix it up."

I was glad to help out and not just stand by gawking at Luca. I needed a distraction. While I was mixing the salad, I heard music coming from the living room. Henry joined us and announced, "Everyone ready for some dancing?"

He grabbed Frida who just set the last wine glass on the table. And they started giggling while Henry was leading her around the dining table and into the living room. I noticed Luca walking towards the dining table with two decanters of red wine. He poured a little wine in a glass and took a sip. It must have been to his liking for he added more wine to that glass and then put it in front of one of the place settings. Then he grabbed another wine glass and left it at the place setting next to him. And looked up and caught me watching him.

He pointed to the chair and nodded at me. I nodded back yes to him. And he was off to the living room to join the rest of the family. I asked, "Claudia can I bring anything to the table?" She opened the fridge door and handed me grated cheese, butter and a jug of water. I retrieved them all from her and placed them on the table. When I turned to go back to the kitchen nobody was in there. I found everyone in the living room. I relaxed in the first chair I spotted and listened to the family carrying on with one another. Max saw me and joined me in the chair next to me.

"Are you having a nice visit Emelia?"

"Yes Max, I am. It's a bit different from when I visited for your wedding. I feel like everyone is more at ease."

"Oh yes, we all were running around preparing for the big day then. This is how it is when the family comes together here."

Rafael saw me and rushed over to me. We embraced and he waved to his fiancée, "Teresa, please come here, I want you to meet Frida's friend from New York, Emelia."

Teresa came over to us. She had long wavy brown hair and was about my height and stature. I also noticed she had a smile as infectious as Rafael's. We exchanged kisses and greeted each other. As we got to know one another, I recall seeing Claudia going back to the kitchen, but first she stopped into the dining room. As she made some last minute adjustments of the table settings, I saw her taking Luca's wine glass. I thought maybe she was bringing it to him. But she placed it somewhere else on the table. Maybe she confused it with someone else's glass. And then I got back to my conversation with Teresa and Rafael.

Just a few minutes passed and Claudia announced lunch was ready. As we all made our way into the dining room, I saw Frida helping her mom in the kitchen so I joined them. Frida handed me a basket with warm bread. As I approached the dining table I saw most everyone had taken their seats. I also noticed Luca picking up his wine glass and walking towards his originally planned seat. At which point he stood there and signaled for me to sit next to him. Frida and Claudia placed the pasta and salad on the table and took seats next to their spouses. Before Luca sat, he filled my glass with wine and asked who else wanted wine. As he filled glasses and passed them around, I noticed Claudia looking towards the two of us. After the wine had been distributed, Luca remained standing and began to make a toast.

His father interrupted him to share his own words. And suddenly Abuelo rose from his chair and tapped his glass with a spoon. I looked over at Frida and she was quietly laughing and I smiled back at her. We all gave Abuelo our full attention. Luca sat next to me and whispered, "The man of the house will give us his blessing."

Abuelo rested his arm on Abuela Lily's shoulder. And he raised his wine glass and in Spanish he shared his blessing. When he was done we all lifted our glasses to Abuelo. Luca tapped his glass against mine. And we enjoyed the delicious wine. Then Rico began his own toast.

"As we begin our Christmas celebration, Claudia and I want to thank everyone for being here together. As we get older and our lives become more complicated, it won't be so easy to have all of us here. Let us embrace the next few days and have a glorious Christmas. My heart is overjoyed by your love and happiness. Salud!"

My tear filled eyes met Frida's and we lifted our glasses to one another. Luca observed our exchange and as he began to tell me something, his hand gently wiped a tear streaming down my face. "Your friendship with my sister is very meaningful." As I tried to compose my tears of joy, "Yes, Frida is like the sister I never had." Henry bellowed, "Are we allowed to eat now?"

Claudia said yes and everyone began to pass around the food. Luca's toast will need to wait. The next hour was spent devouring the scrumptious meal Claudia prepared for us and the family telling stories and laughing.

After Frida and I cleaned the kitchen and table from lunch, we began decorating the tree and the rest of the house while Claudia, Teresa and Abuela were busy in the kitchen organizing some dishes for the Christmas Eve feast. I was so full from lunch I couldn't imagine looking at another morsel of food. Thankful we won't be eating this special dinner until later tonight.

"Emelia once we're done decorating, you might want to take a rest. Tonight will be a long night."

She sparked my curiosity. "What's the plan for tonight?"

"We'll leave for church at seven o'clock and return for dinner and open gifts. Usually we don't get to sleep until well after midnight."

"It all sounds wonderful and thanks for letting me know. I'm beginning to feel a bit tired now. I certainly can use a nap."

We finished spreading Christmas cheer around the house and put the boxes away.

"Where did all the men go?"

Frida smiled, "They're dropping off donations my parents brought from their church back home. Abuelo knows many families nearby that can use some help especially at this time of year." I nodded my head. "Tomorrow we'll go around and say hello to some of the families. When we're not here, they visit my grandparents. So, we like to catch up with them on the holidays. And we'll also go to my Tío Cisco's house. He opens up his house to everyone and feeds hundreds of people on Christmas Day."

I hadn't known any of those traditions before my visit. Frida continues, "My family enjoys doing this every Christmas. That's why our Christmas Eve celebration is more about keeping it just our family."

"Frida you never mentioned this to me before. I'm even more grateful you allowed me to be part of these special moments with you and your family."

"Well, if I told you, I would feel like it's me boasting about it. We've done this since I was a child and it just feels natural to me."

"I understand. It's truly remarkable what you and your family have done."

"We better go to our rooms before they all get back. The ladies are also done in the kitchen and it's nice and quiet." Frida and I walked towards our bedrooms and waved to one another.

I glanced at the clock in my room and it was almost five o'clock it seemed like I could fit in a good rest before the night's festivities. I kicked off my shoes and lied down on the bed. I turned to face the dresser and focused on the flowers in the little jar and I began to drift off.

Chapter 15

I SLEPT ON and off until about six-thirty when I woke from my nap. I took out my clothes for the evening and arranged them on the bed. And I quietly set off to the bathroom down the hall to freshen up. When I entered the hallway, I didn't see anyone and all the doors were closed. I heard music coming from the living room. It was Rico playing his guitar. I stood there leaning against my door frame just for a few seconds to enjoy his music.

"Did you have a good sleep?" Luca softly asked me. "Yes, I feel recharged. And you, did you sleep?"

"I did, I did. Are you going or coming from the bathroom?" He said noticing my arms filled with a towel and toiletries.

"I'm going but stopped to listen to your dad. His music is superb." He nodded yes.

"Oh did you want to use the bathroom?" He shook his head no.

He replied, "You can use this one, there's another near my bedroom." We parted ways to get ready for the evening.

At seven the house was bustling with activity and so different from just a half hour before. We loaded up in two cars for the church. I rode with Max, Frida and Henry. Luca was driving his car with his parents and grandparents.

The church was just a ten minute car ride down the mountain. When we arrived, Frida quickly told me about a priest she wanted me to meet. "He's from Astoria Queens and relocated here five years ago. I think he'll like to meet with you and talk about your neighborhoods." I replied, "Sure, I can't wait to meet him." Frida explained, "The prayers are about to start so, we'll wait until after the ceremony to talk with him."

As we entered I was distracted by the radiance of this church tucked away in this little village. There were statues and paintings everywhere I looked. Flowers and ribbons adorned each of the rows. The church was filling up with parishioners and I heard voices and music coming from an area near to the altar. I noticed Rafael and Teresa already in a row and waved to us. We joined them along with Teresa's family. I found myself sitting between Frida and Luca. The altar table had two bright candles on each end. As other people passed to take their seats, some stopped by our rows to say hello to Frida's family. It was truly a joyous occasion.

"What are you thinking?" Luca asked me.

"I don't know if I'm thinking about anything. I'm just taking this all in."

"The ceremony will be in Spanish. Just signal to me when you want something translated."

"Thank you Luca, is this a Catholic church?" He nodded yes. "Then I should be fine. I will be able to follow along."

He handed me a booklet. "Ok, just remember I'm here if you need any explaining." We smiled at one another.

I whispered, "Just like the movie we went to see." And I winked at him. He looked at me slightly confused and then he remembered.

He laughed a very low laugh. "Oh yes, how can I ever forget?"

I looked over at Frida and saw her and Max holding hands. And I thought, maybe one day, Luca and I will be sitting here holding hands in this church. Henry appeared at the end of our row looking for a seat near us. We made room for him, by shuffling down the bench but it was a tight squeeze. So we were all pressed up against one another. Well, if I couldn't hold hands with Luca I was happy to settle with our closer arrangements.

The mass began and soon we were all singing and praying. We got midway through the ceremony and the overhead lights slightly dimmed. Frida whispered to me, "The children will now proceed to the altar and take part in the living nativity." And one by one the kids took their positions at the front of the church. When they were finished, we got to enjoy seeing the adorable children portraying, Mary, Joseph, baby Jesus, an angel and shepherds with their flock of sheep played by dogs. Then we all began to sing "Silent Night" also in Spanish.

After the mass we stood outside the back of the church. It was like a reunion of sorts. Everyone stopped to say hello and *Feliz Navidad* [Merry Christmas] to the Morales family. I was standing in the middle of Frida and Luca. A couple of young women greeted Luca and as he was conversing with them, they kept glancing at me. I tried to get involved with Frida and the family she was talking with. And Luca touched my elbow and grasped my hand. "I'd like you to meet my friend Emelia. She's visiting with me and my family for Christmas." I smiled at the two ladies and said hello. They said hello and quickly said goodbye to us.

I looked at Luca, "Did I say something wrong?" He laughed and nodded. "No, you were perfectly fine. I needed saving. Someone must have told them I was single again."

I smiled back at him. "We just came out of church and you're telling lies already." Frida looked at both of us. "What are you up to? You look guilty of something." Luca explained. Frida laughed with us too.

"Padre Antonio, Feliz Navidad." Frida welcomed the priest near us. They held hands and embraced. "This is my friend Emelia from New York. She's from Queens too. I want you both to meet."

The priest extended his hand to me. "Father Antonio, it's very nice to meet you."

"Feliz Navidad Emelia. What brings you all the way to our little community?"

"I couldn't pass up this chance to celebrate Christmas with Frida, Luca and the rest of the Morales family of course." I looked over at Luca. "The ceremony was lovely. I will never forget it."

The priest smiled, "Thank you Emelia that was very kind of you to say." The Morales family surrounded Father Antonio and talked with him.

While they were talking Luca whispered to me, "Did you just lie to a priest?" I looked at him giggling and whispered, "No, what are you talking about?"

"Well, it was one thing for me to tell those women you were my friend. They were not priests."

"Oh, now I know what you mean." I placed my hand over my mouth to cover my laughter.

"You are in big trouble."

"Oh no, what I said was completely different from what you said."

"No, it was the same but you said it to a priest." We exchanged sweet smiles to one another.

Frida turned to me and asked, "What is going on with you two? We should leave before you take this any further and make fools of yourselves."

Luca prodded me with, "See I knew you were trouble, lying to a priest." Frida shushed us both as we passed Father Antonio and Luca ran ahead to bring the car closer to the church for his grandparents.

On our drive home from the church Frida reminded Max to drive slowly through the town. And in a few moments I saw the sky light up with fireworks. Frida said, "They do this every Christmas Eve right after the church ceremony."

When we arrived home, Frida insisted we run inside before the others to turn on all the lights. Max, Henry and I followed Frida into the house. We managed to light candles and turn on the Christmas lights. And of course Henry started up the music.

When it was all set, the door opened and Frida's grandparents were the first to enter. Abuela's eyes sparkled along with her radiant smile. Then Abuelo took his wife's arm and they slowly danced their way towards the living room.

All the ladies went into the kitchen to begin the dinner preparations and the men went to the living room. Henry and Luca returned to the kitchen to ask if we needed any help. Claudia directed Luca, Henry and me to arrange the table.

After completing that task, Luca asked me to assist him with the drinks. Once we gave everyone refreshments we joined the rest in the living room. Claudia entered and announced, "We have a while before dinner will be served." Henry jumped up and said, "Let's open gifts now." And Rico walked to Claudia and commanded, "Now, I'd like to dance with my wife. We can open gifts after dinner."

Everyone applauded Rico's direction. For a couple of minutes we all gazed at Frida's parents dancing so gracefully together. Max and Frida began to dance, followed by Henry and Abuela. I felt a tap on my shoulder and saw Luca standing next to me with his hand extended. "Will my friend from New York dance with me?" I smiled and took his hand. "Yes, I would love to."

My heart fluttered and I felt a shiver run down my spine. I hoped Luca didn't feel me tremble in his arms. As he pulled me closer, he whispered, "Don't worry I've got you. It will be just like before. Just let go and feel the music."

He took my hand and placed it over his heart. And when I breathed in his fragrance I got lost in the hold of his arms and the music.

While we were dancing, I asked Luca, "Did you place flowers in my bedroom?" He extended his arm out to spin me around and whipped me back into his embrace.

"I'm not certain, which room are you sleeping in?" And he pushed me away for another spin and pulled me back to him.

"Uh, first room on the right." With our cheeks pressed against the other I felt his beard tickle my face.

"Are you sure that's your room? Could you be staying in another room?"

I tried to push him away to spin him, but his grip was too strong. And with much grace and determination he led us towards the dining area and the entry for the hallway, always keeping to the rhythm of the music. As we danced alone down the hallway I was able to see why he was teasing me and began to laugh into his shoulder. The first room on the right was the laundry room.

"My lovely friend from New York, can you tell me again, which room are you staying in?"

When I finally stopped giggling, I looked into his eyes and replied, "Oh, my mistake, I'm sleeping in the second room."

He led us towards the doorway to my room and dipped me in his arms. And as we both looked into the room towards the flowers, he whispered into my ear, "Then yes, Mi Lia, those flowers were from me to you." And he placed a featherlike kiss on my temple.

Without missing a beat, he whisked me back up and steered us down the hallway to join the others in the living room. Before we parted, I whispered,

"Luciano thank you for such a lovely gesture and the flowers too." And he simply responded by showing me his dazzling smile.

The party continued with a few more songs and we exchanged dance partners. While I took a break from dancing, Frida motioned for me to join her in the kitchen. We filled all the serving dishes and brought them to the dining table. When everything was done, she announced to everyone that dinner is served. Claudia looked quite surprised and thanked us both.

As the family gathered around the dining table, I noticed Luca standing by the two seats where we sat together at lunch and he waved me over to join him. Everyone took their seats but Luca remained standing. "Before I say a few words, let's fill our glasses." Just like our afternoon meal, decanters of wine were being passed around. Henry was sitting to my right and offered to pour me wine. "*Gracias* Henry." And then he passed the decanter to Luca and he placed it on the table.

He began, "Feliz Navidad and Merry Christmas." His toast was in both Spanish and English. "I feel very blessed to be here with my family and lovely friend from New York for this Christmas." He winked at me and I heard Frida giggle and I looked over to her and she was smiling. Everyone else looked a little confused but Luca continued.

"Many of you know my life wasn't easy during these last few months. And I thank you for your love and encouragement. As I leave my old life behind in Caracas, I am now ready to begin this new chapter in Panama with an open mind and an open heart. Please raise your glasses in honor of family, devotion, integrity and the certainty that genuine love still exists. Salud!"

Luca leaned his goblet towards mine first and we looked into each other's eyes and tapped our glasses. Afterwards I tapped glasses with Henry and the rest of the family around me. And Luca sat in his seat to my left. As he settled down and placed the napkin on his lap I felt him take my hand in his and lifted it above the table. Henry took my other hand and did the same. I noticed everyone joining hands around the table when Claudia began her prayer. When she was done, Henry released my hand and Luca lowered our hands still together onto his lap. As platters got passed around he squeezed my hand before freeing us.

Henry leaned to me, "Why did Frida laugh when Luca mentioned you in his toast? What did I miss?"

I giggled at his question. "Well, it was something that happened after mass tonight."

Luca interrupted, "What are you talking with Henry about?"

I smiled at him and leaned back so they both can hear me, "Well he asked; why did Frida laugh when you said lovely friend from New York in your toast? And I was about to explain, but maybe you should. It is your story." I teased him.

But Luca sternly told his brother, "Henry I'll tell you later."

Henry whispered to me, "This should be good." And he raised his voice to reach his sister, "Hey Frida, why did you laugh when Luca said something about Emelia during his toast?"

Frida looked at all three of us and giggled. "Maybe you should ask them what they were up to after the ceremony."

"I did and Luca said he'd tell me later, but I want to know now."

Rafael chimed in, "Yeah me too, what's going on? When we were outside of church tonight two of Luca's friends asked me and Teresa about Luca's new girlfriend from New York."

I covered my face with my hands briefly and laughed out loud. And I reached for my wine glass. I said to Henry, "Yes, this should be good."

Luca sipped his wine too and began to tell the story in Spanish but paused and said to me, "You know how this went, I hope you don't mind if I don't translate for you."

I nodded and replied, "Just as long as you tell them the truth." And everyone laughed.

When they finally settled down, he told them the story. I understood most of what he said except the last part. He lifted his glass to toast me, but before I reciprocated I asked him, "What did you say at the end?" He smiled, "I said and now I'd like to thank my girlfriend from New York for saving me from those inquisitive women at church tonight." We tapped glasses.

Christmas Eve dinner continued with more stories, delicious food and laughter through to midnight. After we cleaned the kitchen Henry finally got his wish to open the gifts. We all found seats in the living room.

As the youngest, we nominated Henry to bring a gift to each person. He found them under the tree and started the process by announcing the name as he handed out gifts. When each of us had one, Henry instructed we were permitted to open them. It was fun watching everyone ooh and ah as they unwrapped their treasures.

Henry volunteered to give out the next round too. He grasped one of the gifts I brought. As he examined it, he joked about how they were wrapped. "Who can this gift be from? Wrapped in this unique tissue paper and ribbon, I don't see a card on it, who is it for?"

In a raised whisper I said to him, "Turn it over!"

"Ah," he said, "the mystery is solved." He spotted all of my gifts and distributed them one by one.

Luca looked surprised when Henry gave him one too. And he glanced at me and smirked. Claudia slowly removed the ribbon and paper from her gift and gently lifted the lid off the box. As she unpacked it I watched her smile. "How did you know I like hot air balloons?" She showed everyone the porcelain candy dish with hot air balloons painted all over the lid and bottom. She walked over to me and kissed me. "Thank you Emelia, it's beautiful. How did you know?" I shrugged my shoulders, "I didn't; just a coincidence, I like them too."

The rest of the family opened their gifts and thanked me. Luca methodically untied the ribbon and finally removed the paper. He held the book in his hand and examined the front and back covers. And when he opened to the cover page he began to read. As if he knew, he thumbed through the first few pages and found what he was searching for and paused. The book I gave him was a popular book back then that I had read, *Like Water for Chocolate*, written by Laura Esquivel. I bought him the Spanish version. I wrote a note on one of the pages to him. When he was done reading my note, he continued flipping through the rest of the book.

Abuela walked over with a little card and handed it to me. My name was written on the envelope and a tiny bow was affixed to it. She smiled at me when I took it from her hands. I smiled back and said, "*Muchas gracias.*" I opened the envelope and inside I found a card that was hand painted with a Christmas design. As I flipped open the card to read the inside, a five dollar bill fell into my lap. The note inside was written in Spanish and was signed by Frida's grandparents. The back of the card explained that it was made in Chiriqui by a local artist. I have cherished that card.

After all the gifts had been opened Henry started the music again and increased the volume. Everyone looked ready for bed. The grandparents were the first to retire followed by Rico and Claudia. Luca sat next to me on the couch. "Thank you for the book."

I looked up to him, "You are very welcome. I read the book and thought you might like the story. They've also made it into a movie."

"I am embarrassed. I didn't give you a gift."

"You shouldn't be and you gave me something already; remember those flowers?"

"Emelia, you are too kind."

Henry tried to coerce us to dance, but we were all very tired. I lost track of time but it seemed late. So I rested my head on Luca's shoulder and Henry left to lower the volume.

I'm not sure of the hour when I opened my eyes and felt Luca caressing my face. He said, "Let's not sleep here I'm sure our beds are more comfortable." I yawned and stretched and looked around the room and it was just the two of us.

"Is that my water?"

He reached to the table and brought the glass to me.

"What time is it? And how long was I sleeping?"

"It's late and I'm not sure maybe an hour or two."

"I'm sorry I didn't mean to fall asleep on you." I took another sip of water and handed him back the glass and said, "Thank you. Did everyone go to bed?"

"I guess so, I fell asleep too and when I woke they were all gone."

Luca stood and extended his hand to me, "Take my hand, I want to show you something." I grasped his hand and we walked over to the kitchen. He unlocked the door and we went outside. "Where are we going?" He hushed me. "You'll see."

When we stepped off the porch and walked passed the cars in the driveway, Luca led us onto a pathway. Being up there away from the city lights, we were surrounded by darkness. My heart was racing with excitement and I was grateful Luca was still holding my hand.

Until my eyes got acclimated I could only make out the shapes of the trees lining the trail and my very determined guide. Only a few minutes before, I was waking from a nap snuggled close to him. And now we're roaming around in the balmy night. As we continued the journey I noticed our strides were more in synch. We walked up towards someplace and I began to see flickers of light ahead. I looked quickly behind us and it was pitch black. Where was he taking me I wondered? "In just a minute we'll be there." I was actually relieved to hear that we were almost at our destination.

"Ok, ready?" I giggled, "Yes!" We took a few more steps and as the tree lined path ended behind us, the night sky in front welcomed us. "Look up," he commanded. And when I did I saw stars everywhere. I almost lost my balance and Luca wrapped his arms around me and I leaned back onto him mesmerized by the illuminated sky.

"Do you like?"

"Oh yes, Luca, I more than like. The stars appear so close as if we can touch them. The view from up here is spectacular. Thank you." I squeezed his arms in appreciation.

"Merry Christmas, Mi Lia."

I smiled and replied, "*Feliz Navidad* Luca."

While we stood bound together under the shimmering sky Luca placed delicate kisses along the edge of my ear and then pushed my hair to one side so that his lips continued the journey across the back of my neck and up along the edge of my other ear. My body reacted and I released a sigh.

Luca twisted me around and framed my face with his hands. My heart was pounding when I looked into his eyes. He declared, "I've wanted to kiss you since we were alone in the fields today. I don't know how I lasted this long. Do you want me to kiss you Emelia?"

My body shivered and I nodded, "Yes, kiss me now." His lips met mine and he delighted me with soft wet kisses. And when he sucked my bottom lip his tongue entered my mouth and for the next few minutes under a blanket of stars on Christmas night my heart sprang to life once again.

When we paused, Luca held me close to him and I caressed his back. "Your romantic starlight kisses are certainly the best present I've ever received."

With my ear pressed against his chest, I heard a muffled laugh and he squeezed me even tighter. "When you fell asleep on my shoulder earlier, I thought about how happy I am when you're around. And it reminded me of this place I discovered years ago with my brothers when we went exploring late one night. I hoped that I could share it with you tonight."

Seconds passed in silence and Luca acknowledged, "I know I let you down this year when I didn't stay in touch."

I looked up at him and placed a finger over his lips. "Before you continue can we just stop the clock from moving forward for just another minute longer?" He nodded in agreement and we kissed.

I didn't want the past few months to bring sadness to this special place from his childhood that he had made our special place too. And hoped our renewed bliss could linger for a few minutes more.

"I won't spoil this night or this place by telling you about my life since we said goodbye at the airport. After you went home last year, I thought about you often and wondered if you still felt the same way for me as I did for you. And then I allowed life to get in the way and got off track. Changes occurred recently that have freed me from my past obligations. I was worried about seeing you and hoped you didn't hate me for being so distant with you. But when I took you in my arms I felt we still have that connection."

Luca released his grip on me and knelt down before me holding my hands in his. "I kneel before you under this Christmas sky promising never to go back on my word with you. You fill my heart with joy and I want us to be together. I know it won't be easy at first, but I know we can make this work. And then one day, I will bring you back up here and ask you to be my wife. Tell me that you will give me a second chance."

With tears streaming down my face I tugged at his hands, "Yes Luciano Morales, as crazy as this may seem I will give you and us a second chance." He jumped to his feet and kissed every inch of my face and while holding me in his arms spun me around.

"We should get back so we can get some sleep." He grabbed my hand. I tugged him towards me, "Just one more second Luca." With him standing behind me, I took his arms and wrapped them around me. Looking at the sky I proclaimed, "For all who will come here after us, I wish them the love and happiness that surrounds us tonight." Luca held me tighter and nuzzled my neck. "Luca I will hold this memory in my heart forever, thank you." Taking our last glance we headed down the path towards the house.

Before going inside Luca pulled me into his arms and kissed me. "Mi Lia I'd like nothing more than to fall asleep with you in my arms tonight. But you know my parents wouldn't understand." Sadly I agreed. "And would you mind if we ease them into this courtship of ours? That way I get to plan more stolen moments with you." I sealed our pact with a kiss.

Chapter 16

NEVER HAVING TOLD anyone about that Christmas night, I don't even know how to or why I should continue telling Jenene about the rest of the trip. When I pause she looks at me and says, "There's more right?" I get up and pace the living room searching for the words to explain all that transpired next. It's difficult for even today, I don't understand what happened.

"The next couple of days with the family were fun. Filled with group activities and when Luca and I had private moments we'd kiss and talk about our future. Since my trip was about visiting Frida, when we left the country house I only saw Luca once more before my flight. He stopped by Frida's home and our relationship remained a secret, it was awkward and a bit sad, since I knew I'd be leaving the next day. He didn't even see me off at the airport. We exchanged addresses and phone numbers and said goodbye in Frida's living room."

"After I got home he didn't call. Even when New Year's came I didn't hear from him. I waited another week and reached out to him thinking maybe he lost the piece of paper with my phone number. I remember hearing his outgoing message on the answering machine and his voice made my heart dance. I left him a quick sweet message and said goodbye. The call was never returned."

"Oh my gosh, never? You never spoke with him again? Maybe something happened. Did you call Frida?"

While nodding I say, "I did and I tried to ask questions without being obvious. She said Luca moved to Panama and was working. So, he must have been okay. He wasn't in any accident if that's what you were thinking. I mailed him a note. Just in case maybe he was feeling strange about not contacting me sooner. You know, leaving the window open for him kind of a move. I still didn't hear from him."

"What a loser, how could he lead you on like that?" Jenene says with such disdain.

"A few months passed and I called Frida for her birthday and we got to talking about life and she told me Luca was getting married. And when I asked to whom, she told me Violeta."

Jenene's mouth opens in shock. "That dog, what was his deal? He was such a liar to you. I don't know why you're even worried about him. He doesn't deserve you."

"Yeah, that's what I tell myself too. But I can't deny my feelings for him and somewhere deep down inside I still believe he truly loved me. But I can't figure out why he let me go."

Chapter 17

PEOPLE OFTEN ASK me before a trip how excited or happy I am to be travelling. And I tell them the standard response something they want to hear. But what I'm really thinking is my true excitement only begins once the plane has landed safely and I have retrieved my luggage from the carousel. Today is no different.

I'm not a regular traveler, maybe two trips a year. So I don't enjoy the frequent flyer or TSA express perks to move me through the airport queues faster. With the exception of missing my flight due to the long lines, I don't stress too much about not having those privileges mainly because I'm an avid people watcher. And airports are one of the best places for this entertainment.

As a single traveler it's just me to worry about, so I do get a kick out of people traveling with family and observe all the junk they bring on the plane, how much food the kids eat in the terminal while waiting to board and how many times they drag their parents to the gift shops or bathrooms mainly out of curiosity.

Now settled in my aisle seat I glance around the cabin to see my neighbors. Today's flight is a mixed group of families, elders and singles. The flight isn't too full and the window seat passenger has opted to move to an empty row nearby and leaving me extra room to travel, a win-win for both.

A quick glance out the window I see rain droplets. A man coughs at his seat diagonally behind me. The pilot has made an announcement to the crew to prepare for takeoff. Even though it is not raining the sky is thick with clouds.

Each day leading up to today I've been filled with mixed emotions. I know how happy I'll be to see Frida and her family I'm just not certain how I'll feel when I see Luca.

I keep telling myself a lot of life has happened since we were together. And that my feelings for him may have changed. Maybe he's not the same man I once knew. And then I think, well am I the same woman? How much have I changed? Or how much has life altered the woman he first met to the woman I am today?

What I do know that hasn't changed, is whenever I'm dating a man whether it be brief or extended my mantra has consistently been, "If Luca came back in my life today would I push aside the man I am with to be with him instead?"

I know it's silly and somewhat juvenile but he was someone that invaded my heart. And even though he never fulfilled the promises he made to me, there has always been a section of my heart reserved for him and only him. It's not like it kept me from loving other men just that I couldn't love them with all my heart.

Even the morning of my wedding Luca came to mind and I pondered if he would reach out that day or appear at the ceremony what would I do? I know the answer is the same as it was when he promised me his heart on that starlit night.

After a short delay we are finally moving towards the runway. The rain slicked path awaits us. The pilot announces we are fifth for takeoff.

That Christmas night is a memory that's imbedded in my soul. There are moments when I despise that memory and moments when it shines a light in that area of my heart that has been left abandoned. Like a room in someone's home that's under lock and key with the contents inside remaining untouched. So that when the prior inhabitant comes back they will feel right at home. But this chamber is unfurnished with only a couple of photographs hanging on the walls and still waiting to be lived in.

Second in line the pilot assures us. As much as I want to arrive in Panama today I feel like the delay is appropriate for how I'm feeling.

The roar of the engines and the plane speeding ahead matches my racing heart. Only seconds and I feel the plane lifting off. At this point of takeoff I begin counting from one to twenty until we reach the desired elevation and I think about planes of yesteryear and how much the technology has improved. And I wonder how much has stayed the same.

Almost reaching number twenty I feel the plane leveling and we're in the clouds. I hear the chimes ring letting me know we have reached the appropriate altitude. My favorite part of flying is starting about now when the white puffy clouds are beneath us and the blue sky above. As if we're hitching a ride on a cloud.

Settling in for my long trip ahead I grab for something to read. Someone I met a few months ago informed me he has written a book or two. I didn't ask Craig much about his writings apart from how long it took to get published. Hesitantly he told me not very long and with a smile whispered, "About twenty years." I smiled back at him and he began to explain, "I haven't been writing for twenty years, just twenty years of life had to be lived for me to tell my stories." I knew from that moment when he seemed his most sincere that I found a true friend.

I located one of his books soon after we met. Each time I open the cover and find my place marker I wonder where the story will lead to next. And I also think, why don't I read Craig's book more, for I'm always entertained by his words. Not only because the story is set near my former hometown in Queens, New York but the familiar Queens voices I hear when reading. Now and again I feel like I'm walking with the characters along the similar streets I once explored in my old neighborhoods.

I brought Craig's book with me on this trip like a security blanket I suppose. Do writers ever think about the people that read their books? And where their books travel to with each reader? Do some books just rest on a night stand or side table? Or in someone's travel bag going from city to city. Does the reader engage fully word for word or just skim each page quickly? And how much commitment is involved? I've stayed up late for hours with a book I can't put down. When others I think of as a special treat to end my day. Reclining in my coach seat I find my place marker in Craig's book and become transported to Corona, Queens.

An hour of reading and snacking has passed and I've put the book away and gear up for a nap. I'm not sure of the plans when I land except that Henry and his family will meet me at the airport. Our flights arrive about thirty minutes apart.

Turning off the overhead lamp I secure my headphones and scroll through the playlists. I smile when I see the one titled, *My Brothers.*

Years before the invention of this supreme device my music companion was the Sony Walkman. Back then it was the greatest portable way of listening to music especially if you were a mixed cassette tape aficionado. Mixed tapes were like the playlists of today. I had tapes for several genres and moods. Movie soundtracks, dance tunes, country music, classical music, exercise songs and the one I always grabbed and listened to the most was the one labeled, *My Brothers.*

Although I have two brothers, this wasn't a mixed tape about them. It was a compilation of some of the artists and groups they introduced to me. Living in our modest home in Queens with older siblings was an experience I would never change. Because the person I am today was molded by those years.

When else can a boy crazy teenage girl get such insight of the male mind? But both of them were so different which left me confused on occasion. Did I rely on their friends that visited regularly? Well yes, the endless amounts of young men that inhabited our home were very interesting. Most all of them treated me like their little sister and when I'd hang around and wait for their conversations to get juicy, rather informative; I was always ushered out of the room when they realized I was all ears. Over the years it's been a joy to watch these young men become husbands and fathers and above all else life-long friends.

My Brothers playlist has some of the music I heard blasting from my oldest brother Marty's stereo while other songs included the tunes Evan introduced me to while we'd spend endless hours in the basement orchestrating our own lip sync battles.

I guess that was the foundation of my musical tastes along with my parents' enjoyment of musicians dating as far back as the 1940's. With their music being played on the turn table in the living room housed in a piece of wood furniture with built in speakers and compartments to store their albums.

When you think of the songs of the 1970's through to the 90's I feel we were entertained by so many different styles, voices and rhythms. As much as

I embraced all the differences this silly boy crazy girl found something even more profound. These brothers of mine sang about love, heartbreak and life. The songs allowed me to get the insight I craved. Do men and women love the same? Do they hurt the same? Do they look at life the same? And so this was how the mixed tape *My Brothers* began.

I sifted through my own brothers' albums as well as mine and also some of our cassettes. I found Zeppelin, Eagles, Genesis, Springsteen, Joel, Van Morrison, Stones, Beatles, Frampton, U2, Stewart, Doors and many many more. And I taped the songs from these wise talented men that would give me some advice, support and hope when I was searching for love, in love or just out of love. Or when I lost my way and needed to get back on the right path again.

And when our technology switched over from cassette Walkman to CD Discman and then to the iPod, I had to box up my favored tapes. Before I did I made sure to remix that playlist on my iPod. And have added other tunes since the 1990's. Looking over it now I see the titles of songs from way back when and their memories slowly enfold. Like the afternoon I heard for the first time Rod Stewart's soulful voice travelling from Marty's room into mine singing these memorable lyrics from "You're in My Heart":

"You're in my heart
You're in my soul
You'll be my breath should I grow old
You are my lover
You're my best friend
You're in my soul"

Or the day I played my first Billy Joel album on my stereo. Slowly taking the album out from its inner sleeve with the words printed on both sides. Sliding the album down the center pin and setting the needle with such delicate accuracy on the initial groove with the anticipation of what's next to come. I would listen from the first track and when that side was completed, I'd flip the record over to enjoy the second side all the way to the last track. And singing and reading along with the words. Billy Joel's song "You're My Home" has stayed with me since the first twenty spins on my turntable.

"If I traveled all my life
And I never get to stop and settle down
Long as I have you by my side
There's a roof above and good walls all around
You're my castle, you're my cabin and
my instant pleasure dome
I need you in my house 'cause you're my home"

These men and others sang to me and informed me of the many aspects of life and love with their honest, passionate, realistic, sometimes harsh and gritty interpretations.

Selecting this playlist, I recline my seat and begin to unwind with the voices of my talented distant brothers as the airplane escorts me closer to my distressing destination. Closing my eyes thinking about the clouds in the sky I slowly drift away.

Chapter 18

Waking up I check the clock on my iPod and see that I slept for close to three hours. With my disruptive sleep patterns these last few nights leading up to the trip, my body just gave in when all I was left to do on this flight is sit back and relax. At least I'll be energetic when we land.

Smiling as I recall the shopping spree with Jenene and how much she got caught up in my past. She is as much as a romantic as I am. I know she'll want me to call her with updates during my trip but I told her I most likely won't contact her. I explained that I want to disconnect completely when I can. And I also confessed that should I need some encouragement at all, I will reach out to her immediately. She's been a kind friend so I hated telling her my communications will be limited. She even said, "I don't know how I'll survive." She begged me to send an email after my first meeting with Luca. I promised I'd send a message. And even when I said it I wasn't sure I actually would. Or if after meeting him would send me into such a depression I would call her and beg her to tell me reasons to stay even though seeing him in his happy life with his family would make me want to board the next flight out.

My ears begin popping and the pilot has announced our arrival just a short time away. Looking out the cabin window at the evening sky I remember the near perfect Christmas night. I've thought about that memory almost every night since I purchased the plane ticket. Keeping it alive has given me the courage to make this trip. I'm thankful for having that most tender memory with him. We were so young and in love. Part of me wants him to address why he let me go without any explanation. And part of me fears any reason would never be enough for how he hurt me. But if I leave there and he doesn't say a word I will feel like he forgot me. Should that be the case maybe I will finally forget him.

The lights of the city are visible now and I hear the landing gear move into place. Before touching down the thought of him still having feelings for me occurs. What if Luca confesses he still loves me? After all these years imagining him swooping in and proclaiming his love has not prepared me for the reality. Probably since I know that would never happen after seeing pictures that Henry has shared over the years proving Luca is happy in his life.

The wheels touchdown, feeling the brakes kick in I begin counting again from one to twenty which calms me until the aircraft comes to a slower pace. Eighteen, nineteen and twenty, the plane begins to taxi towards the gate and the passengers applaud the pilots' steady flight and safe landing.

Pushing that possibility so far back in my mind that I haven't even allowed myself to ever consider what I might actually do if I'm faced with the chance of us having a future. The same concern dims this dream. He lives here and I live there. Now his life is even more rooted than before. Could I ever see myself living here? I've made a life for myself. Am I too old to start a new life in another country? Speak another language fluently? Working here?

We're almost at the gate and I hear mobile phones being activated.

Why would it be up to me to move? Maybe he'd want to move to the U.S.? Or maybe we can compromise and find a place where we both can live. Oh this is crazy. This will never happen, stop thinking this way. It's pure fantasy.

The bells sound and the clicks of the seatbelts announce their release as the race to deplane has begun. I've never understood why passengers do this, maybe they want to stretch their legs, but not all of them. Thankfully I don't have a seatmate; usually I stay put and just wait it out until the row in front of me begins to move ahead before getting up. My laid back ways infuriates some window seat passengers but most just sit back and take my lead.

Exiting the plane I make my way through the terminal after using the restroom and follow the signs to baggage claim and customs. The last visit here I was greeted by Frida and Max. Tonight Henry and his family will be meeting me. I glance at the arrivals board to check which carousel I will hopefully find my luggage. When I travel by plane, in addition to all the other fears, this particular one remains close in thought. The anticipation of waiting for my luggage to appear on the conveyor belt fills me with anxiety. Waiting for the belt to move I glance at my phone to see if Henry has called. I told him I would contact him once I have my luggage in hand. I think he might get the rental car first if my flight arrived much later than theirs.

The lights blink, tropical dance music plays and the alarm sounds to announce the luggage parade is about to start. Looks like half the flight is waiting for their baggage. And if all goes well, I should see my bag in the next ten minutes any longer I know that it didn't get on this flight.

Thinking I secured the perfect viewing spot a very old woman maneuvers her way in front of me. From behind she looks like the little old lady from the *Tweety Bird and Sylvester* cartoons just dressed more stylishly. Petite and helpless but if I reached for her luggage would wallop me with her purse.

Finally I see bags passing through the entry door. The old lady is on the move she must have spotted hers. She tugs the arm of a man waiting and points to an oversized animal print bag. I knew she had a wild side. He obliges and retrieves her bag and sets it down in front of her. Patting him on the shoulder they exchange smiles and she goes on her way. Passing by me I notice her shoes match the print of her luggage and I smile.

Relief washes over me when I see my bag. After pulling it off the belt I walk over to the seated area and rest my belongings down. While I search for Henry's number his number appears on my screen and the phone rings, perfect timing.

I say, "*Hola* Henry."

He laughs, "*Hola* Emelia."

"I was just about to call you, I have my bags and heading towards customs. Where are you?"

"Oh good. Our flight arrived early and we all went to get the car. Call me when you get through customs and I'll get you curbside."

"Good plan. What type and color of vehicle are you driving?"

"It's a white SUV type. Olivia what brand of car is this? That's right, a Ford Escape."

"Ok, thanks, I will hang up now so I can locate customs and move along quickly. Talk soon I hope."

He laughs, "Ok ciao."

Thankfully the line at customs moves swiftly. I'm impressed how a nice smile and pleasant demeanor speeds up the process or maybe it was just the late hour. I will walk away thinking it was the former.

Within minutes of calling Henry I spot a white SUV coming towards me. Peering into the windows I see their smiling faces and wave to them. Excitedly Olivia jumps out of the vehicle and even with her petite size greets me with a tight hug. Henry comes to our side and grabs my luggage. Olivia swiftly opens the back door and joins her sons Mateo and Benjamin. I go to Henry at the rear of the car and we hug quickly. "Welcome to Panama Emmy." "*Gracias* Henry."

Before taking the front seat I say to Olivia, "Are you sure you don't want to sit up here?"

She smiles, "It's all good Emelia. Plus my husband drives like a local here. You'll see."

Securing my seat belt I answer, "Maybe I'll squeeze back there with all of you."

Henry revs the engine and we're off. He says, "Emmy we're thinking we should check you into the hotel first and then we'll grab some light nibbles there too. Does that work for you?"

After a day of travelling and the late hour I say, "Yes, that sounds perfect to me."

The drive to the Westin Playa Bonita doesn't take very long and soon Henry explains to the valet he is dropping off a guest of Luciano Morales and informs the valet he will need his car in about an hour.

With just my luggage in hand the five of us make our way into the hotel lobby. Upon entering we're greeted by this open and enormous bustling area. I see tremendous glass windows in the distance that I'm sure during the day present a breathtaking view of the ocean. Olivia and the boys take a seat while Henry and I go to the front desk.

"*Buena noches*," Henry begins with the very polished lady behind the counter. They exchange a few words and again I hear Henry use Luca's name. She asks for some identification and I give her my passport. A couple of minutes go by when she hands me the card keys to the room, my passport and a map of the hotel.

The porter, Nicolo, immediately walks over and takes my luggage. Henry motions to Olivia and we follow the porter. On our way to the elevators Henry whispers to me, "I think you'll like the room."

I smile at him and say, "If it's anything like the lobby, I'm sure I'll love it."

He adds, "Don't make a fuss and I'll take care of the porter. We can talk over drinks."

Soon we're boarding the elevator and I wonder what Henry means when he said don't make a fuss.

We arrive at our floor and follow the porter down the long corridor. He stops at my room door and I quickly insert the key in the slot and the light turns green. Nicolo takes over again and swings open the door removes a rubber stopper from his back pocket and slips it under the door then pushes the luggage cart into the room. Switching on lights as he makes his way further into the place, the five of us follow him like ducklings.

Now I know why Henry said what he said. Had he not been there with me, I would have thought these accommodations were a mistake. Nicolo starts to explain the layout of the suite and Henry tells him I speak only English.

The porter smiles at me and starts over again, "In this area, you have your dining room and living room and off to the side a full service kitchen."

He proceeds to the glass sliding doors and opens one of them, "Out here is your terrace."

We all follow him. Ushering us back inside, Nicolo directs us to the bedroom. "Would you like your luggage in the master bedroom?" I nod and he takes my luggage from the cart and carries it into the spacious room.

After he leaves my bags in the walk-in closet he opens the door to the other terrace. Nicolo is very kind to go over the light switches and before he leaves, shows me the second bedroom. I am stunned by the considerable lodgings. Maybe Henry and his family are staying with me. But they left their luggage in the car.

When Nicolo finishes the tour, Henry gives him a tip and we all say goodnight to the porter. He shuts the door and leaves us alone. I wait about ten seconds and then say to Henry, "Did they mess up my original reservation? Did they overbook the hotel and comp me a suite? What's going on?"

Henry glances at Olivia and they both laugh and he says, "Let's just say, my brother's name gets some extra perks around here. And this is not just any suite. Emmy you're in the Presidential suite this weekend."

And I know which brother he means. The one I'm supposed to be annoyed with and how can I stay annoyed when I'll be sleeping in a room fit for a queen. It would be foolish and inconsiderate if I asked them to give me a regular room. But I feel apprehensive about staying in a room provided by Luca. Does he think this will make up for the way he's treated me?

I change the subject, "So is anyone hungry?" The boys say yes at the same time. Sarcastically I say, "I wonder if this dump has a decent place to eat." Olivia and Henry laugh at me and after a quick freshening up we make our way to the lobby.

Henry talks with the concierge to find out where we can grab some nibbles and soon we're escorted by another staff member to one of the many restaurants. After being seated on the grand outdoor terrace I allow myself to loosen up, enjoy the setting and my company.

We place our drink and food orders quickly due to the late hour and after the waiter leaves us Henry begins with, "What do you feel like doing tomorrow Emmy?"

I reply, "If our schedule is open I'd say, sleep in a bit and then enjoy what this resort has to offer. I'm sure the beach is amazing. What are your thoughts? And where are you staying? You should stay upstairs with me."

Benjamin says, "Yeah Papá, we should stay in that huge room." Henry glares at Benjamin and says, "Benny, you know better. Thank you Emmy, but we're staying with Olivia's family. But we'll gladly hang around here with you tomorrow. What is good for you?"

I think for a moment, "After ten?" Olivia nods, "Yes that will give us a chance to get better settled at my mother's home."

I smile, "We can leave it open ended. Since we have each other's mobiles, just text me when you wake up and tell me when you think you might arrive. No pressure."

The boys sound excited about the opportunity to spend the day at the beach. Henry says, "Let's plan on us being here about ten and we'll start with a late breakfast. Ok?"

His sons smile and we all agree. Our food arrives and the rest of the night we talk about the party, the family and Henry shares some photos with me.

It's after eleven when I get back to my room. And before retiring to bed I unpack all my things and get completely settled into my home away from home for the next few days. Once I put on my pajamas, I go outside to the terrace hoping the ocean breezes clear my thoughts for a peaceful night's sleep.

Some deep breathing methods and yoga exercises under the starlit sky allows me to push thoughts of Luca out of my mind for tonight and tomorrow. Before I fall asleep I convince myself to stay in the moment which means tomorrow is a Luca free day.

Chapter 19

THE HOTEL PHONE rings. "Good morning, Ms. Caldera, this is Eugenio at the front desk."

"Good morning Eugenio, how are you?"

"Thank you for asking Ms. Caldera, I am very good. And I hope you had a restful night and are enjoying your stay."

"Yes, I did, thank you."

"You have a guest, Mr. Morales; may I direct him to your room?"

"Oh yes, of course Eugenio, thank you for checking."

"I apologize for the interruption; your guest should arrive shortly. Please enjoy the rest of your day."

Before ending the call I say, "Thank you."

I hang up the phone and glance at the clock. Henry is thirty minutes early. Luckily I'm almost ready and I won't make them wait too long.

I open the doors to the terrace, that way he and his family can take in the view while I finish primping. As I dash towards the bedroom I hear a knock at the door. One quick glance in the mirror and I think, this will do for now.

With a twist of the top lock and a firm tug of the heavy door I greet him excitedly with, "You are" I pause and continue "not Henry." I was planning to say you are early and then I saw this was not Henry at my door at all.

"No, I am not my younger brother." He says in his deep voice.

"You certainly are not. Luca this is a surprise."

"May I come in?" he asks with a serious tone.

I nod and open the door wider, "Yes, please come in."

Luca walks in and does a quick study of the living room while I try to look him over without being caught. Suddenly he turns to me and asks, "Do you like the accommodations?"

Feeling anxious I reply politely as if he's someone that I've never met before who has provided a service to me, "Oh yes, the suite is tremendous. But it wasn't necessary. Who can I thank for this very special luxury?"

"My company hosts meetings at this hotel and I asked someone at the front desk to do me a favor."

Raising my eyebrows I say, "Wow, that's a very nice favor."

He still hasn't smiled at me, so I walk towards him hesitantly to extend a gracious hello. "It's been too long can I at least get a hug from an old friend?"

And then he walks into me with his arms wide open. We stay in each other's embrace for a few seconds. I try to take in his scent with hopes his unique fragrance was the same as before. The cologne is a citrus woody musk and traces of his natural essence prevail and captivate me. I don't want this hug to end, it's been ages since we've been together and I'm so nervous I don't even know what to say next.

He's the first to separate us and walks towards the terrace. As he looks out into the distance, I break the silence, "Is Henry downstairs? Are we keeping him waiting?"

With his eyes locked on the view, "No, he's not here. There's been a change in plans. He asked me to meet with you instead. I hope you're not disappointed."

I know it's been awhile since I saw Luca, but I can't figure out his mood. My heart is racing, my palms are moist and I'm feeling lightheaded. I think I'm experiencing shock. I expected to see him tomorrow, not today. And not just on the other side of my door without any warning. I find comfort and support in one of the living room chairs.

Now I gaze towards the terrace doors. "I am not disappointed Luca, I just didn't anticipate seeing you today. If you have other plans, please don't feel obligated to babysit me. I know you must be busy preparing for the party and seeing relatives."

He suddenly turns to look at me but remains so far away. He clears his throat, "Would you feel better if I left?"

And this awkwardness between us is interrupted by a knock on the door. He points to me and commands, "Stay there, I'll get it." I ponder, who can this be, maybe his wife and children? If that's the case, I would feel better if he left.

"Yes, thank you and please place everything on the table." I didn't order any food and yet it's being rolled into my room.

"I'm sorry I think there's been a mistake I didn't order room service," I say nervously.

Luca follows the gentleman towards the dining table. "I did, there's no mistake." The man begins to arrange an assortment of breakfast foods and beverages. As Luca is walking him out and gives him a tip I look over and see fresh fruit, yogurts, breads, two covered dishes, bottles of water, coffee, tea and juice. I remain seated.

Luca walks towards me. "I thought since I arrived early you may not have had breakfast yet and we can enjoy it here with the beautiful ocean view."

Ok, now I get a sense of the old Luca. But I can't stop feeling so anxious. Maybe I just need a couple of minutes alone to collect myself. "I didn't have breakfast yet, so this was very thoughtful of you. I'll join you in a minute, I'll be right back."

With no hesitation, I stand and walk towards the bedroom and close the door. I find my refuge in the bathroom, behind another closed door. Sitting on the edge of the bathtub I begin taking deep breaths while counting. When I reach ten, I feel slightly better. Washing my hands I see my reflection in the mirror and am grateful that I had applied makeup earlier. I soak the washcloth in cold water and hold it in place behind my neck.

I tell myself, "I can do this. This will be fine. I came here for Frida." And my thoughts wander. Why the hell is he here in my room? What is going on? What is he going to tell me? And why does he have to look so good? Alright, before this gets even more awkward I need to go out and face him.

I find him situated at the table on the terrace. I pop my head out the doorway, "Can I bring you anything?" He looks up a little surprised, "Ah, no,

I think I have what I need. I hope you like what I ordered." I smile at him and walk to the mini buffet.

I place a scoop of scrambled eggs on a dish and a slice of toast. Successfully I manage my dish, the fruit platter and a couple of water bottles and lay them on the outside table. He observes me and smirks. I sit and look out at the ocean and inhale the fresh air. This is what I need to clear my mind. Although my confusing and conflicting thoughts still persist.

"You ordered lots of food. Were you expecting more people?"

"Not really. I just wanted to give you a variety. Plus, the hotel is just trying to make an impression."

I look over at his plate. He's enjoying yogurt, oatmeal and orange juice. I relax slightly when I see he's hungry and eating. As I begin to eat my meal, Luca fills the silence with conversation about the events his company has held at this hotel. I'm grateful for the small talk. I pass him the fruit platter and he portions several pieces onto his dish and gives me back the plate. I in turn do the same.

"How was your flight yesterday?"

"It was pleasant with a slight delay. And after the long journey it was very nice to see Henry and his family at the airport. I'm glad we arrived around the same hour."

Luca looks again somewhere else. "Yes, he told me he's been in contact with you over the years and more recently for this visit. It must be easy with him living in Arizona to stay friends."

He looks at me. I smile at him, "Yes, I guess. Plus he's more like a brother to me. No matter how much time passes, I'll always be happy to hear from him or see him. And we usually just start back where we left off."

With Luca's beautiful blue eyes now holding a lock on mine I sense he wants to say something to me. He stands and walks towards the edge of the terrace and tensely holds the railing. I don't know whether I should go to him or remain seated.

A few seconds pass and I join him as we look out at the ocean. I turn my body towards him. "I think of all your family as my family Luca. And when Henry called me a few months ago and invited me to Frida's party, I knew I had to be here. And I also knew that seeing you again, would be difficult. But, I couldn't let that stop me from celebrating my friend."

He places one of his hands on mine and takes a deep breath and begins to finally talk with me.

"Emelia, I lied to you. I called Henry and told him I needed to see you today. I also asked him not to tell you. I'm sorry if you feel tricked. This was the only day we could be alone before the party tomorrow. And I want to explain to you what happened between us. I hope you're good with all this. Are you?"

I knew I shouldn't have eaten. I'm finding it pretty hard to keep my food down right now. He is too direct for me this morning. With his hand now gripping mine, I look at him and say, "Luca, I don't know what to say. I've been confused since you got here. Are you sure you want to do this right now? Maybe you want to take a drive someplace or walk on the beach?"

"No, no, I don't want us distracted and I feel this is the best place. We won't have any interruptions."

"Sure, just let me go sit in the shade and then you can tell me what you came here to say."

He lets go of my hand and I walk over to the table and take a gulp of water. When I finish I reach over for his water bottle and toss it to him. He catches it and smiles, "Thanks I needed this." And something tells me it will be awhile before I see that smile again.

I take my position on the chair. My heart is pounding and I feel a shiver run through me. He walks to the table too, but remains standing. He begins to pace but then grabs the ottoman and drags it over and sits facing me.

"I have so much to say and I don't know where to start. The choices I made in my life years ago hurt you. I knew that then and I know that now. When you first opened the door thinking it was Henry, you welcomed me with your bright lovely smile. But when you saw it was me, a cloud of sadness washed over you. And I know I did that to you. And I also know I have to be honest with you and explain why I didn't fulfill my promises to you. You deserve to know the truth. And for the person you were to me, deserves to know, that it wasn't about you at all."

I sit in my chair looking at this man who appears so burdened by what, guilt, sadness, regret? I remain silent in fear that if I say something I might scare him and never know why he pushed me away.

"We were so young when we met but wise enough to know true love when it happened to us. That night when you arrived in Caracas and my sister brought you to my home I remember when I touched your hand, saw your smile and heard your voice, my heart trembled. I was shocked by my instant feelings towards you so I sat with Papá that first night. But I watched you talking and laughing with the others. I was enamored at how easily they liked being around you. Just like my sister explained to us how much your friendship meant to her. And you left that night and I didn't see you until I drove to Valencia. I remember thinking about you during the long drive and I saw you before we went to the beach waiting outside my parents' home. And I think about all the moments we had together Emelia. I'm not about to reminisce right now with you, but I just want you to know I never forgot them, not any of them. You are not someone I could forget and you're not someone I ever wanted to forget."

I turn in my chair to reach for the water again, hoping that the sorrow building up inside me won't give way to a gush of tears. Not now, he still has much more to share.

"I know on the last night in Caracas, I told you we'd be together after I had sorted out my life. And when I saw you at Christmas my life was in the middle of a big change. I was free of all my previous commitments. I finally felt allowed to start this new chapter here in Panama and then begin building a life with you. I know I made promises to you that I did not keep. I just hope that after I explain you will understand why I made these decisions and disappointed you."

He stands again and walks around the terrace for a minute and back to the table. He grabs the fruit platter and two forks. I smirk at him when he presents the platter and cutlery to me. "Want some fruit?" It was like a peace offering. I snatch a fork from him along with a slice of pineapple. I muse, how does he do it? He eases the tension by offering me fruit. After one bite into the juicy slice my anxiety slightly subsides.

He places the platter on the table near me and remains standing. "With the fluctuating economy and overall situation in Venezuela I decided to relocate to Panama. My family had made the move and they needed me with them. But my job search was long and growing dire. One day, I got a random call from a start-up financial company that was opening an office in Panama. I met with the team and was offered the job. And the plan was to move after Christmas and begin working in January."

Luca sits again on the ottoman. "With my new life ahead of me, I knew I was making my way to a fresh start and I also knew I needed to end my relationship with Violeta. But she ended things first. She said she was in love with someone else. I wasn't surprised just relieved. And so we parted ways."

He takes a moment and continues, "A week before Christmas Violeta's father calls me and asks to meet me. Not sure what this was about, I agreed and we met at his office. That afternoon I learned that he was on the investment board for the company I was to start with in January. Upon him telling me this information, I thought I was out of a job before it began. He explained to me, that my position was secure and I had nothing to worry about. In fact he was disappointed with his daughter for choosing that other man over me. Feeling optimistic I decided to fit in a quick trip before my move and I spent Christmas with my family and you. I didn't tell you all this then, I was happy that it was behind me. Seeing you and being with you confirmed that what I was feeling for you was more intense than I had for anyone else, even Violeta. And when we parted, I knew that once I got settled in Panama in my new life we'd continue our relationship."

Standing again, he paces in front of me, "I returned to Caracas after Christmas and started my relocation to Panama. A few days after I moved in, Violeta showed up at my home. She said she wanted to get back together. That she made a mistake and that it was me she loved. I told her to leave me alone. The next day at the office her father called and asked to meet me for dinner that night, I accepted. That dinner changed the rest of my life."

Luca is quiet and grabs the chair close to me and sits. "You see, it was one thing for his daughter to end our relationship, but it was another for me to turn my back on her. He was looking out for his daughter's best interest.

I respected the man until that night. How could he expect me to put aside my differences, my feelings and agree to get back with her? I went home and thought about it. I spent the next couple of days talking to my family too. And they all concurred under those circumstances, it would be best for me to forgive her and get back together."

With his elbows pressed down on his legs he sits slumped over looking at the floor. He takes a deep breath looks away at first and then back at me, "Emelia, I was confused, I was desperate. I had just left a job and relocated to this country. I didn't know how long it would have taken me to find another job. And my family was depending on me. This was a unique opportunity. You may not be able to understand; you come from a wealthy nation and live in a big city where there are plenty of these prospects. But here in this small country, at that turbulent period, my options were limited. If only she would have stayed with the other man. Things would have been different."

My legs feel numb. I have to get up. I can't listen to this anymore. It's my turn to pace the terrace and get some distance from him. I rise from the chair and immediately feel the pins and needles in my feet and make my way to a corner edge of the terrace. While leaning my elbows on the railing I rest my chin in my hands and close my eyes. The tears start welling up I swallow away a whimper and open my eyes. Looking up at the sky and repeating to myself, be calm, I'll be fine, I've had my life, he's had his, I can get through this, be strong. Just breathe, inhale and exhale.

A few moments pass I turn around to search for him on the terrace. And then I see him returning from inside the room holding two more water bottles. He hands me one and keeps the other. "Thanks but I do think we might need something stronger after this catch up." He shakes his head in agreement. "Yes, but for now, I think its best we stay away from alcohol." We both tap our bottles together. Instantly reminding me of the several occasions we shared toasts.

After we take a few swigs, we both turn to look out at the beach. I feel like if I don't look right at him, it might be easier to hear more.

"Emelia, say something, tell me what you're thinking." He tries to hold my hand and I pull away from him. I step a bit to the left to give us some space.

Give me space. All my thoughts and words are crashing into one another. My feelings are a jumbled mess scattered on the ground beneath me. And having him so near to me is not helping.

He again tries to take my hand. "Please, let me hold your hand Emelia and talk to me."

I now turn to look at him with my back pressed against the railing. With my voice quivering, "Please don't touch me, not now. And talk to you, I don't even know what to say to you. You've had time thinking about all this. Over twenty years. I've had two minutes to absorb it and you want to know what I'm thinking. All these years I've felt so many things towards you and towards me. It was okay for me to be angry with you. Feel played by you, believed in your fake promises. And I experienced similar behavior by other men. So, I just convinced myself to think that's how men are or that I just make bad choices or maybe I'm not supposed to have love in my life. So when you ask me to tell you how I'm feeling and hold your hand, part of me wants to run into the bedroom, lock the door and crawl under the covers. And the other part is telling me to calm down and just listen to all that you need to tell me."

I walk away from him and towards the other corner of the terrace. I just need silence to gather my thoughts.

A few minutes pass, I walk towards him and we meet each other half way. Sinking into his clear blue eyes I begin, "I want to just hate you for all this. I want to blame you for all my sadness. But I can't."

I bite my lip to keep from crying. "What we had back then, was young love and who knows if it would have survived the long haul. You did warn me you weren't good at long distance relationships. You and Violeta were together before I met you. So, you can't take fault in all this. I just wish you would have been honest with me to tell me what was going on. To be left out in the cold like that, no explanation. That was heartbreaking. I thought I did something wrong. Letters and phone calls from your sister were vague. She told me to ask you what's going on. But you never called and you didn't answer my calls. And then Frida wrote less and our phone calls were not as frequent. I do remember she told me you got married. So, it was best for me to just let it go. Let you go. What we had, that magic, that sweetness, that tenderness, was gone. And I had to move on. You left me with no other choice."

I pause for a second and reach for his hands and continue, "Luca I never forgot you. I always remembered our special moments together. And I couldn't truly hate you. I loved you. I never could love anyone as I loved you."

Luca reaches up to wipe the tears cascading down my face. "Emelia, I never meant to hurt you. I just knew I had to meet everyone's expectations and hoped that they were right and that my life would fall into place. And love would come later." Tears trail down his cheeks.

With a tinge of compassion, I say, "And hearing your life story today, made me think so much less of myself. There I was sitting in my wealthy country, with many opportunities and always thinking the worst of you; when all along, you had made real life decisions that affected so many people and over the years honored those commitments. If all that you are telling me really happened, then as you are now and how you were back then, an honorable man."

He grabs me and holds me close to him. It feels so good to be back in his arms even if it's just for today. I want to stay with him like this forever. But I know he belongs to someone else. And I have to respect that. My body surges and I cry uncontrollably. So much time had passed and yet all my feelings for him return; love, joy, sadness, abandonment, disappointment, anger. Feelings I thought I overcame all those years ago.

He begins to rub my back and calmly tells me, "I am here, let it all out, I will never hurt you again. I am sorry. I am so sorry I broke your heart. I won't ever leave you again. I loved you too. And I never loved anyone as I loved you. I've known that all my life. But I thought this was how it had to be." His words begin to soothe me. And slowly my senses return and I try to loosen my grip on him.

We part slightly and I realize my face is soaked and my nose is a mess. He places his hand against my cheek, "Oh no, look at you, let me get some tissues." Luca sprints into the hotel room.

I follow and holler, "I'm in here too." I wander to the bathroom and to my surprise he's sitting on the edge of the tub wiping his tears. "Look at the two of us." I say while tending to my own clean up. When done, I offer him the sink. "I'll meet you in the living room."

While I wait, I distract myself by bringing the plates in from the terrace. Upon my second trip I see him standing in the living room watching me. "Emelia, you can leave all that, when they come to clean the room they'll take care of it."

"I just needed to do something Luca. I really wasn't even thinking."

"Come here, I need to hold you close." I walk over to him and into his awaiting arms. We hold each other for a few moments in silence. I can hear his heart thumping. "Luca, can I ask you something?"

"Yes, you may ask me anything."

"You said that when you made this decision you hoped your life would fall into place and that love would come later. Did that love ever happen?"

He takes a deep breath, "Yes and no."

While we continue holding one another, I look out the windows. He says, "Violeta moved into my home shortly after and a few months passed and we started planning our wedding. I tried to push you out of my mind so that I could be faithful to my wife."

Hearing that, I let go of him and rest on a living room chair. He follows me and sits on the coffee table near to me. Luca continues, "And as our marriage was building, I slowly began to accept this is my life. I know that I found happiness being around my family and friends and advancing my career. And as far as my married life, she was kind to me and cared for me, so I did the same for her. In some ways you could say we loved one another. We started our own family. First our daughter arrived and our son a couple of years later. I love my children dearly. I can't imagine life without them."

He pauses and takes me by the shoulders and he looks into my eyes, "Even though my life was full, I'd feel this wave of regret come over me. These moments would come at the oddest times. And then they would hit me at very specific occasions. When we'd celebrate Frida and Max's wedding anniversary and every year at Christmas. I'd see your face when I closed my eyes and hear your voice and picture that special day in the fields of flowers with you. You were so happy. I was so happy."

Feeling suffocated by his words I take his hands off my shoulders and walk towards the terrace doors. Luca follows me and stands just behind me and continues, "When I'd visit my grandparents' home, every now and then I envisioned you walking out of the bedroom towards me. And a few years ago Henry was visiting for the summer and told me he saw you in Arizona. He said that you were married, but he didn't meet your husband. You had visited him with your parents and that you looked the same. The next year when Henry and his family visited for Christmas, he said he had seen you again. And that time you told him you were divorced. Part of me felt so sad for you and then selfishly I was comforted to know you were single again, as if one day we might have that chance to be together."

Uncertain what to think of all he just shared, I look at him over my shoulder and give him a crooked smile. "So when you ask me did I ever find love, I found love in many ways, but I never found nor felt the love I had with you."

Luca turns me to face him and caresses my cheek with his fingertips. "Henry wasn't completely right, you changed. I find you even more beautiful today."

He trails kisses along my forehead, I close my eyes. His lips travel down the path of my nose and along my jawline. Tilting my head back I feel my own heartbeats increasing and then his hands gently lift my head towards his and our mouths meet. Swiftly the tip of his tongue parts my lips. We lose ourselves just kissing, touching and holding one another. As we slow the pace my mind begins to take control of my body. My fingers caress his neck and his cheeks and his jawline. And we wind down with quick luscious kisses. He opens his eyes and looks deeply into mine.

"We still have it," he proudly flirts smiling at me. I shut my eyes tightly and open them again blushing, "Yes, we still do. But we shouldn't have done this."

Luca looks confused. As he rubs my tense forehead, "Why shouldn't we?"

"I'm not that kind of woman and you're not that kind of man. At least that's what I thought. I can't be the other woman and after all these years, you can't cheat on your wife."

I start to pull away from him but he holds me in place. "No, don't run from me. We just had a perfect moment Emelia. I've dreamed about this. Please don't ruin it."

He kisses me again. I push him away, "Ruin it, Luca, this is not right, we shouldn't be doing this." I break loose of his grasp and try to put distance between us.

I sit at the dining table. He follows me and as he kneels down beside me he forcefully moves me and the chair to face him and I feel trapped. He clutches my hands in place on my lap.

"Oh, my love, you don't know. I thought Henry told you. I'm not with Violeta. Our marriage ended a while ago and I'm just waiting for our divorce to be finalized."

He leans down and kisses my hands and places his head in my lap. Running my fingers through his wavy locks and gently rubbing the back of his neck.

"Henry didn't tell me anything. As far as I knew, you are still married. In fact, he showed me pictures last night of the family at a wedding and all of you were there, including Violeta."

He continues to rest his head on my lap and discloses, "I think that was from a wedding we attended almost a year ago. Shortly after that she asked me for a divorce."

I utter, "I don't understand, what happened, why now?" He continues to talk with his eyes closed and in a tone mixed with irritation and defeat.

"She said she was done with this arrangement. I didn't know at first what she meant. So she broke down and admitted that years ago when she came back to me and professed that she loved me that it was because of her father. He pressured her to make it work with me and even threatened to take away her trust fund and any future inheritance if she continued relations with that other man. So she compromised too. Then over a year ago, she was out to lunch with a friend and seated at the next table was him. The man she left me for all those years ago. They reconnected that afternoon and for months carried on an affair. Then we went to the wedding, she claims to have had an epiphany. When she asked me for the divorce, she said she no longer wanted to live this way. And that we both deserved so much more. That we deserved to be with the ones we love. She said she was sorry for misleading me into this marriage. But felt she had no other option. And knew at the very least I was a respectable man and that our lives would be content. That day when she told me all this my heart shattered into a million pieces."

I glance at his face and see Luca crying. Leaning down I tenderly kiss his temple and grasp his shoulders. "Luca let me get up." He won't budge and his arms tighten around my legs.

He raises his voice to me, "You don't understand. You don't understand Emelia."

I wiggle out of his grip and slide down to the floor and onto his lap. Taking him in my arms and holding him close. "Luca tell me what I don't understand."

"When I said that my heart shattered that day, it wasn't for her. It was for you and for us. The life we could have had. The love that was lost. I was devastated. How could she and her father manipulate me like that? And then I was angry at myself. You praised me earlier for being loyal to my commitments and being an honorable man. I wasn't a man when I hurt you. I wasn't a man when I allowed them to convince me that having a life with Violeta would be better. I wasn't a man when I took the easy way out and worked for that company. After I promised you a future, I should have never let her back in my life. So, I felt I deserved all this now. Because of the pain I caused you. I took what we had and tossed it away. For what, why didn't I just listen to my own heart? I should have believed in us and that we'd find a way to make it work. Instead, I listened to others and took the easy road. It wasn't always easy. And Violeta was right all along. When we'd have arguments and there were many, she'd accuse me of never loving her. She always said no matter what she did someone else had a hold of my heart. And usually I'd storm out of the room. I could not argue with her about that, it was too painful for me. For that was one part of me I knew she would never possess."

I feel chilled and wrap my arms around myself. Resting my head against his chest I close my eyes. Too many thoughts, too many questions and too many feelings are overpowering me. I want to sit here in silence with him just until I get some clarity, if that's even possible.

As if he can read my mind, his arms hug me closer into him. And he kisses my forehead. "My love, I know, I've said a lot. And you need a chance to think. When you opened the door earlier to me, you know what else I saw before you showed me the sadness I brought to you? For a brief moment your smile your spirit made me see the life we could have had together. Tell me I'm not too late. Tell me you're single and we can try once more. We can still love again, you and me. The way it was meant to be. I will never hurt you again and I won't leave you again. I am free to be with you. I'm free to hold you in my arms like this forever." He kisses my forehead again, resting his head upon mine and remains quiet.

We sit on the floor for a few minutes in silence. I slowly pull my head away from his chest and I feel his head move from its resting place. I teasingly say, "If you hold me in your arms like this for another thirty minutes, I don't think either of us can get up without assistance. I am now slowly climbing out of your lap."

He begins to laugh and he releases me. As I reach to get some support from the chair he says, "We're not that old."

I smile back, "We're not old at all, just old-ER. Need a hand young man?" I offer him my hand.

"Hey, we're the same age." He manages to get up without my help.

"I'm six months older than you. Are you sure you want to try again with this older woman?"

He grabs my hips and forces me to bump into him and gives me a sweet peck. "You remember my birthday, that's a good sign." And he gives me his sweet boyish smile and raises both his eyebrows. I giggle and return the smile.

There's a knock at the door. "Did you order more food?" I say exasperated.

He shakes his head, "No. When did I have a chance?" He says defensively.

The person knocks again. Luca walks to the door. When he opens it we see someone from housekeeping. They speak in Spanish. I say, "Luca ask her to give us five minutes." He looks at me with furrowed brows. "Are you sure?" "Yes, I am sure." Words are exchanged and he closes the door.

"Emelia what do you have in mind?"

After taking a much needed sip of water, "Well, it's a beautiful day and we're at the beach. I thought we could let her in the room and we'll take a walk." He nods, "Good idea."

"Hey did you bring a bathing suit? Any chance I can enjoy watching you swim today?"

He smiles, "I came prepared. Actually, I too am staying here."

My heart flutters and I nervously exclaim, "Staying HERE, or at this hotel? Oh forget I asked that."

Luca walks over to me and grabs the water bottle out of my hand and takes a swig. "I know it's been awhile since you've seen me but I'm still respectful of you. I have a room across the hall." He kisses my nose. "Are you ready for our walk? We can swim later, ok?"

I stride towards the bedroom, "I need a minute to freshen up and then I'll be good to go." He yells to me, "I'll go to my room and meet you in the hallway in five minutes." I wave at him and he's gone.

Chapter 20

THE PERSON I see looking back at me in the mirror has transformed since the morning. I expected this trip wasn't going to be easy, but I never anticipated any of what Luca just told me. Well, no need to make any decisions now. I'm here for a few days. I want to believe he's sincere but I also feel guarded because he's made promises to me before that he didn't keep. Now listen, heart, mind and body, it's a team effort, let's be open to this and above all do not be impulsive.

Luca is waiting for me outside my door. As he takes my hand in his we walk towards the elevator. "What were the plans with Henry and the rest of your day?" The elevator arrives and we enter. "I don't know. We only planned to meet for breakfast and take it from there. We worried that if we got too far away from the hotel, we might run into your sister. So we mentioned just relaxing at the beach and walking around nearby." We arrive at the lobby and locate the doors towards the boardwalk.

Once outside my body delights with the sun on my skin and the ocean breezes. Luca lays a tender kiss on my cheek and another on the hand he's been holding so dearly. "This is nothing like the beach I took you to in Valencia. But we'll make the best of it." He says with a sarcastic tone.

We stroll down the ramp and kick off our shoes. My feet immerse in the warm sand and Luca leads the way. For the next few minutes we pass families setting up their chairs and umbrellas; teenagers playing volleyball and children building sandcastles. And as we walk further and further away from the hotel, we encounter less and less people. Soon it seems as if we have our own private beach.

I think he's waiting for me to say something, "It's good to be out here on the beach. I feel more at ease with my thoughts." He releases my hand and tries to put his arm around me but I move slightly away from him. And we continue to walk side by side.

"Emelia, today, I just want us to be together and get to know each other again. I want to hear about your life since we last saw one another. What do you want to do today?"

I lead us towards the water's edge and look out at the horizon. "Me, what do I want to do today? For starters, spending the day with you is completely unexpected. And there have been moments when I feel a rush of anxiety come over me. But I'm trying to work through them. I want to spend today getting to know you again. I don't know what tomorrow will be like or the rest of the week. So, it seems like today is the only day for you and me, right?" I breathe in the ocean air.

He turns to face me, "Yes, all day it's just you and me. I don't have to be anywhere until tomorrow." I smile and cautiously caress my hand down his forearm and reply, "I don't remember us having a day completely to our-selves." He smiles and replies, "Me too. Now I'm feeling a rush of anxiety." We look at each other and share a laugh.

He says, "How does this sound, we take it easy all afternoon at the hotel, lounge at the beach and pool and maybe later go out for dinner and dancing?" I nod and respond with, "Sounds perfect." And we continue our stroll on the beach.

"Did you learn how to swim since our first trip to the beach?" I bump into him to push him away.

"I thought maybe you'd start with simpler questions, but no, you ask me about my swimming capabilities." I exhale loudly. And I reply playfully, "I don't feel like answering your question at this moment."

He stands in front of me to block me from going further. I scoot around him. He tries again. I turn and walk in the opposite direction. He's beside me and whispers in my ear, "It's just a yes or no question."

I stop and fold my arms in front of me. I reply, "No." And then I start again, towards the hotel.

He asks, "So does that mean you don't know how to swim?"

I reply, "Yes."

"Emelia, you've confused me now. I will ask you again do you know how to swim?"

I stand still and I look away. "No, I don't know how to swim. But it's not for lack of trying. Can we go now to our rooms to get changed?"

He puts his hands on my shoulders and holds me in place. "I'm sorry that my question upset you. I was just remembering our first day together at the beach and how annoyed I was with you because you didn't mention this until we got to the beach. I would have packed you something to use that day had I known. So, I thought it was like a private joke now between you and me."

I hold back my tears. "Oh Luca, I'm not upset about your question. I thought, I thought I could be comfortable with all this. All that you told me back in the room. And we'd have this fun day together. But it's just hitting me all over again. And I don't know what to do, how to feel. You hurt me so long ago. And I'm worried that if I allow myself to love you once more, that you'll hurt me again, just like I said earlier, waves of anxiety. Please just hold me right now and let's be silent for a few minutes." And that's exactly what we do, stand together holding one another looking out at the water.

With the sounds of the breakers calming me, a question that has haunted me for years comes to mind, "Luca why didn't you call me all those years ago? I needed to know what happened."

He closes his eyes and inhales deeply and then exhales. Luca first stares at the ocean and then back at me. "That's not a simple question." He pauses and still holding me he continues, "So much time has passed and yet, all my feelings and reasons why I didn't reach out to you churn up again. Selfishly I knew it would have hurt me just to hear your voice and tell you that I'm saying goodbye to you, to us. I knew what I was doing wasn't fair or kind to you. And so I took the easy way out. I was a coward. I hoped if I didn't tell you we didn't have a future, maybe there still would be a chance because I hadn't said it out loud. I actually feared I'd crumble as soon as I heard your voice and your disappointment with me. I couldn't bear it. Later on I told myself, maybe it was better for you too, that I didn't shut the door on us completely, so that you could hope for our future together one day. And now I realize how terribly wrong I was to not be strong enough to tell you the truth. Because I think I caused you even more pain."

I press my forehead against his chest. Now I have his answer to one of the questions that tormented me all these years. Had he told me this back then would I have allowed myself to love differently? Was he the cause of my failed marriage, all of my failed relationships? I can't blame him completely, I should have known better. And I should have let him go.

After a while, I look up at him and ask, "Do you think the maid is done in the room?" He kisses my lips. "Yes, and if not we can wait in my room. Let's go back and get changed." We hold hands and walk silently back to the hotel.

When we arrive on the floor of our rooms, we see the maid's cart at the other end of the corridor. "Oh good, she's finished with the room. I'll need about twenty minutes."

He nods and smiles. "No hurry, just knock on my door when you're ready." Before we part I pull him close to me and kiss him on the lips followed by a quick, "Thanks."

He takes a tendril of my hair and places it behind my ear. Then he swipes his cardkey into the reader and places the card in my hand. "Instead of knocking, just use the key."

Once inside alone in my room I lean my back against the door and close my eyes. I try to manage my thoughts. Basically, there's just two ways this can go today. I can be a weepy emotional mess wrapped up in the past or I can embrace the present by giving my all and have the best time with the man I once loved.

Chapter 21

THE LITTLE LIGHT turns green and the lock releases. I turn the handle and open Luca's room door. Quietly, I close the door behind me and walk through the entry hallway. And I find my Prince Charming sleeping on the bed. Placing my beach bag on a chair and his key on the desk, I tip toe over to the bed, flip off my sandals and lie next to him.

A minute or so passes and he sighs. And then he rolls his body halfway over mine. With his nose nuzzling my neck and his arm resting across my stomach he murmurs, "You smell so good, like coconuts."

I giggle, "It's the suntan lotion."

And he smacks his lips and says, "Mmm, I want to devour you."

I laugh and exclaim, "Oh, no, no, no, no, no you can't lick the lotion."

And he lifts his head off my shoulder and leans his face close to mine, "Then I'll just have to settle for this." He eagerly kisses me and his desire to devour me has been satisfied, for now.

Just like teenagers making out in the back seat of a car, this session must end before we go too far. When we take a breather I say, "I want to look good at your sister's party, which means, I need sun-kissed skin today."

He smiles at me, "I don't want to sound selfish, but you already look better than good right now. But if you insist, let's go to the beach where you will be sun-kissed."

Once we break out of the love nest we find our way back to the beach. Luca locates a double chaise lounge for us. This is beginning to feel like a honeymoon to me.

As we settle into the deep comfortable cushions, under the oversized canopy he says, "This is getting better every minute. Now when I want to touch you, I won't have to go too far." I smile and raise one eyebrow. "Yes, it's like having a bed on the beach, but with an audience." He grimaces, "Oh that's right, I better not forget."

"*Buenas tardes*, Good afternoon. My name is Javier and I'm your waiter." I greet him with "*Buenas tardes* Javier" just when Luca says, "Good afternoon Javier."

"Here is our menu and can I bring you some ice water while you decide?"

Again like a singing duo, we say, "Yes, please bring us the water."

Javier gives Luca the menu and when he leaves, we start laughing like little kids. After I gain some composure, I announce, "You can answer all his questions we're not doing that again."

Javier returns with the water bottles and Luca orders us rum punches to start followed by vegetable and steak skewers. Once we're alone again, Luca kneels up on his side of the chaise. "Want to go in the water with me before he comes back with our drinks?"

"Ooh that does sound tempting. But will you also swim for me today?"

He looks at me like a little boy. "I remember that day at the beach and when I first spotted you swimming. You took my breath away."

"Well, it's been awhile and I'm a bit old-ER, as you would say. Yes, your wish is my command. I hope I don't disappoint you." I lean up to him and we kiss.

He swats my thigh and says, "Let's go." We run into the water and I'm expecting it to be cold like in the Northeast. But it's warm with a cool undercurrent and I quickly dunk myself. Luca lurks around me like a shark.

"It's not very deep right here, I'm safe." He goes back under the water and disappears for a few seconds and he pops his head up and floats on his back towards me. With the sun glistening on his wet body he says, "The water feels great, right?"

I nod yes. "And it's so clear, I can see my feet." He now treads water near me. "Go and swim, I know you want to. I'll stay here safely and admire you."

He nods, "Emelia, you're just back in my life I'm not about to leave you."

I kiss him and say, "Oh Luca, we have all day to be together and you won't be leaving me. Now go and swim."

He kisses me and asks, "Any requests?" I look up to the sky and reply, "Do whatever makes you feel good. But since you asked, maybe you can end with the butterfly?"

My merman swiftly kisses me goodbye and he dives underwater and disappears with his feet as flippers splashing water up at me.

A few yards away his head rises out of the water and he comes into view and waves at me and I wave back. He holds up his index finger and begins his show. His first lap he starts with the freestyle. His arms and legs move so easily on top of the water as he swims in front of me from right to left and left to right. He looks to me again and holds up two fingers. I smile and excitedly give him two thumbs up. Luca's second technique looks like the breaststroke. And I wonder how often he gets to swim, 'cause from here, he seems to be in very good shape. Completing that segment he waves three fingers at me and I clap my hands. Oh, and he's treating me to my second favorite swim style, the backstroke. Placidly he glides smoothly over the water and I'm mesmerized by his strength and form. It appears this might be his favorite too, for he does a third lap of the backstroke. When he's finished he looks at me and shows four fingers and with both arms gestures towards me. He must be preparing for the finale. Enthusiastically I perform the one person body wave to him. I crouch down into the water and rise up with both my arms towards the sky and repeat. I hear him whistling at me in the distance. Luca dips out of view and then his head and shoulders powerfully emerge above the surface as he swims the butterfly towards me. I wish I had my camera. But within seconds he's close to me and circles underwater like a dolphin begging for my attention.

Playfully he arises from the water climbs up my body pulling me against him and takes me in his arms. His force almost causes me to fall into the water but he manages to hold me in place. I am completely drenched. Breathlessly he says, "Did I satisfy your wishes my love?"

His chest rises up and down from his swimming performance, I run my hands through his soaked hair and say, "Yes, even more than I wished for. Hey, for a man of your age, you look like a twenty year old swimming out there. I'm impressed." He winks at me and says, "Around you, I feel like a twenty year old." And then we kiss.

"If I promise to keep your head above water will you trust me?" While trying to figure out what he's getting at I reply, "You're not turning this into a swim lesson, right?"

"No, I just want to have fun with you at the beach and I need to know what you're comfortable doing. For example, if you climb on my back and wrap your legs around my waist we can float together. Or we can do the same but face to face."

I glance around to see how many other swimmers are in the water. Not too many and none that are near us. "I'm good with that as long as if I panic, I can put my feet down and I won't go under water."

He nods, "Yes, of course, we won't go further out than where we are now. I've got you I won't let anything happen to you."

Slightly terrified I say, "Ok, let's try some of your tricks."

He embraces me and soon has me floating with him like when he led me on the dance floor except my feet aren't touching the ground. We travel to the left and then back to the right and when he whirls us around I tilt my head back in the water and squeal with delight.

Luca whispers in my ear, "Ready for another trick?" I smile at my life-guard, "Yes!" He shifts us so that I'm floating on his back. With his careful direction, I should place my hands onto his shoulders and let my body rise up to the surface and he'll do the rest. It took me a few tries and with his boundless patience finally we were peacefully gliding together.

As my trust continues to build my grip eases too. And soon my fingers are resting lightly on his shoulders while my body floats. And I can feel his body swim beneath me pulling us both along. It's so relaxing and sensual and my mind like my body drifts with thoughts of me and Luca giving ourselves to one another.

My imaginings are suddenly interrupted when he stops swimming and steers me into his arms. Alarmed I ask, "Are you ok? Should we go back to the chair?"

He replies, "I'm more than okay now."

With my legs wrapped around his waist he says, *"Bésame Mi Lia."* [Kiss me my Lia.] And we kiss fervently with our bodies rocking to the rhythm of the waves. Soon I feel his arousal pressing against me. And I know we can't give ourselves to one another here. My lips pull away from his and I kiss him on his temples and his forehead and whisper, "We probably should slow things down, otherwise we'll get thrown out of the hotel." He tilts his head back and laughs. "Yes, you are probably right."

With that he kisses me quickly and helps me to balance on my own feet. He explains, "I don't know what happened I was swimming with you floating above me and became captivated by the ease and allure of us moving together as one. It was so calming and intense. And then I didn't feel your hands clasping me and I turned desperately to save you. But you were there all the while Emelia and my fears changed to desire. I know this is happening all too soon. I am sorry."

A quiver runs through me from the top of my head to the tips of my toes. "My love, you're trembling, let's go back to the lounge chair for you to get warm." He puts his arm around me and we walk side by side towards the chair.

When we reach our beach bed, Luca quickly wraps the sun heated towel around me and grabs the other towel for himself. I take a few minutes to dry off and calm my chill. But I know it wasn't the water that made me shiver. It's what I'm thinking about and what I want to tell him that's making my body react this way.

Javier appears with a tray of drinks. Perfect timing, the rum will relax me and give me some courage. I actually wouldn't mind doing a shot right now. Luca says, "*Gracias* Javier, impeccable timing we just came back from our swim. Can you also bring over our food when it's ready?" Javier nods.

Luca takes both cups off the tray and hands me one. I know not to sip yet, I'm certain he will treat me to a toast. He raises his cup to me, "I am suddenly at a loss for words. Since we've been apart I could only imagine a day like today with you. And yet here we are. So, here is to you and me reuniting. Salud." We tap our glasses and I steal a quick kiss from him.

We stretch out on the beach bed and sip our drinks and nibble on the tasty skewers. After a while I turn to Luca and he also turns his body towards mine. Propped up on my side, I reach over to him and with my fingertips trace the angles of his face. "You are even more handsome than when I first met you. And I never thought that would be possible."

Then it occurs to me, "Luca, what happened to your nose?"

He looks at me curiously, "I don't know, what happened?"

I shake my head, "Nothing now, I mean, it's different from before. I loved that little curve."

His eyes widen, "Oh, now I know what you mean. I had it corrected. When I would swim underwater my breathing was challenged and thought it might help to fix it. I had it taken care of not long after I saw you last. Until you just mentioned it I almost forgot about it."

I trace my finger along the bridge of his nose and ask, "When is the divorce final?" He grimaces, "In August."

"I need to apologize to you."

He crinkles his forehead, "Why what have you done?"

My fingers continue their journey to his neck, his collar bone and his shoulder. "When we were together in the water, you made me feel so tranquil and safe with you. This connection that we have is extraordinary. Just a few hours ago you rolled back into my life and out there in the water I wanted to give myself to you. So you shouldn't say you're sorry, I want you too."

He takes my hand and brings it to his lips and kisses the tips of each finger. Then he secures that hand over his heart. "What should we do about this Mi Lia?" he says flirtatiously.

I look towards the water for a moment and back to him. "For starters, I think we only need one room for tonight."

He takes a deep breath and kisses my hand, "How scandalous, go on."

I bury my head into his chest and he hums with delight. I sit up and finish my drink. Javier glances over and I raise my glass and wave two fingers at him. He smiles and nods to me.

"Scandalous is right. Luca, we're practically strangers. We've lived apart for so many years. This doesn't make any sense. I don't know if I even like the man you are now. And I'm still not over you ditching me. Yet, I'm having these thoughts of being with you. It's all so confusing. How are you so certain of your feelings towards me? I'm not the same woman."

When he rises up he also finishes his drink. Takes my empty cup with his and places them on the side table near him. "Emelia, you are right, you may not be the exact woman I knew, but what I'm certain of, I loved your heart, I loved your mind and I loved your entire being. Tell me, do you think you changed for the worse or the better in all the years we've been apart?"

Javier returns with more drinks. I smile at him, "Many thanks Javier." He replies, "With pleasure."

I take a couple of sips and Luca nods his head, "Stop fighting this, you know I'm right. Just allow yourself to be free to love me again. Free, like you were when you floated with me out there. You will see that I'm not very different from the man you first loved. Except now, I'm giving you my all. And I'm not giving up on us and I will stop at nothing to win you back. I can't lose you again."

Wishing I could just hit the pause button and dash up to my room and call Jenene. And tell her all that's happened and tell her all that I'm feeling and ask her if I'm completely crazy to give Luca another chance.

It occurs to me before I can even consider opening myself up to Luca at this level, we need to address something else and I don't know how to bring up the topic. I sit up and glance at the water. He caresses my arm, "Don't be nervous this is a big step for me too. The last woman I was with I'm divorcing and to be very honest, until today, you were the only other woman I've kissed in over twenty years."

I move closer to him and with discretion begin to explain, "My thoughts were about something else. You see, leading up to this trip, I didn't plan on engaging with someone intimately and so I'm not quite prepared."

He smiles and looks encouragingly at me, "Emelia, I am a man and you are a very beautiful woman who takes meticulous care of her body. I'm certain even in *Her* most natural appearance I will desire *Her* as much as I desire you."

What is he talking about? I glance away from him and repeat what he just said in my mind. *Her* most natural appearance, who is *Her*, what is *Her*?

"Luca, I'm a little, oh? Ohhh!" I nervously giggle into his chest with complete embarrassment.

"My sweet Lia, I love your honesty. It makes me want you even more."

I giggle again. And he laughs too. I take a deep breath to gain some self-control. When my giggles calm I look into Luca's eyes. "You're so gentle and considerate with me which makes this even more difficult to explain because I don't want to hurt your feelings. When I said I'm not prepared, I should have said, not prepared *responsibly*. I was not talking about *Her*. And trust me, *She,* is pleasingly prepared and after all this time readily awaits an introduction with *Him*." He looks at me with surprise and uncertainty.

I whisper, "Luca, before we go upstairs, we should discuss protection." He nods his head, "Oh, yes, we're good. I had that taken care of after my son was born, so that concern is settled."

I hoped I didn't have to teach a sex education class today, but since he's been out of the dating world I must inquire. "From what you just informed me, that procedure covers only half of my worries. You are aware of other things that might be exchanged if we don't take precautions?"

He smirks back at me now. "Emelia, as much as I'm enjoying this very delicate topic with you, I must inform you, that my goal is to get to know you very intimately when we are alone. And so that we don't have any more confusion we should speak directly now about your worries."

He is so right about this, but I can't be blunt with him. "Ok, I agree, we should just discuss this openly. Knowing you can't impregnate me gives me some assurance, but, you did say, you were with one other person, who happened to be with two men. There's a chance you may have received something more than divorce papers and I'd rather not get the gift that keeps on giving, that the three of you may have passed around. Now do you understand why I think we should stop at a drugstore and pick up something?"

Luca smiles and gives me a quick kiss. "When we separated I saw my doctor and he ran many tests. Besides having low blood pressure, everything else checked out, my body is healthy. And without sounding too bold, I had tests taken about a month ago again, and I received a shiny gold star."

I lie back on my side of the chaise, fold my arms and close my eyes. My mind is cluttered, I can't find the words. I want to laugh, and scream, and cry and laugh again. I know he means well, but he didn't have to make me feel like such a given. Was this his intent all along? Have I just been fooled by his charms?

I feel him inching closer to me and with his lips near to my ear, "I want to apologize I've said something wrong. All these years I've thought about you and wondered what it would have been like if we had been together. You know, together, together. I was being honest before when I told you I haven't been with anyone. And when my brother told me you accepted the invitation my heart came to life again and I wanted to make sure if I ever got that chance to be with you that everything would be good. I certainly didn't think today would happen. It only occurred to me yesterday to visit you here at the hotel. My only hope was that you didn't slam the door in my face. I never expected all this, just yet. If you're still feeling angry with me or think I'm just using you I will understand and we can keep both rooms and move forward with our plans for dinner and dancing tonight. Or maybe you want me to leave you alone and I'll see you tomorrow at the party." He rolls back to his side of the lounger.

After thinking about all he just said I get up from the chaise and look for my sundress. I find it in my beach bag. I put it on, take a drink of water and walk around to his side. He gets up and puts his shirt on. Does he think I want to leave?

"Are you going somewhere?"

"You got dressed I thought you wanted to leave."

I shake my head, "No, I just wanted to stretch and get dressed but I'd like to stay a bit longer here with you. Do you want to stay with me?"

He sits back on the lounger and opens his arms to me. I scramble over to him and into his embrace. As we nestle together, I say, "What I was feeling a few minutes ago wasn't completely directed at you. I think years of casual relationships have taken its toll. I've been on a break from dating while waiting for the right man to come into my life. A very long break, so in case you were wondering, I too received a gold star during my last doctor's visit. I forgive you if you forgive me." He kisses my forehead and pulls me closer to him.

"Emelia, oh never mind."

I giggle, "It's out there Luca; just say what you want to say."

"Well, it's not what I want to say, it's what I want to ask."

Pulling away from him so I can look him in the eyes, "What is your question?"

He smirks, "How long of a break?"

Nodding my head while I smile at him playfully, "I will tell if you tell." He nods in agreement.

I suggest as if we're ten year olds, "Ok, on the count of three, we just blurt it out." Luca laughs and we both sit up and face one another. Before I start with the countdown, I think back on my last encounter. He says, "I'm waiting." I reply, "I'm thinking." He closes his eyes while shaking his head. Clearing my throat I say, "Ok, are you ready?" Opening his eyes he whispers, "Yes."

With a wave of heat rushing to my cheeks, I don't understand why I'm so nervous to tell him. It actually is a good thing.

"I'll count down now." With three fingers raised I say, "Three, two, one."

Luca says, *"Dos años"* [Two years] just as I say, "Two and a half years."

He covers his eyes with his hands. He says, "Why are you so precise? Now I have to rethink my number."

I rest my head on his chest again and say, "Well, I'm glad that's out of the way."

"Emelia why? You are a smart, fun, gorgeous and loving woman. I'm surprised."

"Surprised by what?"

"Surprised, that no man has made any effort to date you."

"Well, besides dining out, playing tennis, going to the movies or hiking with friends, unless a man appears randomly in my living room, I wasn't putting myself out there. I wanted to focus on just being with me for a while. And if I met someone that I wanted to date, I would have been open to that, but that someone never made an appearance."

"Is it too late to change my number?" he asks.

I giggle into his chest and say, "No, it's not too late."

He says, "Mine is closer to three years."

I pop my head up, "Luciano Morales, you are so competitive, you have to be lying."

"Emelia, first, I had to wait until now to hear you say my name like that. You know what that does to me." He quickly kisses me.

"And second, I am a very proud man, why would I lie about something like this? I wouldn't go around boasting to people that for the last three years I didn't want to sleep with my own wife." Now of course when he puts it that way, I feel terrible.

"Luca, so for almost three years, you haven't been intimate with anyone?"

"Mi Lia, I observed my vows. I felt awful pushing her away, which broke a vow I guess, I didn't want to make it worse by cheating on her too." He pauses, "I thought after I took a break from her, maybe I'd be interested again, but that never happened. And then she wanted a divorce."

Resting again on his chest I take his hand in mine and say, "Well, it's like we're almost virgins again." He laughs, "Oh Mi Lia, I've missed you."

Chapter 22

WE WAKE FROM our beachside snooze and settle the tab with Javier. I grab my beach bag with Luca leading the way and I reach out to hold his hand. My entire body is pulsing with anticipation. In just a few minutes, it will only be us alone in the bedroom. I wonder what he's thinking right now. Is he feeling just as nervous as me? I've had sex before and yet this almost feels like my very first time.

Entering the lobby I look for a distraction. "Do you know what time it is?" And then I giggle to myself, really, you couldn't come up with a better question. He should respond by saying, "It's time for sex." He looks towards the front desk and spots a clock. "It's almost three why?" "No reason, I seemed to have lost track of time with you today."

We find our elevator bank and the doors open to an empty car. Luca presses our floor and the doors close. In tantalizing privacy he draws me near and I rest my head against his shoulder. I count the beeps as we pass each level. The elevator stops and the doors open to our floor.

While walking towards the hotel rooms I get the impression he's waiting for me to give him some direction. We reach my door and I take the plastic key out of the side pocket of my bag and Luca smoothly takes my key swipes open the lock for me and says, "I'll get my things and bring them into your room, I hope you don't mind if I borrow the key?"

I was wrong this man did not need any guidance from me. I smile at him and say, "No, I don't mind." He smiles back and whispers, "I'll meet you in the shower in a few minutes." My eyes widen, "Don't take too long," and I kiss him.

We go our separate ways and I close the door behind me. I glance around the suite not really looking at what I'm seeing, just trying to calm all the thoughts darting in my mind. When suddenly they are halted, when did those arrive I wonder?

Sprinting to the coffee table I stand before the most gorgeous floral arrangement I've ever received. A tall glass vase filled with calla lilies and long stemmed red roses with a card resting between the blossoms. Do I read the card now or wait and have him read the card to me? My heart is pounding. I pick up the card and slowly open the envelope. I sit and read the inscription.

> *My Dearest Emelia,*
>
> *Spending the day with you has been a dream come true. Let's take this leap together and I will bring excitement and joy to your life as you have given me today.*
>
> *I am yours forever.*
>
> *Love, Your Luciano*

I read his kind loving words again and again while glancing at the flowers. Can this really be happening? Can we finally be together after all these years? Can I believe that no one or nothing will stand in our way? Can I trust he won't break my heart again?

Ok, stop all this thinking. Slow it down and let all that's going on now, just happen. Take it moment by moment. Don't cloud my mind so that I won't enjoy being with him, especially now, this afternoon and tonight, before I share him with his family. I close my eyes and breath and count.

I am so concentrated on my breathing I don't hear Luca enter the room. He sits on the arm of the chair and rubs my back gently. "Wow, the flowers arrived so soon. I thought you would have gotten them tonight after dinner." I lean and rest my head on his thigh and place my hand on his knee. He strokes my hair and massages the back of my neck. I raise the card up to him, "Please read this to me."

He takes the card and then I feel his chin near to my ear, "My dearest Emelia, Spending the day with you has been a dream come true." He kisses my temple and continues in a most adoring and gentle voice, "Let's take this leap together and I will bring excitement and joy to your life as you have given me today. I am yours forever. Love, Your Luciano"

I get up from the chair, tug the card out of his hand and place it on the table near the vase. When I turn to him he stands and I take both of his hands and say, "I still feel like this is all a dream." I lean to him and rub my nose against his nose.

I say mischievously, "Excitement, huh, I'll race you to the shower." And I drop his hands and bolt towards the bedroom. He's behind me in seconds and shoves me onto the bed, out of his way and takes the lead and wins. I'm screaming with amusement on the bed and hear him turn on the water.

I grab the extra robe from the closet and place it on the hook near mine in the bathroom. He's leaning against the sink waiting for me wearing a silly grin. "Can you turn the other way for a minute?" He looks confused. I point to the toilet. He smiles and spins around.

While I'm sitting, I say, "You should be disqualified, you knocked me over." He turns to look at me. I grimace and shake my head. But he continues to watch me.

"Ok, I lose. You win. What's the prize?"

I use the paper cloth and stand. I reply, "I didn't think that far."

He trades places with me removes his swim shorts and asks, "Can you look the other way?" I laugh and face the shower.

I hear the toilet flush and I feel him standing behind me. As he unties both of the strings of my sundress it falls to my feet.

He whispers, "You don't need to think about it, I have something in mind." I turn and look at him curiously, "Have you now?"

I unbutton his linen shirt and after the last button, I pull the shirt off from his shoulders and he lets it fall to the floor. He places one finger under the strap of my bikini top and as it drops, he kisses the top of that shoulder and he does the same to the other. Pulling the top down, he cups each of my breasts in his hands and leans his head towards me and trails kisses from my neck down to each nipple. As he suckles each one I feel my body respond and exhale. "Let's move this to the shower," I plead breathlessly. I quickly remove the rest of my swimwear and join him in the steamy double shower.

With both heads raining water on us, we rinse off our day at the beach. I soap up a washcloth and begin to work on his back. I first clean his neck and rub the cloth in circular motions around each shoulder, then shoulder blades, the middle of his back and up and down his spine. As I reach his lower back I am gratified to see two sweet dimples above a perfectly sculpted bottom. I want to cup each of his cheeks so desperately but after adding more soap to the cloth I resume my task with circular motions and continue down the backs of his muscular legs, first the thighs and later his calves.

When I'm done with his back, he turns around and takes the cloth from my hand. "It's my turn." He places the cloth on a hook and takes the shampoo bottle in his hand and motions for me to sit on the bench. I sit and soon his hands are working their magic through my hair. And he ends with a gentle and thorough neck massage. "Now you can rinse off." I go under the shower and rinse off the shampoo and watch him cleaning the front of his body.

Soon he's beside me, "Turn around, I want to wash you." I do as he says. His method is both timesaving and thorough. In longer sweeps and wider circular motions his hands cover both sides of my body. He lingers around my breasts and begins sucking and nibbling my neck, "This is good now, yes, no suntan lotion?" I squeal with pleasure. "Yes!" while giggling. Then he quickens the pace and cleans the rest of me.

He points to the bench again. I obey and take a seat. Kneeling down he scrubs my feet. I grab the shampoo and quickly tend to his very full head of hair. "I must commend you on your techniques shower boy, quick and efficient." He smiles at me, "To be honest, your technique, almost sent me over the edge. And for what I have planned for you, I need to pace myself." I rub my other foot up and down his calf.

When he's done, we both stand under the water and finish our shower rituals separately and rapidly. He exits the shower first and dries himself and tosses me another towel.

I pat down my body and squeeze out the excess water from my hair. With the towel wrapped around his waist Luca leaves the bathroom while I put on a robe. And when he returns he's carrying a shaving kit. I start to brush my teeth when I hear him rummaging through the kit. Soon we're both tending to our dental hygiene. While pouring mouthwash into a cup I sense he's watching me. I offer him some and he passes me a cup to fill. He raises the cup and taps it against mine. These grooming formalities feel like we've been doing them together for years.

When we're both finished he walks over to me and brushes his hand down the lapel of my robe and raises his eyebrow to me. We smile at one another.

"What are you doing? What's that look about?"

He hums, "I'm remembering when I first saw you in a robe."

And now he fondles both lapels and moves his hands down to the belt while holding me close to him.

"Oh yes, at your aunt's house before the wedding. When I saw you, I wished I had worn a robe like this one instead of the one I was wearing."

His hands travel back up and are stroking my breasts over the thick terry cloth material. "I seem to recall, that robe had special effects, for if you were wearing this robe that day, I would have had to do this to see your *tempting tetas*." [breasts]

He unties the belt and slides one side of the robe over and lightly circles his fingertip around an already aroused nipple. While looking in each other's eyes, "Luca, you don't know how embarrassed I was that day. I didn't plan on seeing anyone much less you. Otherwise, I would have put on my bra and panties. I can't believe you remembered that."

His hands have stopped tantalizing me and have found my behind as their resting place. "Emelia, do you know how sexy you looked in that robe? Your hair looked the way it does now, wet and messy. The sun was shining behind you and I could see the outline of the curves of your body. And when you came down a few steps to meet me, I could smell your freshly showered skin and then I saw these."

He opens my robe fully and looks amorously at my breasts. "And you didn't even notice the affect you had on me. That moment was so pure and alluring. I thought about you in that robe endlessly." Placing my hands on both sides of his face I raise myself up on tippy toes and kiss him.

We part for a moment and he says, "Let's hold that thought. I need you to stay in here until I return to get you. Maybe five minutes, ok?"

I look at him curiously. "Can I ask why?"

He shakes his head no. "Ok, I will stay put. I'm sure I can keep myself busy in here."

He kisses me on the forehead and walks out of the room. He comes back in, tosses me his towel, grabs the other robe and closes the door when he leaves.

For the next few minutes, I'm primping and hanging up damp towels. I'm just about finished when I hear a knock. I walk over to the door and open it. Luca is standing before me wearing the robe and his lovely smile.

"My love, are you ready for your prize?"

"Ooh, I forgot about this. Yes, I am ready."

He takes my hand and leads the way. First I hear music, sounds like a trumpet, I know this music. It's Chris Botti. The drapes are drawn, the lights are dimmed and the bed linens are folded down to the foot of the king bed with a large bath towel placed across the width of the bed and a single rose on top. He's standing behind me with his arms hugging me in front. And with his lips nipping at my ear whispers, "Remove your robe and lie down on the towel. I will return to give you a massage." My entire body quakes and I'm not even sure I could move my legs. He leaves me alone in the bedroom.

When I finally gain control, I walk to the bed and pick up the rose. Bringing it to my nose I enjoy the sweet fragrance and place it on the dresser. Tossing the robe onto the slipper chair I arrange myself on the designated massage area and let my head hang over the side of the bed slightly. Trying to calm my racing heart, I listen to Botti's, "When I Fall in Love" and soon my handsome masseur enters the room. Hearing him place something on the dresser I take a peek and spot two water bottles.

I close my eyes again and think about the day. And force myself to only think about the present and not what tomorrow brings. All the years we've been apart doesn't seem to matter when we are close to each other. I couldn't explain it back then and today, I still can't. I'm so overjoyed to be with him. My thoughts pause as I feel him place a warmed towel over my body.

"Are you comfortable?"

"Yes."

"Do you need anything? Are you thirsty?"

"Yes, just a sip of water please."

I rise up on my elbows and he places a bottle in my hand and I take a swig and pass it to him. "Thank you." I settle back down.

Luca folds the towel down to the center of my back exposing my shoulders. He rubs his hands together and soon I feel cool lotion dripping on one arm. The fragrance is familiar, ah, now I know where my bottle of moisturizer went. He begins this decadent treat from my shoulders down to my wrist. Before working on my hand, he kisses each fingertip and then gently kneads away any tensions. He continues the same treatment on my other arm all the way to my fingertips.

Moving the towel to cover my back he bares my legs, and drips lotion on the backs of each thigh. He works the lotion into my skin and massages each of my legs down to the ankles. When he reaches my feet, he gives them the same care as my hands by placing kisses on the pads of each toe. When I think my body has completely relaxed I feel him move the towel from my back and drape it over my legs. I hear him take a gulp of water.

Seconds pass when he joins me on the bed. I first feel the weight of him on my bottom while his legs straddle my hips. Ever so softly his fingertips dance in circles over my shoulder blades, travels down my spine and then to my lower back. And when I think I'll feel drops of lotion he places kisses across my back and as he leans his body closer to mine his body heat warms my skin. After my back has been blanketed with his lips, his hands methodically work on eliminating any apprehensions I had for us being together.

Chapter 23

MY MASSEUR ENDS this relaxing and most arousing indulgence with a kiss on my lips. He's lying on his side next to me and I sit up to rest on my elbow and look at him. With his fingers caressing my face, he says, "Emelia, I've loved you since the night we first danced. Tell me you want me as much as I want you."

I rise and feel the towel slide off the backs of my legs. Kneeling next to him, I tug at his robe and loosen his belt. He kneels in front of me. Grabbing the lapels of the robe I pull him closer. "You captured my heart that very same night when you held me in your arms and whirled me around the room. At some point today my heart danced again for you. We have been apart for too long. Luciano you have been and always will be the love of my life. Yes, I want you completely."

I slowly push the robe off his shoulders and he places it at the foot of the bed. With his hands on my face he brings my mouth to his and I feel his tongue seeking mine. Even though we've been intimate since we stepped into the shower we take several minutes getting to know the feel of one another. And lavish the other with caresses and kisses.

Placing a hand on the small of my back he lowers me onto the bed. He trails kisses down my neck and the space between my breasts as he positions himself on top. My insides are pulsing with desire I raise my knees and wrap my legs around his waist. He resists and pushes my knees back down on the bed. I sigh. His tongue travels from my nipples to my navel. And his hands gently spread my legs. I moan once more and my pelvis rises towards him. I feel his tongue and lips sucking and licking the path from my knee to my inner thigh and then repeats the journey on my other thigh.

When I think I can't hold back any longer, I shift up to see his next move and find him looking directly at me from between my legs. With a delighted smile, he whispers, *"Ella, es espléndida."* [*She* is splendid.]

I fall back on the bed when I feel him place a kiss on *Her* followed by his warm tongue gliding around the Empress and he moans. He gently parts my lips and guides his love spear inside me and lowers his body onto mine. My nipples arouse when his chest hair tickles my breasts I raise my knees up again and wrap my legs around him.

Slowly thrusting deeper inside me I moan with elation having my Luca finally loving me and me loving him. We look into each other's eyes as he quickens the pace. With my hands caressing his back and moving down towards his bottom Luca powerfully pounds into me. Our breaths synchronize with our escalating desires and he leans down and while nibbling at my earlobe whispers, "I can't wait much longer. *Te quiero con toda mi alma.*" My hands cup his sweet bottom pulling him deeper into me with our bodies rocking together. Breathlessly I urge, "You don't have to wait, I'm ready for you my love, my Luciano."

With a few more thrusts I feel him vibrating inside me and when his body slightly stiffens everything I've felt for this man, love, joy, longing, heartache and compassion erupts with his release and we are bound together body and soul.

I don't know how much time passes after we consummated our love, but after coming down from this ecstasy high, Luca is lying sleepily on me and I concentrate on him breathing in my ear. I don't want to move, I just want to stay connected to him forever. Just last night I arrived in this city with so many concerns and hesitations. And here we are, a day that I never could have predicted. Yet one that I wished for and always thought never would happen. Could this really be the beginning of our future together? Or am I just allowing myself to be hurt once again? I feel a surge of panic swell inside me. Don't do this now he will feel your body shiver. Don't ruin it. Think good thoughts, breathe. Think about how happy you were with him today. Think about swimming with him. Just listen to his breath now and float with him.

I feel a kiss on my neck and another and another and another. I caress his smooth back and draw circles and straight lines with my fingertips. He sits up slowly and looks into my eyes and kisses me intensely.

"Oh Mi Lia," he affectionately says. "After all these years, I thought I had to be dreaming but when I opened my eyes and felt you underneath me and was surrounded by your scent I had to make sure this really happened. *Bésame Mi Lia.*" [Kiss me.]

I kiss him with all the love I feel for him. I grasp his upper arms, "This may have all felt like a dream Luca, but it's real, oh so real."

He shifts his body and slowly pulls out of me and moans. Rolling on to his back, he pulls me over to snuggle against him. I sit up first to grab the sheet and blanket. Once we are nestled together under the covers I release a satisfying purr.

Kissing my forehead he says, "You like?" I nod, "Yes I very much like." I kiss his neck and ask, "You like?" He hums, "Oh Mi Lia, my body is still trembling for you. I too, very much like."

After we rest quietly and blissfully, I interrupt the silence, "Earlier you whispered something that sounded like, *Quiero todo alma?*"

He hums, "Oh yes." He takes my hand kisses it and places it over his heart.

"I said, *Te - quiero - con - toda — mi - alma.*" He pronounced each word slowly to me. "I want you with all my soul."

I take his hand now and kiss his palm and hold it in place over my heart and repeat, "*Te quiero con toda mi alma.*"

He pulls me close to him again. And we fall asleep.

Chapter 24

WAKING UP FROM our sex nap, I feel my bladder is about to burst. Trying not to wake Luca, I quietly crawl out of bed, grab my robe from the chair and tip toe into the bathroom.

Behind closed doors, I tend to my needs. Then while washing my hands I look at my reflection. My complexion still has the very satisfied after glow. But my hair is out of control. Before we go anyplace this evening, I will need to tame these curls.

Now, where are my magical styling tools, this mess will entail skillful wizardry? Grateful everything is here in the drawer I switch on the hair dryer and hope my attempts are successful.

Working my brush through my brown locks I am pleasantly surprised things are looking up. That wasn't too much of a struggle and I'm pleased with what I see.

Now what should I wear tonight? Going into the other room I see Luca standing in his robe and he's talking on the phone. Sounds like dinner reservations. The call ends and he turns and looks at me wearing dark rimmed eyeglasses. My older Luca is very hot.

"I made reservations to dine here at the hotel. Are you good with that?" I nod, "When do you want me ready?" He adjusts the volume on the music player and I hear a familiar song. Swaggering over to me he pulls me towards him by the belt on my robe. I gently remove his eyeglasses. Raising one of his eyebrows, "We have a couple of hours. May I have this dance?" Placing the glasses on the dresser he takes me in his arms and he leads me around the room.

"When you left me alone in bed I had a chance to study your music library. I see we have similar tastes." He kisses my neck. "You have quite a collection of Juan Luis Guerra."

I giggle, "Someone I met when I was much younger turned me on to him. And I never seemed to get enough. You have to admit he does have a charming voice."

He spins me and then dips me near the bed, "More charming than mine?" While he's still holding me over the bed I reply, "I'm not sure I haven't heard you sing in ages." He lets go of me and I drop onto the mattress. I laugh, "You are not jealous? Are you?"

He walks over to change the song. I jump up and grab his arm, "Please don't I like that song." I was too late he switched it to another of Guerra's songs, "Bachata Rosa". Luca replies, "I like this song more."

It was a slower paced ballad. And my heart flutters. This was the second song we danced to that night in Valencia and I remember him singing it to me.

I'm in his arms again slow dancing with his hips grinding against mine and soon he's serenading me. We loop around the room a few times and venture out to the terrace. All the while Luca's voice is eliciting tiny vibrations up and down my spine.

Luca leads us back to the bedroom. As we near the edge of the bed, my feet step on his and hold him in place. While he continues singing I lay kisses along his jawbone and chin. Then my lips travel down his neck, his collar bone and I open his robe. With my hands inside I begin rubbing his back and my vocalist doesn't miss a lyric. I tantalize him by sucking and licking his nipples. He breathes in deeply and my journey continues from his chest to his taut belly and then his navel. Sucking and licking along the way. I nudge him on to the bed and he grabs me and we tumble on top of the blankets.

We adjust our positioning and I climb on top of him and continue my adventure from his navel, past his pelvis and when I arrive at the site for my affections he groans. I glance at him and he's observing me. With my tongue swirling around his tip and fingers stroking him at full length his hips buck and he plunges deeper into my mouth. My love has stopped singing.

I allow myself to indulge just a bit longer and he calls out, "Mi Lia." When my tongue tastes a few droplets of him he sternly says, "Emelia!" I slowly release my hold on him lift up my robe and lower my hips down and guide him into me. He yells out my name again and grabs my hips and slowly lifts me up and down. As our pace intensifies he thrusts deeper and deeper and my back arches to welcome the desire building in me. With my climax seconds away he sits up tears off my robe and drives his tongue into my mouth and with multiple powerful thrusts we both explode into pure euphoria.

I rouse to him singing acapella. I nibble his neck. He pauses, "I'm a little confused did you enjoy my singing or were you trying to make me stop?"

I laugh into his neck and then crawl off of him. Evasively I reply, "Or maybe it was the song or Juan's voice." I grab my robe and I jump off the bed. He lunges to me and pulls me into his arms and back down on the bed. Pinning me under him, his teeth tug my earlobe and he whispers, "I'll have to experiment my theory later on." I purr with delight. He lets me go and with a slap on my thigh, he orders, "Let's get dressed for dinner."

Chapter 25

WHEN I'M READY I find him patiently waiting for me on the terrace. As I get closer to him, he turns and extends his hand to me, "*Mi amor, eres tan bella.* [My love you are so beautiful.] Will you do me the honor and join me at dinner tonight?" I smile and take his hand, "Yes, I'd love to."

Walking down the hallway he interrupts my thoughts, "What are you thinking about?" I giggle, "Trying to figure out which date this is for us."

"What do you mean?"

"How many dates we've had together, like dinner and dancing in Valencia could be our first date. And our second was the movie and dinner. Now do you follow?"

We board the elevator with another couple. Luca says, "Buena noches." And they reply back with the same. We stand close holding hands and I listen to the beeps until we reach the restaurant level.

The elevator doors open and we look to the wall signs to find the way. Luca takes the lead and after a couple of turns we see the glass doors leading into the restaurant. The host greets us and Luca tells him we have a reservation. He checks the list for Luca's name and shows us to a table.

They exchange words and it appears the host is presenting us with a few options. My date chooses a table overlooking the ocean. Luca pulls my seat out for me and once I'm settled, he sits in the chair next to me. We both can enjoy the view and still be close together. The host leaves us with menus and the wine list.

"Would you say this is our fifth date?"

I try to think how he got to that number. "I'm not sure, what are you considering dates?"

He begins to count on his fingers, "The two you mentioned, Christmas Eve at the overlook, today at the beach and now dinner and dancing tonight."

Playfully I respond, "I think that's right. So, it took you four dates over two decades to get me into your bed." The waiter suddenly appears, my face immediately blushes wondering how much he just heard and I release a nervous giggle while gazing into Luca's eyes.

He says, "*Buenas noches, soy Paulo y soy tu camarero esta noche. Quieres vino o bebidas?*" [Good evening, I am Paulo and I am your waiter tonight. Do you want wine or drinks?] We both greet Paulo and Luca opens the wine list. After Luca studies the collection he orders champagne and Paulo excuses himself.

Luca leans close to me, "Yes, I have a four date, twenty year rule before I enrapture a woman." Pushing my hair behind my ear he gives me a kiss. And a rush of tingles race up and down my spine.

We look over the menu and I ask Luca if I can borrow his reading glasses, I forgot to bring mine to dinner. Thankfully the dishes are listed in both Spanish and English. There are many delectable selections to choose. We agree to order dishes that we'll share considering it might be fun to sample a few different flavors. Paulo returns with the champagne. He takes our dinner order after filling our glasses. Luca requests for Paulo to take our picture. And then he leaves us again.

Raising our glasses to one another, Luca begins, "Every second I spent with you today, I found myself loving you more and more. Thank you for opening your heart again to me and I promise, I will love you and devote the rest of my life to you to make up for our lost years. Here's to our first official date." Our lips join we tap glasses and take sips of the bubbly.

"Luca, I think we need a redo of our first kiss, especially if we're considering this our first date."

He smiles at me and asks, "Why, I thought that first kiss this morning was very memorable."

"I agree, it was, but that's when I thought you were married, you know really married. It was a stolen kiss. I felt like a thief."

As he leans towards me, I back away from him. Placing my hand on his chest to hold off his advances, I say, "Maybe we should wait for a more private moment?"

Luca rests back in his seat, "Ah, Emelia, you know how to hurt a man." He places both his hands over his chest as if I jabbed a sword into his heart.

"Luca, you'll survive." He smiles and winks at me.

As we wait for the appetizer, we talk about the view and our day at the beach. He leans close, "Being with you today was so incredible. I know that it was not easy for you and there were moments I feared you might change your mind and just ask me to leave. But you didn't. And I'm so grateful for that."

I smile at him and he continues, "Years ago, on that Christmas night I promised you a life together. I felt such strong feelings for you, and knew we had to pursue this. And I also knew it would take time. You still have tonight and the rest of the week to decide how you feel. But I want you to know I am committed from this day forward."

I turn to him and say, "Very powerful dinner conversation for our first official date Mr. Morales." He smirks at me.

"I appreciate." Then I pause, "Oh that word sounds so trite. Today I told myself to be completely open to you and to the possibility of us. I cannot deny I have had the best time of my life with you. And knowing you're committed and giving me the space to be certain and to trust you again, is exactly what I need."

Pausing again I take a drink of water. "But I also realize the dynamic will change when we share ourselves over the next few days with your family and your children. And I don't know how receptive they'll be to us. I need to tell you all that because I want you to know all that I'm thinking and feeling. And I also want to say, if it was just about you and me, I'd say yes and ask you when can we start this adventure?" I kiss his temple.

Our first course arrives and is placed in front of us. Before we start he takes my hand, "Emelia I know we don't have all the answers tonight. But you'll see things will fall into place this week. My children will love you. Tomorrow when they meet you they will know you as their aunt's friend. And when we go to Chiriqui and they get a chance to hang around us, we'll get a sense on when it's best to tell them. You should be having these thoughts, but I hope it helps, when I tell you, there is nothing to worry about, they will embrace us. I'm not even considering the rest of my family. Remember, they advised me years ago and I know what I want and it's you and I'm not giving up on us. Now let's eat."

After tasting each of the dishes for our first course I suggest we take a break from talking about the future. Luca begins, "Tell me some of what you've done since I last saw you."

I think how best to summarize the last twenty something years. "Well, I moved into Manhattan. First I lived in a one room apartment and absolutely enjoyed the energy, people, how close I was to everything I wanted to see and do. I made great friends. My job was interesting, challenging and fun. I worked with a team from a previous fashion retailer and they opened their own boutique and I followed. I recall putting in lots of hours, but I didn't mind, we were all building something together. It was great for a few years and then it changed. The team split and I followed a couple of them to a designer. That was good for a while until they stumbled over some hurdles. So, they left but I stayed and even though everyone was very nice and I enjoyed my job, I didn't have that same feeling of being part of a team. So, it became just a job."

Sipping on the champagne I continue, "But during those years all of my jobs provided money and opportunity to travel. I went to Italy, France, England, Spain, Greece and Aruba. My summers were spent at the beach with family and friends. I went to the opera, ballet, museums, plays and concerts. Living there was just what I expected and so much more."

"When you talk about Manhattan you sound like my sister. She loved it there. I often wonder if she had stayed if her life would have been much different. I've been there on a few occasions. And considered reaching out to you, but I thought it would be too painful." I caress his arm knowing what he means. He continues, "Did you meet your husband there?" I nod no. I think about what I should say about my previous marriage. Paulo returns and takes away our dishes. Another waiter brings our next course.

"Do you mind if we wait to talk about that part of my life?" He grasps my shoulder and rubs it, "I don't mind. You can tell me when you're ready." I nod to him and say, "Thank you."

"What is your profession now?" I smile and begin with, "It's the best job that I ever created for myself. After working for years with designers and clothing stores I began my own service. Basically I shop for people, better known as a personal stylist."

He grins, "You shop for people, what exactly does that entail?"

"I met many of my clients over the years having assisted them with putting together their wardrobes at high end retail stores when I figured I could branch out and do it on my own. I began with five clients and now I have about twenty regulars but around forty overall. So with the regulars, depending on their status, wealth, I fill their closets with clothes that they need or will need for a future event. Some come with me to fashion shows and others I meet for an afternoon and I advise them while they try on clothes. Others, I look out for pieces that I think they will like. And the next appointment I see them, I show up at their door with these purchases and they usually love their new additions. The non-regulars call on me at change of seasons and we shop together or I just go out and shop for them. My hours are very flexible and I like the spontaneity of it. And the perks from several of the boutiques that I send my clients to, well they are pretty nice."

"You must have a lot of patience."

"Yes and no. I mean in the beginning with a new client it takes some effort finding the right blend between their personality and their style presence. But once I zone in on those aspects, it becomes very natural for me. For instance I can be out and about in a boutique or a retail store and pieces catch my eye and immediately I see a particular client wearing it."

"Do you get tired of spending other people's money?"

"Good question. I never looked at it that way. However, when I'm busy filling their closets, they're also busy donating their lightly worn garments. So a couple of mornings a week I visit women's shelters. And I advise some of the ladies there about the clothes they should wear on job interviews and at the job once they get hired. We put together outfits from these and other donations. The best part is when I get the chance to see someone all dressed up before they leave for that interview and they have that shine, that confidence. And I know then I'm doing something right."

A tear or two gets trapped in the corners of my eyes. Luca brushes his fingertips across my forehead and down my face, "Emelia, you are a compassionate woman who feels so deeply. This tender heart of yours astonishes me and how it survives in a world that can be so harsh. I'm grateful to have the chance to share my life with you." He leans to me and gently kisses my lips.

After our sweet moment I look down at our dishes and say, "Ok let's switch." He appears confused. I smile and point, "Well I want to try some of your food. I thought that was the idea." He gets serious, "Oh, you want some of this?" I nod and say, "Yes please."

We start to feed one another. I ask, "So do you know the plans for this week after the party tomorrow?" He places a forkful of food near my lips and I oblige.

"Monday we drive to Chiriqui. I think Frida will want you in her car. I will drive my car with my parents and the kids. Henry will drive his car with his family. But if you want to ride with me, we can move people around."

I think he sensed I was feeling pushed aside already. But I know he's thinking about his sister too. I feed him and say, "Thanks for giving me that option, but I think you're right, Frida will want me in her car so we can talk during the drive. But I will consider your offer for our return trip. Tell me more."

He feeds me again, "Ok, so drive Monday, Tuesday we'll go wandering. We have a tradition, a new one since you've been there, the kids like to get out and explore the area. We did it with them when they were younger. And now they're older and not always together, they make a big deal when all the cousins are around. We leave after breakfast and are gone until late afternoon. And we manage to get lunch someplace in the village. They also like to cook and play games. So, I hope you're up for that. I'm not sure what's planned for Wednesday yet. And then we drive back Thursday."

I feed Luca some more and he feeds me. "Your flight is Saturday right?" I nod yes. "Are you staying here again later in the week?"

"I wasn't sure what to do, so I asked the hotel to hold me a room and that I would tell them by Monday what my plans are. I was leaving it up to your sister."

He places a fork to my lips and I open my mouth. "You can tell the hotel that you won't need the room. You're staying with me."

I quickly swallow. "Thank you for the invite, but I'm confused. Well, I never actually asked you about your living arrangements. And it just occurred for me to ask now. Why did you get a room at the hotel?"

He laughs, "I guess it does seem odd that I took a room here. Well, Frida stops in at my place on the weekends and since the kids are with their mom I thought it would be fun to get away, hopefully be with you, and I didn't want to run into Frida before the party."

I reply, "Ah that makes sense."

He continues, "I moved into my own home last year. The kids are with me two weeks per month. And we've been fairly good with juggling schedules. When I travel she's somewhat agreeable to keep them longer, we manage. This will all change soon, my daughter is going away for college. And that just leaves my son. He'll probably come and go whenever he wants."

Paulo returns, takes our completely empty dishes and tries to tempt us with dessert and leaves us the menu. "Now you know about my setup, will you stay with me?"

"Yes, but do you think Frida might find it strange that I'm staying at your place and not hers?"

"She'll realize by then, you and I are together."

I smile. He opens the dessert menu for both of us to peruse. "Ok, then yes, I will stay with you at your home." Paulo returns and we decide to share a dessert.

When Paulo serves us the key lime pie Luca asks him about a dance place. We are informed we can stay here at the hotel and go to the bar lounge where they should have music.

"My love, if the lounge isn't any fun would you mind if we go back to the suite?" I nod and reply, "I won't mind at all, I was sort of hoping you'd suggest that." He raises his eyebrows and smiles. I ask, "Before we go anywhere, can we walk off some of this dinner?" He nods in agreement and rubs his belly, "Yes, I feel the same way."

Luca settles the bill and we say good night to Paulo. "I know this hotel very well, so I can lead the tour if you want." While we explore, Luca fills me in briefly about his company. Some of the doors are locked to the banquet rooms but then one door to a ballroom was left open. We sneak in.

Even though the lights are dimmed, I can see the room is tremendous. Tables are folded and stored in carts and chairs are stacked. The dance floor is empty and across from where we entered is a wall of glass windows and French doors. We go over to them. Outside the doors is a terrace. My guide turns one of the knobs and the door opens. The terrace is the entire width of the room and overlooks the ocean. I can't see much of the water since its dark out but I hear the crashing waves.

Luca takes me in his arms and begins to hum a song and soon we're dancing on the terrace. During our second turn around the terrace he pauses and suddenly dips me. When he pulls me back up to him I smile and he kisses me gently on my lips. When we part, I giggle and then bestow him with another kiss. After our first kiss redo, Luca begins to sing the song he was humming and we continue our dance. All my concerns are at rest dancing under the stars with the love of my life with my hand in his resting upon his heart.

Chapter 26

———————

NOT SURE WHAT wakens me the sunlight streaming in from the windows or hearing Luca singing in the bathroom. I close my eyes and stretch from head to toe in this huge bed. My body feels great and well rested. I wonder what time it is and how long I've slept. Reaching over I grab his pillow and hug it while turning over on my stomach. I breathe in his fragrance, close my eyes and listen to his lovely voice.

My suite-mate is now joining me in bed and lies on my back. Kissing my ear he whispers, "It's bad enough you hogged the bed but now you've taken my pillow, what else do you want from me?"

I giggle as he covers me with kisses and he shifts me under him. With his deep morning voice, his adorable accent sounds even more sexy, "Good morning my love and how did you sleep?"

I prop myself up on our pillows and I admire this very handsome man. With his wet hair combed back I caress his clean shaven face and notice he's used my mouthwash too. I smile at him, "I slept like a rock." He lifts up my pajama top and exposes my stomach and places kisses around my navel.

"Did I really hog the bed? I'm sorry." Looking up and pulling the fabric down, "I didn't notice until I woke up this morning. I've never seen someone sleep diagonally in a bed." I open my mouth, "I've never done that before. Maybe I wanted to make sure you weren't far from me."

"What time is it?" He replies, "I think it's almost ten." I stretch again and yawn. And I feel his hand travel from the top of my head, over my face, past my neck, touching my ribs, running past my hips and resting on my thigh.

"My sweet, between yesterday and this morning I've been admiring you, I mean really looking at you and I know how old we are and I must say you've aged delightfully."

Covering my face with my hands, he says, "I remember a young woman with a natural loveliness that looked even more perfect at the beach without any makeup. Here you are, just waking from sleep and I still see that same face, but with years of many emotions telling me your story." I lower my hands and I gaze into his eyes.

Luca begins to trace the skin near my eyes. He continues, "Your eyes that once conveyed this energy a sparkle from within that for me was infectious. That magic, the sparkle was gone yesterday morning when I first arrived. And yet, I've seen it reappear, a few times since." I close my eyes and open them again and continue watching him.

"These lines, what do you call them, crow's legs?" I giggle, "Crow's feet." He laughs while touching the lines near my eyes. "These crow's feet, tell me how much you've laughed over the years. And when your face is serious, they also tell me, how much you've cried. And to me, it appears, you've laughed more." I nod to him with a tender smile.

His fingers move to my mouth. "Your smile, your multitude of smiles, intrigued me then and intrigues me more now. Your mouth, well, that too tells me some secrets. The lines here are so deep and pronounced when you're happy, and yet, very soft when you are serious. Making me hope, you haven't experienced too many troubling moments." Luca gently kisses my lips. He continues, "And so Mi Lia, your beauty has intensified for me in so many ways."

With my fingers I trace his face. "I can say the same about you too. Although I owe you a massage so that I can examine you as closely as you examined me." I play with the silver white tendrils near his temple. "I especially like these. I have a thing for mature looking men." I wink at him. He replies, "Well, my love, it's hereditary and you won't see more than that for the next ten years at least."

I show him my hands, "These are the real give away you can always tell someone's age by their hands." He takes them both in his and kisses them. I smile and look into his eyes, "I'm so grateful we're still young enough to grow old together."

His eyes glisten and he replies, "Hearing you say that fills my heart with hope." He rests his head on my stomach. I wiggle down to meet him and we start the day how we ended our night.

After our blissful morning activities I begin getting ready for the day. "When should we leave for the party?" He glances at his phone, "Good question, let me call Henry." I walk past him on my way to the bathroom, "I'll take a shower now."

While brushing my teeth I look over to Luca's sink and I notice all his personal things are packed in his shaving kit. I wonder if he's going back home after the party. Or is he just neat. I'll ask him about it later. Now that he's been here with me I don't want to be without him. But maybe we need to be on our own to think about all that's happened between us.

Before I see him in the living room I spot his suitcase outside the bedroom door. I find him in one of the chairs wearing his glasses and concentrating on his phone. I join him on his lap.

"Henry said we should get there no later than one o'clock. I ordered room service while you showered so we won't feel rushed, ok?" I nod, "Yes that's a good idea. Are you planning to go home tonight after the party? I thought you might come back here with me."

He moves a tendril of hair behind my ear. "Well, I wasn't sure. I only packed for one night. And tomorrow I have to do a few things before driving out of the city."

I nod, "I understand, but if you change your mind, know that I would like you to stay the night."

He smiles, "If I stay, I'll probably leave very early and I'll try not to wake you, yes?"

I shake my head no, "If I promise not to delay you, please wake me before you go."

He leans in and kisses me. "For your happiness, I will stay with you tonight."

I hug him and dance in his lap. He laughs, "You're like a little girl so excited and I love it."

After removing his glasses I treat him to about ten kisses all over his face. We hear a knock at the door.

Hopping off him I run towards the bedroom, "Do you mind answering the door while I get ready?" He waves me away as he's walking to the door.

The morning flies by, with breakfast again on the terrace and a quick walk on the beach. Soon we're in Luca's car with my gift in hand and driving to the party. Suddenly I'm nervous. I can't wait to see Frida and the rest of the family, but I'll also be meeting Luca's children today. And then my thoughts drift, if I'm with Luca who is bringing his kids?

"Do you know how many are expected at the party?"

He fiddles with the radio, "I think my mom said almost sixty."

"And your children are we picking them up? Or is someone bringing them?"

"Their mom is dropping them off. They were at church this morning."

My stomach does a flip. Will I also see her? He rests his hand on my leg. "Don't worry, everything will go smoothly, she may or may not stay."

I look out the side window. "Do you think she'll bring her boyfriend?"

I feel the hand on my leg tense. Placing my hand on his, I copy him, "Don't worry everything will go smoothly." We both grumble and laugh.

He pulls my hand to his lips and kisses it. "None of that will matter today, because you'll be by my side."

I think about his statement. "So, about that, are you still planning on just being friendly with me today? Or are we going into the party holding hands and such?"

We're stopped at a red light and he glances to me. "Oh right, yes, we will just be friends today. Now I'm even happier you convinced me to stay another night with you."

The light turns green and we're off again. "So, how much longer until we arrive?"

"About ten minutes, why?"

"Just wondering and preparing myself for seeing EVERY-one."

Listening to the music on the radio as Luca sings along we journey the rest of the way with very little words spoken.

Luca makes a turn and drives down a narrow street and shifts the car into park. "Are we here?"

He shakes his head, "No, it's just on the next corner. I need another moment alone with you before I have to share you." He unfastens his seat belt and moves near me. "The thought of not doing this with you for the next six hours will drive me crazy."

He takes my face in his hands and kisses me. I click loose out of my seat-belt too and grasp his biceps. When our sweet make out session comes to an end, my heart is racing with excitement. I reach to him and fix his hair. I tell him in a low voice, "We might have to plan a secret meeting place at half time." He laughs, "Let's synchronize our watches and agree on a code word."

Chapter 27

THE VALET OPENS my door first and I wait for Luca under the canopy. Once he receives the parking voucher he walks with me to the front door. As he opens the door for me he says, "After you madam." With a quick wink I say, "Why thank you sir."

Proceeding to the hostess stand Luca waves at someone in the distance. I look around, there's a bar on the left side with about twenty barstools and maybe six counter high tables. Behind the hostess I see a small dining area and on the right side a hallway towards Luca's friend. He speaks with the hostess and she points towards the room where that person is standing. While the two of us meander down the hall I feel Luca's arm brush against mine. Until we reach the room our arms subtly remain connected. This secret between us will be spine-tingling for the day.

Inside the private room I see balloons and streamers and a big sign that reads, *Feliz Cumpleaños.* [Happy Birthday] There are round tables with multi-colored tablecloths with flowers and candles. Frida will love this, I hope she's surprised.

Luca gently places his hand on my back and leads me further into the room with him. I look to see if there's anyone I recognize. And immediately Henry is walking over to us with his family. I feel like it's been ages since I've seen them but I only just saw them on Friday night. Luca takes my gift and brings it over to the gift table. And Henry hugs me tight and whispers, "I hope you're not angry with me, Luca was so insistent about seeing you." "No worries Henry, everything is good."

We pull apart and he looks at me and tilts his head and smiles. "Wow, everything IS good. I'm happy for you both." I shush him and shake my head.

Olivia smiles at me and hugs me too. She tells me, "I missed you yesterday but we'll catch up this week in Chiriqui." I squeeze her tightly, "Yes, I look forward to it."

Their sons, Mateo and Benjamin extend their hands out to me. I shake each and say, "Very nice to see you Mateo and Benny and you both look handsome in your party clothes." They snicker at each other and run to the other guests. I look at Henry, "Did I embarrass them?"

"No, I pulled them away from their cousin to come over to say hello to you and their uncle. And they just went back to him."

I notice Luca greeting other guests. "Henry, who else is here from your family, I'd like to say hello." He leads me and Olivia to one of the tables. I see his parents, his brother Rafael and Rafael's wife Teresa standing in a circle near the table. Rafael is the first to see me and pulls me into his arms with such force I thought I was going to fall. "Emelia, Emelia, Emelia. It's so wonderful to see you again. It has been too long." He squeezes me even tighter. When he finally lets go he kisses me on both cheeks and reintroduces Teresa to me. I smile and nod, "I think we met before you were married when I was here for Christmas." Her smile is just as radiant as Rafael's and she agrees. We kiss each other hello.

Next to Teresa is Claudia. I politely extend my hand to her and say, "Claudia I'm truly glad to see you and Rico and thank you for including me in Frida's birthday celebration." I can't figure out her demeanor, she's smiling but she also looks near tears. I move closer to her and place one kiss on each cheek.

She increases her grip on my hand and says, "Emelia, it's lovely to see you, I'm happy that you and Frida will see each other again." And she brushes a tear from her cheek. And before I say hello to Rico she extends her other hand and touches my face. "You look like you did many years ago life must be good for you." I just smile at her.

Rico opens his arms to me and says, "My wife is right, you look terrific. Thank you for coming all this way. And Frida will enjoy spending this week with you, we all will."

I kiss him too and walk into his embrace. He pats me on the back and when we part I see Luca standing next to his dad and he's watching me.

"Emelia, would you like something to drink?" Luca asks.

"Yes maybe, what are they offering?"

"Not sure, you want to come with me to find out?"

"Ok" and I turn to the family, "Can we bring you back some drinks?" They all look at me smiling and almost all at once, say no. I sense they're on to us or maybe I'm just being paranoid.

We walk towards the bar together. Luca doesn't stop to talk with anyone just says quick hellos along the way. At the bar, he introduces us to the bartender. And tells the bartender I speak English.

"Hello Emelia, what would you like?"

I do a quick inventory of the bottles, "Hello, Pietro, I will just have a soda, do you have one that is lemon-lime?"

Luca taps my hand, "Pietro if the lady doesn't mind, I would like to suggest your special drink for the day, Frida's favorite."

I nod in agreement towards Pietro, "Ok I will have the Frida special please."

While Pietro prepares our drinks I ask Luca, "What's the special drink?"

He smiles, "I know you will like it. It's a rum drink you had at the beach."

I smile at him in relief, "Good I was worried my old friend now indulges on some powerhouse cocktails."

Pietro places the two drinks near us. We both thank him and before leaving the bar we tap our glasses together and say, "To Frida!"

Ambling back to his family, Luca stops to say hello to the guests and introduces me as Frida's friend from New York. Most spoke Spanish with Luca and I just smiled and nodded.

Olivia and I make eye contact and she comes over to me. "Emelia, can you help me with something?" I look at Luca and I reply, "Yes of course."

She leads us to the gift table. "The plan for today is that Frida will arrive very soon, we're just waiting to get a text from Max when they're on their way. When she does come into the room we thought you can stay sort of behind all of us, so she doesn't see you right away. We think she'll be very shocked by the party at first and as she's making her rounds to say hello to everyone we thought it would be fun for you to be the last person she greets. What do you think?"

All of a sudden I got goosebumps thinking about seeing her after all these years. "Yes, that sounds perfect. Just tell me where you want me to stand or hide. Do I have a few minutes to dash to the ladies room?"

Olivia glances at her watch, "Yes, you have about fifteen minutes. Do you know where it is?" I nod, "I saw them when we first arrived, unless there's one here in the room?"

I'm glad I asked, she pointed to a couple of doors in the other corner of the room. We walk to the family's table and I leave my drink there and head over to the restroom.

When I exit the ladies room I catch Luca lingering outside the men's room. "Hi, are you looking for me?"

He looks around and kisses me quickly. "Yes, Olivia told me she mentioned the surprise plan to you. Are you on board with it?"

I smile brightly, "Yes that works for me. That way Frida's not distracted by me and greets the other guests first. I get it. Is that why you're waiting for me?"

"Yes and um my daughter and son just arrived."

"I can meet them later too, if you want or now. Whatever you think is best. Did their mom stay?"

"I'm not sure. When I was walking back here to find you that's when I saw them enter the party room."

"Ah, you think we should go back to the party separately?"

"No, not at all. We can join my family near the table. I'll go look for *mi niños* [my children] and I'll bring them over to you, yes?"

"Yes." I smile at him.

Luca leaves me at the table and I locate my drink where I left it. I take a few sips and find Teresa and Olivia. While looking at her phone, Olivia tells me, "Frida will be arriving in about five minutes. Her brothers are telling the rest of the guests. You just follow me when we gather towards the door. You can hide behind her brothers for a while. But make sure you can sneak a peek at Frida when she comes in."

I smile and think, I wonder which brother I will take refuge with and laugh to myself. "Yes Olivia, I got it."

I glance around the crowd and see Luca talking with a young girl and boy. Wow, they all resemble each other, it's so striking. I can't wait to meet them. And then I see their mom. I think that is Violeta. But she's not standing with them, she's talking with a few women and they're all smiling and nodding to one another. She's just as stunning as I remember her. Tall and slim and wearing her dark long straight hair to one side. The body hugging beige dress certainly compliments her figure. While she's chatting with the ladies a man approaches holding two drinks and he passes one to her. And now he stands next to her. Did she really bring her boyfriend to the party? That takes nerve. If it wasn't for the kids, I'd walk up to Luca right now and show her he's moved on. Instead I will stick with our plan and keep our relationship a secret.

There's a commotion at the door and all of a sudden everyone quiets and takes positions. The way they all fall into place you'd think they were practicing this for weeks. Olivia takes my elbow and ushers me to stand behind the three brothers. As I skulk near them I whisper, "Hello." They all jump and turn around quickly and laugh. I put my finger on my lips to silence them. Clearly they forgot this part of the plan.

I stand between Luca and Henry. I check out who else is near me and I see the coast is clear. I rest my chin on Luca's shoulder and I feel him sway back into me. While we wait for Frida I'm granted a few intimate moments with my love.

We all stare at the door waiting for the guest of honor. This part of the surprise is so nerve racking. And then two people enter the room followed by Max and Frida. All at once, everyone yells, "*Sorpresa!*" [Surprise!]

There are two rows of people in front of us, so I doubt she can even see me at this point. I see her smiling and laughing and shaking her head. And she covers her face. Her parents are the first to hug her. My eyes fill with tears and from here she looks the same. Luca turns to me and quickly wipes a tear. Henry exclaims, "I think we got her, she looked very surprised." I nod, "Yes, you guys did a great job keeping it a secret."

As she makes her way through the crowd, Henry and Luca keep a look out and update me on her status. Luca jokes, "At this rate you should pull up a chair, we might be here until six waiting for her." I don't mind at all. Luca's been holding my hand since he wiped my tears.

I can hear Frida's voice getting closer to me. When Luca releases my hand I'll know she's near. I hear people laughing and kissing. Minutes pass and Henry whispers, "She's close by, this is more exciting than the original surprise."

Luca tightens his grip. And then he lets me go. *"Oh, Luca. Dónde has estado? Fui a tu casa ayer y no estabas allí."* [Where have you been? I went to your house yesterday and you weren't there.]

Henry steps in front of me and Rafael also blocks Frida from seeing me. She joyously screams, "Enrique!" They hug and kiss. He's so clever he spins her around so she can't see me. Rafael whispers, "I think he's about to tell her."

I see Henry say something in Frida's ear and he turns her around and she first looks at Rafael and then focuses on me.

Her face changes from confusion to disbelief and she begins to cry, *"Oh, Dios mío, no puede ser"* [Oh, my God, it can't be.] And she charges at me and into my arms and we both are crying like babies. We hold each other so tightly I almost can't breathe.

Soon Henry joins our hug and I feel Luca too and then Rafael and we start laughing hysterically about the group huddle. And the brothers all pretend to be crying with us saying silly things. When I open my eyes, I see Olivia passing around tissues to everyone. I'm sure Frida and I look a mess, but what the heck.

The party guests start clapping and cheering Frida's name. One by one we split apart and Frida and I grab tissues from Olivia and we laugh again.

"Oh, Emelia, I can't believe you are here! This is all too much. I must be dreaming."

I wipe her tears and say, "I am here with your family and your friends to celebrate you, Happy Birthday my sweet and lovely friend!"

And we hug once more. Frida asks me, "How long are you staying?" I pull away from her and smile, "I'm here until Saturday we have all week to catch up. Now enjoy your party!"

She nods, "Do you know where the bathroom is I want to clean up." I nod and take her by the hand. We grab a few more tissues from Olivia and she follows along.

In the ladies room the three of us quickly wipe away the mascara smudges and reapply some makeup. As we talk excitedly like teenage girls in front of the mirrors, we are startled when we see Violeta exit from one of the stalls. The chatter quiets down.

While Violeta washes her hands Frida continues to talk about how surprised she was entering the party. Trying to keep the mood less awkward I ask, "Why were you coming here?"

As Frida is about to answer, Violeta walks up to both of us and says directly to me, "I remember you. You are Frida's friend from when she lived in New York. You were at her wedding."

Stunned, I just stand there and quietly watch Violeta. Frida intervenes, "Violeta, this is my friend Emelia."

Violeta's green eyes glare at me and she says, "Yes, Emelia, Emelia." She looks to Frida, *"Estaba trayendo a los niños a la fiesta y pensé que debía parar para saludar a algunos de la familia. Espero que no te moleste. No planeé quedarme tanto tiempo. Feliz Cumpleaños, Frida"*. [I was bringing the kids to the party and thought I should stop in to say hello to some of the family. I hope you don't mind. I didn't plan to stay this long. Happy Birthday, Frida.] And she leaves us alone in the room.

After the door closes behind her, we look at each other in silence. I blurt, "I don't know what just happened and I'm sure you can tell me another day, but this party is all about you. So let's just focus on that, right?"

Frida grabs me and Olivia and pulls us close to her, "Emelia, you are completely right. It's so good to have you here with us again." Olivia responds, "Come on girls, let's party!"

We laugh and link arms and join the guests as the DJ's music lifts the mood. The guests have spread out, some are at tables, dancing or congregating near the bar. A waiter approaches us with a tray of what I believe to be the Frida drink. We help ourselves and go towards the family's table.

Max, Frida's husband finds me. He looks the same too, just some sprinkles of grey hair. Frida joins us and puts her arm around me. "I'm still shocked you are here. I don't want to let go of you. Tell me again, when are you here until?"

"Frida, I'm here until Saturday. As much as I'd love to stay by your side today, you have so many people that also want to be with you."

She tightens her grip on me. "Ok, but I won't rush to them yet. When did you arrive and who told you about the party? And where are you staying?"

I smile at her and giggle and try to deflect her questions for a bit, "You seem very surprised, you didn't know anything about this party? I arrived on Friday. Henry told me and I'm staying at an amazing place on the beach. How did they get you here?"

She laughs and looks at Max, "I was completely surprised. Max's sister is getting married and this is a place they are considering for the reception and asked us to view the space with them. You came on Friday, have you been alone since then? Or has my family been with you?"

I take a sip of the special drink. "Frida your signature drink is yummy. And yes I've had the joy of being with your family since I arrived."

A young man stops by and luckily Frida's questioning pauses. The three of them speak in Spanish and Frida introduces us. "Emelia this is our son Victor."

He extends his hand to me and I grasp it and smile at him, "Hello Victor, I'm thrilled to meet you. You look so much like your mom and you have your dad's eyes. My goodness, how old are you?"

He looks at his parents and they nod to him. "Tengo diecisiete. I am so sorry, I am seventeen."

I smile at them, "Wow, I can't believe you're parents of a seventeen year old. An embodiment of how much time has passed. I experience it when I'm with my nieces and nephews. We may not feel the years pass so much in ourselves, but these babies growing up before our eyes remind us every day that time is a gift."

Frida's eyes fill with tears and mine follow. Luca appears, "You are both not still crying?" Max hugs Frida and we all laugh. And I feel my suitor's hand gently caressing my back.

Frida continues, "Luca, earlier I asked you where you were yesterday, I went by your house twice and you weren't home. Where were you? Were you with Emelia?"

His hand stops like it's been caught in something. "Yes, I met her at the hotel. I couldn't bring her to my house and blow the surprise."

The waiter returns with more drinks, Luca takes one and tries to change the topic by toasting Frida. I feel his hand leave my back.

I practically finish my drink and Frida continues, "That's good, I was concerned that she was alone in the hotel. Thanks for taking care of my friend. I hope you managed to have fun. Oh, just want to let you know while we were in the ladies room we met Violeta. Is she staying for the party or did she leave? Now that was uncomfortable."

I wished I hadn't finished my drink so quickly I almost want to steal Luca's. I look around to see if the waiter is nearby. Victor bored with our conversation slips away and I want to follow him. I'm impressed how Frida is at ease with her brother to discuss such precarious topics with him.

I reply first, "Actually we did have fun yesterday we lounged on the beach and grabbed dinner." Luca chimes in, "Yes, it was enjoyable to be at the hotel and not working there. And I don't know what Violeta's doing, I didn't get a chance to ask her and I haven't seen her since they arrived."

Frida continues her questioning "Is her friend here with her too?" Luca shakes his head, "No, I didn't see him, but I did see her brother. He stopped to talk with me and said they were all at church and he assured me his sister only wanted to say hello to some of the relatives and they'd be on their way after you arrived."

I spot the waiter and we make eye contact. He's over in seconds, thankfully. Max and I both help ourselves to a drink but the other two keep talking.

"I understand she'll be in our lives especially at functions for Jules and Marcos, but this was the first event since your split that I've seen her, I was a bit startled and especially when she approached Emelia first. Wasn't that creepy Emelia?"

I can't believe Frida is going there right here and right now. But she and Luca were always close, so maybe she wants to be straight with him. I take another sip and tilt my head pretending to think about the encounter.

"Well, I haven't seen her in ages so I don't have much to compare. Maybe she was just as shocked as you were to see me. Remember what we said, today is about you. Let's have fun!"

Luca places his hand on my shoulder and pulls me close, "Yes, Emelia that's a great idea who wants to dance?" We place our drinks on the table and find an open space on the dance floor. It was a freestyle dance, so for now, the four of us are dancing in a group.

Soon Henry and Rafael bust in with their wives too and everyone is smiling and laughing. Luca and I sneak glances at one another and I feel so happy being with him and Frida. The song changes and the DJ announces something and I hear Frida's name. Suddenly she's cheering at the DJ and Max whisks her away from us and they're dancing together to the next song.

I feel someone tugging at my arm and when I turn around I see Henry. "Would you like to dance with me?" I smile and tip my head back and giggle, "Yes, of course."

I see Luca dancing with Olivia. Henry leads me around the dance floor. His approach is slightly different than Luca's but equal in ability and he has terrific rhythm. We get some distance from the rest of them when he starts talking with me. "So, are you and Luca an item? You can tell me, I won't say anything. Olivia and I think it would be great."

Not sure what to say to him, I squeeze his hand, "Henry, you've always been like a brother to me, so I trust you. We reconnected yesterday and I think we're in a good place. There are many things, people to consider and we're just taking it slowly. So, we're keeping it very private."

He spins me with excitement and laughs, "I didn't think about this when I invited you, but when we saw you on Friday, afterwards Olivia and I said you would be perfect for my brother. And he called me that night and asked me lots of questions and demanded that he should be with you on Saturday.

I wanted to call you first to check with you but I figured you'd be fine with seeing Luca. And I didn't understand why he was so desperate to see you. He made me promise not to call you. So, I figured you had my phone number and if there was a problem, I knew you would call me."

I reply, "Thanks for being an understanding brother to him. I don't think this year has been easy for Luca. And I'm glad he looked to me as a distraction."

Henry pulls me closer to him, "You're right, this year has been hell for him and my family has been torn apart about what happened. Luckily I was neutral since I never knew what took place years ago when they got back together. Recently Luca confided in me. But left out an important part of the story, of which I only pieced together when I saw you with him today. You were the woman he fell in love with years ago. I know this because I haven't seen him this happy."

A tremor shoots through my body, I interrupt him, "Henry, please stop, I'll be crying in your arms in another second if you continue."

He dips me. "Ok, I'll stop. I just want you to know, Olivia and I are ecstatic about the two of you and if you need any support you can lean on us. I understand why you want to keep it quiet for now."

The song ends. I hug him, "Thank you Henry, it's so comforting knowing I can confide in you while I'm here."

He whispers, "When you get Luca to move to New York, me and my family will have a place to stay."

I laugh at him. "That's what this is all about free lodging in New York? You know you always have an open invitation whether or not I'm living with your brother."

We meet up with Olivia and Luca near the table. "Are you hungry? The food is set up over there and we should get on line." Olivia informs us. I follow Henry and Olivia, Luca walks beside me, "Save me a seat near you, I want to check on my kids first." I reply, "Ok, see you soon."

Standing with Olivia and Henry we make small talk, mainly about the party, the weather and the music. I ask, "Henry, I haven't seen your brother Nicolás, is he here?" He nods, "No they couldn't come. His wife Carla is pregnant and shouldn't be travelling at this point."

The line moves quickly and soon we're filling our plates with the assorted offerings. I pretty much have taken a little of everything. If I can't finish, I'm hoping Luca will eat some.

I walk back to the table with Olivia and Henry is sidetracked by a guest. When we get there, Luca is sitting proudly with a full plate and a huge grin on his face. He gets up and pulls the chair out for me next to him. And he does the same for Olivia.

I smirk at him, "I'm confused, you didn't stand in line with us but you're here at the table before us with a dish of food. How did that happen?"

He remains standing, "Easy, I was looking for Julieta and Marcos and I found them getting food. And the guests didn't mind me cutting in front of them. I'm headed to the bar can I get you ladies a drink?"

I nod. He guesses, "Lemon-lime?"

I nod again. "Thanks!"

Olivia laughs, "Same for me Luca, I've had too many of the Frida drinks." I laugh with Olivia and point to myself lipping, "Me too."

While we're sitting alone Olivia leans over to me, "I know Henry spoke with you but I also want to tell you personally that I'm so happy to see the two of you together. Emelia, I've only met you on a few occasions but I've always known you were someone special to this family and you've always been so kind to me. I think you and Luca are perfect for one another. No reason to rush things, he's a very good man and I see that he's in love with you. He will wait for you. And don't let his first marriage get in the way. In all these years that I've known him, he never looked at her the way he looks at you."

I smile and grasp her wrist, "Olivia I truly appreciate all that you're telling me, I'm so overwhelmed at this point. But I know being with him feels so right. And he is giving me the space to figure things out. You also should know we're trying to keep this private, mainly so his kids get to know me first as just me and not as their dad's girlfriend."

She shakes her head in agreement. "I understand but you shouldn't worry, after they spend one day with you they will be asking you to move here. They are really nice and easy going."

Luca returns and serves us our drinks. And Henry finally sits with us too. Luca jokes, "My you have some appetite my friend from New York."

"It all looked so delicious I thought I could take a little taste of everything. And maybe you can help me?"

He nods excitedly, "I was hoping you'd share. It's like I have my own buffet at the table." I giggle.

Frida and Max take seats across from us. And I'm amazed at the pile of food on their dishes. Henry exclaims, "What's going on there, you've got food for ten people." Frida howls with laughter. "I'm the birthday girl! They wouldn't stop giving me food. Please help yourselves to our plates."

Rafael and Teresa sit next to Frida. And once everyone is enjoying their food, the conversations change from one topic to the next with heated debates and laughter. The siblings carry on like they did so many years ago and it's good to hear the spouses holding their own too. And it's funny how they drift from Spanish to English and back again. To the point that I begin to easily follow what's going on.

Olivia begs Henry to tell us a story about one of their recent trips. And as he begins recounting the events, he can't control his laughter. She joins him and they both can't speak. We all look at each other and are just laughing because of them. We don't even know what they're laughing about. "I promise, I will tell you all when we're in Chiriqui this week. I just..." And again he breaks into laughter.

Frida sits up in her seat and looks at Max and then looks at me and Luca, "Who's going to Chiriqui? Are we all going? Are you going?"

Max says, "Yes Frida, another surprise, we're all spending a few days in Chiriqui to continue the party."

She raises her hands above her head and cheers "YES! I can't wait. When do we leave?"

Before she gets the answer, we hear *"Tía Frida, Tía Frida vamos a bailar!"* [Aunt Frida let's dance!] And Julieta is pulling Frida to the dance floor.

Luca whispers, "My daughter, she loves Frida." Olivia taps me on my shoulder, "Want to dance?" Luca squeezes my knee and pats my thigh. "Yes, of course I need to work off all this food." When I get up I look at Luca, "Please take whatever you want." With his fork in hand, "I was intending to."

Flo Rida's adrenaline boosting song "Club Can't Handle Me" promptly entices more dancers. Olivia and I find some space on the dance floor not far from Frida and Julieta. As we get into the music I notice Frida slowly making her way towards us. Not long, the four of us are dancing together. "Jules, this is my friend Emelia. You remember when I told you about my life back in New York? She's that friend I mentioned." Julieta nods her head. "Emelia this is Julieta Luca's daughter." We both say our hellos. Introductions have been made and we continue dancing. Somehow I suspect that was Olivia's plan all along.

Another fun tune follows and the rest of our table is up dancing with us. It's so sweet to see Luca and Julieta grooving together. With high heels, Julieta appears as tall as her dad. She has his hair color and long beautiful waves and his strikingly blue eyes. Julieta has her mother's slender yet curvy body shape and her facial features are a mix. At this close distance I notice a little cleft in her chin.

Frida comes over to me, "Do you remember our nights at the Monster dance club?" I laugh with her and shout, "Yes! Vividly, like it was last month!" We dance in step with one another. Henry also dances close to us. And we take turns switching partners and then it's me and Julieta.

She tries to copy my steps and soon we're synchronized, I shout, "You're really good, a quick learner." She smiles, "My Tía taught me years ago. I dance with her a lot." Rafael tries to get between us and we laugh at his silly dance moves.

The song fades and a slower paced song starts. Julieta grabs me and Frida and pulls us to the table, "Tía, I've got a great idea. When I start college, you plan a trip to New York and when you're there, you and Emelia take me to that club you always talk about."

Frida looks at me, "Do you think it's still around?" I shrug my shoulders, "I don't know, but one quick search on the web and we can find out."

Julieta runs to her dad. She comes back with his phone. I scream with delight. "Oh Julieta, you are something, I love your enthusiasm. It's contagious."

"Ok, tell me the name again, is it Monster something?"

My mouth opens wide, "Frida, your niece has quite the memory. What else did you tell her? Yes, Julieta, I think it was the Monster Dance club."

I whisper to Frida, "You did mention it's a gay club?" Frida nods yes. With just a few key strokes Julieta's eyes widen and she shoves the phone screen in our faces, "Is this the place?"

I squint and beg, "Can you enlarge it I can't see it without my glasses." She rolls her eyes with impatience and says, "You're just like Papá." I giggle, "Yes we are older. But still can have fun."

She giggles with us. "Is this better?" I review the website and smile at Frida, "I can't believe it, the club is still around."

Julieta does a happy dance. "Ok, then it's a plan, you are both taking me there for my birthday."

I give Frida a worried look. Frida replies, "Jules check to see if they have an age restriction. You might have to be older to get in." Thankfully Frida read my mind.

"I'll check later Tía. Either way, I'll find a way to get in as long as you both are with me." She runs back to her dad with his phone.

I hug Frida, "So, I will finally see you in New York again?" She grimaces, "We'll see."

We get back to the table and notice everyone must be up dancing. I sit and rest for a bit. Grateful all the plates have been cleared. I don't think I have room for another morsel. Well, maybe dessert.

Frida is talking with some friends and I sneak to the ladies room. I'm glad when I get inside there's no line, in fact nobody is in here. I freshen up and apply some lip color. With the exception of my run in with Luca's soon to be ex, today has been a truly special day.

Passing the dance floor on my way to the table to drop off my purse, Julieta and Luca dance towards me. She asks, "Emelia, would you mind dancing with my Papá?"

"No, I don't mind as long as he's okay with it."

"I'll take your purse to the table if you want. And can you tell him about our plan?"

I raise my eyebrows, now I see her motives. "Sure, of course."

She leans in and kisses my cheek, "Thanks Emelia." And she passes me off to her dad.

He spins me around and I see Julieta skipping to the table. Back in his arms our bodies are pressed together and he's gliding me around the floor and singing in my ear. He is energized and concentrated. I don't stumble and I get lost with him in the moment. So much so, I didn't notice the song change until midway through. My choreographer releases me and tugs me back into his arms again and again. It's like we've danced for years together. When the song concludes he pulls me close and whispers, "Mi Lia thank you." I kiss him on both of his cheeks and we walk to the table.

"So, tell me about this plan you have with my daughter."

Julieta appears in seconds. "Did you tell him?"

I laugh, "I was just about to. Or would you rather?"

"No worries, you can tell him now or when we're all in Chiriqui this week!" She flits away.

He tugs me close, "I see you made a friend."

I nod, "Yes, it appears so."

We take our seats and he replies, "One down one to go. Hey do you still take pictures?"

He remembered. "Yes, when I'm inspired. Why?"

He rests his hand on my knee, "My son also takes pictures. Maybe you'll be inspired when we're out hiking together?"

I hold his hand under the table. "Yes, I think that can be arranged."

While sitting together cooling down from our recent activity I hear a very familiar tune. Frida appears suddenly and smiles at me, "Ready my friend, I requested this for you and me."

I jump up and follow her to the dance floor. I haven't heard this Soup Dragons "I'm Free" song in years. We seem to be the only two that know it. Thankfully Max joins us followed by Julieta and now I'm feeling less self-conscious. Henry and Olivia also share the floor with us. As the energy increases we're all singing and dancing to the music. What a blast!

At the end of the song, the lights dim and the waiters roll out a huge birthday cake with candles and sparklers twinkling.

The DJ leads us all in song, *Feliz Cumpleaños*. Everyone stands and we form a ring around Frida, Max and Victor. I've got Henry on my left and now Luca and Julieta on my right. It's a spectacular moment. When the sparklers burn out, Frida attempts to blow out all the candles. And she manages all but two and Victor blows them out with her. The revelers applaud the birthday girl.

Chapter 28

LUCA AND HIS brothers bring Frida's gifts out to Max and he carefully puts them all in the trunk of his car. Frida hugs me before getting in the car and tells me, "I've got your mobile number and the hotel information. We'll pick you up around noon and travel together to Chiriqui, yes?" I nod, "Sounds like a fun road trip I can't wait." I hug her again and Max waves to me from the driver's seat.

Luca and I are the last to leave. The valet drives his car up and Luca holds the passenger door open for me. He settles into his seat closes the door and leans towards me. Cupping his face in my hands I look into his eyes and admire his playful smile. He says, "I've waited patiently, please don't make me wait any longer. *Bésame mi amor.*" [Kiss me my love.]

I torment him with three little kisses and finally give into his wishes. He kisses my nose and after he puts the car in gear proclaims, "I am all yours for the rest of the evening. What do you want to do?"

I giggle with surprise and say, "I really don't know. I hadn't planned that we'd be on our own so early. How did that happen? I thought for sure we'd be dropping off your kids or going back to Frida's."

He melodiously laughs and informs me, "The kids have school in the morning and technically this was their mother's weekend. My father offered to drop them off at Violeta's on their way home. And Frida has to pack for the next few days away with the family. So, I'd say we lucked out."

I copy his laugh and say, "Oh yes we did. Now what should we do? This is your city, any suggestions?"

Letting a yawn slip out, he says, "I'm sorry, I was just thinking about our week ahead and that we'll be on the go until Thursday. Maybe we should have a relaxing evening at the hotel. Start with a drink or two at the bar. Or maybe just go up to the room and watch a movie. I still owe you a movie night."

Happily I say, "I was hoping you didn't really want to go out. Is it selfish of me to want you to myself tonight?"

He takes my hand and kisses it. "No, not selfish at all. I'm glad to hear it."

I recline and shift in my seat so that the rest of the drive to the hotel I can observe him. I felt the car slow down and he looks over to me and gently caresses my face and smiles. I close my eyes briefly just so I can cherish the simple joy of being with Luca in his car travelling to our home away from home. A week from today I'll be thinking back on these special moments. So right now, I want to appreciate every second I have with him. I open my eyes again take his hand and kiss it sweetly as we continue our drive to the hotel.

Before going to our room Luca suggests we take a stroll on the beach. As we approach the doors to the deck area we see the vibrant glow of the sunset through the glass doors. Kicking off our shoes once we hit the sand we walk along the shore hand in hand taking in the setting sun. It's a dazzling ending to a fantastic day. With Luca standing behind me and his arms wrapped around my waist, he holds me in place as we stand together watching the day come to an end.

Luca spins me so that we're looking at one another. "Your silence worries me, talk to me."

He knows me so well and yet doesn't have any idea what I'm thinking about. In his defense usually I have several thoughts dancing around in my head.

I swallow and look into his concerned eyes. I don't know what to say first. So I muster, "I'm just enjoying the sunset with you. Thinking about how today was almost perfect and how comfortable your family makes me feel. So I anticipate the next few days away with them will be lots of fun."

"But?" he asks.

I shake my head, "No but. I promised myself that I will give you my all this week. Plus this is our special place and until tomorrow, let it just be you and me."

He pulls my face close to his, "Are you sure? You said today was almost perfect. I'm certain I know who made it less perfect for you. Please talk to me Emelia."

"I haven't had an experience that involves someone's ex-wife, so this is all new to me. And I guess it was better to have it happen sooner than later. But the way Violeta spoke to me and her expression is very concerning. Why would I matter to her, I'm just your sister's friend, unless she knew about you and me from before."

Luca takes a few steps away from me, "It's frightening how accurate the phrase is *'the truth always comes out.'* I never made her aware of you and me during our marriage. After we split I was moving to my new house and boxing up my things, she was separating some of our personal items like pictures, music, movies and books. She came upon the book you gave me for Christmas. I always had it in the library in my home office, but somehow it appeared in the bookcase in the living room. She waved it up at me and asked was it mine and I looked at it in her hand and I guess my delayed response caused her to open the book. When I got to her, she was reading your inscription. She kept repeating your name and asked me who you were. I snatched it away from her and didn't answer and continued to pack my things."

I walk up to him and he puts his arm around me. "And when your sister introduced us today and said my name, she realized I was the one who gave you that book."

We stood quietly for a minute. "I think she's still in love with you Luca."

He takes my hand and leads us back to the hotel. "No, she's not in love with me, never was. She was just shocked to come face to face with the woman that stood between us all these years."

If he's right about that, then I'm astounded by what took place today. We walk in silence up to the hotel veranda. Before entering the lobby Luca stops and says, "So did that help clear your thoughts?"

I look up to the sky and back at him and say, "I don't know if that bit of information helped or caused further anxiety. I just know that there's no reason for me to think about it tonight. Agreed?"

He smiles, "Agreed."

We pick up snacks and beverages from the hotel shop for our movie night before going to the room. It looks like we hadn't eaten for days. We get into our pajamas and arrange our assortment of goodies on the coffee table. Grabbing a blanket from the closet I join Luca on the couch as he's pulling up the movie menu on the television. We search through new releases, older titles and some classics. It wasn't an easy task for two movie buffs. We settle on the film *About Time*. He hadn't seen it and even though I've watched it before, I insist it's worth seeing again. I know he'll love it.

With the lights dimmed we snuggle on the couch as the movie begins. He kisses my forehead and says, "Thank you for giving me another unforgettable day with you." Placing my head on his chest he squeezes me tight.

The end credits are rolling and we're both sobbing. I grab the packet of tissues from the table and pull out a sheet for him as I take one for me.

"I can't believe I never saw that film. It's such a tender story." He blows his nose.

Handing him another sheet, I smile back at him and grab the used tissue and fling it to the floor. "I know I was so moved the first time I saw it. And each viewing since it gets better and better." I blow my nose too and toss the used tissue.

He wipes his face with the other tissue, "How many times have you watched this film?"

I laugh, "I think this was my third."

"Did you ever see it while on a date?"

I shake my head, "No, never on a date, until now." He leans towards me and kisses my lips.

I dry my face with a clean tissue crumple it and toss it to the floor. He begins to laugh. "Emelia, why do you keep throwing the tissues on the floor?"

Giggling I reply, "It's just something I do after watching tearjerker movies. I feel like it's a break from the norm and allows me to just be free to enjoy a good cry. And then when I'm ready I walk around and put them all in the garbage bin."

And he crumples up a tissue and does the same. "I see what you mean." I laugh and say, "You are now officially a member of the chick flick club."

I stand and stretch. While locating the bin I inquire, "What did you like most about the story?"

He sits quietly thinking about the film, while I get rid of the used tissues. "Well, I can easily say, the entire movie was delightful. As a son and a father with a son, obviously I enjoyed that storyline most followed by their love story." Luca reaches for my hand, "Why do you like it so much?"

Placing the container on the floor next to the table I kneel partly on the couch beside him. Looking into his eyes I play with his hair.

"I agree, it's a delightful film and before watching it with you I most liked the father son story as well as the love story. But tonight, being here with you after the last two days we've had, the ability to travel back to our past and try to redo a part of my life or relive it, really touched me deeply. I'm so relieved that after all that's happened, somehow you and I are together again. And maybe we just have to believe this was the plan all along."

He lowers me onto his lap and nuzzles my neck. "Emelia, I can't believe that just yet. My heart is still recovering from not having you in my life all these years. Each moment we spend together, I feel it healing little by little."

Closing my eyes I nervously tell him, "I know what you mean. My heart feels so vulnerable when I'm with you. It's like it wants to love but is either unsure about how to love again or so afraid of being crushed again. And it desperately wants to let you in on the secret treasures hiding deep inside."

"Mi Lia, what are these secret treasures?"

"They are my thoughts, my fears, my hopes and my dreams. You see, if I reveal just one of them to the wrong person, I believe I can never get it back the same way."

Luca looks into my eyes, "But if they are shared with the right person?"

"I don't know. There hasn't ever been a right person."

Luca kisses the area just above my heart and lowers us both down on the couch. Wrapped in his arms with my head against his chest I rest quietly listening to his thumping heart as we lay tangled together in comforting tranquility.

A few minutes pass and Luca rises from the couch, "Do you mind if we take this to the bedroom? After tonight, we'll have to be on our good behavior and I'm hoping to overindulge with you until the morning." I quickly stand and he whisks me into his arms and carries me into the bedroom.

Chapter 29

TAKING A LAST glance I'm thrilled knowing that in just a few hours Luca and I will be together at my home. I've waited for this day for so very long and can't believe it has finally arrived. I grab my car keys and open the front door. Sitting in my car and setting the GPS for the airport my mobile rings.

It's Luca, he can't be that early. "Hi, did you arrive already?" No response.

"Luca, are you there?"

Silence, "I can't hear you. Call me back." The line is dropped.

I refresh the airline flight status page on my phone and his flight hasn't landed yet. The phone rings again.

"Hi! Luca?"

He clears his throat, "Emelia can you hear me?"

"Yes, I can hear you. Where are you?"

"Have you left for the airport yet?"

"No, I'm in the car just ready to get on the road. Why, what's going on?"

I hear him take a deep breath, "I won't be coming today. I didn't get on the plane. I wanted to make sure you didn't go to the airport. I don't know what to say, except I am very sorry."

He's quiet. "Wait, don't hang up, please talk to me tell me what's going on."

"I have to go."

The phone connection remains open and I think I still hear him. I gently say, "Oh my love, if you want to come here another day don't worry. I know it's a big step. I will understand. Please talk to me, tell me what you're feeling. We'll get through this together you and me, just like you told me when I was there with you. Remember the day at the hotel? It was a perfect day."

I still hear him on the phone. "Goodbye Emelia." The line disconnects.

I turn the car off and in a daze I wander back inside the house. After closing the front door I slide down to the floor and grasp my knees into my chest and cry uncontrollably.

When my eyes open I'm in the dark. Where am I? My heart is racing and when I touch my face it's drenched from sweat or tears. I sit up in bed and realize I'm not alone. He's snoring lightly, it's Luca. I sneak away.

In the privacy of the bathroom I try to control my emotions. It was just a dream, I tell myself. It was just a dream. He's here with me now. We have the week to see how this will play out. Be calm. I splash cold water on my face.

Unlocking the bathroom door I enter the bedroom. His light snoring assures me he's still sleeping. In the darkness I look for my robe. I can't find it and give up. Wearing only the racy nightwear Jenene picked out with me I head to the living room and directly to the terrace, I just need some fresh air to clear my thoughts.

Walking over to the terrace railing I see the stars above me and hear the waves. Why did I have that terrible dream? What is my mind trying to tell me? Should I not trust his promises again? Should I doubt him? It feels different now. What will it take to believe he won't abandon me again?

Placing my elbows on the railing I rest my head in my hands and close my eyes. Just listen to the waves and silence the thoughts. The ripples start from the left and travel to the right and a split second of silence. And it starts all over again. I don't know how long I concentrate on the waves when I feel cocooned in Luca's arms and a blanket around us. And he rests his chin on my shoulder. I hear him take a breath. I tremble and he hugs me closer.

I ask, "Did I wake you?"

"No, I don't think so. I woke to use the bathroom and when I returned to bed, you weren't there." He kisses my shoulder. "So I came to look for you. Have you been out here long?"

I nod, "I'm not sure, maybe a few minutes."

He loosens his grip a bit but I still feel protected. "Want me to leave you alone?"

"No, please don't."

He leans close to my face and kisses my temple. "Why are you out here?"

"I had a dream and when I woke up I couldn't go back to sleep. And I didn't want to disturb you. So I came out here."

"Do you remember the dream? Want to talk about it?"

"It was a silly dream."

"But it kept you awake that doesn't sound so silly to me."

I move my body to turn to look at him. After re-wrapping ourselves in the blanket I search for his eyes.

"From what I remember, I was at home and getting ready to pick you up at the airport. And when I got in the car, you called me. Told me you didn't get on the plane and that you were sorry. I tried to find out why and you simply said goodbye. And the phone went silent. I woke up in our bed in complete darkness and my face was wet with tears. At first I was disoriented. And then realized where I was. I went to the bathroom to calm down and felt I needed air to clear my mind. I came out here to listen to the ocean and then you joined me."

He pulls me close to him and caresses my back. I rest my head on his chest and he rocks us back and forth. "Emelia that's a good dream, it's telling you that you want to be with me and you'll be sad if we're not together."

I push him away from me. "No, no, no, that's not what that dream meant. It's reminding me how I felt before. Like when we first met and you promised me we'd stay in touch and you took me to the airport and when I boarded the plane I was sad to leave you but very hopeful we'd be together again. And that didn't happen. The second trip, you promised me again and I convinced myself, it would be different. I believed you and trusted we'd be together. I got on that plane all alone but with such confidence that what we had was real and that we'd find a way to be together and make it work. Do you know how I felt each time those promises were broken? The first time, well I thought maybe it was too soon to believe in us. So, I visited for Christmas. And our spark our connection was even greater and I fell for your promises. I opened my heart again for you. Those feelings of rejection and abandonment keep coming back to me and I tried pushing them away just so I can give you, give us another chance. And as much as I tried to bury them, they came back to me in the dream."

He takes the blanket off and drapes it on my shoulders. "I'll be back." While he goes into the room, I pull over two chairs and settle into one of them.

When he returns, he's wearing a robe and has two water bottles and hands me one. He sits across from me and scoops up my feet to rest on his legs. "I understand why you have these fears just tell me what you need from me to take them away. I will do anything for you."

I take a sip of water and look at him. "This is crazy. We shouldn't be talking about this just yet. Who knows, by the end of this week, we might not even like each other anymore, much less love one another."

He grabs my foot. "Don't say that. You know that's not true. You're just trying to avoid this conversation."

I challenge him, "Ok, I've had less than forty-eight hours to contemplate this possibility and you've had more than that. What was your plan, how did you see us making this work? I mean you live here and I live there. And you have two children. See what I mean, why should we be talking about this now? And yet, it haunts me. I feel I can't completely let go of those fears, but I'm trying to push them away to look towards our future."

He caresses my legs, "Ah, now I know what's driving all this, the uncertainty of it all. Luckily I have been thinking about us and I have some ideas. First, I will be able to work from here and the New York office whenever I choose. I am just like you Emelia. This will be all new to me and we'll build our future together. I can either stay at your place or a hotel when I'm in New York."

I take a deep breath, "And what about your kids? Won't they mind you being away?"

"Not really, my daughter will be at school in New York, I will see her there and when I'm back I will see my son. Now can you believe in us?"

I guardedly nod yes.

He moves my legs off of him and stands and then pulls me up to him. "Now I don't believe you, talk to me," he commands and wraps his arms around me.

"I've always believed in us, it's just something happens after I get on the plane, your life gets in the way. I just have to trust you once again, but I won't know that until after I'm gone."

He looks up to the sky, "I hurt you deeply Emelia and I promise you won't have those fears and doubts when you fly back home, I will make sure of that, you will see. Now please promise me that you will not think about any of this and just open yourself up to me this week."

I look into his eyes, "Yes I promise to give you my all this week." He leans down and his mouth finds mine. The blanket drops to the floor and his hands are all over my body. My hands explore him and I feel his arousal building and I slowly open his robe and he breaks us apart. Luca looks around the terrace and says, "Give me a minute." He removes his robe and places it on my shoulders.

First he takes the cushions from the lounge chairs and places them on the floor of the terrace and picks up the blanket and tosses it over the cushions. He returns to me, takes my hand in his and kisses it. As he leads me towards the makeshift bed he whispers in my ear, "I want you now and I want you here." I place my hand on the back of his neck pulling him close and eagerly my tongue finds his.

We hastily remove one another's pajamas and lie down on the cushions. While Luca rests on his side he begins to explore my body. Outside here with Luca on the terrace, lying naked in the darkness, I feel so exposed, so alive and so very aroused.

His head lowers down and his tongue circles each nipple and his fingertips dance over my belly and journey to the tops of my thighs. I run my hands through his hair while he continues licking and sucking. He rubs my sweet spot and inserts one finger inside. With the stars shining down on us I become intoxicated by the ocean air and Luca's natural fragrance while listening to the waves crashing on the shore. As he continues his rhythmic seduction he inserts a second finger and circles them around and around and deeper and deeper. I moan blissfully. My senses are overwhelmingly stimulated and my need for Luca continues mounting.

He whispers, "Your desire for me makes me want you more." Luca resumes pleasuring me and says, "Your body tells me you want me. I need to know, do you want me? Do you want all I want to give you?" I moan, "Yes Luca, yes."

With every movement of his fingers my pelvis lifts to meet him. Ravenously he says, "I want to hear you let go of your fears, I want my mouth to feel your surrender."

Removing his fingers he crawls down and begins kissing the insides of my thighs. Lifting my hips he rests my legs over his shoulders and his mouth begins to liberate me. With each stroke of his tongue and thrust of his fingers my mind and body begin to let go. And suddenly I quiver from head to toe and the force between my legs takes over and for several sensational moments I am free of all anxieties.

While my insides are still throbbing Luca drops my legs and pulls me up towards him. As he eases himself into me, I cry out and he puts his mouth on mine. When I gain control of my movements I rock up and down bringing him deeper and deeper inside me.

"Free your mind. Tell me Emelia, what do you want?" My mouth finds his nipples and I suck and nibble and he moans. I feel him pulsing and I quicken my pace. He grabs my ass and quickly pushes me down onto the cushions and pulls himself out of me.

He looks desperately into my eyes and says, "I'm waiting, tell me."

Breathlessly he gently slides his hardness in and out of me, taunting me as I'm about to climax again. "Luca I want you."

He pulls out again, "Oh Mi Lia, I know you desire me, but what else do you want?"

He plunges into me. I cry out, "I want us to love again. I want you never to leave me. I need you Luca. I want you Luca. I love you Luca."

His tongue thrusts into my mouth and with several more jolts I climax again as he empties inside me.

After a few minutes, I open my eyes and with his body lying heavily on mine my heart and soul find solace from making love with him under the moon and the stars. I kiss his shoulder and close my eyes.

I feel his eyelashes tickle my neck and not long after he detaches us, he sits up. With a moan he says, "I always knew we had this strong passion between us, but I never could imagine this intensity. It will be very difficult to keep my distance from you the next few days."

I smile and nod. "Yes, we'll have to find ways." He stands and extends his hand to me, "The bed will be more comfortable let's go." With his help I stand and we gather our things.

We snuggle in bed with arms and legs entangled. "When you come to New York, I'd like you to stay with me. But can we get a hotel room on occasion?"

His laugh is throaty and sexy. "Ah, we've had a good run here. Yes, I think that can be arranged. And I like that you're making plans for our future." He kisses my nose and my lips. "Now we should get some sleep, tomorrow will be a very hectic day."

I kiss him back, "Good night Luciano, my love."

And he whispers, "Buenas noches mi cielo." He places a tender kiss on my forehead and says, "My heaven."

Chapter 30

THE STRUMMING OF guitar strings playing from Luca's phone wakes me from my slumber. Slightly the mattress shifts as he reaches to silence the alarm. Quiet once again he envelopes me with his bare body and kisses my shoulder. I simply reply with a murmured purr. We lie there entwined for a few minutes. I don't want our romantic reunion at the hotel to end just yet. I take his hand that's been cupping my breast and treat him to several drawn out kisses and return the hand to where I found it. He responds with his own gentle purr and increases his hold on me.

"Good morning, mi amor. I look forward to waking with you like this for the rest of my life. I never want to start my days without you ever again."

I trail kisses from his wrist to the crook of his arm while turning to face him. "Well, for the next few mornings, you'll have to settle with seeing me first with your family at the breakfast table."

He plays with my hair. "Oh my dear, have you forgotten when I snuck in and out of your room and we didn't get caught?"

I giggle, "Now I remember and how shocked we were when your sister wandered into my room mistaking it for the bathroom. That was close."

He kisses my forehead, "Well, I have a plan, to LOCK the door." I kiss him on the lips, "But no funny stuff ok?" With squinted eyes he asks, "Funny stuff?"

My hands travel from his chest down to the tops of his thighs and I start caressing him, "You know like this, we should be on our good behavior."

As my touch encourages him I ask, "How much time do we have until you need to leave?" He advances towards me and passionately kisses me as my hands continue their seduction. Within seconds, he parts my legs and thrusts into me. Nibbling on my ear he says, "I will always make time to love you."

My body awakens to those words and him pulsing inside me. Eagerly he groans, "I'm close my love how about you?" Without answering, he works my sweet spot rapidly and begins sucking my nipples as we savor this last morning alone together. With our bodies bucking for the other I moan and breathlessly answer, "Yes, very very close now."

My declaration lures his mouth to mine and I feel his hips take over as he plunges deeper and eagerly inside me, one, two, three more times and we both reach a wondrous morning climax.

Moments following our newly desired escapades a thought crosses my mind. As I stroke his back I whisper, "For the amount of sex we've had these three days, I'd say for two old-ER people we're certainly making up for missed indulgences."

He gives me a low carnal laugh, gently raises my chin while tracing my lips with his fingertips, and replies, "I intend to make that our new life's goal." While I look curiously into his eyes, he continues, "So, if we'd been indulging for the last twenty years, we should multiply that by the number of times per year the average couple has sex...maybe two hundred?"

While I laugh and nod about his inflated number, he asks, "Too much or too little?" I whisper, "Sadly I think, your number is too high."

Naughtily he replies, "Oh Mi Lia, that is sad and you might be right. Thankfully by my experience since Saturday, I can report we are not average."

I smile, "Yes, we are certainly not average."

With his raised eyebrow he flirts, "By my new calculations I would estimate, we need to make up for two thousand pleasurable decadences." I reply, "That sounds closer to the average."

Suggestively and cheerfully he announces, "We could reach that goal in less than three years." I laugh into his chest while trying to figure out his crazy calculations. Still laughing I reply, "Are you saying to achieve that goal, we simply need to do what we just did a few minutes ago, roughly twice a day for three years?"

His teeth bite down on my shoulder, "I'm shocked, not only are you quick with numbers but you also like it rough." He clutches my bottom. I squeal, "I challenge you and if you play your cards right Mr. Morales, we might just reach that goal within two years."

With that provocation he slips under the covers. My very competitive team captain lavishes me with kisses down to my navel and with his very skilled methods sets out to bring us closer to our revised and ambitious goal.

Chapter 31

I SNEAK AWAY to the bathroom after round two. If we continue at this rate, Luca will certainly be late for work. I wash my face and brush my teeth and armor myself with a big fluffy white robe before going back to the bedroom.

The bed is empty and I don't see Luca but I hear his voice in the distance. He must be on the phone. Glancing at the clock I see it's almost eight. I must remember to call the front desk to inform them I'll be checking out at noon and won't need a room later this week. After Luca leaves, I could go back to sleep. Although I should do something more productive like check out the hotel gym or walk on the beach.

Wandering out of the bedroom I walk towards the terrace doors. Luca is sitting on a chair in the living room when he looks up to me and points to his phone while continuing his conversation. I wave and open the door. Closing the door behind me I make my way to the terrace railing. Breathing in the ocean air I'm grateful for waking up again next to Luca and another beautiful day awaits us.

As I'm watching the waves I feel my love's arms embrace me. While he rests his chin on my shoulder I say, "Earlier when I commented about how much sex we've had, I wanted to say, before you got me off course." He squeezes me gently. "In addition to our desires and stamina, I'm surprised that I've never once felt uneasy or self-conscious being with you. My heart and body have been overwhelmed by wanting to love you more and more. That it hasn't mattered to me that the first time we've completely shared ourselves wasn't with our twenty something bodies, it was with our older slightly weathered forms."

I pause and continue, "For so many years I've endured this love hate relationship with parts of my body that I thought were far less attractive than other areas. But with you, until now, telling you this, I hadn't thought about them and only focused on being with you and finding ways for us to reach higher levels of passion. It's like my body thrives on loving you. I wonder then, is this what true love making feels like? Not thinking about our imperfections and just pleasing the other; if it is, then this is happening to me for the first time in my life."

Luca holds me tighter and says into my ear, "Emelia you are a very beautiful woman. This beauty stems from deep in your heart and extends to every part of your body. That's why I desire every piece of you. And I want to erupt inside of you when I hear you and feel you tremble with ecstasy, because of what I can do for you. I too, am feeling this for the first time in my life."

I turn to look at him and he kisses me gently on my lips. Holding my face in his hands he looks deeply into my eyes and says, "I was sitting in there watching you while I was on the phone and I couldn't even concentrate on the conversation. As I watched you, I was feeling so much love for you and was also feeling anxious about how you see our future. I ended the call and came out here to be near you and hold you in my arms. Without even asking, you opened your soul so tenderly to me that you managed to take away any anxiety I was feeling just a few minutes before."

Luca pulls me close to him and my face presses against his chest while we look out at the ocean. Holding him securely in my arms I say, "Before we go our separate ways today, I want you to know that I am honestly considering a future with you. I just need to continue feeling that I can trust you again with my heart. So keep doing what you're doing and I'll keep doing what I'm doing and hopefully we'll get where we want to be before I leave on Saturday."

I look up into Luca's eyes. He pushes my windblown curls aside, kisses my forehead, the tip of my nose and my lips. Luca whispers, "I would be honored to be the keeper of your heart for the rest of my life." We kiss again in the morning sunshine on the terrace where just a few days ago our young love that was disrupted decades ago was given another chance at forever.

"Mi amor, I must get ready for work. We have a full day ahead of us and the sooner I start my day the sooner I can see you later." I smile at him, "Yes, of course, I promised you that if you stayed with me last night, I would not make you late." He hugs me once more before we leave the terrace.

Luca quickly showers and packs his overnight bag while I begin taking my clothes out of the closet and drawers to fold and put away in my suitcase. He smiles at me when I drag my luggage out from the closet. "That will soon change," he says looking at my oversized bag.

"What will change?"

While smirking he says, "The size of your luggage, since you'll have a home here too and won't need to pack as much."

I smile back at him, "The list continues to grow."

He looks confused, "What list?"

I stand close to him and flirt, "You know, the pros and cons list. Why I should or shouldn't be involved with you."

He squints his eyes at me, "And which side of the list does having two homes fall on?"

"Hmm, at first, I thought it would be a positive but now that you have me thinking…"

He takes me in his arms and dips me towards the floor and I laugh and try to squirm but I give up, he's too strong for me. While he attacks me with kisses he shouts, "Stop thinking, it's a positive reason."

I giggle from his enthusiasm. "Yes, yes, I give up, I'll stop thinking. Now will you stop?"

He lifts me up and says, "I will never stop kissing you my love. It has quickly become one of my favorite enjoyments."

I tease, "Oh yes, your kisses, another one for the list." I run from him and hear him laughing in the bedroom.

I look around the living room to find what else needs to be packed. Glancing at the floral arrangement, the flowers still look fresh. Luca enters the room.

"Can I bring the flowers to Chiriqui? Or do you want to take them for your house? They're still so beautiful and I don't want to toss them just yet."

"Either works for me, whatever you want to do."

"Well, if I bring them today, you know your sister will inquire about them."

"Oh, yes, just say they were a welcome gift from me."

I nod in agreement, "Sounds good to me."

Pulling me into his embrace, he says, "My sweet, I must go now. I should see you later around dinner." He holds my chin and kisses me slowly and passionately and as I gasp for air we continue with our goodbye kiss. When we stop he looks into my eyes, "I just wanted to make sure my kisses remain on the good side of your list."

I brightly smile back to him, "That kiss is now emblazoned on that side."

He pats my bottom and I reciprocate and demand, "Now get out of here before we start something we'll want to finish." He laughs, "Yes, I'm going."

I walk him to the door. "Enjoy your drive with your family." He opens the door, "I'm sure Jules will be talking about you during the drive. Have fun with Frida. Good bye."

He gives me a quick peck on the lips. I say, "Bye my love," and close the door. Leaning my back against the door I look at the flowers on the table. There's a gentle knock from the other side. I open the door quickly, it's Luca. He pounces on me and hugs me tightly.

"It's crazy I started missing you immediately when I was walking away without you. I just need one last moment with you."

I hear him breathing in my scent as I do the same, citrus, musk and my favorite, Luca. He takes my head in his hands and runs his fingers through my hair and caresses the side of my neck with the tip of his nose. He whispers, "I don't want to forget your intoxicating fragrance." And then he dashes out into the hallway.

Watching him walk towards the elevators, I whistle my appreciation melody to him. He turns quickly around and says, "That was you?" I laugh, "Yes good looking, that was for you." He laughs and continues to the elevator. As we wait for it to arrive we watch each other from a distance until the chime of the elevator interrupts us and he waves at me and I wave back.

Closing the door of the hotel room again, I am alone in my thoughts. I have about three hours until Frida arrives. First I should shower and then order room service. Suddenly I feel my stomach growling. I rummage through my bag for my phone. I haven't checked it since Luca arrived on Saturday. He's kept me so preoccupied. The battery is low and I should charge it up before I leave the hotel. While I locate the charger I see I have some emails. I connect the phone to the charger and I sit at the table quickly reviewing my mail. I count two from Jenene and one from Henry. There are several random emails from other friends that will have to wait. Henry's message is from Saturday.

To: Emelia Caldera
From: Enrique Morales
Subject: My apologies

Hello Emelia,

By now you must know from Luca the plans have changed for your first day in Panama. Please accept my apologies for not contacting you sooner. My brother said he would take care of everything.

See you tomorrow at the party.

Please don't be angry with me Emmy. I'll explain when we see each other.

Abrazos y besos,
Henry

Scrolling to my next messages, I see Jenene's emails from Saturday and Sunday.

> **To: Emelia Caldera**
> **From: Jenene Caro**
> **Subject: Arrived Safely?**
>
> Hola Emelia,
>
> Just checking in.
>
> JC

> **To: Emelia Caldera**
> **From: Jenene Caro**
> **Subject: VERY Curious Friend**
>
> Hey Emelia,
>
> How was your flight to Panama? I emailed you yesterday and you haven't replied back. Maybe you're not getting service.
>
> Anyway, I hope you're having fun. You BETTER email, call or text me at some point during your trip. Don't make me wait until you return to hear about your first meeting with Luca.
>
> From your very VERY curious and impatient friend,
>
> JC

I put the phone down and smile. While I shower I'll think about what I should tell Jenene. Everything so far with Luca is going blissfully and as much as I want to let her know, I also want to just keep it between me and Luca.

When walking around the suite alone it seems so big and quiet. I'm glad he stayed the extra night. Otherwise I think I would have felt so lonely here. Odd, I've lived alone for so many years and yet, I can't recall when I've missed someone like this that invaded my space.

Entering the oversized shower I remember just a couple of days ago when we were here together. And we explored each other for the very first time with such tenderness and reverence. I really have enjoyed being with him. I wonder how the rest of the week will play out. So much has happened since Saturday and we still have five more days until I leave.

Ending my calls with the front desk and room service I arrange my clothes for today and pack the rest of my wardrobe. It's always such a breeze to repack, probably since all the guess work has been done. Glancing at the clock it's approaching ten and I'm making great timing. I will certainly walk on the beach before the road trip.

There's a knock on the door. Looking through the peep hole I see the room service waiter. Opening the door I greet the gentleman, "*Buenos días.*" "Good morning Ms. Caldera. Where would you like your breakfast?" I swiftly walk towards the terrace, "Out here please," and I open the door to assist.

He pushes the cart out and sets down the breakfast tray on the table. He hands me the bill holder. I add the tip and my signature, "*Muchas gracias.*"

"You are most welcome, enjoy your day." I walk the waiter to the door and before I close it I hang the Do Not Disturb sign on the outside door handle.

Alone on the terrace I sit and eat my breakfast of eggs, toast, fresh fruit and yogurt. I just remembered, I should reply back to Jenene's email. Pausing from my meal I go inside to grab my phone. It's not fully charged, but this will do. I disconnect the phone and bring it out to the terrace.

I munch on two pieces of pineapple and think about when I had that fruit on Saturday morning while Luca was professing to me his life choices. If I keep looking back I won't be able to embrace all that's happening now. Focus on the email to Jenene.

To: Jenene Caro
From: Emelia Caldera
Subject: Short but sweet

Hola Jenene,

To my very curious friend, thank you for your concern. I arrived safely on Friday. And since Saturday morning my world has been turned upside down and today was the first day I glanced at my phone. All I can say or want to say is that I'm very happy that I made the trip.

Now I must find the courage to allow my heart to love freely again.

Hugs from your Elated Friend,
Emelia

P.S. I will be forever indebted to you for the XXX baby dolls you convinced me to buy.

I re-read my email repeatedly before hitting send. I hope my note won't drive her mad for more details. Well, if that doesn't satisfy her curiosity, she'll write me back or try to call.

Before that happens, I walk the phone back inside and reconnect it. I want it fully charged before the road trip. Oh no, Luca and I didn't exchange phone numbers. Well, I can always contact Henry for it. Or I'll just have to go all day without hearing from him. My heart flutters when I think about seeing him later today. It's so silly and different to be feeling this way again for someone and especially Luca. The last few years my life has been fairly predictable with meaningless relationships. There are some advantages to those types of affairs, one that stands out is when they end I don't feel crushed and trust rarely plays a significant part. I was convinced the heart racing, tummy flipping kind of love had sailed away years ago.

I walk towards the terrace railing. What if all these shallow relationships changed me, weakened me? Do I have it in me to make a life with Luca succeed? Do I have what it takes to be there for him and his children? I've been swept up with the romance of it all, but when the fairy dust settles, will I have the courage to entrust myself to Luca and have faith in us? He seems to believe in us and has all the answers. Maybe the moment has arrived to let someone take the reins for a while and doing so will allow me to dismantle the walls protecting my heart. My heart that has been left isolated for so long. Will I ever know if Luca is the one to let back in? Or in order to live, love and trust again I have to leave the past behind and run towards the future with my arms open wide no matter the consequences. It's all or nothing. And I want it all. Luca IS the all that I want.

Chapter 32

"Thank you for visiting us while staying in Panama Ms. Caldera," the lady at the front desk tells me while I checkout. "Your hotel is exceptional and your team is most accommodating. I will come back here again and recommend your hotel to others. Thank you and enjoy the rest of your day."

The hotel bill is settled which doesn't add up to many charges, just the movie and a few incidentals. I guess Luca handled the rest. Heading towards the exit I see Frida walking through the front doors. I wave to her and she waves back.

We embrace, "Great timing, I just settled the bill."

She replies, "I hope you're ready for the road trip."

"I am I took a long walk earlier. I forgot; how many hours is the drive?"

Outside I see Max and Victor standing near their SUV. She says, "Without traffic usually six hours."

Approaching Frida's family I say; "Good afternoon, nice to see you again Max and Victor." I hug them both. Max takes my luggage, the flowers and adds it with all their bags in the trunk.

Frida and I climb into the backseat while the men sit in the front. Frida announces, "Today's trip will be piloted and co-piloted by my husband and son. That way I can sit with you and catch up." I grasp Frida's hand and squeeze it and say, "I can't believe I'm sitting here with you. I think we'll cover about ten years of memories during the first leg of this trip."

The men look at each other and laugh. I joke, "Hey, hey, don't laugh I'll be asking you both all sorts of questions too, you're not off the hook."

Frida laughs and Victor increases the volume of the stereo. And we all crack up. "Oh you are a comedian Victor, I like you already." I grab his shoulder and shake it a bit.

Frida comments, "Where did you get the flowers? They are beautiful."

"Oh, they were a welcome gift from Luca. I thought we can all enjoy them at the house."

"How much of the city have you toured while here Emelia?" I subtly take a deep breath and hope my face doesn't flush with embarrassment. I can't tell Frida all that I've been up to since Friday.

"Not much. Friday night I dined with Henry and his family. Saturday I was sequestered to the hotel grounds and Sunday was your party."

"The reason why I asked I wondered if you thought it looked much different from when you were here last."

"Maybe at the end of the week we can walk around. But besides your old apartment and your parents' place, my only other vivid memories are Chiriqui and the famous Canal."

As Max drives us out of the city to the highway, Frida points out areas that have been transformed since my previous visit.

"How old are you Emelia? I forget are you my age?"

I smile at her, "I will be thirty-nine until I show my real age."

Victor turns around with a confused look on his face. "How old do I look Victor?" He glances at his mom and then me and blurts out quickly, "Twenty-nine."

I applaud him and say, "I am adopting your son." I high five him showing that I am certainly from an older generation.

"All kidding aside, I am younger than you by three years."

"Oh then you must be the same age as Luca."

How do I play this? "Yes, I think so. Frida you could pass for thirty. It's crazy that you are about to turn fifty. What is your secret?"

She glances at Max, "A loving marriage, a precious son and I enjoy my work."

Max reaches back and grabs my knee. Frida laughs, "*Mi esposo,* [my husband] you have caressed my friend's knee, is there something I should know?" Max quickly removes his hand.

"Papá, before you get us in an accident, please keep both hands on the wheel."

The entire car roars with laughter. I add, "Max, I love you as my friend's husband, but you're not my type." Victor turns around and smiles at me.

"Emelia we'll stop in a couple of hours and get a quick lunch. We won't be eating supper until everyone arrives later, unless you're hungry now." I shake my head, "No, I had a decent breakfast. That should hold me over until then."

"Frida, what is it that you do? You mentioned enjoying your work." Victor turns to me, "It might take my mom the entire car ride to tell you what she does. Be prepared." Frida takes a hold of his shoulder, "Did I say precious son? It's not too late to change that, right?" Everyone giggles.

"Depending on the time of the year, I teach art classes a couple of days a week at a local college. Give tours at the Art Museum as well as the Bio Museum. And volunteer at a children's hospital in their art program. Oh, and I run a small company from home, designing personalized stationery and gifts that I sell online."

"Victor you were so right!" Frida laughs. "My friend, that is impressive and how do you fit all that in?"

"Well, it's easy, each of those don't require a full day's work. They are broken down a couple of hours here and there. I like it, I'm never bored. And I've been at the school for many years, so I'm able to make my own schedule."

"From what I remember about you, I think each of those jobs suit you perfectly. Especially the museum tours. Victor, your mom and I would visit the museums in New York City and I always felt I had a private guide. On my next trip back here, I will sign up for one of your tours and in English of course."

"Yes, I do give tours in both English and Spanish. Oh, when is your next visit?"

I am almost caught, "When you extend the invite."

"Our home is your home Emelia and we'd love to have you again for Christmas. Do you think you can get away again for the holiday?" Beaming I reply, "Yes, I would love to."

Frida clasps my wrist, "Each Christmas when we're together in Chiriqui someone always brings up your name, mainly Henry. We pull out the pictures and the kids ask the same questions. We tell them all the stories and we enjoy some laughs and cherished memories."

I ask, "Victor, tell me your favorite story involving the annual Christmas tree hunt."

Frida and Max laugh out loud. "You remember that?" Frida yells.

"Yes, when your father's car got stuck and the guys had to push it out of the mud or something and then he left Luca on the hill. We had to give him a ride back because your dad didn't want to stop the car."

"That truly happened? I thought my family was telling me tales all these years." Victor exclaims.

"Victor that really happened, I witnessed it myself. The best was watching your Uncle Luca just standing there alone waving goodbye to your grandfather and great grandfather."

More stories and laughs fill the hours until we stop for a stretch, fuel and lunch. For the next segment of the drive, the ladies navigate while the men relax in the back seat.

"I like your modern ways Maximo. I'm impressed you don't mind the ladies at the controls."

"Ah, Emelia, I am still a traditional man in many manners. But over the years, we've made this drive and I'm too exhausted at the end when I drive the entire way. I welcome a second driver, even when it's a woman."

Frida chuckles quietly, "Emelia, don't let him kid you. He handed the wheel over to me just ten years ago. For the previous ten I had to listen to him complain how tired he was and ignored my pleas to share the driving. It was only when he twisted his ankle during one of our hikes he had no choice but to let me drive home."

Max says, "Yes, and you proved your abilities that day."

Frida snickers, "Oh yes, I think I had the longest driving test in the history of driving tests. Six hours convinced him I was at his skill level."

Max clears his throat, "I never mentioned you were ever at my skill level. I simply agreed you could handle the drive."

He reaches forward and caresses Frida's shoulder as he teases. "Good thing you didn't touch Emelia again. Otherwise I would have pulled over and left you at the side of the road." We all chime in with laughter.

I ask, "Any special music requests from the passengers riding in the cheap seats?" Victor replies, "Not really, can you and Mamá tell me again how you became friends? And why I'm only meeting you now?"

I blast the radio and Victor taps me on the shoulder. I lower the volume, "Yes?" I ask. "Come on, I'm serious. Over the years I've heard stories about your visit here, but don't remember how you met. And we've been to New York a few times, why didn't we see you when we were there?"

I clear my throat, "I can't answer that question, maybe your mom and I can start from the beginning and she can fill us in later."

Frida begins by telling Victor about our mutual friend Phil. And when he left to serve in the military, how our friendship developed. And then when she needed to move back home because her visa was expiring. I fill in some blanks with fun stories of adventures. When we are done reminiscing, we notice both Max and Victor napping.

In a low voice I suggest to Frida, "I guess we should stay quiet a bit and let them sleep." She replies in a soft but direct tone, "Emelia, that's a good idea, but I feel I should clear the air about why we lost contact all these years. For I know it was most of my fault and I first want to apologize."

I touch Frida's shoulder, "As much as I appreciate you saying that Frida and maybe one day, I would like to know why; please don't feel like you have to get into that now."

She takes a deep breath and following her exhale begins, "I'm not sure when you and I will be alone again, so if you don't mind, I'd like to explain."

Hesitantly I reply, "Ok, I'm listening."

"When you were here last, for Christmas, I remember how much my family enjoyed being with you and noticed your special connection with Luca. I thought maybe it was because you were both pushed together when you visited for the wedding. I had been distracted with the preparations, then leaving for our honeymoon and my brother stepped up and took care of you. So it seemed only natural that you would develop a friendship."

Frida pauses and then continues, "There were subtle hints though that it was more than that, but I wasn't sure, until one morning when I wandered into your bedroom. I quickly realized my mistake and when I turned to leave,

I thought I saw a reflection of my brother in the mirror. I told myself, I must have been seeing things. And when I returned to my bedroom, I peeked into Luca's room and he wasn't there."

My heart is racing with panic. I don't know what to say, so I just let her continue. "I went to bed, but couldn't fall back to sleep. Emelia, I was confused. So many thoughts crossed my mind. First, I thought, how could you? You were my friend. And you took advantage of our friendship and slept with my brother. I then thought, how could he do that, and in our family's home. I tried to put all that aside and be open to the possibility that maybe you both cared for one another and I should be pleased. If it all worked out, you, my best friend, would move here and we'd be one big happy family. So later that morning and that afternoon, I observed you both. In an attempt that either of you might reveal the nature of your relationship. I was sure you had seen me in your room that morning and I expected one of you would explain the situation. But neither of you did. So, I had to rely on your body language. Although you both continued to show the sweet friendship that I had once thought developed, sadly I let ill thoughts cloud my judgement and convinced myself you both were just carrying on this illicit affair."

Frida becomes silent as she maneuvers around a truck. Settling into the left lane she says, "And after Luca moved back to Panama, Violeta suddenly came back into his life. He called me one day and asked me for advice and what he should do about Violeta. That's when I confronted him about you. He first tried to deny it and when I told him I had seen him in your bed, he brushed it off and said, 'Not everything is what it seems.' I was confused, hurt, angry and disappointed and advised him to try to make a life with Violeta."

I hear Max stretching in his seat. I turn around and his eyes are closed. Looking at Frida, I'm not certain if she wants to continue or does she want me to say something. "Frida that was ages ago, why are you bringing that up now and why didn't you ask me about all this back then?"

"Seeing you with Luca at my party and knowing he was with you on Saturday and he brought you back to the hotel last night, had me thinking about all this. And I sensed the two of you still have that connection. Was it always just physical with you or was it something more?"

Geeze, she gets right to the point. But there's so much more to all this and we shouldn't be getting into it now. I fear our passengers might be listening.

"Frida, don't you think maybe we should talk about this when you and I are alone?" She quickly glares at me. "Alright, I'll do my best to explain, respectably. I just don't want all this getting back to your niece and nephew. Do you understand?" She nods at me.

I lower my voice even more hoping Victor doesn't hear me. "When your brother said not everything is what it seems, he was trying to send you a message in more ways than one. You were right, when you said, that Luca and I developed a friendship during my wedding visit. We had a spectacular time. And we fell in love. But we only kissed, kissed a lot. You knew me back then. I would not have just slept with your brother. We made promises that we'd keep in touch and see what happens the next year. Well, he didn't stay in touch. But then you and I made plans for me to visit for Christmas. And when you thought he wouldn't be there for the holiday, I was sort of relieved not to see him, because I felt like he betrayed me. Yet, he did show up and first acted as if nothing happened. Little by little he won my heart again and on Christmas Eve he promised me that once he moved back to Panama we'd work on building our relationship. Since he promised that to me before and didn't come through I agreed to give him a chance but I couldn't trust him at that point and I certainly didn't engage in what you thought you saw. We simply shared a bed in your family's house."

She looks at me again expecting more I guess. I continue, "And you know what transpired next. I tried reaching out to him and you. He shut me out. I couldn't tell you what he promised. That was our secret. Then you informed me they were getting married. I was devastated when you told me. You and I talked less and less. So I lost our friendship too. I never knew until this past Saturday what actually happened."

I look out the window and we ride in silence for a few minutes. "Frida I never meant to jeopardize our friendship. You were my best friend. But I fell in love with your brother. And he fell in love with me. We just needed to sort all that out before involving your family. We didn't think you saw him that morning in my room. I am so very sorry our actions made you feel that way. I wished you would have asked me back then."

I hear Frida flip the turn signal and feel the car slowing down as she veers us over to the rest area. Parking the car, she unlocks her seat belt and moves towards me and hugs me tightly.

"I am so sorry Emelia; I ruined all of your lives with my foolish misgivings. I feel so terribly about this. I hope one day you can forgive me."

My friend is crying in my arms and I squeeze her and rub her back to console her. "Oh Frida, you didn't know, this is not your fault. From what I understand, there were many people involved with this mess. You are not to blame."

"Where are we? Is it our turn to drive again?" Victor inquires. "Yes, Victor, let's stretch our legs for a bit," Max suggests. Frida and I separate and I hand her a pack of tissues while she looks at Max and nods her head to him. "When we come back, you two can take a break." We both shake our heads in agreement towards Max. And we are left alone in the car to speak more freely.

"How are things now with you and my brother?" Frida asks. I don't know how much to tell her. But I don't want to keep secrets from her. Had we all been honest years ago life may have gone differently.

"We're in a very good place. On Saturday he surprised me at the hotel. And he explained everything to me. Now we hope to make a go of it. After all these years, we still care deeply for one another. But we want to be sensitive to his children. This year hasn't been easy for any of them and especially the kids. So, when we're all together, Luca and I will present ourselves more like friends. And we hope sooner than later they will be comfortable enough around me and accept us as a couple." I think that's all I should say at this point. I don't need to tell her all the intimate details from our weekend.

Frida leans back on the driver's side door and looks out the windshield. Looking at me now, "I can't deny seeing how happy Luca was when you were around him, all those years ago and yesterday when I watched you both at the party. You are right this year has been a rough one. Luca confided in me a few months back, the pain he experienced when Violeta finally told him why she returned to him and insisted they get married all those years ago. He spoke about someone that he loved and hurt but never told me who she was.

I had suspected you were the woman he loved years ago, but didn't have the nerve to bring up your name to him. Mainly out of guilt and my old feelings of betrayal. Emelia, he's been hurt deeply. I can't watch him go through that again. Do you really see yourself with him? And can you take on all the challenges like, relocating, being with his children and dealing with his ex?"

"For the past three days, my mind has been filled with those considerations and many more. He and I have discussed all of this extensively and have come to an agreement. We will take this slowly. I know I love him and he's expressed his love to me. Now it's about making it all work somehow."

She watches me as if I have something more to say. "Can you for one moment just be my friend and not Luca's sister? So I can totally be honest with you?" She nods her head and I continue, "If you only knew how many times I thought about him over the years. I never could have imagined we'd be together again. I feel like all that's happened in my life has brought me to this exact place. Would I have liked to have been with Luca the last twenty something years, shared a life and made a family with him, yes, absolutely. But I would have missed out on the life I did have, so I can't wonder about that anymore. My focus is on the fact that Luca has given me this gift, his love. And I want to love him too. I'm just so afraid that he'll hurt me once again and choose someone or something over me."

"My family is walking back towards us we should get out to use the bathroom and stretch." Opening the car doors I see Max and Victor approaching. Exchanging smiles, Victor says, "Next shift starts in a few minutes ladies, don't take too long." We laugh and reply together, "We won't."

While walking side by side to the restrooms, Frida places her arm around me, "I know we have more to catch up on but I'm glad we cleared the air on this subject." I nod my head, "Yeah, let's not keep secrets anymore; promise?" We embrace quickly. "Promise," Frida replies.

Returning to the car, Frida and I spread out in the back seat. Maybe this last portion of the trip I can doze off. And with my eyes closed, I can think about all that Frida said to me earlier.

"Any requests from the cheap seats?" Victor flashes a smile to us asking. I reply, "I'm open to most anything, plus I think I'll try to nap for a bit. How about you Frida?" She says, "Same with me, I didn't get much sleep last night and a nap sounds great. So I'm good with whatever you both choose."

I roll up my sweatshirt and use it as a pillow against the door. Staring out the window as we pass the cars I try to sort through all that she said. I can see why she reacted that way after finding me and her brother in bed together at first. But why didn't she ever confront me? Wasn't it worth saving our friendship? Why is she only seeing that Luca was hurt in all this? Has she not recognized I too was hurt? I lost two relationships that were so important to me and yet, she's only concerned about Luca. Is there something more that I don't know? Well, I can't figure this out now. I'm sure this will be another late night. As I gradually drift off I picture Luca on the terrace with me this morning.

Chapter 33

OPENING MY EYES I see signs for Chiriqui. My neck is very stiff. Slowly I straighten my back and do a few neck and shoulder rolls to loosen the kinks. With a quick glance towards Frida I see she's still asleep. Catching Max's eyes watching me in the rear view mirror I wave to him. He waves back. After a couple of yawns and stretches I search for my water bottle. Once hydrated I find my mirror in my bag, what must I look like? Yikes, thankfully we'll be arriving before Luca.

I check my phone for messages, hoping to see a hello from Luca knowing that would be nearly impossible since we didn't exchange information. No new texts or emails. Putting the phone away I set my sights on the scenery. My heart pulses faster thinking about Luca and that we'll be together shortly. How will we keep our distance? Right now I want to run into his arms when I see him. And talk with him about what Frida and I discussed. And how much I need him to hold me and tell me he still loves me and all this will work out.

As Max navigates through the towns nothing appears familiar. I was here so long ago. I'm sure to remember the house, the church and the fields of flowers. I hope Luca sneaks us out of the house to gaze at the stars again. I also wouldn't mind seeing the ridge during the day, just to get my bearings.

Frida begins to stir. "We're almost there, I slept a lot," she exclaims.

I look to my friend, "I did too. It was a nice rest."

She asks, "Max, should we stop at the market first?"

"Tío Henry texted and said they did the shopping and they're waiting for us at the house."

"So, let's take the back road, no need to go through town."

Max replies, "Are you sure, I thought maybe you wanted Emelia to see the town."

She looks over at me, "Do you mind if we skip that today? Tomorrow we'll be hiking and you will surely see all of this then."

"That works for me let's take the back road." Max makes a sharp turn and Victor yells, "Woo! Hold on to your seats ladies, it's gonna be a rough ride."

Victor wasn't kidding; the rest of the drive is a dirt road with several bumps and holes to drive around. I can feel the water swishing around in my stomach. Grabbing hold of the door handle to stay balanced, I'm like a kid on a safari ride while looking out all the windows. But each view is the same, trees all around and a dirt path.

A couple of minutes pass and the road feels smooth again. "Do you recognize anything yet Emelia?" Frida asks. "Not really. Maybe after being here a few days, memories will come back to me." Two more turns and I see houses ahead of us.

Frida points, "Just up that way." We're heading up a hill when Max turns the car into a driveway. Another tree lined road surrounds us and a house in the distance gets closer and closer. I notice a white SUV parked near the house. I guess Henry and his family are the only ones here so far.

Max parks behind Henry's car in the very wide circular driveway. I release my seat belt and jump out for a good stretch and fresh air. My body feels so tight after this last part of the drive. Everyone follows my lead and we look like an uncoordinated exercise class.

The front door opens and Henry and his family rush to greet us. After everyone exchanges hugs we all gather the bags and march into the house.

We enter through the kitchen and the layout from here looks familiar, but the interior has been upgraded tremendously. Still carrying our bags, Frida leads me through the kitchen and says, "A lot has changed since you were here before. Over the years, we've renovated and enlarged the house. Luca mostly took care of the changes. He always loves being here."

Henry joins us and he takes hold of my luggage, "May I?" he asks. "I've managed this far, but if you insist, yes, thank you."

"I want to show you to your room and give you the tour." And then he winks at me. I wonder what's up his sleeve.

"You're in good hands Emelia, I think. I'll leave you for now as I go to my room and unpack." Frida walks away from us.

"Let's first start at your room and we'll continue the tour after I drop off your luggage. Luca was right, you don't pack light." He smiles at me.

"Hey, that's not fair; I had to pack for a week." We both laugh as he leads me into what I think is my old room.

"My brother called and instructed me to give you this room."

Once inside I look around. "Who usually stays here? I don't want to boot them out."

"This room had been closed off for years. Mainly it stored all the furniture during the renovations and then it became a junk room. The extension added more bedrooms and the loft is for the kids. This one finally got an overhaul just a few months ago. You might be the first one to use it. I even hurried in here earlier to make sure everything works. I was surprised Luca insisted you take this room."

While placing my smaller bags on the window bench I scan the room quickly. "I think I stayed in this room before, but I'm confused, wasn't the laundry room next door?"

Henry's eyes widen, "Wow, good memory. Yes, the laundry room was the first room followed by this room. But that's been moved further back of the house." He walks towards a door near a corner of the room and opens it. "This room now has its own bathroom. It was the old laundry room and don't worry, this is the only entrance to it. So you will have complete privacy."

I peer inside the bathroom while Henry holds the door open for me, "What a treat. Are you sure I'm not putting anyone out?"

"Emelia, don't worry, we have plenty of rooms. You'll see. Oh, and I should tell you the kids will be surprised to see someone using this room. They always joked that it was haunted or something."

Startled I reply, "Haunted? Maybe I should burn some sage leaves in here to neutralize the energy."

Henry is moving close to the bedroom door and says, "Let me show you the rest of the house."

Before we leave, he backs up and says in a lower voice, "Now after you told me you previously stayed in here it's all making sense to me. I can't wait to tell Olivia. She always wondered why Luca was protective of this room. I was in my own little world back then, what else did I miss?"

I grab Henry before we continue the tour and while I hug him I profess, "You may have fared better than all of us blissfully inhabiting your little world." He grabs my shoulders and looks into my eyes, "Emelia, what's wrong?"

His sincere concern touches me deeply and my eyes quickly fill with tears. I will not crumble right now. Not when everyone is due to arrive. It's just too much to get into with him. And I don't think I should burden Henry with all my thoughts and insecurities.

I nod, "It's nothing. Coming back here brings up a lot of memories for me. And I'm just so happy to be with all of you." He lowers his head and continues, "Don't say it's nothing, I may have been clueless when I was younger, but I know you're holding back. You can trust me."

I exhale, "Your sister opened up to me about some events from our past and I just need to process."

He hugs me tightly and whispers, "This will all work out. You will see. I know my brother loves you and you love him. That is all that matters now. Talk with him later and you'll feel better."

There's a knock on the door and thankfully it's Olivia. She hurries in and closes the door while joining in on our hug, "What's happened?" Henry and I giggle. "Great timing Olivia," I reply and separate from them.

"Frida talked with Emelia about something that upset her and I'm trying to find out and help. Maybe you'll have better luck." I interrupt, "Soon everyone will be wondering where we are and I don't want them asking me questions. So, let's let it go, for now. And let's move on with the tour."

As I try to leave the room, Olivia takes a hold of my hand, "I told you, we're here for you whenever you need to talk. We can easily just get away for a walk or make up an excuse to drive to the market. Yes?" Wiping my face, I nod yes, "Thanks you guys. You're the best." I grab tissues from my bag and erase any remnants from my mini meltdown.

The three of us walk along the main hallway and Henry points out each of the bedrooms. "I don't remember all these rooms. But then again, I didn't frequent them, probably only viewed them on the original tour."

"After Abuela Lily died, Luca had a sitting room converted into a bedroom for Abuelo near to the front of the house. That way he didn't walk down this hallway when he was here alone. But that's changed too. He lives with Raffy and his wife nearby. And when we're all visiting, Raffy brings Abuelo over and he stays with us. It's also a nice break for Raffy and Teresa."

Making our way to the other part of the house I say, "Oh that's wonderful I can't wait to see your Abuelo. How is he?" Henry smiles, "He's old. But he's doing fine. I'm not sure if he'll remember you. He'll just be happy to see all the children."

Walking into the dining area, it looks much bigger than I remembered. But the wood floors and vaulted high ceilings are the same. Henry points out the expansion so that the table fits the entire family. And then he points up to the loft.

"Do you remember the loft?" I shake my head and say, "I don't remember going up there. I just recall seeing it from down here. I didn't think anyone used it back then."

"You're right, it was just for storage. But we had an idea the kids might like bunking together when they're here. So, we raised the roof and now they all have a bed to sleep in. "Want to check it out?" Smiling I reply, "Yeah sure."

The staircase seems almost hidden, located after Abuelo's room and another bathroom. "Now I can see why this room was better for your grandfather. It's so close to the kitchen and the living room."

As we climb the stairs we hear music and laughter coming from the loft. It's funny that we didn't hear them when we were downstairs. We find Mateo, Benjamin and Victor upstairs playing cards.

"What are you playing?" Henry inquires. "Poker," Victor jokes. I smile, "I don't see any money. What are you playing for?" Then I notice a pile of little folded pieces of paper in the center of the table.

"No money is exchanged. We play for favors, chores or snacks and desserts during the time we're here." Victor explains.

I walk over to the table and ask, "Do you mind if I sneak a peek?"

Victor replies, "Take a look."

I grab a folded note and see that it says, *Clean up table after dinner on Monday.* I fold that one and put it back and grab another, *Enjoy three of my cookies,* signed Benny. I smile and put that one back while I look at Benjamin. I take another and it says, *Wake up early first morning to help make breakfast.*

When I put that one back, I ask, "So, how does the chores thing work?"

Victor explains, "We only play for one hour. At the start of the game, we fill out twenty bets each. Let's say I win this game. I take the entire pile. During the next game, I bet some of those. And when the hour is over, we get to keep our winnings. And while we're here, I can give let's say Benny one of the chores to do instead of me doing it."

"I like this game. Who made it up?"

Victor answers, "Me and Jules."

"Oh, so, why didn't you wait for her to arrive to play?"

"I'm just warming them up and we play this game lots while we're all together."

I exclaim, "I love it. Should we leave them alone, the game IS timed?" Henry nods and we let the boys continue their game.

Before heading downstairs, I study this marvelous room and see two bunkbeds in each corner and four single beds paired two by two on each side. The boys are sitting on bean bag chairs and I notice a couple of bookcases crammed with books and games with model planes, cars and ships resting on top. There are a few handmade mobiles, birds and butterflies hanging from the ceiling. I proclaim, "This loft is awesome. I'd want to stay here if I was them. This was a fantastic idea."

Finding our way downstairs, Henry tells me, "We were concerned they'd grow out of it at some point especially Jules, being the only girl cousin that stays here. But she still wants to be with them. I think she likes this home as much as her dad does."

Henry finishes the tour in the living room. "I remember this room but this looks bigger too. Usually when you go back to a place from your past, the rooms somehow are smaller than you imagined." Henry laughs, "You are right, but we enlarged this room too. And when everyone is here, it fills up quickly."

"Well, thanks for the grand tour Henry. I hope I won't get lost. Now if you don't mind, I want to unpack. Please tell Olivia and Frida to get me when they start preparing dinner. I'd like to help."

He nods and says, "Yes, I sure will and Emelia, remember what I said. This will all work out. You belong here with our family. You'll see." I grasp his shoulder and whisper, "Thank you."

Before going to my bedroom I discover the bag containing the flowers from the hotel. I fill up the vase with water, trim the stems and arrange them. Once I'm done I place the flowers on a table in the living room. At first I wanted to place them on the dining room table, but figured they would get too much attention there. While cleaning up the area of the counter I had been working on, I see a slender petite container in one of the cabinets. It gives me an idea. I hurry back into the living room and snag some of the flowers. Two roses perfectly fit in this cute vase and I deliver them to Luca's bedroom. My heart is pounding when I reach his room. Quickly I rest the flowers on his dresser and sneak out before anyone catches me. When I get back to my room, I'm grateful I didn't bump into anyone along the way.

Leaving my door ajar unhurried and alone I slowly look over the room. Two walls still have wood paneling now painted off white and the other two walls are a light shade of blue. Some of the furniture pieces look the same, like the armoire and dresser. I'm not sure about the headboard and nightstands. The bed linens are very feminine with wild flower print and several pillows. Doesn't seem like Luca's style. But what do I know I haven't seen his home yet. I do appreciate the private bathroom. I bring my toiletries and makeup and leave them on the cabinet in there. Back to the bedroom, I unpack my clothes. I set aside the envelope of pictures I brought to show Frida. Swiftly I return to the bathroom to wash and look more presentable for Luca. It has been a long day and right now, it shows on my face.

Chapter 34

FEELING SLIGHTLY REVIVED I join Frida and Olivia in the aromatic kitchen. "Ok ladies, put me to work, otherwise I might fall asleep standing up." They both laugh.

Frida replies, "We thought it was just us, are you tired too? We must be getting old."

I smile and say, "Old-ER ladies, just older."

Olivia instructs, "Ok, we are going for something simple yet satisfying. Do you like chili?" I reply, "Yes, one of my top favorites. Who doesn't like chili?"

Olivia adds, "We've also made vegetarian chili for Julieta."

"That sounds yummy. Can I also try that one?"

Frida says, "Yes, we've made plenty."

"Ok, what can I do?"

Frida walks over to the cabinets, "Emelia, you can set the table, I'll put all the dishes, glasses and cutlery on this counter. There are tablecloths and napkins in the breakfront over there."

I find several types of linens and decide on a navy cloth with a pattern of yellow and orange flowers. Not sure how many will be seated for dinner I grab a stack of matching napkins. Henry comes to my rescue and assists me with the very large tablecloth. We both return to the kitchen and my eye catches some movement out the windows. Henry rushes to the door and says, "They're here. Olivia, please tell the boys to join me outside." She goes towards the loft staircase and I hear her say something while Henry goes outside.

Not sure what I should do, I just grab the stack of dishes and continue setting the table. Counting fourteen dishes I place each accordingly. The very large table allows everyone to have ample space. Returning to the kitchen for the utensils, I first see Claudia and Julieta entering the house. Julieta quickly embraces Frida and they exchange words. Claudia glances at me and I walk towards her and she greets me with a kiss.

"Good evening Claudia."

"Hello Emelia how was your ride here?"

"It was long but my companions made it fun. How was your trip?"

"It was long and I slept for the last half of the ride. The party yesterday tired me out."

Frida tells Claudia, "Mamá, all you need to do is unpack and relax we've got dinner covered tonight."

Claudia kisses Frida, "*Gracias*, it's a pleasure to have you lovely ladies in the kitchen."

"I second that!" Luca exclaims. I didn't even see him enter the kitchen as I was focused on collecting the utensils.

Julieta stands before me and I gently place the forks and knives on the counter, and she attacks me with a very energetic hug.

"I'm so glad you're here Emelia. Meeting you at the party wasn't enough to get to really know my Tía's friend."

I squeeze her and respond, "I feel the same way Julieta, I look forward to getting to know you more over the next few days."

We stand apart looking at one another, "I love the card game you and Victor made up, it's so original."

She laughs, "Oh the poker game. As the oldest of the cousins that stay here, we had our reasons. And it's all in fun. Maybe we'll get the parents in on it too and you of course Emelia." She gives me a sweet half smile.

Julieta skips away with her satchel over her shoulder towards the loft. Luca must have gone back to the car, I don't see him. And then it's a parade of men, young and old carrying luggage and bags filled with more food. I continue with my task and make way to the dining table. Down to the last few place settings I sense Luca standing behind me.

He follows me closely as I lay down the next fork and knife, he whispers, "I want you to know how much I love seeing you in this house again." His voice near to my ear and what he just said sends tingles up my spine. I move to the next plate, he adds, "I've dreamt of this moment. My heart is bursting with happiness."

Continuing to the next seat, he goes on, "Thank you for making this dream come to life." I want to turn and take him in my arms but fear being caught by some onlookers. Shaking slightly, I place the final fork and knife down and back into him gently. He spins me around and gives me a bear hug.

"Great to see you, how was your day? When did you get here?" he says loudly.

With our hearts pounding against each other, I don't want to let him go. But we disengage and I begin placing napkins next to each fork and he takes a stack and follows my direction.

Looking into his eyes, "We arrived a couple of hours ago I think." When we're standing across the table from one another I lean in and whisper, "My morning was exceptional and the ride here, well, it felt like forever."

With him leaning towards me he says, "For me too. I'll tell you more later. Did Henry get you settled?" We finish distributing the rest of the napkins, "Yes, thank you for arranging my accommodations once again." He's finished before me and says, "I'll be back I just need to do a couple of things."

We go our separate ways and I reply, "Sure, see you in a few." Going to the kitchen to get the glassware I turn back and see Luca has disappeared again. He's fast. Done with the table settings I ask Olivia, "What else can I do?"

"Nothing for now, everything is all done, we're just waiting for Abuelo to arrive and then we'll eat. Rafael said he'll bring him by shortly. Just sit back and relax."

Luca is carrying a box into the kitchen. When he places it on one of the chairs he begins pulling out bottles of wine and after he reads each label puts the bottle back in the box. Finally he finds the one he was looking for and locates another and leaves them both on the counter.

He announces, "These should pair well with the chili." Olivia replies, "Luca any wine you choose, I'm first in line to fill my glass." While he's uncorking one of the bottles he looks at her and smiles, "Thanks Olivia." Luca glances at me, "Do you want wine tonight?"

"Yes, sure, from my recollection I never turned down a wine you were offering." He pours wine in a glass and tastes it then replies, "Wow, such nice compliments from the lovely kitchen ladies. We might have to make this a regular thing."

Olivia laughs and adds, "Let's see how you feel about that tomorrow morning when we're watching you and my husband make breakfast for us all."

Luca awards Olivia with a hearty laugh and pours wine in each of our glasses. "Oh very good Olivia, but what I actually was saying, I'd like to see the two of you here in this house more."

Olivia rises from the kitchen stool and walks over to embrace Luca. "Luca you know we love coming here. But with the boys' busy school and sports' schedules and Henry's work, it's not so easy getting away. Hopefully we can be here more this year. How about you, if you visit us in Arizona, maybe that can be a regular thing too?"

They both turn and watch me. I remain quiet while we all look at one another and then I say with a smile, "I didn't say anything, why are you looking at me?"

Luca says while handing me a glass of wine, "Just making sure you're also planning to make this a regular thing." I look to Olivia and then to Luca while lifting my glass to them, "I would be honored."

The three of us clink our glasses together in a group toast, and Luca announces, "To all the beautiful women in my life. Salud! And may they always want to cook and feed me."

Luca takes a sip while Olivia and I burst out in laughter. I have to place my glass back down so that I don't spill it.

Julieta appears and asks, "What's going on? What are you toasting and can I have some?" While her dad fills a glass for her I reply, "Let's make a toast to your dad's playful humor. Salud!" As we all tap our glasses, Julieta blurts, "Him, Papá, he's always so serious."

I finally take my long awaited sip of wine and after the tense drive here I take two more sips discovering all the essences while surrounded by Luca and his family.

"You see, my daughter agrees, my toast was not humorous, in fact I was serious."

Henry enters the kitchen finds himself an empty glass and places it in front of Luca. "What are we doing? I'm starving is there anything to nibble on?" he asks.

Luca exclaims as he passes Henry a full glass, "We're enjoying some wine with the lovely kitchen ladies."

Olivia responds with, "Yes and I told your brother how much we'll enjoy the two of you here in the kitchen tomorrow making us breakfast."

I clear my throat, "I must be honest with all of you, the credit goes to Olivia and Frida, I only took care of the table."

Luca follows with, "Olivia, we might have to rethink the proposal we made earlier. Your so called friend over there is separating herself from the cooking crew. I suspect in case the meal isn't any good."

All of us explode with laughter including Julieta. She taps her glass with mine, "You're right, Papá is funny." And we look at each other while enjoying a sip of wine.

"Tell me what proposal and I'm still hungry," Henry barks lightheartedly. Olivia goes to the refrigerator and pulls out a platter of vegetable crudité and places it in front of Henry.

He kisses Olivia and says, "That's what I was looking for, thank you kitchen lady. And what's this about a proposal?"

Olivia shares with him, "Luca was telling us we should make this a regular thing, you know, all of us being here together at the house. And I told him that's a great idea, but he also should make visiting us in Arizona a regular thing too."

Henry taps his wine glass with Olivia. "Yes, I second that." Julieta announces, "Well, I'll be in New York for the next four years, how about we move this party to New York? You'll come too, right Emelia?"

So touched by how kind Luca's daughter has been with me. I lift my glass to Julieta and the rest of the family at the kitchen counter. "Yes, I would clear my calendar." As everyone takes a sip, Luca and I make eye contact.

While we continue telling stories and sharing laughs I notice Frida and her parents emerging from the corridor of bedrooms and they appear very serious. I wonder if I'm the subject of their expressions, more specifically Luca and me. Why would Frida tell her parents about us? Isn't it our place to discuss this with them? Luca is watching me and I give him a sweet smile. He raises an eyebrow, most likely questioning what I was thinking about. I shake my head subtly at him. And he nods at me. He snatches a celery stalk from the platter and I take a carrot stick.

Claudia and Rico join us at the kitchen bar and take seats on the stools. Frida and Max enter moments later. "Music, this party needs music," exclaims Henry. He and Julieta go to the living room together. Luca says, "I wonder what music those two will agree on." Olivia laughs, "Be thankful my sons are not playing their music."

Rico says to me, "Emelia, we're so happy to have you at our home again. We're glad that Henry convinced you to extend your trip."

"Rico thank you. I'm very happy to be here with all of you. I'm just sorry that your mother is not with us anymore."

He places a hand on mine, "Very kind of you to mention my mother, she liked you too. My father will be joining us soon. We'll explain to him again who you are. But please don't be hurt if he doesn't remember you." I shake my head, "No, I won't be. But thanks for preparing me."

Music fills the room suddenly and we all smile at once. Our DJ's decided on The B52's "Love Shack." And then we see them bopping in from the living room dancing to the fun beat. Even though most of us are tired, I sense this might be a late night.

Victor surprisingly enters the room and joins his dad and cousin. He must have been upstairs with Mateo and Benjamin and now they come into view as well but they walk over to their mom and grab some veggies. Luca comes towards me and instead of asking me to dance he sits between me and Rico. Marcos is the last to join us from the loft and stands between his dad and grandfather. Having not seen him much at the party I get a chance to look at Luca's son now. With his long arms and long legs, I'm sure he'll be just as tall if not taller than Luca when he's done growing. His face actually resembles Rico but has greenish blue eyes and a little chin dimple too. He's wearing his brown hair very short, so I can't tell if he has his dad's wavy hair or not.

Marcos says something to his dad I think he's asking about supper. "Marcos, you remember meeting Emelia at the party yesterday." Luca reintroduces us.

Marcos nods at me, "Oh yes, hello."

I smile, "Hi Marcos, good to see you. Were you playing cards with your cousins?" He looks at me slightly confused. I add, "Victor showed me earlier a poker game they were playing. And I thought maybe they started another game when you arrived."

"Oh yeah, we finally got all our bets on paper but then the music started and Victor left us. We'll play later."

Marcos puts his arm around his dad's shoulders and Luca points to the vegetable platter. His son perks up and grabs some veggies and walks over to the fridge. Luca leans to me, "Usually our first night here is an early one. I think the drive drains everyone."

I ask, "Do you think we should start with dinner then?"

"Yes, plus I don't think Abuelo will eat much this late. I'll put together a small plate of fruit and cheese for him. Follow me and we'll help Frida and Olivia put the food out."

Luca uncorks another bottle of wine and brings it to the table. When he returns he places the box of wine bottles under the little table in the corner and grabs another bottle and leaves it on the counter. He empties the original bottle of what's left into both our glasses. And he proceeds to tell Olivia something, I see her nod yes and opens the fridge door. Between Luca, Frida and I we start a procession line and bring whatever Olivia hands us to the table.

When all the dishes have been arranged, Luca goes into the living room and shortly after I hear a track change. He has put on some dining music. Our dancers boo the temporary DJ's efforts. Olivia announces, "Dinner is ready. Bring your dish from the table and we'll serve you from the stove."

Luca hands me my glass with just a sip of wine left and I empty it before he takes our glasses and sets them down on the dining table and returns with several dinner dishes. He shows his parents that he brought their dishes over and then gestures to me. Olivia begins to spoon out the chili. Luca hands her the dishes meant for Rico and Claudia. She places a small portion for each and looks at them and asks, "More?" They both say, "No, that's the right amount." Luca takes their dishes, adds a scoop of rice on each and brings them back to the table. His parents follow and sit while all the kids are grabbing their plates. I wonder if they have designated seats.

Luca is back and the kids line up. He takes the large pot from the stove and sets it in the sink and grabs another ladle. He and Olivia team up and portion out chili and rice for the hungry recipients as I stand by and watch all the smiling faces pass me with filled plates. Julieta approaches and Olivia points her to the smaller pot on the stove. Frida and Max help themselves as well as the rest of the kitchen duty team.

I follow Luca to the table and he pulls the chair out for me and after I'm seated he sits next to me. He fills our glasses with wine and passes the bottle to Henry. Just as Luca stands to make a toast, the door opens and in walks Rafael and Abuelo Manny. Rico advises everyone to remain at the table and Rafael waves at all of us and walks alongside his grandfather towards the table. He pulls the chair out for Abuelo and when he sits, Rafael pushes the chair closer to the table.

Olivia asks Rafael, "Are you hungry?" He smiles, "If it's what I think it is, yes! I always have room for your chili." She tells him to sit and goes to the kitchen and fills a plate for him.

Returning to the table she brings both Rafael and Abuelo's dishes to them. "*Gracias Olivia,*" Abuelo tells her and touches her hand. She places a tender kiss on his cheek. "*Hola Abuelo.*"

Luca instructs me to fill Abuelo's goblet with a few sips of wine. When I begin to pour the wine Abuelo looks at me and I stop. He says, "*Más vino,*" [more wine] and waves his hand. I look at Rafael and he nods yes. I continue for a bit when Abuelo flattens his hand and says, "*No más.*" I give the bottle to Rafael.

Abuelo takes my hand and looks to me, "*Mi nieto es tu novio, sí?*" [My grandson is your boyfriend, yes?] Luca leans towards me and closer to his grandfather and replies in a low voice, "*Abuelo espero que un día ella diga que sí.*" [Grandfather I hope one day she will say yes]

With that, his grip tightens on my hand and whispers to me, *"Mi chica no le hace esperar mucho tiempo."* [My girl, don't make him wait very long.]

I turn to Luca and am surprised when I see his entire family watching us and listening to what I thought was a somewhat private conversation. I look across the table and find Julieta smiling at the two of us and shaking her head with hopeful agreement.

Luca translates what he and Abuelo were saying. "Abuelo asked if I am your boyfriend and I told him, I hope one day you will say yes. And he said to you, my girl, don't make me wait very long." I whisper to Luca, "Please tell Abuelo, I will say yes now, if I can call him my Abuelo too."

Luca looks at me with sparkling eyes and kisses my cheek softly. He translates to Abuelo, *"Voy a decir que sí ahora, si puedo llamarte abuelo también."* Abuelo takes my hand and gives it a delicate kiss and replies, *"Cuál es el nombre de mi nieta?"* [What is my granddaughter's name?] Henry gets up from his seat and taps his wine glass with his spoon *ting-ting-ting* and yells, *"Abuelo se llama Emelia. Woo Hoo!"* [Grandfather her name is Emelia.]

Abuelo looks to Rafael and gestures he wants to stand. He releases my hand and with Rafael's help he rises to his feet. Rafael hands Abuelo the goblet and we all take his lead and lift our glasses towards him. Luca places his hand on the small of my back.

"Sus ojos expresan un amor profundo que usted tiene el uno para el otro; el tipo de amor que transpira para toda la vida. Debería saber, me sentí así por tu Abuela Lily y todavía lo hago. Emelia quiero darte las gracias por traer la felicidad al corazón de mi nieto. Bendigo este nuevo amor en nuestra familia. Que tengas la devoción, la pasión y la alegría que tuve con el amor de mi vida, Liliana. Salud." [Your eyes express a deep love that you have for each another; the kind of love that transpires over a lifetime. I should know, I felt like this for your Abuela Lily and I still do. Emelia I want to thank you for bringing happiness to the heart of my grandson. I bless this new love in our family. May you have the devotion, passion and joy I had with the love of my life, Liliana. Cheers.]

Luca tells me what Abuelo toasted to us. And when he's done I notice that almost everyone is now standing and clinking their glasses and cheering, "To Luca and Emelia. Salud!" We both stand and tap our glasses with Abuelo's and the rest of the family too. Julieta is standing across the table from us and looks at me and her dad and says, "I thought there was something going on but I wasn't sure. Now I am." She taps her glass with ours.

Luca pulls me close to him and says, *"Bésame mi novia."* [Kiss me my girl-friend.] He kisses me quickly on the lips and we tap glasses and sip our wine. Rafael shouts, "I'm glad I stayed for chili. Although Teresa will be upset she missed all this." After all the excitement quiets down, Marcos implores, "Can we eat now?" We all laugh and pass around the chili fixings.

I'm grateful everyone is so hungry their attentions slowly fade away from us and their conversations move into subjects from vacations, our trekking adventure tomorrow and what's planned for dinner tomorrow night. All the while Luca's hand goes from resting on my knee or rubbing my back during intervals between eating and talking with his hands. I'm thrilled that we no longer need to hide our relationship from his family. I just wonder if Luca should have a talk with his children. Seems like we just dropped this news in their laps and surely they'll have some thoughts about it. Julieta couldn't hide her excitement, so, my guess is she's accepting of all this, but he should talk with her anyway. I haven't been around Marcos much and from the moments I've observed he seems like a nice young man. Maybe Luca was right, when he told me not to worry about his children. Were all my fears about nothing? Can Luca and I finally enjoy life together? Presently, yes, and I will embrace each and every minute.

"Does my girlfriend want more wine?" Luca asks while holding the bottle near my glass. "Is my boyfriend having more?" He smiles and nods. I reply, "Ok, just give me three sips. I want to be in good form tomorrow." He pours a little amount of wine in my glass then whispers, "For you my love, anything." And then he pours just about the same in his glass. "I will take your lead, we will be on the go all day."

As dinner winds down, I notice Victor and Henry's sons exchanging little pieces of paper. Oh, I think I know what they're up to. Benjamin receives one from Victor and he covers his eyes with his hands and passes a bet to Victor and he laughs. Mateo hands each of them little papers and they reciprocate back to Mateo. I see Benjamin talking with Olivia and she nods and waves her hand over the dishes. Benjamin stands and begins clearing the dinner plates from the table. Upon his third trip back from the kitchen, he approaches me, "Are you finished? Can I take your dish for you?" I smile, "Yes I am, thank you Benny. Do you need help?" He smirks and says, "No, I can do this on my own. But thanks. Tío Luca, are you finished?" Luca nods and hands Benjamin the plate.

A few moments later Henry and Luca continue cleaning up the table and I see Victor and Mateo on dishwashing duty. I look to Julieta, "Seems like you're off duty tonight, does that happen often?" She smiles, "Now, that I'm older, yes. But when I was their age, I helped out just like them. I lend a hand usually. Plus I didn't play poker yet."

We both are startled when we hear Abuelo snoring and glance towards him. He's sitting back in his chair with his eyes closed and in deep slumber. I yawn and Julieta giggles at me. I say, "Your great grandfather has got the right idea."

"Yes, I hope to go to bed soon after dessert and our late night walk."

"Late night walk?"

"Yes, my Papá and Tíos would go for a walk after supper when we were much younger but never allowed us to go. And then one night, Victor and I snuck out of the house and followed them. It was so dark and I started getting scared when we couldn't see them in front of us. But we were determined to see this secret place. So Victor held my hand and we started running to catch up. We thought for sure we were going in the right direction, there was only one pathway. Finally we reached this opening at the top and the sky was lit with stars and the moon was full that night. I couldn't contain my excitement at what we both stumbled upon that I twirled around and around and around to take in the magnificent night sky. And when I stopped spinning, Papá was standing in front of me and I almost fainted. He grabbed me in his arms and rested me down on the bench."

"Did you and Victor get in trouble?" She grinned and nodded, "Not really. They were more worried that we could have gotten hurt or lost in the dark. Dads are like that you know. Our moms would have screamed at us. And after that night, they always include us in their late night walk."

"Do you go to the same place each night?"

"Yes. And when the other boys got old enough they were allowed to come along too."

"Do the moms ever go?"

"No, they were always too tired. But if you're not too tired, you can join us tonight."

My heart fluttered, "Sounds like a super way to end the day. If the rest of the group doesn't mind, I'd love to tag along. But I will understand if they don't."

"I'm sure they'll be fine. Plus it will give them a chance to tell you about their first ventures to the secret place. I better go and help with the desserts. Otherwise it will get too late for the walk tonight."

After Julieta leaves me, I stand and grab the last of the dishes and bowls left from dinner and head to the kitchen.

Looks like the young men have a terrific dishwashing system going. I scrape off the dishes before handing to them and they seem pleased at my efforts. Luca motions for me to join him. As I get closer he takes my hand and we dash outside together.

The cooler temperatures awaken me immediately and he rushes us away from the house. "Where are we going?"

"Not far, just over there."

We stop beside a tree and Luca looks back towards the house. "This will do for now." Pressing me against the tree trunk he traces my jawline and lips with his fingers. "I've thought about kissing you since I left early this morning. And when I got here tonight, I couldn't wait to get you alone."

He begins with sweet little pecks along my jaw and when I tilt sideways he treats me to more kisses down my neck. "I want to be with you every second of the day. I can't miss another moment with you. Tell me again, I want to hear you say it to me and only me."

I lean in and kiss his chest over his heart and look into his eyes, "You are awfully hard to say no to. So I guess I have to say yes, my love. Only if you promise never to break my heart again, I will be your girlfriend."

I smile and find humor at the thought of being someone's girlfriend at this age. He hugs me and treats me to countless kisses all over my face. I feel like the cat in the cartoon with the very amorous skunk.

I laugh while trying to push him away. His grip tightens and he stops kissing me. We look at one another and I trace his lips with my fingertips. "I've wanted to do this among other things with you all day." I gently kiss his lips and slide my tongue into his mouth and he accepts my affections with a melodic hum.

We pause after a few seconds and he holds my chin in place, "What other things?" He asks with much flirtation while grinding his hips against mine.

"The kinds of things that we shouldn't be doing with a house filled with your family."

He laughs and takes my hand and suddenly we're on the move. We rush towards the cars in the driveway he raises his right eyebrow and points to the back seat of one of them. I whisper, "NO!" And I laugh.

We run to a barn or shed and he extends his arm like a game show host showing me what's behind curtain number two. "Please no!" I shoot that idea down too.

"My dear, you are high maintenance."

Nervously giggling I say, "Your family would be out here in a second viewing our activities. I am not high maintenance."

He starts laughing and hugs me, "I know I was just playing with you." And whispers, "I promise never to break your heart again and I promise I will have my way with you later."

He kisses my ear and pulls me back to the house with him. My face immediately heats up to a very rosy shade. Lucky for me when we go back inside, nobody is there to welcome us.

First I smell the aroma of coffee brewing and then I hear someone playing the guitar in the living room and notice a platter of cookies and pastries on the counter.

"They're waiting for us," Luca says quietly and still holding my hand he leads us into the living room.

We sit on the loveseat as soon as we enter the room while everyone else has their attentions towards Rico and Marcos sitting near the unlit fireplace each playing guitars. While listening I take the blanket hanging over the arm rest. Draping it over my shoulders, I offer some of the blanket to Luca, but he nods no. Then setting it in place, Luca grips my shoulder with one hand and with the other picks at my hair. He lets go of my shoulder and shows me a piece of tree bark he took out of my hair. We laugh quietly. And I comb my fingers through my locks to make sure that was the only piece. He clears his throat and whispers, "You're fine." I sit back and rest my head on his shoulder. He purrs with contentment and interlaces my fingers with his.

In my comfortable place nestled with Luca listening to the soothing music, I look around to see who else is enjoying this private performance. Henry and Olivia are cuddled on the couch next to Claudia, Victor and Julieta. Across from them I see Rafael, Frida and Max. It's so sweet to see Frida and Max holding hands. Abuelo must have gone to bed and Benjamin and Mateo are missing and most likely are in the loft. The room is softly glowing with the dimmed table lamps and candles of different shapes and sizes scattered along the mantle and coffee table.

I glance up to Luca and see his eyes are heavy with sleep. Settling deeper into the soft cushions I feel my breathing syncing with his. The music begins to fade and when they finish, Victor and Julieta gently applaud their talented efforts. If Luca wasn't holding my hand, I too would have joined in the applause.

Julieta views us and waves to me. I wave back and smile. She gets up and walks over to us. I squeeze Luca's hand and when he opens his eyes Julieta is standing next to him. He and I move to the right to offer space for her to join us. She sits next to Luca and he places his arm around her shoulders while she rests her head on him, he then places a kiss on her forehead. The three of us are closely snuggled on the love seat. This moment was but a dream only twenty-four hours ago.

Rico starts strumming again and Marcos waits to join in. If Luca told me last night the three of us would be sitting together like this, I don't think I would have believed him. I'm so relieved Julieta seems to approve of us being together. I just don't know what the rest of the family is thinking. But I won't let any of those uncertainties take away from this special moment. I close my eyes and let the music fill my mind.

Drifting back to reality, I hear Luca and Julieta whispering. I think they're talking about doing something later. He tells her if she can round up others he will go too. I'm not sure, I missed the first part, but I think they're talking about the nightly walk. She gets up and leaves the living room.

Lifting my head I lean back onto the cushion. "Did we wake you?" Luca asks.

"I don't think I fell asleep, I was floating with the music."

"Oh, that's what you were doing," he smiles. "Do you have the energy to float away with us to the ridge?"

I yawn. "I think I might. Who's going?"

"Not sure, I'm leaving it for Jules to put the group together. But from what I see, I don't think she'll have any success."

Julieta enters the room with the tray of desserts and another tray filled with mugs of coffee. I smile at Luca and say, "You have raised a very clever young lady. She's tempting everyone with caffeine and sugar. Once that kicks in, she won't have any problems finding volunteers." He grunts and stretches back into the spot Julieta vacated, "You may be right. I forgot about the after dessert sugar high."

Within seconds Mateo and Benjamin bolt into the living room looking for some treats. It was as if they had been monitoring the room all along, how did they know? I look to Luca and we exchange smiles. I joke, "I better fuel up so you won't have to carry me back to the house later." Luca stands, "Do you want some coffee?" I nod, "No thanks, but I will indulge on some goodies." He extends his hand and helps me up. We join the rest of the family foraging the dessert tray.

Sure enough, Julieta triumphs and has organized a group for a late stroll. I go to my room first to use the bathroom and grab a light sweater. When I return to the living room, Frida tells me, "If you're tired you can stay back here with us." Julieta enters, "No Tía, Emelia said she's coming, right?" I nod, "Yes of course, plus I need to work off those scrumptious cookies I just devoured." She takes my hand and I smile and wave back to Frida and Olivia.

"I found her we're all ready to go now." Julieta announces to the group already walking up the path. Luca helps me with my sweater as Julieta runs ahead to lead the way.

With the rest of them a few feet away, I ask Luca, "Jules explained to me earlier this walk has become a tradition with the dads and kids are you sure you want me to come along?"

He pulls me close to him as we continue walking and whispers, "I've only shared this place with my brothers and the kids, nobody else. This is our special place too, you and me." He kisses my temple and grasps my hand as we increase our pace to meet up with Rafael and Henry.

"Earlier, Jules told me about the night when she and Victor first followed you up here. Were you surprised?"

Henry laughs, "How could we be, they were so loud. We just pretended we didn't know they were behind us."

Rafael continues, "And they reached the age for us to pass the torch."

"Why isn't Max here?" I ask.

Rafael laughs, "He's afraid of the dark."

Luca replies, "No, Rafael it's not that. We started coming up here when we were young boys after everyone went to sleep. And when we got older, before the kids were born it was just something the brothers did. Most nights it was after we had a few drinks and by the time we set out, Max and Frida were in bed. When Victor and Jules joined us, we then decided we should ask Max to come along. I mentioned it to Max the following day and he pulled me aside to inform me he has poor night vision. But thanked me for inviting him."

I inquire, "Is Victor sad that his dad can't come along?"

Henry answers, "In the beginning he was bummed but has gotten past it."

Rafael interrupts, "I told him no outsiders are allowed on this nightly excursion, just blood brothers and sisters."

Henry questions, "You didn't say that, did you?"

Rafael responds, "Well at first, I wasn't sure he knew about his dad's vision problem. So I wanted him to feel he was part of a special club."

I interjected, "Then he could have asked his mom to come along."

Henry clears his throat and looks towards Luca. Henry replies, "Since we're all being honest here, right? Frida was never interested when it was just her brothers and like we said, most nights she was asleep when we snuck away. Later on when we were all married, we, more like Luca, asked Frida to suggest to the wives, more like Luca's, that this was a brothers' tradition."

I wonder should I be here with them. "So, tonight when Frida suggested for me to remain back with them, I should have said yes?" Luca increases his grip.

Rafael replies quickly, "No, not at all. If Luca didn't want you to come along, you wouldn't be with us."

"Rafael," Luca says sternly to his brother.

His brother continues, "Plus we already know this is not your first foray up to the ridge. Our brother broke the code with you years ago on Christmas night, right? Since we're all being honest."

Luca inhales and replies, "Yes, my brothers, since we're all being honest. Emelia is my past love I told you about that I brought up here and proposed to."

"Yes!" exclaims Rafael and he high fives me.

Henry replies, "Raffy, you just figured that out now?"

He smiles, "Yes, actually yes."

We burst with laughter. The kids who are much further ahead of us stop and look our way. We compose ourselves and walk the rest of the trip joined together with arms around one another. Every so often someone says, "Raffy, YES, actually YES," and we giggle.

Just before we get to the ridge Luca slows us all down, "Gentlemen, please remember to keep this between us. They should believe this is Emelia's first visit here, right?" Both Rafael and Henry respond, "Agreed."

Not long after the brothers promise to keep my prior visit a secret, we arrive at the peak. Luca assists me up the dirt path with his brothers in front of us. The view takes my breath away. It has been too long since I was last here. So much of life has happened since that Christmas night. And yet here I am, with Luca holding hands. I inhale and take in the refreshing night air. Once where there was one bench, now I see three. The sky is so clear with millions of stars and the half-moon overhead.

Strolling over to the center bench, Luca and I take our seats for the late night show. Julieta joins us and sits next to me.

"What do you think of this place?"

"Julieta, I think it's breathtaking. Thanks for inviting me."

"I thought you might like it. You know you can call me Jules if you want."

"I will and please call me Emmy if you want."

Marcos sits next to his dad. Luca asks, "Any of the regulars out tonight?" As Marcos points out constellations to his dad, Julieta talks with me.

"Do you have places at home like this you visit?"

"Well, there's this old observatory in my town. I get to it once or twice a year and it has this tremendous telescope and I spend an hour or two there while the operator points the scope to planets, star clusters and constellations. And there's a place in the mountains where I vacation with my family and at night before going to my room I look up at the sky. Without the city lights interfering, it's an opportune chance to see many stars. But, I haven't been to a place like this at home. I'm sure there are plenty but I'm too scared to find them on my own in the dark of night." Luca squeezes my hand.

"Do you go camping?"

I reply, "I haven't been camping in ages. Have you gone camping?"

"No, we haven't, but Papá said, we'll go next summer after I complete my first year of college. If you're still dating him, maybe you can come too."

I smile, "Yes, that sounds like fun, if we're still dating, I'd like to go." Luca begins to rub his thumb against the knuckle of my thumb. Is he listening to both conversations?

Julieta leans towards Luca, "Marcos when we go camping next year, we'll have a different night sky perspective. You better do some research before we go."

I ask, "So Marcos, the stars and constellations I see here tonight are they very different from the ones I see back at home?"

The two men snicker. Marcos says, "Yes and no. There are many points to consider. If you specifically are saying tonight versus any other night of the year, then yes. Meaning if you were home tonight and called me when I was here and we looked up at the night sky, we may not see the same stars or constellations at the exact moment. Depends on the time of year and since we're north of the equator we see some of the same and we also see more than you do."

Julieta adds, "Sounds like you need to study up on this too before we go."

I laugh, "Yes, you are right. Honestly, it's been awhile since I observed the night sky so far away from home, to wonder about the differences. I'm sure at some point in my school years, I learned some of this, but that was a while ago too."

Luca laughs, "Yes, Emelia, we are old." Now it's my turn to squeeze his hand. And then he adds, "Old-ER."

We sit quietly observing the night sky. Luca tells us, "Marcos has been studying astronomy for many years. And it's become a favorite hobby for the three of us. So recently we've been planning trips to destinations where we can geek out. Like a trip to see the Northern Lights."

Marcos asks, "Would you like to geek out with us too Emelia?"

"I would, but as your sister pointed out, I need to read up on all this before geeking out with you and especially with a view as spectacular as this one."

Marcos adds, "Yeah this place got me hooked and Papá. He knew lots of stuff then, but now, he asks me questions."

Luca laughs, "I know lots of stuff now, but yes, you know more about this then I do."

I say, "I'm sure all three of you can school me on this."

"Tomorrow night, we can come up here earlier and we can show you lots," Marcos announces.

"Tomorrow we'll have a full day maybe we can do this again the next night," Luca suggests.

Julieta then replies, "Ok, then that's the plan."

Henry walks over to us, "We should start heading back, Mateo is about to fall asleep and I don't feel like carrying him to the house."

Marcos stands quickly, "Don't worry Tío; I'll perk him up for the walk back."

"Not too much, we don't want him up all night." With that Marcos runs to Mateo.

Before we walk down the path, Luca and Julieta take my hands and we form a row linked together with the rest of the nighttime explorers. I look to my right and see, Henry on the end followed by Benjamin, Mateo and Julieta next to me. Looking to my left, Rafael is on that end followed by Victor, Marcos and Luca next to me.

Henry proclaims, *"Para todos los que vienen aquí después de nosotros, les deseo una buena vida."* [For all who will come here after us, I wish them a good life.] He raises his hand linked with Benjamin's.

Benjamin replies, "Delicious cookies like my mom's."

Mateo adds, "A soft bed."

Julieta says, "A loving family," she raises our hands.

With my heart pounding, and tears streaming down my face I say, "Pure Kindness." I raise my hand clasped to Luca's he says, "Forgiveness."

Marcos adds, "Knowledge."

Victor says, "Friendship."

And Rafael ends with, "Peace."

As we lower our arms and begin descending to the house, Luca takes my hand to his lips and kisses it gently. When he looks into my eyes he proclaims, "You see, that Christmas night has remained in my heart and I've kept your wishes tradition alive all these years."

I wipe my face and reply, "Luca it was so long ago, I can't believe you remembered. You keep surprising me." He says, "I intend to for the rest of our lives if you let me." Kissing me quickly on the lips we run down the path to the others.

Rafael says goodnight and hugs everyone before he gets in his car. When he embraces me he whispers, "Thanks for coming back to us, especially to my brother." He tightens his embrace. "Thank you for welcoming me back." Before parting he kisses me on both cheeks. Luca whispers, "Enough, she's MY girlfriend." Rafael pats his brother on the shoulder, "Don't screw it up again brother." They embrace. And Rafael drives away from the house. We see lightning bolts in the distance.

Reaching the front door, Henry puts his finger to his lips, "Be quiet when we get inside. We'll see everyone at breakfast." One by one, we go into the house silently like little mice.

Julieta hugs me before joining her brother and cousins in the loft. "Thanks so much for including me tonight, Jules." She replies, "Emmy I'm glad you weren't too tired."

Henry, Luca and I walk down the hallway. I stop in front of my bedroom door, Henry turns and mouths good night and I wave to him.

Just the two of us now standing together alone, Luca runs his fingers through my hair and holds my head in the palm of his hand. "If you want, I'll come back in a few minutes, I just need to change." I nod yes. He leans close and gives me a gentle peck before disappearing down the hallway.

Going through my evening routine I think about all that happened today and how much I need to talk with Luca. Before climbing into bed I switch off the table lamps, but keep the bathroom light on with the door half open to provide a lit path for him.

The bed sheets are refreshingly cool and I'm glad Luca will soon be here to cuddle next to. Closing my eyes while I wait for him I begin to hear droplets of rain outside my windows followed by flashes of light and rumbles of thunder. We got back just in time.

Within a minute or so, Luca turns off the light in the bathroom and he crawls under the top sheet with me and my body is cocooned with his. He whispers, "*Hola mi amor.* I'm so happy you didn't fall asleep." I purr and reply, "With *mi novio* protecting me, I'll soon be in dreamland."

Pushing my hair aside he kisses the edge of my ear then down the side of my neck while his hand travels under my pajama top. He has quickly memorized the pathway to igniting my internal flame. "What are you wearing? It will take me forever to get you naked," he whispers with displeasure.

With the rain getting louder, I shift to face him, "I am wearing slumber party pajamas. Luca we should talk and you promised no funny stuff while we're here."

He removes his t-shirt and says, "I promise my plans for us in the next few minutes will not be funny. We can talk afterwards. Now be very quiet so I can show *mi novia* how much I desire her."

Squirming out of Luca's arms I climb out of bed and walk over to the window bench. "Emelia, come back here," he says in a loud whisper.

"I'll only come back if you don't break your promise." I stand looking out the windows with my arms folded.

Hearing him moving around in the bed, he tiptoes over to me and sits on the window seat.

"Emelia, what is wrong? I remember what we said this morning about not having sex while we're here, but I wasn't sure if you were serious or being playful with me. And earlier when I kissed you outside, I sensed you wanted to be together too."

"Luca, I'm not saying I don't want to have sex with you, I'm just saying, it's not appropriate here, with your family all around." He pats the cushion next to him and I take a seat.

"Mi Lia, the door is locked and my children are on the other side of the house upstairs in the loft. The rest of my family is down the far end of the hallway. We have privacy and if we aren't loud nobody will hear us."

The words from the car ride with Frida keep repeating in my head. "Luca, I have something to talk about with you."

"What else is on your mind Emelia?" Flashes of lightning shine into the windows. Nervous from the storm I say, "Maybe we should go back to bed." He takes my hand and we crawl slowly onto the bed.

Luca puts the pillow behind his back as he sits up resting against the headboard. And I sit across from him with my legs folded. "During the drive here today, your sister wanted to clear the air."

"About what?" he asks.

"About what happened when I was here last and why our friendship ended."

"Emelia, go on."

"She said she saw you that morning when you were here in my bed. Because of that, she was confused which led to bad feelings for you and me. She felt I betrayed our friendship. She told me a few months later that she confronted you about it and your answer was cryptic. So, when she advised you about your relationship with Violeta, over the years she realized her advice was wrong, for she allowed her feelings to get in the way. And that she's sorry that her actions kept you and me apart."

With my concerns aired, I'm feeling tired all of a sudden. I lie back down on the bed and close my eyes.

"And that's why you don't feel comfortable messing around with me?" I reply, "Oh Luca, that's part of the reason. And after all that's happened the last few days, I just need to be alone with you. Not just to mess around, you know."

Luca slides deeper into the bed beside me, "Can I?" I nod yes. Now with his head resting on my stomach I begin to unwind with my love dozing off on me.

Chapter 35

THERE'S A CLAP of thunder and my body startles with the crashing sounds of the storm. Not certain how long we've been sleeping, I try to reposition and realize Luca is still resting on me. Feeling him move from my stomach to his pillow, I say, "I'm sorry Luca." Groggily he says, "Mi Lia, what are you sorry for?" And when his head settles into his pillow I turn sideways to look into his eyes. "I'm apologizing for waking you up just now." He purrs and slowly his eye lids close.

Now that I'm wide awake I lie there admiring my Luca. This man that has promised me he won't give up on us, this man who has opened his heart again to me and this man who proclaimed our intentions to his family. My man that I loved once before and during the last few days I find myself loving again. My man who makes every fiber of my being come to life just when he enters the room, looks into my eyes and says my name. My Luca, who's gentle touch or kiss triggers sensations that I haven't felt in so long.

With my heart fluttering, I lick my lips and take a deep breath. My fingers run through the soft hairs on his chest and he sighs. Slowly my hand travels down from his chest to his stomach and his body stirs. Luca wakes with a full stretch and focuses his eyes on mine.

While my hand continues touching Luca he smirks at me, "Why aren't you sleeping?"

"The storm outside is so wild and getting louder I can't sleep."

"Are you scared?"

My body shivers, I whisper, "No," and I lean in to kiss Luca.

Luca parts us and looks at me and says, "Yes?" I nod at him and say, "Oh yes."

He forces his tongue into my mouth and our hands fumble with the other's pajama bottoms. When I free him from his pants, I feel his desire pressing against my hand and I gently massage him. "Oh mi amor, your touch electrifies me. I must delight in you first."

I quiver and quietly he shifts down the bed raises my legs and completely removes my shorts and panties. The quick bolts of lightning illuminating the room allow me to admire Luca and his next moves. Bringing my legs down he parts them open and I feel him blowing gently on the insides of my thighs as his soft wavy locks tickle my skin.

I whisper, "Oh Luca."

"Yes, Mi Lia, tell me do you like this?" He surges his tongue around and around sucking gently while slowly easing his fingers inside me. Controlling myself not to moan I exhale and inhale deeply.

He halts, "Or do you like this?" Methodically his fingers are circling and pulsing in and out of me as he continues sucking and soon my insides begin responding to him. Between breaths I whisper, "Oh Luca, I like everything you do to me. Please stop, I'm getting close my love."

I rise up and run my fingers through his hair. He whispers, "*Silencio!* Now I know what pleases you, lie back and be very quiet."

He doesn't stop and I can't speak anymore in fear I might cry out and wake everyone in the house. Gripping the sides of the bed while his fingers vibrate and delve deeper and deeper, with his tongue swirling against my very sensitive spot my climax takes over. My body erupts in multiple waves that seem beyond my control.

As the quakes lessen he removes his fingers and slides himself inside me and before I let out a moan he covers my mouth with his. Between the thunderous evening storm and Luca's exquisite seduction my mind and body are somewhere in the clouds trying to recover from the various sensations.

When he stops kissing me, he whispers, "My darling, allow me to show you how much I love you, want you and need you." He glides his hardness in and out of me while sinking deeper and deeper. My body has completely surrendered to him I can no longer resist his need for me as I yearn for him even more.

Leaning up I kiss and nip and lick his chin. Stretching my neck my mouth finds his shoulders and his forearms. And when I reach his nipples I lick and suck and gently tug them with my teeth while caressing his back first with my fingertips and then gently grazing him. I feel my passion building again for him. I move my hands and clutch his curved bottom helping him get closer to orgasm. Wrapping my legs around him, looking into his eyes that are watching me, I whisper, "Luciano, oh my Luciano I am yours forever, I want you now my love."

Mightily and intensely Luca plunges inside me again and again and again. With our hungers near to climaxing he whispers, "Mi Lia, you are the only woman for me. I don't want to live without you. Let me love you like this forever."

And after one more thrust my body shakes as he shudders and our orgasms are only heard by our rapid breaths as the roaring storm outdoors splendidly conceals the sounds of our love making.

Tears are trickling down my face as I recover from another body shattering climax with the love of my life. Luca lies heavily on me and I savor each and every moment of him securely inside me.

Even though we just made love, I'm craving him even more. He and his lanza magnífica have aroused the beast in me. Maybe we should take the mattress off the bed. Or we can attempt other positions around the room. I smile and think of him earlier pointing to the back seat of his car and the barn. Are those options still on the table? And I must rename Luca's lanza. I laugh to myself thinking about that night with Jenene. Actually, that name is perfectly suitable.

He slowly lifts his chest off mine. "Oh, please don't go yet," I beg. Kissing my shoulder, "I'm right here. I won't leave you." When he pulls out of me my body shivers and he rolls me over onto him and holds me snugly to him. Our legs are entangled and I rest my head against his chest.

"I love this chest of yours. And I can't get enough of you tonight Luca."

"Oh, now you know how I've been feeling since I first touched you on Saturday. You are like a drug to me. And now that my family knows about us, I feel free to hug you, kiss you and touch you anytime anywhere whenever I want."

I look into his eyes and kiss his lips. Nuzzling back into my favorite place I listen for the thumping beats of his heart as I glide my fingers against the soft hairs on his chest. Earlier I wanted to talk with him about so much, but now, all I want to do is just be here alone with him sheltered in his arms.

"Emelia, can I ask you a question?"

"Yes Luca."

With his hand caressing my back, "Do thunderstorms often have this effect on you?"

I smile and look at him, "Yes and snowstorms too."

He moans while placing a kiss on my forehead and says, "I'm suddenly thrilled we're here in the middle of the rainy season." I giggle into his chest.

"Mi Lia, before we go to sleep, we should set the alarm." Reality slithers between us. "Is there a clock in this room?" I ask. Feeling like my mind and body are stuck in a trance I can't even remember seeing a clock in here before.

He laughs and yawns. "I don't recall either and I don't want to turn the lights on. Where's your phone? We can use the alarm on that."

Oh boy, reality is now poking at me until I get up to look around. Beginning to get feeling back in my arms and legs, I plan to get out of bed and use the bathroom and then take care of the alarm.

"Where are you going? Tell me where it is and I'll get it."

"I wish I could tell you, but there are a couple of places it could be. Plus I need to get dressed."

"Why get dressed?"

I reply, "In the event someone walks into this room, we should be clothed."

"Nobody is coming in."

"Why are you so sure?"

He announces, "I'm so sure since I locked the door."

"So then why am I getting up?"

He laughs, "You are so cute my love. Either you are very tired or you're in a sex fog."

I growl gently into his chest, "Yes, a little of one and a lot of the other." He tries to move me off of him. "Now what are you doing?"

He takes my head in his hands and before kissing me says, "My sweet, I'm looking for something to set an alarm."

I giggle in mid kiss. "You're making me crazy, I forgot about the alarm, argh!" I bolt out of his arms and into the bathroom.

Closing the door I switch on the light. I cover my eyes with my hands from the terribly bright light as I find my way to the toilet. Contemplating my next move while I sit there and tell myself this room needs a nightlight. Maybe I can get one tomorrow. Washing my hands I glance at my reflection. How come after sex, my hair always look like I just got out of a wind tunnel and his hair stays perfectly styled? As my fingers try flattening my tresses I hear a tap at the door. He'll be blinded if I open it now. I turn off the light before letting him in.

"Are you done? I need to go too. Why is the light off?"

Even when he whispers his voice sounds so stern. "Do you have sunglasses with you?"

He replies annoyed, "No, why?"

I simply answer, "Cover your eyes?"

"Emelia, I know what you look like naked."

I exhale loudly, "It's not about me." I flip the switch.

He covers his eyes, "Why is it so bright?"

I pat his bare bottom, "Blame the decorator for not installing a dimmer or nightlight."

As he relieves himself he says, "I guess I'm to blame. Tomorrow we'll get a nightlight."

"I'm going out please leave the light on until I find my phone or the clock."

Locating my purse on the chair near the dresser, I fumble inside it and feel for my phone. Oh good, it's here. Now I hope the battery didn't drain. Rubbing my finger against the screen, my phone lights up and the battery is pretty full. I hear the faucet running. Quickly locating my pajama shorts and panties on the bedroom floor I turn them right-side out and put them on.

Luca swings the door open more, "Did you find it yet?" I reply, "Yes." He turns off the bathroom spotlight. I use the flashlight on my phone to give Luca some direction.

"Thanks, my eyes haven't adjusted yet for the dark; I still see the glow of the bathroom light in my eyes."

He finds the bed and starts to get in when I ask, "Don't you want your pants?"

With my phone light dimly shining on me, he replies, "It's still thundering outside so I thought we'd try for round two before going to sleep. Why are you completely dressed again!?" He whispers with displeasure.

In my giddy state I let out a squeal of laughter and he shushes me then tosses a pillow at my face. I throw the phone and his pajama bottoms at him as I continue giggling uncontrollably into the pillow.

Every time I think the giggles will cease, I hear Luca's demanding voice in my head saying, "Why are you completely dressed again?" and the wave of giggles takes over once more. Twice I try to tell him why I'm laughing but I have to stop and muffle my silliness with the pillow. I sense he's losing patience and it makes it even harder for me to stop.

Walking over to the dresser, I get a packet of tissues. Blowing my nose and wiping my tears of laughter I see Luca standing near the bed putting on his pajama bottoms. I feel I ruined the mood.

Finally composing myself, I scurry towards him and kiss his shoulder blades tenderly. He tenses with my touch. I rub my face on his back and my hands travel to his front caressing his chest and stomach. My lips continue kissing the line of his spine down to his cute dimples while my hands show him how interested I am to start round two. Slowly I feel his body relax.

"Tell me Emelia, why do you only love my chest?" I purr as I continue touching him. "I love every inch of your body Luca." He hums, "Tell me more."

As the rain storm continues I whisper in his ear while my hands rub his chest, "Well, your chest muscles are impeccably defined and I love that you don't wax or shave away your hair. It's so soft and when our bodies are pressed together I love how it tickles me." He hums.

After I enjoy exploring his chest, my fingers travel to his arms. "Your arms, I think you've gotten stronger over the years." He whispers, "I didn't think you noticed."

"Oh Luca, I noticed." Moving along I say, "And your abs are thankfully no longer an eight pack otherwise, I don't think I'd be naked in front of you." He quietly laughs.

I playfully say, "And your sexy subtle six pack and this trail of hair leading to here…" My fingers continue their journey from his navel to his most playful place. "Brings me to *Him*."

He turns and takes my face in his hands we look into each other's eyes. Kissing my temples and the corners of my mouth, I lick my lips and I feel his tongue searching for mine. My fingers slip under his waistband as he presses his pelvis into me. With my wandering hands I stroke his length with my fingertips and circle the head. He releases a moan in my mouth. While massaging him, I continue, "We briefly had one on one time the other day, but I'd like to get to know *Him* even more." With my fingers gliding along his hardness Luca moans again.

I gradually kneel down and free him of his clothes. Glancing up at him he looks at me with lust. My tongue is the first contact and he exhales with my hands caressing his inner thighs from front to back and my mouth envelopes his mighty magnitude. Meticulously my tongue swirls deliberately around him and when I reach his tip I treat him to a lingering suck and repeat my seduction again and again and again. His body staggers and he pulls out of me.

Racing to the window he tugs the large bench cushion off the seat and places it on the floor. He pulls me towards him and I crawl to the cushion. Kneeling next to me, we begin to kiss. He raises my arms and removes my pajama top above my head. Sucking my nipples my hands find him again. He mutters, "No," against my shoulder and turns me away from him bending me over towards the top end of the cushion. Peeling my shorts and panties down to my knees he spreads my thighs further apart and thrusts into me like a bolt of lightning. Releasing a breath I slide further down the cushion. He catches me and pulls me towards him forcefully. One hand massages my nipples and the other is between my legs. My bottom rocks gently towards him and our bodies sway against the other as his finger increases the tempo on my sweet spot. With my legs quivering, he pulls out of me and slides into me again, I moan. With the pace increasing he hovers his chest over my back and grabs my breasts with both hands. Thrusting into me again and again, I hear the sounds of our bodies pounding against each other and my ache for him continues to build. I can't hold on much longer.

I turn to look over my shoulder and whisper, "Oh Luca, I'm close and I want to see you." He lets go of my breasts, pulls out of me and turns me over to face him yanking my bottoms off entirely. I straddle him and he lies back down on the other end of the cushion. Guiding him into me, his pelvis lifts up and I take over.

Lifting my hips up and down I hear him say, "Mi Lia, I'm almost there and you?" His thumb finds my pleasure spot and with rapid pulses he induces my desires once again until I whisper, "Yes, now, Luca, yes." He sits up and I wrap my arms around him with his hands guiding my hips up and then grinding down taking him even deeper. I muffle my moans into his shoulder as our passions erupt just seconds apart.

He collapses onto the cushion and takes me with him. With our chests heaving against the other I feel completely satisfied and can only think about sleeping. Exhausted I whisper, "Luca, at this moment you have absolutely gratified me."

I sit up and kiss the tip of his nose, "But if we don't get into bed immediately, I might just crash here on the floor all night." He lowers me back down against him and I nuzzle my nose and lips against his neck.

"Wait Emelia, this sensation of your body lying replete on mine gives me so much pleasure. With you I'm beginning to feel like a new man."

I remain silent so we can savor this feeling of fullness, love and elation. As I begin to drift off Luca's fingers dance across my back. "Mi Lia, let me take you to bed."

Slowly I ease myself off of him and when I stand I offer him some help. He squints and smirks, "I'm good, gracias." Once again I gather our nightclothes off the floor. I place his on the bed and I take mine in the bathroom with me.

Entering the bedroom I feel my way to the bed in the darkness. "Luca are you still awake?" He mumbles something.

"Where's my phone?"

Whispering he says, "On the night table."

Crawling under the blankets I reach over to the table and find my phone. "When should I set the alarm for?"

He growls, "Six."

Now it's my turn to growl. "Ok, the alarm is set."

I slide over to him and he opens his arms, "Come closer my love." After we kiss, I rest my head on his chest and we nestle into the other. I whisper, "Luca, you know how to love a woman, this woman." He purrs and replies, "Oh Mi Lia and you know how to love a man, this man."

Chapter 36

THE DELICATE CHIMES sound and within seconds I hit snooze. Luca remains in deep sleep. The early morning sky casts a blue glow in the room. I stroke the back of my hand along his jawline and the stubble tickles my skin. My fingers trace his hairline making elongated circles on his forehead. They continue their path down his nose and rest along his cheek and I sweep his skin back and forth until he makes some movement. He purrs. I continue gently waking him while I delight in watching him.

Licking his lips and then he swallows; and his eye lashes flutter when he opens his eyes. Treating me to an affectionate smile he pulls me into his chest and he purrs again. "I don't want to ruin this moment with you, but the alarm went off about five minutes ago." He kisses my head. "I can linger for a minute or so and then I will leave you." I hug him tightly and breathe in his scent.

"Remember breakfast is around nine. You have a couple of hours to get more sleep."

While setting my alarm for eight I ask, "Are you sure it's nine?"

"Absolutely, 'cause I'm the one making it." He winks at me and kisses my lips.

I moan, "I'm the lucky one today, 'cause I slept with the chef."

"See you later my funny girlfriend."

"See you later my hot boyfriend."

He unlocks the door and opens it slowly. He looks to the left and the right and waves to me as he closes the door gently.

Placing my phone on the night stand, I roll into Luca's warmed section of the bed. The second best thing about waking up in Luca's arms at six in the morning, knowing I have two more hours of sleep.

Chapter 37

AFTER MY SLUGGISH start this morning, I managed to shower, dress and tidy the room shortly before nine. As I walk towards the door a wave of anxiety comes over me. Seems only a few family members don't seem as happy as the others about our relationship. Maybe if I don't make eye contact with them this morning, I'll ease into the day. Inhale and exhale, inhale and exhale, now open the door.

Leaving the hallway behind me, I first see Luca sitting at the table talking with his father and Abuelo with Henry busy in the kitchen. The men appear very serious. "Good morning Emelia," Henry exclaims from the kitchen. With his announcement, the three men look up towards me and Luca smiles. He stands and comes over to me. Kissing me lightly on my lips, "Good morning my love, how did you sleep? Was the room comfortable?" He winks at me.

"Good morning. Yes, very, I could have slept for days in there. How was your rest?"

He takes my hand and we go into the kitchen. He whispers, "Not long enough." Passing Rico and Abuelo, I say good morning to them and they reply back.

"Hi Henry!"

He smiles, "What can I get you to drink?"

I ask, "Juice or water. What are you offering?"

"I've got coffee, tea, apple juice and water."

"I'll have some juice for now. Where's the rest of your family?"

Luca informs me, "Frida and Max have gone for a run. Olivia is upstairs with the boys and Jules, and my mom is still in her room."

My tension eases. "Can I help you with anything?"

Luca caresses my back, "No, we got it all covered. Just sit here and keep us company." He pulls out one of the counter stools for me and I sit.

"It smells delicious, what are you guys making?"

"Breakfast burritos," Henry replies rolling his r's with confidence. "They are quick, easy, healthy and filling."

I respond, "And I bet very yummy."

Luca pours a glass of juice and brings it over to me. Henry slides over a platter with sliced loaf bread. "Olivia made this, zucchini corn bread. Want a piece?"

"Sure, I remember how much I liked the corn muffins she made on my last visit."

Luca passes me a small plate and fork and cuddles me from behind. "This kitchenette has very nice service. I might have to stop in again tomorrow."

Henry smiles and Luca kisses my ear and whispers, "Thank you for sharing your flowers with me. When did you put them in my room?"

I whisper, "Yesterday after I arrived. When did you notice them?"

"Just this morning, I was lying in bed thinking about you and suddenly they were in my line of vision and it was like you were there with me."

I turn and we look into each other's eyes while I caress his jawline. Henry clears his throat so I turn back around and help myself to a piece of the loaf. After tasting my first forkful, my mouth waters with delight.

"This is delicious Henry; I'll have to get the recipe from Olivia." Luca leans over my shoulder and I feed him a piece. As he's chewing, I prepare another on the fork for me and just when I'm about to put it in my mouth he takes my hand quickly and guides the fork to his open mouth. I smile and he runs his index finger down my nose to my lips and I kiss it sweetly.

I say, "I told you it was yummy." Luca begins to boast, "Olivia makes this for me. She knows it's one of my favorites." He feeds me a another piece.

Henry laughs, "No, my brother, she makes it for me."

Rico steps into the kitchen, "My sons, my sons, Olivia has confided to me, that she makes this loaf especially for me."

We all laugh and suddenly Olivia appears. She smiles at us, "What did I miss?"

I reply, "You missed a lot. The men are fighting over your luscious loaf."

Olivia takes the seat near me. "I'm lucky these men are easy to please. Whatever I cook, they devour." Henry brings over a mug of coffee for Olivia and kisses her on the lips.

"Hmm mi esposo, I'm not complaining, but you're so amorous this morning. Maybe we should visit more often."

Henry smiles, "You are most worthy and you should have seen these two a few minutes ago. They're not the only romantics in this house."

While giggling nervously I cover my eyes and turn a light shade of red and look towards Luca. He takes my hand and kisses it. With that gesture, Henry takes Olivia's hand and treats her to a flurry of kisses from her wrist all the way to her shoulder.

She screams, "Henry" with delight. Claudia enters the room and Rico walks over to her and takes her in his arms, slightly dips her and kisses her on the lips.

We all applaud the loving couple. Rico helps Claudia stand up straight, steadies her and takes a bow. "Ladies, my sons learned from only the best." Claudia looking shocked has no idea what's going on.

Shortly after, the kitchen swarms with hungry patrons and the very handsome kitchen crew takes charge and soon everyone sits at the big table with plates filled with burritos, Olivia's delicious loaf and fresh fruit salad.

The conversations are not that easy this morning, they switch from Spanish to English and English to Spanish so rapidly and are talking about a few topics all at once. I'm following for the most part. But am grateful to just listen, observe and dine on the delectable meal that my love and his brother have prepared for all of us.

Seems everyone is energized for the day's activities, when after we finish eating, the kitchen cleanup starts immediately. Marcos and Julieta take charge. Most of the diners bring their plates to the kitchen and scrape them off before handing over to Marcos. I help Julieta with clearing the table and within a few minutes, the kitchen looks like it wasn't used since the night before. Luca comes in from outside and looks surprised. "Wow, you guys are quick."

Julieta replies, "Yes it went faster with Emmy's help."

I smile, "Thanks Jules but you both did the brunt of the work." And I ask Luca, "When should I be ready?"

Luca looks at his watch. "About twenty minutes. Does that work?"

"Yes, it does."

He smiles, "I'll come get you."

Once in my room, I quickly brush my teeth again and prepare my little backpack. Glancing at the clock that I spotted earlier on the dresser I have ten minutes to spare and lie down on the bed. My brief morning nap comes to an end when I feel Luca get on the bed next to me. He first twirls locks of my hair and gently secures the strands behind my ear. Rubbing my neck with the back of his hand it travels to my chest and rests against my heart.

"My love, are you ready?"

I reply, "Mm-hmm."

"I promise later when we get back, you can sleep for a bit before dinner."

Opening my eyes I see him watching me. "So when you say a bit before dinner, define a bit please."

He informs me, "Probably no less than two hours unless the kids entice you to play some games with them."

I think, "If that's the case, I'll plan to sleep for one hour and play for the other."

There's a knock at the door. "Sí," Luca answers and moves his hand away from me while sitting up on the bed.

The door opens and we see Julieta. "The crowd is getting rowdy out here."

We smile at her. She steps further into the room and looks around. Luca says, "Yes, we're good to go."

"Papá this room came out nicely. How was it sleeping in here Emelia, Emmy?"

I joke, "You mean in the haunted room?"

She giggles, "Papá told you?"

"No, your Tío Henry when he gave me the tour."

She looks surprised. "How about when we leave on Thursday, you can tell me why you think this room is haunted. I don't want to know before then."

She sits on the bed with us, "Sure. But I never really thought it was haunted. It just was never used. Where did you stay when you were here last?"

I look at Luca and then to Julieta, "That was a long time ago and your dad has made so many changes to the house. I think either this room or the one next door."

She scoffs, "It couldn't be the room next door, that's a closet followed by the laundry room."

I nod, "Oh, well, I do remember the laundry room and then my room was next."

As Julieta walks around the room admiring her dad's decorating efforts she says, "Emmy then I suppose this must be the room you stayed in, because the old laundry room was where the bathroom is now." I reply, "Then you must be right."

Another knock on the open door and before anyone can reply, we see Victor standing in the doorframe. "Hi, are you ready?" We get up from the bed. With eyes wide open, Victor says, "Ooh, Emmy you stayed in this room last night?"

Luca, Julieta and I look at each other and laugh. "Yes!" I reply. And add, "I don't want to hear about any ghosts until we leave on Thursday, deal?" Victor raises both hands at me in surrender and says, "Deal."

Chapter 38

ONE BY ONE we venture outside leaving Claudia, Rico and Abuelo at home. The group is quite large and Luca told me that we'll be meeting Rafael, Teresa and their daughters when we arrive in town. Luca is walking beside me with Henry and Olivia in front of us. I look to see who is leading the pack. Victor and Julieta are our guides, followed by Marcos, Benjamin and Mateo. Frida and Max are between the kids and us. I try to count heads but Benjamin and Mateo keep weaving and I have to start over. There must be eleven of us now and fifteen in total when we meet up with Rafael. No wonder the cousins enjoy this outing.

Luca's hand brushes against mine and then he interlocks our pinkies. I break the silence, "How old are Raffy's daughters?"

Olivia responds, "They're turning twenty-one this year."

"Oh I didn't realize they're twins."

"Yes, Gabriela and Graciela," Luca tells me.

I ask, "They weren't at Frida's party, right?"

Henry answers, "Right, they went to a wedding on Saturday and they also stayed back here with Abuelo. He doesn't like to make the long drive twice in one weekend."

"Twins always fascinate me or any multiples for that matter. I've only met twins, have any of you known triplets or greater?" They all respond no. I ask, "Which side of the family has twins?"

Henry laughs, "All sides. Well, both sides for Raffy and Teresa. The Morales family has twins on both sides too."

"Wow! What was it like when they were babies, were you able to tell them apart?"

Luca replies, "They were lots of fun especially since they were the first babies for the family. We kept mixing them up. But, that was just for the first year."

Olivia replies, "I'm not sure Teresa would agree with you about twins being lots of fun. Our sons are two years apart and sometimes it was challenging to take care of both. I can't imagine what it would be like with twins especially during the baby stages."

I add, "I know what you mean Olivia, but some parents like the idea of getting through each stage all at once. When I was married, I pondered those same thoughts and also, feared childbirth like most women. Often thinking, maybe it would be better to have twins, so if I didn't want to go through the birthing again, they'd have a sibling. Either way, taking care of children is a lifetime mission."

Henry says, "Too bad you and your ex didn't have kids, you'd be a great mom. How long were you married?"

Luca gently taps Henry on his shoulder and I mouth to Luca, "It's okay."

I answer, "Not very long, on paper a little over a year, but we split a few months before our first anniversary. So we were just beginning our marriage and having children was not the priority those first few months."

Henry says, "I'm sorry Emmy, I didn't mean to put you on the spot. I just remember how good you were with our sons when you visited. And I see how you interact with all the kids here."

Luca slides his hand into mine and holds it firmly. "Henry, I'm open to you asking me questions about my life. For the most part I will tell you and there might be an occasion when I don't want to get into it. And I'll tell you that too." Then I add, "Since we're all being honest here."

Henry stops and turns to me with a laugh and squeezes my shoulder. "I do enjoy having you around Emelia, since we're all being honest. I hope we see you more often now."

I look to Luca and then at Henry, "This is all so new to us and wonderful and complicated. I can't speak for your brother, but I'm trying to figure out how we can make this work. And then I get overwhelmed with all the elements. And yes, I hope to see you and Olivia more often now too."

Luca clears his throat, "And I keep telling you, don't worry. We can make a life together very easily. Just let me show you how."

Henry slows down and walks next to me placing his arm around my shoulder, "Emmy, if anyone can make this work, it's my brother. Listen to him and you will see. You may think this is challenging, but it is not. The hardest part in life, is finding someone that you love, someone that makes it all worthwhile. And you and Luca have that love. I see it and so does Olivia. Just trust it Emelia."

Olivia stops and now we all stop, she says, "First I want to say, we're not going to talk about this all day. Let's just enjoy being together. Second, my husband is right. You must trust this extraordinary love you have for one another and everything else will fall into place around you both. You will see."

Henry steers the four of us into a group hug. Our support circle is interrupted by hoots and hollers from the crowd ahead of us. We quickly react and increase our speed to catch up with them.

"What's the plan today?" I ask Luca.

He replies, "Why, do you have to be somewhere?"

I squeeze his hand, "No place but here. I just want to know to pace myself."

"Uh-uh, soon we'll arrive in town and meet up with Raffy. He usually tells us our next stops. Most likely we'll visit some relatives and friends. Check on them to see if they need any help and they tell us all that's going on in their lives. We'll grab lunch and afterwards make our way back to the house." I nod my head.

"When were you last here?"

Henry turns around and smiles, "We were last here for Christmas. But Luca's been here many times since, working on the house and the guest room."

Olivia tugs on Henry's arm and he turns back around. I look towards Luca and I joke, "Little brothers have *grandes bocas*." [Big mouths]

He nods in agreement, "I was here just last month. But I didn't get a chance to see many of the neighbors, if that's why you were asking."

"Yes, actually that was why. I remember the house a little bit from my previous visit. I vaguely remember something where we ran out of water or had to wait for the well to fill up. Or maybe it wasn't this place."

"You might be right. We had that repaired. We also have a backup system just in case."

"From what I see now, the house is perfect for all your families. Seems everyone fits comfortably and all the renovations were well planned out."

Luca says, "I always loved coming here when I was a little boy. And all the fun memories I had with my siblings. Of course the Christmas with you was extra special. So when my kids were born, I made sure they also created memories up here with the family. Their mom didn't like it much and before they were teenagers, she started to only come here for Christmas. And I would take them here once a month and for their school holidays. She said she liked having the break for herself and I enjoyed being with Julieta and Marcos without worrying she wasn't having fun."

I add, "So a win-win for everyone."

"I guess under those circumstances," he replies with a slight lilt in his voice.

"I'm glad you've taken care of this house. Last night you had four generations under one roof. You must realize the lifelong memories you're all making here at this home. And you all should be proud. These days, it's not easy keeping families so connected. But you seemed to have managed to do just that with such ease."

Henry turns around, "If it's safe to talk now, I'd like to add, Emmy it may look easy, but over the years we had our challenges. The renovations have added to the ease, and it also takes certain personalities to like this lifestyle. And right now, it's a perfect blend." He smiles and continues, "You know I'm right brother."

Luca replies to his brother, "Yes, not everyone likes the rustic appeal or the family togetherness."

Olivia turns, "In the beginning I had a love hate relationship with this place. I hated the kitchen. And not long after, the kitchen was renovated."

Luca remarks, "That expense was a win-win for everyone." He winks at me and rubs Olivia's shoulder.

She laughs, and says, "The privacy, there was none. But then with the expansion and locks put on some bedrooms doors, I began to feel more at home here and started to love being here."

Henry jokes, "Yes, I loved it even more and then Benjamin was conceived. Made in Chiriqui."

Luca clears his throat, "We got the point, *gran boca*." And Olivia and I giggle.

Coming around the curve I see a town in the distance. Olivia announces, "Emelia we're almost there, you see?" Jokingly I reply, "Yes, I see. And thankfully, otherwise Henry might be inclined to tell us when and where Mateo was conceived."

Olivia turns to me and says, "Aha Emmy, you feel my pain." Henry replies, "Hey, I'm just being honest and Emmy is practically family. She was commending us on making this house a home of special memories, I thought she should know, how truly special some of them are."

He stops to hug and kiss his wife. Luca puts his arm around my shoulders and treats me to a few sweet kisses and whispers, "I love our special memories too." I kiss him on the lips and softly say, "Me too."

When we continue walking towards the town I remember the song Henry played for us last night and giggle. I joke with Henry by singing to him some of the lyrics from the song "Love Shack." Henry spins around and gives me double high fives, holds my hands and looks to his brother, "I love this girl, Luca she's a keeper. As soon as your divorce is final, you better marry her. In fact you need to lock it in before."

Olivia grabs her husband again and says to us, "I'm sorry; he's out of control today."

Luca pulls me close as we keep walking and whispers, "My brother the romantic, with his advice to lock it in." I giggle and hoping to change the subject I say, "Oh is that Raffy over there waving at us?" Olivia answers, "Yes, I've never been more grateful to see him."

All the cousins, aunts and uncles are exchanging hugs and kisses. Even though we all saw Rafael last night he's the one they mainly flock to. Teresa pulls me over to her, squeezes me tightly and whispers in my ear, "Rafael told me the surprising news. Welcome to our family. I'm sorry I missed all the excitement last night. We'll make up for it today."

I'm feeling a bit awkward I wonder what Rafael exactly told his wife. To make sure Teresa knows Luca and I are just dating I quickly say, "Yes, last night was a big step for us telling everyone we're dating."

We separate a bit and she smiles at me and replies in a gentle yet determined tone, "I've known my brother-in-law for many years and what you have together is more than just dating. I can understand why you want to take it slowly. That ex of his is not an easy person and she'll try to make his life miserable. Don't you worry about her, with Luca's wealth, integrity and love for you he'll make sure you have a wonderful life together without her interfering."

Suddenly my mouth feels dry. What is Teresa talking about? What don't I know about Violeta? All along I've assumed since the divorce was her idea she was fine with it and happy to make a life with her boyfriend. What hasn't Luca told me?

"Now I've worried you. That was not my intent Emelia. Since you saw her at the party the other day, I thought you knew about her ways. I just wanted to assure you not to be concerned with Violeta."

Rafael interrupts us, "Hello Emelia," he says while hugging me. Immediately I reply, "Raffy it's so good to see you again. Please introduce me to your daughters." Figuring his wife will stop talking about this once we're surrounded by other family members.

Rafael leads us towards the twins and I glance around to find Luca. His back is to me when I see him talking with his children. With my heart pounding nervously we approach the girls and I promptly mask my unease with a smile.

"Graciela and Gabriela I'd like you to meet a delightful friend of our family, Emelia." I look them both over and smile, extending my hand first to the lady on the right, "Hi, nice to meet you." She replies back, "Nice to meet you too, my name is Gabriela but most call me Gabby." I do the same with Graciela.

"I met your parents years ago, before you were born. It's a joy to meet you both." I study the girls as Rafael explains my connection with the family to them. They are the same height and body shape, tall and lean. Gabriela is wearing her dark brown hair in a ponytail that sits high on her head. Graciela is wearing her equally dark tresses in a right side braid. With their hair pulled back I notice their facial shapes differ slightly. Graciela's is long and slender where Gabriela's is more rounded. Their eyes are a gorgeous blue like their mom's and their lips are beautifully plump like their dad's.

"And last night Tío Luca shared with the family that he and Emelia are officially dating. And if everything works out, she will be your new Tía."

My cheeks heat with embarrassment and I feel hands grabbing my shoulders from behind and hear Luca's voice, *"Hola mis sobrinas favoritas."* [Hello my favorite nieces.] He lets go of me and embraces the girls together. After an exchange of greetings Luca takes my hand and says, "Did Rafael introduce you?" I smile, "Yes he did." Luca pats Rafael's shoulder and says, "Now brother, tell me where are we going today?"

We walk over to the porch and sit on the steps. Although I hear Luca and Rafael discussing the plans for this afternoon I'm caught up in my thoughts to actually listen. I reach into my backpack for a water bottle. After taking a much needed sip, I stash it away in the pack.

"Emelia, do you want to use their bathroom before we go to our next stop?" I nod and Luca takes my hand and leads the way into Rafael's house. When I'm finished I find Luca in the living room waiting for me. I ask him, "Do you need the bathroom?"

"I used the other one down the hall, but thanks. Come here." He takes me into his arms, kisses my forehead and I rest my face against his chest with my arms around him. Breathing in his citrus musky fragrance to calm me he begins to talk while rubbing my back.

"I know my family can be overpowering but know it comes from a good place. They're trying to make you feel like you're one of us. The last few months when I was coming here to the house, Rafael and I got closer. And I told him some things about you and me from before. He wasn't surprised because he was around us more than the others. So he's happy for me that you're back in my life again. If they're making you feel uncomfortable, I will tell them to stop."

I look up to him and he takes my face in his hands and runs his fingers through my hair. I share with him, "They're just being who they are and I can't ask you to make them someone they're not. I love that our relationship is out in the open and they feel compelled to verbalize their acceptance. That's a very good thing. I'm sure we will be old news in a couple of days."

He leans down and treats me to a very short yet passionate kiss. When he finishes I smile at him. He flirts, "Just a sample of what to expect tonight when we're alone again in your room." I lick my lips and reply, "I'll be thinking about that kiss all day." He swiftly plants two more kisses on my lips and whisks us out the front door.

The younger ones have started walking through the town when we get outside. Rafael gives his directions, "The kids will meet us in an hour at Tío Cisco's house. We can get started on his projects before they get there."

The four couples quickly pass the shops and food places and arrive at Tío Cisco's house located just a quarter mile from town. Luca explains Tío Francisco is Rico's oldest brother and has experienced some health issues the last couple of years and needs assistance with household tasks.

When we approach the house I notice a man sitting on a chair on the porch. His nephews greet him first and the man welcomes them with a huge smile. The ladies all stand back near to the front door waiting for an opening to say hello. Luca helps Tío get up from the chair and Rafael hands him a walker. Tío looks a little like Rico, he may have been taller, but he's leaning on his walker. And his striking white hair reminds me of Abuelo. As Tío steps gingerly towards us, each of the family members embraces him and he says something to them separately.

When it's my turn he looks at me with his dark brown eyes and smiles. Luca comes right away and stands beside me. *"Tío Cisco, esta es mi novia Emelia."* [Uncle Cisco, this is my girlfriend Emelia.] I extend my hand and say hello. He takes my hand and pulls me close to him for a hug. I was surprised by the firm grip and strength of his gesture that I stumbled slightly with the walker between him and me.

"Bella, Bella Luca. Sé amable con el corazón de mi sobrino. El es muy querido para mí." [Be kind with my nephew's heart. He's very dear to me.]

Rafael holds the front door open and we follow Tío into his home. The ladies take direction from Teresa while the men follow Rafael and Tío. When the kids arrive at Tío's house, team Teresa managed to put clean linens on his bed, tidy up the kitchen, bathrooms, sitting room and communicate to the kids to stop off at the market and purchase groceries to fill up his refrigerator and pantry. Olivia wished for another hour to whip up a dish or two to leave with him. But Rafael was concerned with the weather and said we had two more places to visit.

Saying our goodbyes to Tío Cisco, Luca holds my hand as we walk away. I felt like we made a real difference for a man that at some point in his life was young and vital as we are today. My eyes tear up agreeing with Olivia's wishes. Maybe she and I can sneak away tomorrow and prepare some meals for him.

I let go of Luca's hand to search for a tissue. When I finish dabbing my eyes and cleaning my nose, Luca holds me close while we keep the pace with the rest of the group and he whispers, "*Mi cariña* [My darling] your heart is as compassionate as mine. Maybe you and I can visit Tío Cisco on another occasion so you two can get to know one another." With my arm around Luca's back I grip his hip with my hand and reply, "Yes, I'd very much like that."

And then I think about when I visited for Christmas. "Luca, when I was here before, we went to one of your uncle's homes on Christmas Day. I recall he opened his house and served so many people that day. Which uncle was that?"

"Oh Emelia, you have some memory. That was Tío Cisco. He and his wife did so much for the people here. Now that she has passed and his health has declined, he moved to a smaller house and well, he can't do much for himself let alone the people they once supported. That's why my family and I try to care for him whenever we can, so that he can live comfortably and with little worries."

"Luca you are all so thoughtful and generous. I'm feeling very fortunate to be included in your family."

"Mi Lia, after all my terrible mistakes, I am the fortunate one."

Our grand troop of fifteen is heading to the next destination. "Who's next on the list?" I ask Luca. He replies, "I'm not sure in which order, but we'll be stopping at Yolanda and Consuela's homes. They are my Abuela's friends and their husbands passed a couple of years ago. They don't have as many chores as Tío Cisco. Mostly they just want to see all the kids and hear about their lives and give them sweets.

We swoop into Yolanda's home first. After she says hello to everyone, Luca introduces me to her. For a woman that boasts about her youthful spirit at ninety years of age she doesn't look a day over seventy. She stands with terrific posture at about five feet high with a slender petite body, white as snow hair pulled into a bun and with light green eyes. Yolanda's beautiful face shows minimal signs of her age. I wonder what creams she uses. After our introductions she hurries into the kitchen with the speed of a six year old. Within seconds, she's offering us all a tray of goodies. Henry takes the tray from her and places it on the coffee table then Rafael takes Yolanda by the hand and escorts her to a chair in the middle of the living room.

Everyone takes a rest on chairs, couches and the floor. And the conversations start and are mostly all in Spanish. This gives me a chance to look at each and every one of Luca's family members as they take center stage telling Yolanda a story or two. There is lots of laughter especially when Benjamin and Mateo stand up and delightfully act out a story for all of us to enjoy. Luca translates for me a little after each person shares something while Yolanda observes us.

I hadn't realized there was some order to this game when suddenly all eyes are on me. Luca says, "It's your turn." I look at him slightly puzzled. He places a hand gently on mine, "Go ahead and I'll translate for you."

I hear Yolanda clear her throat and she says, "Luca does your friend speak English?" I look to Yolanda surprised that she speaks fluently in English. "Yes, Yolanda, she speaks English and very little Spanish."

She smiles at me, "Oh this will be a nice treat for me. I haven't spoken English in a while and welcome the challenge. Go on dear, please tell me, how you've come to know Luca."

I take a deep breath wondering where I shall start. "First Yolanda I want to thank you for hosting us today in your home. I met Luca through his sister Frida. Many years ago when Frida lived in New York we became friends. And when she returned to Panama, met Max and soon after they got engaged. She invited me to their wedding in Valencia. I previously met Henry when he visited Frida in New York and then I met the rest of the family including Luca during my stay in Valencia. Luca was kind enough to keep me company while Frida was wrapped up with the wedding and honeymoon activities and before I went home a friendship developed. The next year I came here to Panama and Chiriqui to spend Christmas with everyone. Over the years life sort of got in the way and caused us to lose touch. Except for me and Henry since he and his family live in Arizona and I would see them occasionally. A few months ago Henry called me and invited me to celebrate Frida's birthday. And I accepted and arrived last Friday. The next day Luca surprised me and kept me company once again."

Pausing I look to Luca and he smiles. I continue, "It didn't take us very long to realize the connection we had years ago was still there and very much worth pursuing at this point in our lives. And now here we are."

"Thank you Emelia for telling me this story, I'm curious as to why you and Luca lost touch years ago, but that's not important now. It's beautiful to see you've been blessed with a second chance." I exchange smiles with Yolanda.

Luca quickly starts his story. And little by little I begin to understand he's telling Yolanda about the night he and I went to the movies in Valencia. Right when he tells her the movie was in Japanese with Spanish subtitles, the room erupts with laughter. Once everyone composes themselves, Rafael ends the round with a story.

Luca and I are the last to bid farewell to Yolanda. She hugs us both and tells us, "When you are next here, I want just the two of you to visit so you can tell me more about your love story." She smiles and kisses us both goodbye and we leave her porch hand in hand and meet up with the rest of the family for Consuela's house.

When we arrive at Consuela's just a few homes down from Yolanda's we are welcomed by a houseful of guests. Some are sitting on the porch and others are inside. Most of us remain outside so we don't intrude on Consuela's party.

Frida and I are waiting together near the bird bath located in the front garden. Besides a few words exchanged over breakfast and when we were at Tío Cisco's, this is the first chance that we are sort of alone, since our discussion in the car yesterday and Luca's announcement last night. And I'm not certain what to say. I sense Frida along with her mother are still not very happy with our current status.

I begin with a neutral question, "When you come here do you always visit with family and friends?"

Frida nods and replies, "Usually yes, other times we host a lunch at the house and people stop by during the afternoon. It's like an open house gathering." She looks away and then adds, "I bet you didn't plan on doing this on your vacation."

I smile, "I seemed to remember going to people's homes on Christmas Day. So, I figured we might be doing the same again. As far as helping out your Tío, that was a gratifying experience."

Max ambles over to us. "The kids are getting hungry, how about you ladies?"

I grin and say, "The cookie I devoured at Yolanda's made my stomach crave for more. It's been growling ever since, so yes."

Frida laughs and says, "Me too. Did they suggest where they want to eat?"

He tells us, "Gabby told them about a new place that opened, said she knows the owners and they're waiting for us. It's not far from here."

Luca appears and advises us, "Let's grab lunch and if we're feeling up to it later and the weather holds up, we can visit Consuela on our walk back home." He takes my hand and we are mixed in the middle of the group with Frida and Max just in front of us.

Luca says, "I heard Gabriela has organized something delicious at a new place for us. I'm so hungry I could almost eat anything put in front of me, how about you?"

I giggle, "Yes, we were just saying the same thing. I'm famished."

During our short stroll to the restaurant Luca tells Frida, Max and me about what was happening at Consuela's house. I'm grateful he was able to fill the silence with a light topic.

Gabriela directs us to the side entrance to the restaurant. A young woman greets Gabriela with kisses and she leads us all to the outdoor dining area. As we flow into the courtyard, Gabriela introduces us each to our hostess

Giuliana. We take our seats and Giuliana announces that Gabriela has chosen the menu for today's lunch and shortly she will bring out the first course. Two waiters appear with trays filled with cocktails.

While I wait for my drink I take in the décor. We're sitting on a collection of rattan chairs and benches adorned with navy and turquoise striped seat cushions. There are trellises situated along the perimeter of the dining area that have sheets of cloth with circular shapes sweeping underneath and with each gust of wind they wave overhead producing a cool breeze to the patrons beneath. Luckily we're sitting under these trellises and I'm appreciating the shade and cool breezes. The tables in the center have turquoise umbrellas to shield them from the afternoon sun. Lanterns hang along the back brick wall and tall lampposts are positioned intermittently throughout. I can imagine how romantic this place looks at night.

Sitting at the head of the table, Rafael stands and taps his glass with a spoon to get our attention. Giuliana and a couple of waiters appear in the doorway with trays filled with dishes for our first course, but remain still as Rafael begins speaking.

"First I'd like to toast my lovely family including you Emelia, for our productive morning; second, to our daughter Gabriela for making our lunch arrangements at this superb restaurant; and finally to Giuliana and her team for preparing and serving us this soon to be delicious feast. Salud!"

We raise our glasses and tap them with each person near to us. As the plates are distributed to each I discover we're dining on Greek cuisine. And my stomach flips with excitement. Each of us has a sampling of three of my favorites on our dishes I don't know where to begin. My mouth salivates after each forkful of the divine salad with olives, feta cheese and tomatoes, the slice of spanakopita, followed by a three bean salad. This crowd went from chatting wildly to silence once the food was placed in front of them. All I hear are the flapping sheets above and cutlery gently gliding on the dishes. Everyone appears as hungry as me and the delicious delights put in front of us are a fine reward for the busy day we just accomplished.

Upon finishing my second cocktail, I reach for my water glass. I was so thirsty earlier that I downed the first drink and within seconds, a waiter presented another. Feeling the effects of both drinks, I decide to continue with water the rest of the meal. Not sure why they hit me so quickly, could be the lack of sleep, the three mile walk into town or the drinks were practically all alcohol. The waiter returns with a third and I politely refuse but Luca offers to take it for me. I smile at him when he takes a sip from the glass.

He whispers, "Is my girlfriend drunk?" I giggle and squint at him, "No, but if I have the third drink I certainly will be."

Offering me a sip I give him a shocked look and whisper, "Is my boyfriend trying to get me intoxicated?"

He nods and says, "I don't recall ever seeing you tipsy. Come on, let's have fun today. We're just going home after this."

I shake my head, "We still have to walk all the way home."

Again he offers me the glass, "Precisely, after that walk you'll be clear of mind and ready for your afternoon nap."

I take a gulp of water and reply, "You are a terrible influence."

He places the rim of the glass on my lips and says, "Just share this one with me."

I give in and with my slightly parted lips he tilts the glass and my boyfriend smiles while dispensing a swig of booze into me.

The second course is equal in taste to the first and upon completion I excuse myself to use the restroom. Olivia accompanies me and when we get inside, I determine we're alone.

Taking care of business, Olivia says, "How many drinks have you had?"

I reply quickly, "Ugh, two and a half. What were they?"

She laughs, "I don't know, but I feel the same way."

At the sinks, I glance in the mirror. My complexion is rosy and my hair is out of control. The humidity has made me look like a wild woman.

Looking at Olivia, "Why can't I have your hair? It's as straight as it was when we left the house this morning."

She looks at my hair and begins to laugh. I pretend to be shocked and insulted. She places her hand over her mouth and tries to apologize. Taking her by the elbow I drag her out of the bathroom while she continues giggling. Clearly the drinks affected Olivia too.

Returning to my seat next to Luca I quietly observe everyone at the table. And I spot Olivia laughing with Henry while pointing to her hair. Henry looks at me covers his eyes and shakes his head. A giggle releases immediately and Luca leans to me, "What is so funny that has my love laughing all by herself?"

I smile at him and take his hand in mine, "Seriously, of all the women in the world, why do you want to be with me? Look at my hair."

He begins to laugh as much as Olivia did just a few moments ago. I let go of him and hide my face with my hands and Luca puts his arm around my shoulder and draws me close to him. "Mi Lia, I wasn't laughing at your hair. I was taken by surprise with your question. I was about to tell you all the reasons why and then you were focused on your hair. Making me realize, my love is a little drunk. That's why I was laughing. You are so adorable."

Coming out from hiding, Luca offers me the water glass. I take a big gulp and say, "I may be a little drunk, but even if I was sober, I'd still comment on my wild hair. You don't mind if I rest my head on your shoulder for a moment or two as I envision my awaiting nap and shower." He kisses my head and says, "Not at all mi amor."

A second wind rushes through me after Luca and I shared our ice cream dessert. He's looking relieved that I'm energized for the walk home. I'm sure my quiet respite a while ago had him thinking of alternate ways to get me back, since he was the one pushing me on the third drink. Leaving the restaurant we all thanked Giuliana and her crew.

"How are you? Are you up for walking?" Luca asks.

"Yes, I can't wait to walk off that most delicious lunch and dessert. We have to go back there one night. It's a great place. What do you think?"

He grins, "Yes, yes whenever you want."

Our pace through the town seems fairly quick and when I think we're reaching the end, I ask Luca, "Would you mind if I stop inside the store, I've run out of water and I'll need some for the walk back."

"I don't mind at all, it's a great idea. I'll get some for both of us." He yells ahead to the group and asks if they want anything. Most say no except for Henry as he points to Olivia.

I sit outside on the bench when Luca goes inside. His family continues moving along. People watching while I wait for Luca I'm surprised by the hustle and bustle in this little town on a Tuesday afternoon. I set my sights to the other side of the road, when I notice a woman standing in front of a shop across the way looking directly at me. And suddenly I realize this is not just any woman, it's Violeta.

Behind my sunglasses, I don't think she knows that I've spotted her so I turn my head slightly to the right while watching her from the corners of my eyes on the left. What is she doing here? This can't be her. I only saw her quickly the other day, I'm sure it's someone that looks like her. Why would she be here? I continue watching her watching me. This is so bizarre. I wish Olivia was here with me now. A hand grabs my shoulder and I practically jump off the bench.

"Emelia it's just me, ready?" I look for Violeta when I stand and I don't see her anymore. "What's the matter, what are you looking at?" Luca asks. I scan the people on the street and she's disappeared. I grab the bottle from his hand and pop open the top swiftly and take a swig.

"I don't know, but I think I just saw Violeta. Or someone that looks just like her." He asks, "Where?" I point to the shop she was near and neither of us sees her now. Confused and slightly disappointed I say, "Let's go and meet up with your family."

Luca grabs my arm and hands me a little brown paper bag. I look at him curiously and peek inside. "Aha, a nightlight, you are the best." I give him a quick peck on the lips. We catch up to Henry and Olivia and Luca hands them a water bottle.

Luca and I don't discuss the possible Violeta sighting for the rest of the trip back. I'm grateful, for I don't want Julieta and Marcos hearing about it. Not that it's a bad thing it's just confusing to me after Luca said she didn't like coming here. Who knows, maybe she's away for the week with her boyfriend and they're staying somewhere nearby.

When we finally reach the homestead I graciously excuse my departure and head to my bedroom. Upon entering the room I go immediately to the bathroom and plug in the nightlight. After using the toilet I wash my face and hands and prepare for my much needed snooze by stripping down to my undergarments and slip on my robe. Opening the bathroom door I am pleasantly surprised to see Luca sitting on the chair in the corner of the room.

"How are you?" he asks. I smile while lowering the window shades, "I'm feeling tired. Just looking forward to some sleep. How about you, you must be tired."

"Yes, I am. I hoped maybe we can siesta together."

Popping two aspirins followed by a sip of water I scramble onto the bed, "I'd like that as long as we are just sleeping. But what will your family think? Should we keep the door open?"

He joins me on the bed and we cuddle, "Right now, I don't care what anyone thinks, I just want to be alone with you in my arms as we fall asleep." We exchange kisses and within a moment or two we drift off.

Chapter 39

Opening my eyes I see that it's still daylight, oh good, I haven't slept the night away. Closing my eyes I check with my hands to find my sleep-mate. With him not nearby I indulge in a full body stretch. Realizing I'm lying diagonally across the bed, I wonder what happened to Luca. I couldn't have shoved him off the bed. I whisper, "Luca, Luca, are you here?" Rolling over to the edge I check the floor. I'm relieved when I don't see him suffering on the hard wood. I check the other side just to be certain and he's not there either, I let out a sigh. I guess he went to shower. I must have been in a deep sleep, I don't remember him leaving. Checking the clock it's almost six-thirty. Stretching once more and feeling invigorated by the hour long sleep I make my way to the shower.

Applying the finishing touches of the most minimal makeup application there's a knock on my door. Before I have a chance to get to it, the door opens and Luca enters. Quickly he closes it behind him and embraces me and deeply inhales.

"Mmm you smell so scrumptious I don't want to share you with the others just yet."

I giggle and take in his fragrance. "You smell very yummy too." I squeeze him firmly and ask, "Did you sleep well?"

"With you in my arms my love, I always sleep well." He kisses me passionately.

When we part I mention, "When I woke you weren't here, when did you leave?"

"I'm not sure a little after six. I released you and then you rolled over and spread out across the bed. I got up and left you alone. I showered and when I came back you were showering. Desperately I wanted to join you, but figured I better not."

I nod, "Yes, good behavior, we've already broken a few rules. Let's not push it."

His hands slip under my skirt, grabs my bottom while his pelvis presses against mine. "Oh, we're pushing it again tonight. So you better leave that armor in the drawer later." I smile and add, "You better hope for another thunderstorm."

After a quick peck I say, "You have a way with my body."

He murmurs into my neck. "I want to have a way with your heart too."

I kiss him fervently. Splitting us apart Luca begs, "Stop or I'll have to take you now and neither of us will be quiet about it."

I take his hand and lead us to the bathroom, "Let's do a kiss check we don't want to look that obvious."

Luca splashes water on his mouth and then points to his very evident enthusiasm and says, "Got any tricks for this?" I look into his eyes and brush my hand against him, "I can think of some for later, but for now, try cold water."

He points at me to leave the bathroom, "You are not helping." Before exiting I say, "I can tell you what caused my laughing fit last night, that's a mood killer or possibly seeing your ex in town." He growls, "Both seem to be working, get out." Luca closes the door and I walk away giggling.

Alone in the bedroom I search for the envelope of pictures I brought from home. Hopefully catching up Frida about my family will alleviate the friction between us. Applying some lip balm, Luca comes back into the bedroom. "Ready? Please keep your distance for now. And at some point I do want to know what caused you to laugh hysterically. I was jealous."

Chapter 40

THE FAMILY SEEMS scarce when we enter the dining area and I only see Henry and Olivia busy in the kitchen. They greet us with smiles. "How was your rest Emelia?" Olivia asks.

"So good, I needed that and now I can help you in the kitchen and party later. Did you get to sleep at all?"

She nods, "Yes, between those drinks we had and our morning activities, I was a walking zombie."

Henry laughs, "She was even talking in her sleep. We'll have to find out from Giuliana what was in those drinks."

I laugh, "Do the Morales brothers want to get their wives intoxicated again?" I put my hand to my mouth and exclaim, "I mean women, their women."

Luca takes my hand and rapidly places several kisses on it when he whispers, "You said you're my wife. I will drive there now and buy a pitcher of those drinks for you ladies. So I can lock it in."

I laugh out loud along with Henry and Olivia. Hugging Luca I whisper, "You are so funny. Oh, is it safe to touch you again?"

I hear a laugh erupt from his chest. "Yes."

Henry points to his brother, "You see, I got you thinking."

I clap my hands twice, "Olivia put me to work, enough lounging around here. And Henry, hush."

Luca swats my behind, "Ok mi esposa, I mean my woman, get busy in the kitchen while the men search for something else to do." He winks at me.

After the brothers leave us, I ask Olivia, "Where is everybody?"

She hands me two types of salad greens, red peppers, grape tomatoes and hearts of palm. "Can you make the salad?"

"Yes, point me to the bowl."

Olivia takes a huge bowl from the cabinet and I start to wash the greens in the salad spinner. She tells me, "Frida and Max are still in their bedroom. The kids are in the loft. And Claudia, Rico and Abuelo drove to Tío Cisco's. Claudia prepared some meals for him and they're dropping them off. They should be back for dinner later."

"Oh, that's great Olivia. Now we won't need to do that tomorrow." She nods, "Yes, I'm thankful he's taken care of."

While I'm at the sink, Olivia stands close and says in a low voice, "I noticed you and Frida are not so talkative. Anything I can do to help?"

"It's that noticeable? Thanks for offering, but I think she and I need to find our own way back again. Hopefully between tonight and tomorrow we'll begin to reconnect. With what she told me in the car yesterday and then Luca telling everyone we're an item, she's put some distance between us. I sort of understand why, but I'm sure we can work all this out. And there's Claudia. I can only imagine her reasons for disapproving our relationship. Years ago, I felt she picked up on our attraction and wasn't thrilled then."

Taking my frustrations out on the salad spinner, I'm sure the greens are spun dry and I begin slicing the palm. Olivia folds her arms and leans close, "Trust me, Claudia has her reasons and they're not all about you. She's against the divorce, they married in the church and she believes they should stay married. She's angry with Luca for going ahead with it. She still keeps in touch with Violeta. Is convinced they will get back together. She never thought Luca would start up again with you thus causing all her plans to be ruined and you are also divorced."

Olivia reveals all of this so quickly to me that when it settles in I'm shocked and my mouth pops open. Olivia touches my chin and pushes my mouth closed.

Tossing the greens and sliced palm in the bowl, I wash the red peppers before dicing. "Stay strong Emelia, Luca wants only you. If you hesitate or push him away, he might stumble and fall back into his old ways and follow his family's wishes. You don't want that for him. He was miserable. I can't see him that way again. That's one of the reasons why Henry is being so silly around you both. He's got good intentions but is trying to be playful to get Luca to seize the moment."

I look into her eyes, "Dare I ask how everyone else feels about this, all of this?" Rinsing and drying the tomatoes, they get added to the big bowl.

"That's the amazingly strange part about this, all of this. Everyone else including his children wants to see Luca happy except for his mother. She's siding with the church over her son's happiness."

I nod my head and blurt out, "This has nothing to do with me personally; if she doesn't support the divorce, she'll never support her son being with anyone other than his wife. I thought she just didn't like me."

I look into the sink and turn off the running water, I whisper, "Olivia, promise me you won't tell anyone besides Henry, but I thought I saw Violeta today in town."

Her mouth pops open. I raise my hand to her chin and gently close her mouth. "I promise, I may not even tell Henry. Are you sure? Where, when?"

I continue, "It was when we stopped to get water. Luca went into the store and I waited outside on a bench. After looking around at the people passing in front of me, I glanced across the road and there she was. Or some-one that resembled her. Standing in front of one of the shops staring at me, I pretended to look the other way and she continued watching me until Luca came back. Then she disappeared."

Olivia seems concerned, "Did you tell Luca?" I nod yes. "What did he say?" I shake my head, "What could he say, he didn't see her. After the drinks I had, he probably thought I was just imagining things. I let it go and then we joined you."

While I clean the salad spinner and strainer, Olivia paces the kitchen and then stands close to me, "I bet Claudia has a plan. I wouldn't be surprised if we see Violeta in this house before we leave on Thursday."

Confused, I say, "But Luca told me she hated it here. Why would she come now?"

She grabs my shoulders, "To put a wedge between the two of you. If you loved Luca before and you love him now, don't let them push you away. You must assure Luca that you love him too. And he will stand up to them. But if he doubts your feelings at all, he may cower to them."

My head is revolving like the salad spinner. I thought we had time to work on us, build this relationship. This week with him has been fun, but I don't know how we'll be in the day to day. Olivia motions for me to sit on the kitchen stool, "Tell me what you're thinking?"

Not sure where to start with her. I rapidly reply, "This is happening all so fast. He's been very understanding about giving me room to decide. I thought we'd try making this work as boyfriend and girlfriend before taking more committed steps. Are you suggesting he wants more from me now? And if I don't, he may not go forward with the divorce? That's crazy. We know so little about one another."

I place one hand over my eyes trying to work out some type of strategy. Ugh, strategy, I sound like them. This is about two lives, actually four when you count his kids. We just can't jump into this so recklessly because his mother and his ex are pressuring us.

Olivia removes my hand, "I don't think you have to commit to marriage just yet with him. But you have to assure him of some kind of future. And should Claudia or Violeta talk with you, be sure to hold your ground and tell them you are serious with Luca. Do not waver otherwise they'll use that against you with him."

I shake my head, "You make them sound like monsters. I can't imagine they'd talk to me."

Olivia clutches my wrists, "I want you to be ready in case they do. And if Henry and I are around, we'll support you and Luca and stand up to them. Let's hope it doesn't come to that, as this might divide the family."

I look at her shocked, "Divide the family? How, it was just Claudia not wanting the divorce, right?"

Olivia says, "I'm just saying, there will be friction between you, Luca and Claudia and then Rico will need to be the peacemaker or side with his wife. Luca was talking with Rico and Abuelo earlier and they agree with Luca. Maybe Rico will find a way to convince his wife."

I stand, "I can't talk about this anymore. Otherwise I'll be sick when I see Claudia later. I'm going to my room to count to one hundred or a thousand. And then I'll be back." Olivia hugs me before I have a chance to bolt. She whispers,

"Remember we are here for you. After all Luca has done for his family we want you both to finally be together. I believe you and Luca will work all this out."

I sneak away into my room, close the door and find my way to the window seat in the dimly lit chamber. While my eyes focus on the trees outside, I try to make sense of all that's going on. I partly feel responsible for all this animosity between a mother and son. Had they given him better advice years ago, maybe now we all wouldn't be in this predicament? Divorces happen. I thought Violeta wanted to end the marriage. What's happening now with her to want him back? Luca hasn't told me any of this. Maybe he's not as concerned and he's moving ahead no matter what. So, maybe I don't have to make this decision by the end of this week or sooner. He knows my feelings. It's only been three days, he can't expect more from me. Why has Frida been distant? Is she aware of her mother's intentions? Luca and I are not the enemy here. We're just trying to get back what we lost.

Don't cry, don't cry, don't cry. Inhale and exhale, inhale and exhale. We are a united front, Luca and me. I've got his back and he's got mine.

I use the bathroom before going back to Olivia and while washing my hands I think about how moments ago I proclaimed the value of cold water for other fixes. A wave comes over me, Luca and I will be just fine. We've been given a chance to make this all as it should be now and forever. It has to work, I have no doubts. We were perfect for each other back then and even more perfect now. I apply another layer of lip balm and before leaving I look around this room that Luca so carefully prepared for me, where we made love in last night and slept peacefully together this afternoon. Never again will we allow anyone to stand in our way.

Closing the door behind me I'm feeling more confident as I head back to the kitchen. Olivia is placing two large pans in the oven when I go to the sink to finish cleaning my mess from earlier. But I see the spinner and strainer drying on the rack. "Thanks for finishing up for me." She pats me on the shoulder, "With pleasure."

"Did I miss anything?"

"Not really, Henry came by and I told him to go back to Luca. I didn't want Luca wandering in looking for you. Everything is all set here now. We can go find them if you want."

Before leaving the kitchen I inquire with Olivia, "You said something before about Henry, and having seen Luca miserable for so many years as one of the reasons why he's advising Luca to seize the day with me. Are there other reasons?"

Olivia tilts her head and looks to the floor. "Emelia, Luca is a very proud man surrounded by a family of proud men. So, you must promise me, you won't tell anyone I shared this with you." I nod, "I promise Olivia."

"When Luca moved back to Panama all those years ago, it was to be closer to his family."

"I know that, he told me."

"But did he tell you why?"

Whispering, "He mentioned they depended on him but he didn't elaborate."

Olivia looks at me with concern, "Well, Henry was still in college, Rico was working at another job earning half his previous salary, Raffy was just beginning his teaching career and Nicky, well, he was interning in the states."

Looking into Olivia's eyes I say, "So when he told me they depended on him, they actually were financially relying on him?"

Olivia nods, "Yes he supported his family during a critical period. Eventually they all pulled through but he's never accepted any payment in return. And sadly this year and since you arrived, we're all just realizing how much he sacrificed when he agreed to get back with Violeta and marry her."

I sit on the kitchen stool stunned by Luca's devotion to his family. Olivia holds my hands with hers, "Now you know what truly happened. And you also know why, we want you both to finally be together and live the life you should have had."

Tears streaming down Olivia's face I say, "Oh Olivia, I never knew to what extent his family needed him. Pride, they should all be proud of themselves now and for all they endured."

Olivia wipes her tears and says, "I agree, but you know these men. Now let's go be with them." She smiles at me and I nod and we join them in the living room.

Luca pats the seat next to him on the couch. I sit with him and he places his arm around my shoulders. "I was just about to open a bottle of wine, will you have a glass?" I nod yes. He gestures to Henry and Olivia and they too will have some. "Save my spot, I'll be back." He kisses my forehead and leaves the room.

Frida and Max join us and sit on the couch across from me. "Did everyone sleep this afternoon? Or are we the only lazy ones?" Frida asks.

I laugh and reply, "I slept for a good hour and then showered. I'm feeling revived." Olivia adds, "Us too. We're getting old." We all laugh.

I stand and ask Frida and Max, "Do you want any wine? Luca just went to the kitchen to open a bottle or any other beverage?" Frida puts her hand on her forehead, "I'm not drinking tonight. I still feel a bit woozy from lunch today. What were in those drinks?" I giggle, "How about you Max, wine or something else? I'm up so I'll be happy to bring you back a drink." He smiles, "I'll have whatever Frida is having." Frida replies, "Two waters please." "Ok, I'll be right back. Anyone else want water?" Henry and Olivia raise their hands.

I meet Luca in the kitchen. He's arranged four wine glasses on a tray and is uncorking the bottle. "Missing me already?" he asks. I touch his hand, "Always. And I'm here to bring in some water for the group. Frida and Max are up and they don't want wine. Is there another tray? I think I'll need about five cups or six if you're having any."

He hands me the tray of wine glasses, "Bring these in and leave them on the table and return with the tray. I'll begin filling a water pitcher." I tease, "Ah, you're handsome and smart. I'll have to remember to add those to the list." With an amusing tone he responds, "If you weren't balancing that glassware I'd smack your very tempting bottom." He waves me away. I place the four glasses on the coffee table and hurry back to the kitchen. I grab the envelope of pictures and the wine bottle while Luca manages the tray with water pitcher and cups as we join the family in the living room.

I start pouring the water into the cups and pass them around while Luca takes care of the wine. Henry asks me, "Hey, how is your mom? She looked great when we saw you both last."

I smile, "Thanks for asking Henry. She's puttering along. You know she's about to turn eighty-five.".

"Does she live near you Henry?" Frida inquires.

He laughs, "Yes, very close, we realized many years ago. I still remember that day when you called me Emelia." I look at him slightly confused and then I nod when I remember what he's alluding to.

"Your dad was a big surprise to me. I still laugh when I think about him and how I found them." Frida interjects, "What are you talking about?" Henry looks at me, "Do you want to tell them or can I?" I suggest, "I'll start and then you take over, ok?" He nods.

"So, this was after a severe rain storm. I heard from my parents from what I remember on their mobile phone not long after the storm wiped out the power and they said they were doing fine. But I couldn't connect with them for two or three days after that. Figured they couldn't charge up their phone, right. And that's when I reached out to Henry."

He eagerly continues the story, "I think you emailed me and then called me. Either way we finally spoke on the phone. And you asked me, if I could drive over to their place to check on them and have them talk with you on my mobile. So, I drove over with Benny and after we parked the car, began to search for their apartment. We didn't need to look for too long, as we approached their place, we saw people sitting on chairs outside of their homes enjoying the cool weather. We told them who we were looking for and they directed us. I knocked on the door and your Dad opened it. I quickly re-introduced myself and Benny and your Dad immediately hugged me and insisted we go inside. When we went inside we saw your Mom and she was so thrilled to see us. I explained why I was there. Your Dad offered me a cup of espresso. Looking at him confused he pointed to this device that campers use and your Dad was making espresso on this portable stove top grill. Immediately I thought Emmy did not need to be worried at all and began to laugh. I dialed your phone number and handed the phone to your Mom, while your Dad and I sat back and enjoyed a delicious cup of espresso." Everyone was left smiling after Henry told the story.

"I loved going to your home Emmy, especially when your whole family was there. In some ways they reminded me of my family. And they always treated me like I was related." Frida informs the group. "Your parents were always cooking something delicious in the kitchen. Tell me, how is everyone?"

"Well, I brought a few pictures, that way you can see how they look now." Frida gets up and sits next to me and Luca on the couch. She immediately recognizes each of my family members and then I inform her of the new additions.

The final picture is of my family on vacation in the summer. "This was the last time we all were together for vacation." She laughs, "Why were you all cracking up?" I giggle and stand up to explain. "Well, the friend that was taking the picture was being very precise about our positioning and our smiles. And after the first picture he took of us, his wife who was standing near to him suggested he takes another. So as he started counting from one to three, his wife lifts up her shirt to flash us and we all burst out with laughter. Thankfully, she was wearing her bikini top underneath."

Frida passes that picture around first and each time someone views it they laugh too. Frida says, "Your Dad looks good in that picture. He was always so funny and welcoming to me. I'm sure you all miss him."

My eyes water a bit, "Yes, he's incredibly missed. It's always so touching when people go out of their way to tell me how much they liked him. I mean he was my Dad, so I thought he was the greatest man on Earth. Even now, after so many years have passed, people will tell me how much they miss him and tell me a story. It's still a strange feeling how one day a person who was in your life since the day you were born is no longer there. So, I tell myself that he's just a phone call away."

Luca passes me a tissue box from the side table. I look at him and smile and mouth, "Thank you." Frida snatches a tissue from the box along with Henry and Olivia. Olivia dabs her eyes and says, "I met him that day when you all came to our house and I remember him as such a kind and warm gentleman."

"Did he continue painting? I remember we had that in common," Frida asked. "Yes, he painted a lot. When you come to visit I'll show you some of his art." Frida says, "Henry told me that when he saw you a few years ago your Dad had passed, but he didn't know why, would you mind telling me?"

Uneasy about how much I should include, I begin with, "I couldn't tell you exactly what occurred in my life two weeks ago. And yet, the last week I had with him, I could replay each and every moment. But I will spare you all the details."

I pause, take a sip of water and then continue, "For a couple of months towards the end of that year, he had been in the hospital for a week at a time and then would go home and a week or two later, go back in. So after the New Year, he was admitted once again to the hospital. I planned to visit them when he was about to get out, so I could help him recover at home. Arriving a couple of days early I met him at the hospital and he looked great. Except physically his legs were weakened by all those hospital stays and the medications he was on. Other than that, he had a terrific appetite, his spirits were high and he was looking forward to going home. They suggested he transfer to a rehabilitation facility so that he can get more hours of physical therapy to improve his strength. Sadly, after one night at the facility, he called home the next morning, I answered, and he begged to be brought back to the hospital. My mom was out and I told him we'd get there immediately. When we arrived, his face looked gray and he told me they hadn't given him the proper doses of medication that he needed. He suffered from lung disease and the levels of medication that he required, could only be administered in a hospital setting. We had him transported back to the hospital and when he was in the emergency room his doctor provided the meds to stabilize him. The doctor pulled me aside and informed me that my dad does not have a DNR, do not resuscitate, on file and that we should discuss this with him. First I thought, are we really at that point? And second, let's get him feeling better before we slap him with this. He'll be sure to think he's dying and won't have the will to get better. I called my brothers and they arrived the next day."

Luca places his hand on my knee and I grasp it with both of my hands and continue, "The following three days we all spent together in the hospital with him talking and laughing and just being a family. Making plans for his recovery, getting another facility lined up that can give him the meds he needs. And my brothers left on Monday and I left on Tuesday with plans to return the following week to check on him at the new place. I even recall speaking with him while I waited on the tarmac at the airport for my flight to take off. Joking with him about a certain physical therapy exercise that we called, butt clenches. I ended the call and the flight took off. I flew the day of the President's Inauguration. Every television screen on that plane was tuned to the ceremony. Anyway, after touching down and in the car on my way home I called him again and he sounded in good spirits."

Pausing, I take another sip of water. "The next day, while I was at work, my mom called and said that my dad signed the papers to be transferred to hospice care. He was convinced that if he couldn't live outside of a facility, then life wasn't worth living at all. I understand that now just not when it was all happening. She passed the phone to him and I tried to talk him out of it, but his mind was made up. Later that evening I called him at hospice and I spoke with him."

After a brief pause I continue, "When people wish they could have had a chance to say goodbye to someone they loved, they don't know how truly earth shattering it is, when you actually are afforded that chance. Ending that call was the hardest thing I could do."

Luca puts an arm around me and Frida places her hand on my shoulder. I make use of the tissues on my lap and pass the box around.

After wiping my face, I add, "Wait there's a happy part." They all smile at me with tear filled eyes. "He died the next day. That's not the happy part." I smile and say, "You see, my Dad, to me had such a tender unique voice. When we talked on the phone or in person, most times he had a happy voice and an infectious laugh. And if something was really funny to him, he'd have his handkerchief out wiping his tears. Anyway, a couple of months passed and I kept thinking how much I missed hearing his voice. One night when I went to sleep, I dreamt about him. In the dream, my family and I were all out at my parents' house and the telephone rings and I pick it up. I said, 'Hello' and it's my Dad and he's calling from Heaven. I remember saying things like, 'How can this be, they let you make a phone call?' And he said, 'Yes, I'm allowed to make one call.' I told him it was so great to hear his voice and that I missed him. He asked if he could talk with the rest of the family and we all passed the phone around. And then I got another chance to talk with him before hanging up and I remember I asked him, 'So can you tell me what is it like?' And he said, 'It's the most glorious place you can imagine. I'm having a marvelous time. And they keep me busy, busy, busy.'" I pause, "That's a phrase he would always say. So, that's the happy part. After that dream, although I miss him very much, I know that he's waiting happily for all of us to join him one day and he's just that phone call away."

Frida passes me the glass of wine and after I take a sip she takes the glass from me and takes a sip too. I smile and say, "Now Henry, after I've brought the whole room down, I'm hoping you can finally tell us that story that had you laughing so much at Frida's party, that you couldn't even verbalize it."

Henry raises his wine glass to me and I reach for mine and we tap glasses. He smiles and says, "In honor of your Father. Yes, I will try my best along with the help from my wife and tell you all what we had to endure at the airport a few weeks ago."

Henry looks around the room and takes a seat on the couch next to Max and across from Frida, Luca and me. And he asks Olivia to sit with him on the couch. "Ok, now, let's pretend we're all sitting in the waiting area at the boarding gate at an airport. Bench seating and we're here and the passenger we encountered is sitting across, like where you three are, got it?"

And we all nod. Max says, "What should I be doing?" I giggle. "You're good just pretend you're reading a book." Max takes his two hands and simulates holding a book. Frida says, "Which one of us is that passenger?" Henry nods his head, "Oh, Frida and Luca, move away from Emelia. Like to the other ends of the couch. Emmy is the outrageous passenger." I laugh out loud and blurt, "Thanks Henry."

With all the characters in place, he starts, "So, we're just waiting for the boarding process to begin. When this woman strolls into the gate area with her bags and sits across from us. I don't think much about her and I continue reading the paper and Olivia is reading a book. A couple of minutes go by when she unzips her luggage and rummages through her things. All the while she's talking with someone on her phone. As she searches through the luggage, she begins placing clothing items on the empty seats next to her. Other passengers arriving to wait at the gate pass her and need to walk around her open bags and she apologizes to anyone who wants to listen."

Henry alters his voice to impersonate an American female, "I'm sorry that I'm making a mess, but someone packed my things for me and I'm trying to organize them. My sister went into early labor and I'm racing home to be by her side."

We all giggle at his near perfect impression.

"I continued reading my paper or pretending to, while making funny faces to Olivia." At this point, Henry and Olivia show us what they were doing and we laugh. "I tried not to look, but I couldn't help it. The woman begins this odd display of dressing and undressing in front of us all. I was actually impressed by her flexibility."

Frida laughs, "Flexibility, what the heck was she doing?" I add, "Don't ask me to undress in front of all of you. I'm just representing her location."

Henry goes on, "She removes her shoes and then her stockings. I don't mean socks, I mean her stockings. Then she takes a pair of gym pants out of her luggage and puts them on, one leg at a time, while still on the phone. And when she stands she pulls the pants up to her thighs and under the skirt she is still wearing. Quickly she removes the skirt and her pants are completely on. And we never saw her panties if she was in fact wearing any."

We howl with laughter and begin shouting out questions.

"How were you watching all this?"

"Olivia can you believe your husband?"

"What were the other people doing?"

As Frida inches closer to me Max moves his make-believe book up to his eyes. Henry clears his throat, "Look I had no choice in this she was sitting directly across from me. We were in close quarters. And everyone else was baffled by what we all had to observe. But I tell you, this clothing change was impeccably choreographed. The skirt is removed and the pants are on fine. She puts socks on followed by sneakers. Now she changes her top."

I place my hands over my eyes and bend over with laughter. I ask while peeking out to Henry, "Was it like the scene in the movie *Flashdance,* when she removes her bra in front of that guy in her apartment?" Henry looks at all of us with disappointment and says, "No, that was a pretty hot scene. This was weird and uncomfortable." We laugh again. Frida now sitting next to me yells, "Tell us what happened next!"

Henry gets up and announces, "I'll be right back." We look to Olivia she says, "Oh, you are in for a treat. That's all I'm going to say." I ask, "Did he record her on his phone?" Olivia screams with laughter, "No, but now, I sort of wish he did." Luca slides back over to me.

Henry returns and he has an article of clothing with him. With confidence he says, "Ok so I've been practicing." He pulls a sweatshirt over his head and doesn't put his arms through the sleeves but yanks the material down over him. And in Houdini like moves, appears to be taking off his button down shirt under the sweatshirt.

Frida and I are now huddled together watching him behind our hands like we're seeing a scary movie while giggling like little girls. I'm afraid Henry might pull his arm out of his socket while we watch him struggling. Luca watches his brother with a silly grin on his face.

Henry now stands and within three very quick moves, his button down shirt falls to the floor and he pushes his arms through the sleeves of the sweatshirt.

Henry takes a bow while we stand and applaud his hilarious performance. When we settle down we hear someone behind us clapping even louder. We turn and see Rico, Claudia and Abuelo are standing in the doorway of the living room. What we hadn't realized, they arrived exactly when Henry put the sweatshirt on and watched with curiosity as he removed the other shirt underneath.

———✑———

Chapter 41

THE FUN, LIGHT amusing tone continues through to dinner. We take turns filling beverage glasses, setting the table and checking on another aromatic dinner, that Olivia has prepared cooking in the oven. In between preparations,
Henry and Luca take charge of the music. When a song that I had never heard
before fills the house, the kids come down from the loft and join the older
folks dancing around the dining room and living room.

During Julieta's song choice of Coldplay's "Viva la Vida," she enters the
kitchen and dances and sings along with Frida, Olivia and me. Soon we're
all bopping, singing and letting loose when suddenly the kitchen door flies
open. We shriek from surprise and watch Rafael entering with his family and
he immediately dances with us along with his daughters. The kitchen dance
party gets even louder and Luca rushes to us from the living room to see what
made us scream. Rafael grabs his brother to join in the fun. All of a sudden
Teresa is at the door trying to balance two covered dishes appearing slightly
bothered because her helpers left her alone to dance like fools. Olivia and I
quickly grab the plates from Teresa and then Frida takes Teresa's hand and
brings her into the circle of silliness. Teresa sidles up to Rafael and gestures to
the door. He nods his head and exits with Luca.

The song ends and the next tune doesn't provoke the hullabaloo as the
previous crowd pleaser. Olivia removes the trays from the oven and tells us
dinner is ready. Frida informs the rest of the family dinner will be served and
to come to the kitchen.

Henry goes to check on his brothers and upon opening the door I see Luca
and Rafael embracing on the porch then Henry wraps his arms around them.
The three come in from the outside and Rafael is carrying a brown paper

bag. I wondered why he needed Luca's help, when I notice Luca slipping away heading towards the back hallway.

I walk over to Olivia, "What can I help you with?" She instructs, "Let's place each of these trays on the counter. I will slice portions of one while you work on the other. Everyone can then help themselves more easily." We place the glass trays on trivets on the counter and begin to remove the foil coverings. "You made lasagna?" She nods, "Yes, one with Bolognese sauce and the other is vegetarian." While I focus on my task, I see Luca lighting the candles on the dining table. Rafael removes loaves of bread from the brown bag and after cutting pieces of the bread places them in a few baskets.

Completing the finishing touches, the family is congregating in the kitchen waiting to fill their plates. Abuelo strides directly over to one of the bread baskets and grabs a piece. With his cherished possession he studies the counter tops and upon finding what he was looking for, goes directly to the stove and splits the bread apart and dips each half into the sauce in the pan. Olivia quickly provides Abuelo with a napkin and he smiles at her while he makes his way to his seat at the table. Victor meets Abuelo at the table and holds his chair out for him. They exchange words and Victor takes Abuelo's dinner plate and brings it to Olivia.

"Tía Olivia, Abuelo would like a small slice of your lasagna." Olivia places a smaller portion on the dish and sprinkles it with grated Parmesan cheese adding an extra spoonful of her sauce on the side. As Victor leaves to bring back the dish, Olivia says, "He just loves dipping the bread in the sauce." I reply, "Who doesn't? I think I'll do the same."

When the last dish is filled we all take our seats at the table. I follow Luca's lead and notice that almost everyone is situated the same as last night. With the exception of Teresa and the girls, they are sitting across from me and Luca. Julieta is now sitting on Luca's left while I'm on his right. Rafael distributes the three bread baskets and places the one on our end near to Abuelo and his eyes light up. Rafael certainly knows his grandfather. Before taking another piece of bread Abuelo passes the basket to me, "*Emelia quieres pan?*" I smile and remove a slice, "*Sí, gracias Abuelo.*" He gestures for me to circulate it but I offer him the basket first, he smiles and helps himself.

Luca stands and excuses himself as he dashes into the kitchen. When he returns he hands Henry one wine bottle and Luca begins to pour wine from the second bottle in the glasses on our end of the table. Before taking his seat Luca taps his glass with a spoon to get everyone's attention. While pushing his seat further back and taking a step away from the table, I guess so Julieta and I have a more comfortable view of her father, we both turn in our seats and look up at him.

"Many, many years ago I stood here before you, well not all of you; some of you weren't born yet, sharing my gratitude for helping me through a challenging period in my life with your love and support. Tonight, I'm joined with my dear children Julieta and Marcos. As you all know, this year in our lives, has been very difficult for the three of us. But again with all of your love, kindness, support and understanding we've been able to overcome and accept this new family arrangement and our new lives. We want to thank you all for helping us get through this, now we're even stronger and more confident to see what our futures hold." He raises his glass to everyone and we all take a sip.

Luca continues, "When I reflect on my future, I can't help but think about my past. And earlier when I mentioned working my way out of a tough period in my life I also was embarking on a new start. I made a promise to someone here at this table. But due to my lack of better judgement and circumstances that will remain private, I sadly had to break that promise. Just three days ago I was given the chance of a lifetime to make amends of my awful behavior to Emelia. Each moment that she has bestowed on me since our reunion has been a gift, a gift to someone who is so far less deserving. And yet, she's opened her heart to me once again. Last night, we casually informed you of our relationship, but in my heart, I know, I want to share with all of you the joy and love that I feel for Emelia."

Luca kneels before me and holds out a ring. "That Christmas night with the stars all around us I promised you we'd build a life together. I was a young and unstable man that should not have been making such commitments that I was too cowardly to fulfill. I am a different man today and even more in love with you than I was then. Earlier this evening, Abuelo gave me this ring to give to you. When Abuela Lily finally agreed to go on a date with him, he gave her this ring. And he promised from that day forward as long as she agreed to continue dating him, he will prove his worth and one day, he will ask for her hand in marriage. Emelia, I know that my situation is not ideal at this moment, but please accept this ring as a symbol of my love and devotion to you as we begin our new journey melding our lives together. I promise to never ever let you down again."

As Luca remains kneeling in front of his entire family with my tearful eyes locked on his I reach out and hold his hands in mine. The only words after his tender and loving declaration that I can utter are, "Luca, yes, yes I accept your promise. It will be my greatest honor to receive this meaningful remembrance from Abuelo as a symbol of your love for me. And with accepting this ring, I too promise to love you as we begin this new chapter in our lives, *all* of our lives."

Luca kisses my hand and slides the wide silver band adorned with floral patterns onto my left ring finger. With the ring secure he pulls me into his arms and I tumble onto his lap. We exchange kisses amidst a chorus of whistles, applauses, cheers and glassware tinging.

Chapter 42

"Two nights in a row Luca, I'm a bit worried about dinner tomorrow night. Maybe someone else can be the floor show." I joke with my boyfriend. He laughs, "Yes, maybe we should get up off the floor now. Plus I'm sure certain family members are growing tired of me telling them about our intentions."

As Luca helps me stand we each take our glasses of wine tap them together and take a sip while looking into each other's eyes. Before I take my seat I go over to Abuelo and place my hand on his shoulder and give him kisses on each cheek. "*Muchas gracias Abuelo*. Whenever I look at this ring I will forever think of the love between you and Abuela Lily." Rafael repeats my words in Spanish to him. Abuelo takes my left hand and kisses the ring and rubs his thumb on the silver band while holding my hand. "*Por favor, ser cariñoso y fiel uno del otro, el resto caerá en su lugar. Creo en ti.*" [Please be loving and true to each another, the rest will fall into place. I believe in you.] Rafael interprets for me. I look into the older man's eyes and I know that loving Luca will never be a challenge for me. It's the part about being completely true to him that concerns me.

I settle back into my seat between Luca and Abuelo. Looking down at my dish I suddenly don't feel as hungry as I was before the big announcement. Grateful that the family is engaged in multiple conversations and enjoying the food and we're no longer the center of their attentions. Luca places a hand on my knee. "You haven't touched your dinner yet, is there something wrong?"

I reach down and place my hand on Luca's and answer him, "Nothing is wrong, I'm still feeling so moved by your Abuelo's gift to us and all that you said." I squeeze his hand as he clutches my knee.

"I know what you mean. He surprised me with it and I knew that I had to give it to you right away. I want to be alone with you after dinner. Be ready for me to snatch you away, yes?"

I shake my head, "Yes, I look forward to it."

He removes his hand from my knee, "Now eat!" I put some lasagna on my fork and smile at him before placing it in my mouth.

The remainder of the meal seemed like a typical dinner and when all the dishes were getting cleared from the table, Teresa motions for me to join her in the kitchen. I tell Luca, "I'm being beckoned. I'll be right back." Taking the rest of the plates from the table I join the cleanup crew. I go over to Teresa while she's unwrapping the platters she brought. One is a birthday cake for Frida and the other is filled with cookies and brownies.

"Wow Teresa, when were you free to bake all these?"

She replies, "This morning before you came to the house. I'm blessed with daughters that love to bake as much as I do. The three of us whipped all this up. And we decorated the cake after we got back from lunch."

"What can I do?"

"Can you bring the plates and the forks to the table and leave them where I'm sitting? When you come back, bring the cookie platter too. I will look around for the fruit bowl that Frida arranged." Taking the plates and forks to the table I reply, "Got it."

I take care of my tasks and when I get back to the kitchen Teresa points to the fruit bowl as she's inserting candles into the cake. Teresa gives orders to the twins to get everyone back in the dining room. I glance at Teresa, "Besides the fruit bowl, is there anything else I can bring to the table?" She nods her head, "No, you can just enjoy sitting next to your lovely boyfriend." And she winks and smiles at me. I blush a bit and smile back while saying, "I will do that quite happily."

The lights dim and the music gets turned low when Max enters the room with the cake and candles burning. Everyone starts clapping and singing "*Feliz Cumpleaños*" to Frida and I sing along with the words I remember. Frida is all smiles as her family surrounds her with love and good wishes. When the candles are blown out, Teresa swoops in and takes the cake from Frida and brings it to her place at the table and begins slicing out portions. I get the sense that we're suddenly in a rush. Or maybe everyone is tired from the long day and will be going to bed early tonight. I would like to get to bed early tonight, but after Luca said he wants to get away with me, I'm not sure what he has in mind. And how can we sneak out with all of his family here?

The celebration quiets down after everyone has devoured the delicious sweets. I notice the older kids grouped together in the kitchen and observe that Victor and Julieta have changed their clothes. Julieta comes back to the table. "Papá we're ready to go, where are your keys?" He stands and says, "I'll be right back."

Julieta bends down to me and kisses my cheek, "Emmy, we're going to a party I'm not sure if I'll see you later, so I want to say good night. And I look forward to doing the walk to the ridge again with you tomorrow."

I take her hand before she dashes, "Wait a second, I want to look at what you're wearing." She spins for me and I say, "You'll do great in New York. You certainly know how to dress."

She kisses me again, "Thanks Emmy. *Buenas Noches.*"

I whisper, "Have fun and be careful."

She squeezes my shoulder and hugs her dad when he passes her the keys. As the foursome heads out the door, Rafael and Luca walk outside to see them off.

Teresa gets my attention from across the table, "This is when I know I am old when the kids go out just as I feel like going to bed."

I laugh, "I know what you mean. What are their plans?"

"Graciela and Gabby's friend is having a party and Jules and Victor were invited too. I do like when they can drive themselves but I also worry."

We turn to Abuelo when we hear him snoring. Teresa whispers, "I guess we're not that old." I giggle and raise my finger to my lips to shush her.

Luca and Rafael return and they both look at their grandfather and smile adoringly. Luca whispers to me, "Let's help Abuelo to bed and then we can sneak out." I look at him surprisingly, "Really? I need to go to my room first, give me a minute, yes?"

"Yes, for you my love, I will give you five minutes." We smile at one another.

I use the bathroom quickly, freshen up and tie my sweater around my waist. It feels like ages since Luca and I have been alone at least outside of this bedroom. And yet, it was just yesterday morning when we were at the hotel. Life with him has been very interesting to say the least. It will be good to finally be together to talk freely. Suddenly I feel my heart racing more from anxiety. Everything will be fine I tell myself. Just be loving and true to one another. If I remain in this room any longer, I'll talk myself out of going. A quick swipe of lip balm and I scurry out of the room.

Arriving in the dining room I see Luca talking with his parents at their end of the table along with Frida and Max. I take my seat and I look towards Teresa and Rafael. I ask, "Where are Henry and Olivia?"

Rafael points up, "Making sure the boys get into their pajamas. They were disappointed they couldn't go out with the older kids."

I realize Abuelo has left the table too. I glance at his empty seat, "Oh, I'm sorry I missed Abuelo."

Rafael says, "Don't worry he knows you and Luca will stop in to say good-night before you go out."

I guess Rafael knows of Luca's plans. I feel hands on my shoulders gently massaging my tension. Luca whispers, "Ready mi amor?" I touch one of his hands, "Yes." We say goodbye to everyone and Luca takes my hand. He pulls me towards Abuelo's room. "First, we are to say goodnight to Abuelo, yes?" I nod yes.

Luca knocks on the door and we hear, "Sí." He opens the door slowly and we see Abuelo sitting up in bed wearing a checkered green short sleeved cotton nightshirt. I smile when I notice his bare legs from his knees to his toes. Luca pulls a chair over to the bed for me to sit and he rests on the end of Abuelo's bed. Abuelo points to a picture frame on his dresser and I reach over to pass it to him. It's a photo of Abuelo and Abuela on their wedding day.

"Mi amor Liliana está sonriendo sobre nosotros esta noche porque ella está feliz de que su anillo ha encontrado un hogar con la mujer correcta. No se enoje conmigo Luciano, estoy siendo honesto con usted y Emelia. Haznos sentir orgullosos y encuentren un camino para que sus corazones estén juntos sin importar los obstáculos. La vida tiene sus dificultades como todos sabemos. Tener el mejor socio a su lado, le da la

fuerza para pasar por esas etapas. Ese compañero también hace los momentos felices que mucho más."

[My love Liliana is smiling down on us tonight because she's happy that her ring has found a home with the right woman. Don't be angry with me Luciano, I am being honest with you and Emelia. Make us proud and find a way for your hearts to be together no matter the obstacles. Life has its difficulties as we all know. Having the best partner by your side, gives you the strength to get through those stages. That partner also makes the happy moments that much greater.]

He hands me back the frame and I look at the photo and see their younger selves and my eyes tear up.

Abuelo opens the drawer of his nightstand and takes out a white handkerchief and gives it to Luca for me. His sweet gesture makes the tears come faster. Placing the frame back on the dresser, I take the cloth from Luca and before I use it, I examine it gently. My fingers caress the soft weathered linen with yellow embroidered edges and a blue bird embroidered in the corner. I raise it up to my face and dab away the tears. I look to Luca first and then Abuelo, and say, "You have filled my heart with such joy. You don't even know me and yet, you've given me this ring that has meant so much to you and your wife. I hope to be with you even more so that I can also show you such kindness in return."

After Luca explains to Abuelo in Spanish, he replies, *"Querida, espero con ansias tus visitas y estar contigo. Y cuando no estás conmigo sabiendo que tú y mi nieto están juntos me traerán felicidad. Ahora deja que este viejo duerma un poco."* [My dear, I look forward to your visits and being with you. And when you are not with me knowing you and my grandson are together will bring me happiness. Now let this old man get some sleep.]

We smile at him and we each kiss him goodnight. Abuelo grasps my hand that's holding the cloth with the sweet bluebird and he closes his hand over mine. I caress his forehead and his cheek and nod to him. *"Gracias Abuelo y duerme bien."* [Thank you grandfather and have a good sleep.]

We leave Abuelo's room, Luca keeps the door ajar and we make our way to the outside, not even looking back towards the rest of the family. Taking my hand, Luca leads the way. I don't ask him where we're going I'm just feeling so relieved to be alone with him and taking in the cool night air.

We stop suddenly after we pass the barn and Luca cups my face in his hands. "I want to be with you and only you at the ridge tonight. Are you good with this? Or do you want to go someplace else?" He kisses my forehead and I answer, "Yes, honestly, besides the church I really don't know any other places." He laughs and sets a gentle kiss on my lips. And before the kiss can go any further he whisks me up the path and we swiftly make our way to the ridge.

Why is everyone rushing tonight? I sort of don't mind us making this journey quickly. I'm feeling drained from all the side conversations that I haven't had a chance to discuss yet with Luca; which by this point are probably meaningless since he has voiced his intentions numerously. His mother has to start excepting us by now.

We arrive at the ridge in record speed. Makes me think it's not as far from the house as I originally thought. Either way, the quick jaunt and the silence between us allowed me to sort through my thoughts. Upon arriving Luca takes me in his arms and we dance around the open area for a minute or two while he hums and sings a familiar tune in my ear. When the song is over he dips me and kisses my lips. He takes my hand and leads me to the center bench and when I take a seat he sits next to me. I rest my head on his shoulder and he stiffens. "You're not getting sleepy are you?" I reply, "No, not yet, I just wanted to get more comfortable to look at the stars." I feel his tensions ease slightly and he rests his head on mine.

Without a sound we observe the night sky. I try to focus just on the stars and being alone with my love but I begin to feel restless. I remember him saying how he felt undeserving of my affections; if he only knew how much I feel the same about his feelings for me. During these days of getting to know each other, we haven't shared much of our pasts. Well, I know more of his past than he knows about mine. Isn't that part of the dating ritual, getting to know one another over a period of time? But I feel having known him long ago, and all that's happened the last few days, we've sort of jumped forward. He lifts his head off of mine. And I move mine off his shoulder.

Luca stands and walks towards the other bench and paces in front of me between the two benches. By the second roundtrip I begin to feel uncomfortable for him. I go to him and he stops walking and looks at me. "No, please sit back down. I'm just preparing." I return to the bench.

Another minute passes and he stands near me. Then he sits and faces me. "I never realized how dark it is up here until just now. I feel like such a fool. Emelia I should have planned this out more thoughtfully."

I smile and I take his hand, "Luca, it IS dark up here I don't know what you have planned, but it's just me. I thought we were coming up here to be alone and to talk. Talk to me, what has you so jittery tonight?"

He rises from the bench and kneels on one knee on the ground. While he fumbles for something in his pocket I realize what might be happening. He places a hand on my knee while the other is holding something that I can't see. "I wanted this to be what I promised to you on Christmas night. So on Monday morning after spending two amazing days with you I decided then I would propose to you this week here in our special place under the stars. But now that we're here, I feel like you deserve a proposal more romantic than this and especially one with better lighting where you can see the ring and I can see your lovely face more clearly."

I smile and place two fingers across his lips. "Oh Luca, don't say anything more. Please get up and sit next to me."

"But Emelia let me finish."

I caress his jawline, "That's just it I don't want you to finish, yet." He reluctantly joins me on the bench and I turn my body around and curl up into him.

"Luca you've already given me this ring from Abuelo and before you give me another one tonight, we should talk."

I feel his body slouch and he says, "Oh, I've pushed you too much, too soon, I've ruined all this and you don't want me."

I grab his hands and feel the little velvet box in one of them. "First, please put this away, I don't want it to get lost." He does as I ask.

"Luca, it's not that I don't want you. I fear you won't want me. You see, we've spent four wonderful days together and haven't had a chance to really talk. You know, about the things that couples talk about as they get to know one other. Yes, it does feel like we're on this fast pace. And I also have gotten swept up in it. But we'd be making a huge mistake if we get so caught up in the romance, the sex, the beyond exceptional sex and jump ahead and make promises to one another that maybe one day, we might have to break because we realize we've been with someone that we really don't know."

Even in the darkness I can see Luca's confused and concerned expression. I move my legs off of him and say, "Ok, now I need to think." I walk across to each of the other benches like he did and back to him and without knowing even where to begin I just allow my jumbled thoughts to pop out of my mouth.

"It's so incredible how our connection is just as strong as it was back then, our passion, our energy, our love. But it doesn't erase the fact that we've lived a lifetime apart. And during that break we've had experiences without the other. Some good, some bad and some that probably should be forgotten. But whatever they are, they makeup who we are today. And until we can be honest with one another about all of that, I don't feel right, making these types of commitments to you, because, because maybe I'm not the woman who you fell in love with years ago."

I walk away and take a deep breath and I feel his hands on the backs of my shoulders. "Emelia, you are right about us not knowing all that's happened in our lives while we've been apart. And I'm sorry we haven't had the chance to talk more this week. I just figured that will happen sooner or later. No matter what you tell me, I will still love you and want to be with you and grow old with you. Remember when you said, you're grateful that we're still young enough to grow old together? Well, our past is in our past and our future is ours to make it whatever we want it to be. I know this heart of yours and there is nothing from your past that would make me love you less. Talk to me mi amor. Tell me what worries you. The sooner you tell me, the sooner we can begin this life together, you and me as husband and wife. The way it should have been all along."

Maybe he's right the past is in our past. Or that's just a coward's way out of this. We should start our future on the right foot, honesty all the way. I suggest, "Let's sit, this might take a while."

As we get settled on the bench he holds my hand and says, "Emelia, have you murdered someone?"

I reply, "No."

"Have you stolen money?"

"No."

"Have you hurt anyone intentionally?"

"No, not intentionally."

"Do you have any children you were worried to tell me about?"

"No."

"Have you any addictions?"

"No, not in the sense you're suggesting."

"So whatever you want to tell me is nothing compared to any of those challenges, right?"

I take a deep breath and continue, "Tonight, Abuelo advised us to be loving and true. I agree with him and that's what I plan to do. You keep saying how unworthy you are to have me, because of the one thing you did to me. And honestly I forgave you on Saturday after you explained to me all that happened. But you seem to put me on some pedestal like I've lived this pure life for the last twenty something years while you lived married to one person and sleeping with that one person."

He interrupts, "Oh, Emelia, if you think I will judge you or love you less for having past relations, you're crazy. I may have been married and sleeping with just one woman during that period, but you seem to forget, I had a single life too, before I met her and you. You want me to tell you all about those women now? Do you think that is of any importance to who we are today?"

He holds my head in his hands and brings my face close to his and whispers, "When I look at you I see the beautiful woman I met in Venezuela who invaded my heart and soul. The same woman who came back to me just a year later but here in Panama and allowed me to love her again and promise her a future together. No matter what happened since then, won't ever change how I feel for you."

Now holding my hands in his, Luca continues, "Actually hearing you talk tonight about you and your father, made me love you even more. And I just wish I had met him and I'm sorry I wasn't there for you during your painful moments." Pulling my hands up to his lips, he kisses them tenderly.

Luca says, "Do you know how much having you back in my life means to me? Being with you, these four days has changed me tremendously. I'm feeling more like the man I was meant to be. From a life which seemed out of my control, I suddenly feel as if all the pieces are beginning to fall into place. With you by my side, my heart beats stronger for you. When our bodies touch even if it's just to hold hands, I feel this force go through me that I have never experienced with anyone else but you. When we make love, my heart bursts knowing you desire me as much as I desire you. This makes me want you more and more and more. And when you rest your head on my chest at night, I lie awake waiting for that humming sound you make, for I know you're just seconds away from falling asleep. Then I am comforted by the solace you have found with me."

Grabbing a hold of my shoulders he continues, "I was living for so many years in a loveless marriage and became this ghost of a person that just went through the motions of life and allowed myself to believe this was all there was for me."

I caress his face and he looks at me with concern, "Do you know how much my own mother despises me for my broken marriage; to the point, where she doesn't care about my happiness as long as I don't go against the church. That's absurd, but what's even crazier, I started feeling like it's not worth fighting with her anymore and disappointing her. But, what about me, who or what gives me happiness?"

I interrupt, "Don't you see that you just settled for that life and if Violeta didn't have that affair and ask for the divorce, you would still be in that marriage. But now you're almost free. Free to be the person you are meant to be, standing on your own two feet. And this worries me; you are hurrying into another relationship with someone you barely know, before you're even divorced. I don't want to be your rebound relationship. Maybe I should give you the freedom to get out there and see what your life is like on your own."

He huffs at me, "Rebound? Rebound. What you and I have is far from a rebound. In order for this to be a rebound, I would have had to love my wife and be devastated by her affair and her need to divorce me. I feel exonerated, freed from that life. I was a prisoner that in some ways also controlled the duration of the punishment. Never having the courage to stand up for myself and break out of there. So, you, us, this is not a rebound. You are who I'll run to after a long day at work. You are the woman I want to hold in my arms every night and wake up next to every morning. And when we reach one hundred years old, you are the woman I want to lie entangled with as we take our last breaths. I can't give you back the last twenty years but I can promise to give you the next fifty. We are on the verge of the best part of our lives, because of the depths of the love we have for the other. It survived all these years doesn't that mean something to you? It means the world to me. You mean the world to me. Now stop with all this nonsense and tell me you love me and that you believe in us."

I stand and walk back and forth I have something else that needs to be discussed. "Can we just press pause for a few minutes and then I will answer you?" He growls, "Yes, just pause. What else is on your mind?"

This is too disturbing for me to sit so I remain standing, "I am going to say all this quickly and I hope you can keep up. I'm new to this whole ex-wife thing or soon to be ex-wife drama. And so I have zero experience on any of the proper ways to handle such dealings. With that said, I haven't discussed any of this with you until now because it wasn't the proper time and I thought maybe it would sort itself out and I don't want our life to be a soap opera. So, please don't be angry with me for bringing this up."

He clears his throat, "What do you want to know?"

"Well, it's not what I want to know, it's what I've been told and first you must know, I really like Olivia and Teresa, I think they are both wonderful and they've just been so kind with me. So don't take this out on them, I think they just feel like I should know some things."

"What things?" he asks gruffly.

"I won't name names I will just tell you what I've been told. Someone said that Violeta will try to make our lives miserable but not to worry you are in control of everything. That person thought since I had seen Violeta at the party that I had already known about her tricks. And then tonight someone asked how things are going with Frida. I'm sure you noticed our friendship is a bit strained for now but I think it can be repaired. But I asked that person, how I should win over your mom, I sense she's not thrilled about us being together. And so this person went on to discuss how your mother and Violeta have remained in contact, which is fairly normal I think, right. But to the point that worries this person they might be planning to get you to stop with the divorce. And that maybe I wasn't seeing things today, when I thought I saw Violeta in town. There's a chance she will come here and try to come between you and me. Well, I just need to tell you all this and hear your thoughts. And say, if you and I are going to be a couple you should know you can discuss this with me. Don't feel like you need to keep it away from me. This is something you and I need to get through together."

He growls deeply and inhales and exhales before talking with me, but I wait patiently for his response. "When have you and the other women talked about all this? I've been with you practically most of your visit. Did they huddle with you in the bathroom or something? *Dios Mio!*"

I giggle and he continues, "I am aware of Violeta's tricks. I was with her for over two decades and I'm also aware of her tendencies. She can try all she wants, but the divorce will be final in August. No matter what she and my mother have up their sleeves, I'm not interested. This is all happening since her situation with that guy is not what she hoped it would be and she wants me back. And as for my mother, she never even liked Violeta. But she's more focused on the laws of the church. Those are her religious beliefs and not mine. Like I told you the other night when you were worried about our future, nothing or no one will stand in our way, I promise you that. What else do you want to ask me about?"

I sit straddled on his lap running my fingers through his hair and I place a kiss on his lips. He wraps his arms around me. "Earlier you mentioned a proposal. What might this proposal involve?" I hear and see him smile. He looks away for a moment and then faces me.

"The other night at the hotel after your dream you told me how you felt previously when you went home from here and you feared opening your heart to me this week because of how you'll feel on Saturday when you go back home again. You promised you would let go of your fears to give us a chance and I promised I would do my part to assure you this time will be different. First, I went out and got you this ring, so that when you board the plane, you will go back home knowing my intentions for our future. Second, I have announced to my family that you and I are together. Something I didn't do before. And third, was a surprise even for me when Abuelo gave me Abuela's ring to give to you. That is his blessing for you and me. Even though some may see him as an old man who forgets things occasionally, he and I have gotten closer over the years and especially the last few months as I was preparing the house for your arrival. Both his ring and the ring I still haven't given you are my way of expressing that I'm devoted to you and building our life together. When we're as old as Abuelo and we look back on this week that reunited us after all these years, marks the start of our new lives when we let go of our fears, our constraints all those outside noises in order to be the two people we were meant to be for one another."

He takes my hands in his, "And for me, so far, I'm having the time of my life with you. Most of my family is embracing us and for those that haven't yet, they will come around and all will be good. I will not let any of that ruin these moments we have together." I sit contemplating all that he just told me hoping his words can ease some of my concerns. He interrupts my silence, "Now I notice you've been quiet, what else are you thinking?"

Looking into his eyes, I ask "How long exactly have you been planning my visit?" A low laugh vibrates inside of him, "Emelia, I've dreamed of your return over the last twenty years. But the idea came to fruition over Christmas when Henry and I were discussing Frida's birthday. I hadn't told him at that point. I waited to suggest inviting you when we were planning the guest list. And Henry actually said it to me first."

"What if I had a conflict and couldn't come?" He smiles, "We would have scheduled it for another date when you were free." I kiss him tenderly.

"I'm thinking you've been very busy assuring me of your intentions. And I've been observing and enjoying your very direct declarations. All the while I have been giving us a chance but not showing you or telling you what I'm feeling. I guess I realized each circumstance that we've been tossed together it's while we're on vacation. So we've only known our vacation selves and not the stressful grumpy people we are when we're home. I worry is this just a vacation romance."

Before I can give my heart to Luca, I need to share with him some concerns. "Luca, I have very high expectations when it comes to this type of commitment. And maybe that's why I've been single for a long time." He says, "Emelia, tell me what you expect of me and I will honor your wishes."

I reply, "First, I despise deceit. I have zero tolerance for lies. Second, I don't accept cheating. If you want to be with someone else, just be a man and tell me. And I will step aside. I'd rather share my life with someone who wants to be with me and only me than with someone who cowardly hides with someone else. Third, I will not be involved with someone who does drugs, gambles or abuses alcohol. And finally, never raise a hand to me. If you do, I will immediately walk out of your life."

Luca studies my face for a second or two in silence and then wraps his arms around me and pulls me against him. I rest my head on his shoulder and we sit quietly together.

While caressing my back he whispers, "Oh Mi Lia, my heart hurts thinking about all you may have endured because I failed you before. Please know I will always cherish you and protect you and give you the assurance of my love every day for the rest of my life. I promise to exceed your expectations and be the best man I can possibly be for you."

I whisper, "So Luca, do you think you will still love me when you realize I'm a neat freak and I voice my frustrations at you if you turn out to be a messy slob?"

He hums and says, "Yes Emelia, I will still love you."

"Do you think you will still love me when I burn our dinner and I need to order us pizza?"

He laughs and whispers, "Yes I will. And actually I do like pizza and I do like to cook."

"Or when I'm driving you someplace, you do know that I drive. And a nasty person cuts me off and I swear at them like an old truck driver? Will you still love me?"

He howls with laughter, frees me from his hold and when he finally collects himself looks into my eyes and says, "What words do you say?" He laughs even more and whispers, "Yes I will still love you, but might fear you at that moment."

I giggle too and whisper into his left ear, "I know this time around, I can believe," and I switch to his right ear, "in you and me and us." I take his hands and press them against my chest, "I entrust my heart with the man I have loved since the moment we met. I love you Luciano Morales. Thank you for finally bringing me back to you."

With our foreheads pressed against the other he whispers, "Mi amor, are you sure, don't you have more questions?"

Smiling I say, "I have over fifty years to ask you questions, but for tonight, I am done. And now I want to just be with you and only you under the stars."

"I have a question." I smile at him and say, "Luca, what is your question?"

"Before I propose marriage to you, I'd like to call your mother or your brothers to discuss. Are you good with that?"

I giggle and cover my eyes with my hands, "Oh Luca. I love your ways."

"Emelia, why are you laughing at me?"

"Let's see, how would that phone call go?" I pretend to hold a phone to my ear and I begin, "Ring-ring, ring-ring," using my mother's voice, "Hello?"

And in my best Luca impression I say, "Hello is this Mrs. Caldera?"

"Yes, this is she, who am I speaking with?"

He giggles as I continue. "Mrs. Caldera this is Luciano Morales, you may not know me, but I am a friend of Emelia's."

"No, I don't know you Mr. Morales. Why are you calling? Is there something wrong?"

"Well, she is vacationing with my family here in Panama as you know and I'm calling for I want to marry your beautiful daughter."

"Is this a joke call Mr. Morales? Am I on some radio show?"

Luca grabs the pretend phone from my hand and says, "No, I assure you this is no joke. I love Emelia and I want to marry her and spend the rest of my life with her." I laugh out loud to Luca and he tosses the imaginary phone behind him. "Luca, you just hung up on my mother!"

I move to rise up from his lap and he pushes my hips back down. "Where are you going?" he asks and kisses me longingly. His hands caress my back and I stroke his neck and gently run my fingers through his hair. His fingers travel down my spine and suddenly they are sliding under my skirt to my upper thighs. I rise up again and he squeezes my legs, we stop kissing and he says, "Where do you think you're going?" As I catch my breath, "I thought we'd continue this back in the bedroom."

He adjusts his hips under me and says, "But I want to make love to you here, at our special place where you have finally given your heart to me." Resisting him I say, "But my love, this is also your favorite place to be with your family. We shouldn't do this here." He inhales and removes his hands from my legs and places them on my shoulders. "Emelia, this is not sacred ground and I'm almost certain we're not the first to do this here."

I look around and with my head turned I feel his lips kissing my neck while his fingers unbutton my blouse. Even in the dark he locates the front clasp of my bra and quickly pops it open. His mouth tugs on one nipple while his hand fondles the other. I sigh with anticipation and my pelvis presses against his while my hands slide under his shirt and I find his chest and begin caressing him. Helping him remove his shirt we look at one another.

"Are you sure this is okay here?" He moans and with his head resting on my breasts he growls and I feel him trying to dress me. He fumbles with the clasp, "Help me, I'm very good at taking these off, but…" I kiss his forehead and reply, "I got it." He pulls my blouse back over my shoulders and buttons each button. I assist him with his shirt and he says, "I've got another idea. Let's get out of here."

Before we run down the path I tug at his arm, "Wait. Remember?" We step back up at the ridge and with his arms hugging me from behind I proclaim my wish, "For all who will come here after us, should you give your heart to someone and then they lose their way, never give up hope. For as long as you still love them, the sound of your beating heart will lead them right back to you."

Chapter 43

HAND IN HAND we run down the darkened pathway back to the house. As we get closer we see headlights from a car driving up the private road. "The kids must be back," Luca exclaims. We arrive at the top section of the driveway as they are parking. The lights from the car blind us and we shield our eyes with our hands. Approaching the driver's side, the engine shuts off and Julieta smiles when she sees us. Luca opens the door for her and I see Victor pop out of the passenger's side.

Julieta laughs and says, "Papá we didn't expect to see you there. Does this mean we missed the walk?" He takes her hand as she exits the car. Gives her a hug and says, "How was the party? You're back so soon." The three of us walk towards Victor. "It was fun. But we didn't know too many people and we were tired. Plus you said tomorrow we'll be on the go again." Victor says, "Were you going or coming back from the walk?" Luca answers, "Just coming back." Julieta says, "We were planning to sneak up there and surprise every-one. Was it just the two of you?"

I smile at Luca, he smirks and replies, "We went out to talk and suddenly we were at the ridge. Yes, it was just the two of us." Julieta smiles, "Ok good then we didn't miss anything. We're on for tomorrow night?" Luca answers, "Yes of course, tomorrow night."

He opens the door and we enter quietly into the kitchen. The house is dimly lit and it appears everyone has gone to bed. Julieta and her father kiss and say goodnight. Before Julieta hugs me she takes my hand and looks at the ring from Abuelo.

"I remember seeing this on Abuela Lily's hand for as long as I knew her. But I never asked her about it. I love seeing it again, it's like she's here with us, you know." I nod my head and smile at Julieta. She continues, "I don't know what I'm supposed to say to you about being with Papá. I knew one day he'd be with someone else, but never prepared myself on what I should say or feel."

I interrupt her while she's still holding my hand and I place my other hand over hers, "Jules, I don't know what I'm supposed to say to you and your brother. This is all new for me. Maybe we should allow all of this saying and feeling stuff to happen naturally as we get to know one another. One thing I do want to say to you and Marcos, I love your father and since you and your brother are a part of him I care deeply for you both. I don't plan on taking your mother's place she is your mom and always will be. Just know that I'll be here for you too."

Julieta steps closer and while we hug she whispers, "Thank you Emmy for making my Papá so happy again. Good night." And we go our separate ways.

Luca walks me to my bedroom door and whispers, "Can we have another sleep over tonight?" I nod my head, "Yes, I've been hoping you'd ask." He checks the hallway and kisses me, "I'll be back soon."

Finishing my bedtime rituals, I flip on the nightlight and leave the bathroom door open all the way so the glow from the little light pours into the bedroom. Sliding under the sheet I lie on my back waiting for Luca. While I'm alone I replay some of the night's events in my mind. And then I think of the ring box.

I hear the door open and Luca closes the door and sets the lock. The mattress rocks slightly when he climbs on the bed and as he inches closer to me I feel his arm rest across my belly.

Luca hums and nuzzles my neck and inhales, "This must be my love, but she's not wearing her armor tonight, let me check for sure if this is truly you." I giggle when I feel his hand cupping each of my breasts, "Yes, I can recognize these even in the dark." His hand moves down to my stomach and rubs my tummy from hip bone to hip bone, "Yes, this is your lovely belly." I growl and his hand moves further down, "Oh and I know this part of your body very very well, Mmm." I turn to my side and face him as I grab his roaming hand.

"I thought I'd surprise you tonight."

"Mm-hmm, you can surprise me like this every night." He pulls me closer to him and rests his hand on my bottom.

"Did you set the alarm?" I answer, "Yes. Hey when we were at the ridge tonight and I ruined your plans was this your alternate plan?"

He hums no. "No, this is plan C. And I'm grateful you stopped us."

"Yes, me too, so what was plan B?"

"Well, I was hoping to sneak you into the barn but then the kids arrived."

"The barn? I don't think I've ever been inside the barn. What's it like?"

He shifts out of his pajama bottoms, "I'll show you tomorrow. For tonight I must concentrate on my enchantingly naked girlfriend right here and right now."

I hum while he lavishes me with kisses and we finish this day of surprises tenderly loving one another.

Chapter 44

WAKING FROM A dream my eyes pop open and the first image of the day is Luca looking back at me. I cover my face with my hand. He pulls it down, kisses my palm and rests it over his heart. Lying there side by side in the stillness of the morning we silently observe the other and when my eyes land on his once again I see tears streaming down his face. I take my hand from his chest and gently wipe the tears.

Moving closer to him I whisper, "I know, I know," and I kiss him. When our lips part he whispers, "It's too much, you and me, here together, after all these years, after so much pain, after so much loneliness. All I had to do was reach out to you. Why didn't I do this sooner? Why did I wait so long?"

I pull him closer to me and he rests his head on my chest, "Shh, shh, we're together and that's all that matters. We have to believe there's a reason why it's all happening now."

"What you said to my daughter was so kind and from your heart."

"I truly meant it Luca. Your children, you and me, one day, we'll be a family. It's important to make them understand we all have a part in this and that it's just not us and them; it's the four of us. I know it won't always be perfect, but I want them to know they can count on this new family. I'm sure they're wondering where they fit into all this."

He raises his head and watches me, "Before the alarm goes off allow me to simply admire you without all of life's obligations getting in the way. I've waited so very long to just be with you and only you. Promise me that every day we will be with one another just like this, my heart thrives on loving you and you loving me."

I turn away from him and reach for the phone. We have a few minutes before the alarm sounds and I turn it off. Putting the phone back on the table I respond, "I look forward to fulfilling that promise." And for the next ten minutes in between kisses we tell the other about some of the moments from the last four days that helped to bring us closer together.

Chapter 45

I AM NOT a morning person to begin with and when I don't get six or seven solid hours of sleep I feel like I'm dragging. That is the one thing that I will look forward to when I go home, sleeping late on Sunday morning. I know that will be the only highlight. I feel it now, as I lay her alone in the bed waiting for the alarm to sound. Luca went back to his room a couple of hours ago and I feel like a part of me is missing.

The refreshingly cool shower invigorated me, thankfully. I wonder what's planned for today. Our last full day here in Chiriqui and it seems like things are coming together nicely. Although we're moving very quickly, most of the family is embracing us. Today I hope to get some moments alone with Frida. Last night it seemed like old times with her.

Why do I get anxious when I'm about to leave this room? Maybe I should wait until exactly nine o'clock to go wandering around the house. And just as I'm about to sit on the chair I hear a knock. I bounce over to the door and open it. It's Luca, "Good morning" he says. Feeling relieved I smile at him, "Good morning Luca."

Closing the door behind him, he embraces me and kisses my shoulder. We stand holding one another for a few moments. I inhale and breathe in my love's irresistible scent and I ask, "Are you just going to breakfast?"

He releases me and goes into a full body stretch, "Yes, I slept later this morning."

I run my fingers through his damp hair, "When your hair is wet like this, you look even younger than when I first met you."

Squinting his eyes at me he says, "The flock of men you previously dated how many were much younger than me?"

With a slight giggle I take his hand and pull him towards the door, "I'm starving let's go get breakfast."

Before I can turn the knob he tugs me into his arms, "Lucky for me those young men didn't know how to treat a woman like you. Otherwise you wouldn't be free for the taking."

He indulges me with one of his flaming hot kisses. When he lets me go I say, "I must admit Luciano, when it comes to kissing, you are in your own league."

He smiles and quickly traps me against the wall with his body pressing against mine, "Only kissing?"

With my fingertip tracing his always enticing pillow soft lips, "My body trembles even at your slightest touch. You must have figured this out on Saturday that you have magical powers over me. No man has ever mastered my desires like you have and we've only just begun." I seal my sincerity with my own version of a hot kiss.

He pushes off of me and waves his hand at me, "We should have had sex this morning instead of talking. Now all I'll be thinking about today is that kiss, your body and everything I want to do with you."

I smile at him and say, "You're right, any chance we can sneak into the barn?"

He starts to laugh and whispers, "No forget the barn. I'm thinking about the various ways I will master your desires at home tomorrow when we are finally alone."

"Aha, you were paying attention."

"Yes, mi amor, you are my number one focus. Now let's get out of here."

Chapter 46

THE BROOD SEEMS more energized this morning than yesterday. Are they all drinking gallons of coffee when I'm not around? There are people spread out between the kitchen, dining room and living room. Maybe they were waiting for us. Luca and I greet everyone quickly and we immediately go into the kitchen.

I learn today's breakfast has been arranged by Frida and Max and it appears to be more of a continental buffet, which suits me just fine since I'm overtired and all I want to do is graze. Taking a seat at the counter, Luca places an empty glass in front of me, "Juice?" he asks. I give him a tiny smile, "Yes, thank you." He brings over a pitcher of juice and pours some in my glass.

Olivia sits on the stool next to me. I nudge her and say, "Hey." She copies me and we giggle. And she takes my left hand and rubs the floral band. "I always wondered what Abuelo did with this ring. I'm glad he decided to pass it down." She lets my hand go and I look at the ring and spin it around my finger. I say, "He must really love Luca to part with it."

Olivia leans closer to me and starts in a whisper, "Teresa told me after Abuelo and Rico discussed with Luca his intentions yesterday morning, Abuelo asked Rico to help him find the ring in his bedroom. But they couldn't locate it in his bedroom here. So yesterday when we were all out, he insisted Rico bring him to Rafael and Teresa's house. And he and Rico finally found it in a drawer in his bedroom that has many of Abuela's personal belongings. When Teresa arrived home, she found a note with the ring asking her to shine it up and bring the ring to the house last night."

Admiring the ring again, I picture those two men searching for Abuela's ring for me. "Olivia, thank you for telling me all this, hearing about what they

349

did, makes this ring even more special and I think it's remarkable it fits me." Olivia smiles and whispers, "It is fate Emelia, believe in it."

I take a sip of the juice and my tongue flips with excitement. Expecting it was orange juice it tastes like a blend of several fruits. Taking another swig I try to figure out the mixture. I look to Olivia and ask, "Who made the juice? It's delicious."

She glances at Frida, "And she won't tell us what's in it."

I laugh, "What do you mean? Nobody has watched her make it?"

Olivia nods her head, "I swear she concocts it in her room at night and sneaks it in here in the morning."

After another sip I say, "Mmm, I'll try to get it out of her."

Breakfast is informal and relaxed today. With the buffet we just fill our plates and take seats throughout the house. I find myself sitting on a couch between Frida and Olivia in the living room. Luca, Henry and Max are sitting with the kids at the dining table. And after each wave of laughter I look up and catch Luca glancing over at me. The older generation is having their breakfast at the kitchen counter.

It is calming sitting with the ladies in the sun filled room. "Do either of you know what's happening today?" I ask.

Frida begins, "Max, Victor and I are visiting with a friend in town this morning and I think we're all supposed to meet back here about two o'clock for games and stuff."

Olivia smiles, "The boys want Henry and me to take them to a couple of stores. Usually they find some interesting things here they don't get at home. And yes, they told us we must be back for the afternoon fun."

Luca enters the room and sits across from us. After all our intimate moments this week, it feels very different to not be sitting next to him. When he asks Frida about something I watch and admire him. His voice and mannerisms are what first attracted me to him and now as an older man, his voice is deeper and his posture displays more confidence than in his younger years. With the exception of Christmas when he had a full beard, usually he's been clean shaven. His three day scruffy look is very sexy. The relationship between him and his kids seems solid, kind, loving and warm. And even though we're facing many compromises, I can't imagine sharing my life with someone other than Luca.

"What do you think Emelia; do you want to see if it's still there?" My eyes give me away first and without knowing what I'm agreeing to I quickly reply, "Yeah, sure."

He looks at me curiously and adds, "Ok then, you should change into your swim gear."

Looking confused at him I smirk and wonder should I tell him. I ask, "Swim gear?"

He laughs, "I knew it. You were somewhere else when I was just talking. You didn't even hear a word I said."

The ladies laugh along with him. I laugh nervously, close my eyes and feel my cheeks blush.

Placing my empty dish on the coffee table I get up and walk over to Luca to sit next to him. "Yes, you are right, I completely zoned out." I lean closer to him and whisper into his ear, "I am sorry. You caught me falling more in love with you."

He turns and looks into my eyes and I nod slowly and part my lips with a tender smile. Placing his hand on my cheek he caresses it lovingly and gives me a sweet kiss. He whispers, "Ok, you are forgiven."

I laugh, "Thank you. So where are we going?"

Luca says, "I thought you might want to go back to the place with all the flowers. But Frida isn't sure if it's still there."

Excited I reply, "Oh yes, let's go and try to find it. Do you think Jules and Marcos want to explore too?"

Smiling at me Luca says, "Yes, I already mentioned it to them and Marcos wants to take pictures today so we'll venture around to other places afterwards."

"Sounds like a good plan. Did Frida give you the directions?"

He laughs and takes my hand in his and brings it up to his lips, "You really weren't listening. No, we didn't get that far." I look over at Frida and Olivia and they are smiling and giggling at me.

I confess to them, "My apologies to you all, I was enchanted by my boy-friend's charisma." Olivia says, "I understand, it still happens for me with

Henry, not as much as when we first were in love, but it still takes me by surprise."

Julieta enters the room and sits on the couch next to Luca, "So, are we going to find the wild flowers?" Luca nods, "Yes and no. Tía Frida is unaware if it's still there, but we will go and search. Maybe you can call Tía Teresa and ask her for other places we might want to visit."

Julieta stands and before leaving us, takes all of our breakfast dishes and heads to the kitchen. "Ok, I'll call her from the house phone and let you know what I find out." Luca yells, "And get directions from her please."

We sit back on the cushions and I rest my head on Luca's shoulder while we hold hands. The sunlight in this room and cuddled next to Luca is a tempting invitation for a late morning nap. Frida says, "We are getting old, I only woke up a few hours ago and I would love to take a nap."

Olivia replies, "I agree. I keep thinking I'll sleep when I get home, but that won't happen until Sunday."

To keep from closing my eyes I ask, "When do you fly back?"

"We leave on Sunday. After our drive on Thursday, we'll be staying a few days with my family. How about you, when do you go home?"

Luca's hand squeezes mine. "My flight is on Saturday morning." Glancing at each other I suggest, "Should we start cleaning the kitchen?" He leans down and kisses my forehead, "Yes, let's go."

Luca and I manage breakfast clean up duty while the rest of the family gets ready for their excursions. We are the last to load up our car and with a page of directions from Teresa and Frida in Julieta's hand we are eager and ready to spend the next few hours touring the area. I offer the front passenger seat to either of the kids, but they already had placed some of their belongings in the back seat and declined. With Luca holding the car door open for me, I take my seat and he closes it securely. Suddenly I feel nervous thinking this is our first daytrip as a family. I lean over the driver's seat and flip open the door for Luca. When he settles into his seat he looks at me and says, "Thanks."

I think since I'm the newcomer to this trio I will take the lead from them. Luca requests, "Jules pass me the directions." The paper appears between us and suddenly I hear her voice in my ear, "The directions for the mysterious flower fields are on top followed by three other places Tía Teresa suggested we check out."

While Luca reviews the information I put on my seatbelt. "Do you have a pen?" he asks. I dig one out of my bag and hand it to him.

"We'll drive to the fields first and then the others in this order." He writes numbers next to each of the places. "Jules since you wrote them, would you mind being my copilot and reading them off for me?"

I turn around, "Are you sure you don't want to sit up here with your dad, it might make it easier."

She nods, "Yes Emmy, stay where you are. I know my way around and can direct him from back here."

He passes the paper back to her, starts the car and secures his seatbelt. Luca exclaims, *"Vamos andando!* [Let's go wanderers.] If anyone sees other points of interest let me know."

As we travel down the bumpy road I look out the window and enjoy my surroundings. Julieta says, "Emmy, I wrote the directions in Spanish and it's easier for me to read them to Papá that way, I hope you don't mind." I reply, "I won't mind at all. And I'll test myself to see if I can follow along."

While Julieta directs Luca I think about when we first visited this field. That day's events were so unexpected and filled with innocence and joy. I never would have imagined returning one day with Luca and his two children. Had he never been back? Surely Frida must have stopped there over the years.

Luca navigates down a narrow bumpy road and says, "I think it's not far from here so look out for the house." A building comes to view on the right side of the car and as we get closer I point it out. The driveway is less rough and Luca parks the car. Before getting out of the car he says, "It doesn't look like anyone is here."

With a quick glance up to the house I suddenly see a woman. I say, "Look over there, I see a lady on the porch. Maybe we should talk with her?"

We all get out of the car and Luca says, "Julieta and I will inquire with her. You two can stay here at the car." Marcos and I look at each other and shrug our shoulders and nod as they walk towards the house.

We watch our fearless leaders while the lady walks down the steps to meet them. They shake hands and we hear a lot of talking. Luca points towards us and the lady nods her head. She says something to them and waves her hand and points in the area behind where Marcos and I are standing. Luca and his daughter turn around and gesture the same to her. They shake hands again and wave to the lady when they walk back to us.

Luca and Julieta are holding hands while smiling and talking to one another. When they get near us Luca says, "You two, get your cameras." I smile to him, "Really? We can go and find the calla lilies?" Marcos and I grab our cameras from inside the car and the four of us find our way to the trail the lady explained to them.

"What did she say? And why does this place look deserted?"

The path appears as if nobody has been here for a while. Luca replies, "She explained to us that the blooming season for the lilies is in a few months. But we might see some flowers that grow all year round. She also had been sick for the last year and is now recovering. She promised that if we come back for Christmas it will be just as we remembered."

We arrive at a fork and a small closed up shack. Then I remember when we were here with Frida and Max, they went to the right and we went to the left. "Let's go this way," Luca says while leading us towards the left side of the path. Just a few feet in and we are surrounded by rows and rows of purple blossoms. I don't remember these at all. And there's another opening and the grounds dip down from here and we're able to see the sections of flowers that await us. I sigh and say to Luca, "My goodness, this has changed quite a bit since we were last here."

Marcos asks Luca, "Can we run ahead?"

"Yes, as long as you and Jules watch out for the other. I don't know what we might encounter here."

Luca takes my hand and we wander around looking at all the new flowers that were added. "Will you take any pictures?" he asks. I nod and say, "You set my expectations so low that I wasn't sure what we'd see. And now, I just want to take everything in before I look through the lens."

I tug at his elbow and throw my arms around him squeezing him tight and whispering in his ear, "Thank you for bringing me back here today." I treat him to several kisses on his neck.

"Are you happy?"

I smile at him and say, "Anywhere I'm with you Luca I'm happy. And this place with you and your kids, I'm overjoyed." He takes my hand again, places a kiss on it and we're off exploring.

Catching up with Julieta we find her watching Marcos taking pictures. She proclaims, "I bet he's taken about a hundred." Luca laughs, "Emelia has taken about half as much." Marcos joins us. Luca asks, "Ready to check out the other field?" Julieta smiles at her dad and says, "Yes!" Marcos looks disappointed to leave. Luca explains, "Marcos, don't worry, if you're not pleased with the other section we can come back."

We quickly make our way to the fork and take the other path. Luca and Julieta are whispering about something. I wonder what the owner told them about this place. I ask, "Marcos does your camera have a macro setting?" He looks at me curiously and I show him what I mean on my camera. "Oh yes, I forgot, thanks. Now we have to go back to the other field before we leave."

We come upon coral colored flowers and I think they might be hibiscus. I hear Marcos' shutter click away. And then I see a somewhat shaded area with white flowers with big green leaves and blue flowers speckled amongst them. I get closer to the white flowers when I'm startled by some movement on the leaves. Julieta is standing close to me now and whispers, "Do you see them?"

Concentrating on what I first thought were blue petals are butterflies. They flutter about on the leaves and flowers. With further observation it looks like hundreds of blue butterflies. Luca is standing behind us now with his arms around our shoulders. He instructs, "The owner made us promise not to disturb them." Marcos walks over to me, "What are you looking at?" I whisper, "Just watch and you'll see."

He inhales when he sees them flying around. Marcos exclaims, *"Hay tantas y son tan hermosas."* [There are so many and so beautiful.] Julieta whispers to all of us, "Don't anyone move, let's experience this magnificence in silence."

Luca rests his head on my shoulder and extends his arm to include Marcos. Standing there quietly together, we observe these blue winged delicate ethereal creatures rise and fall with the elegance and agility of hundreds of prima ballerinas. A few of them fly up towards the sky and glide down hovering over the flowers and repeat the aerial performance again and again. I am astounded by nature's grandeur and the realization that moments like these are as fleeting as the lifespan of a butterfly. My soul is embraced with elation and gratitude. And suddenly a tear or two travel down my beaming face.

Luca whispers to Julieta and me, "Do you ladies need a tissue?" We giggle and look at each other and we both wipe away our tears. Marcos says, "I have an idea, let's try to take a group picture with the butterflies behind us."

I suggest, "Let me take a picture of the three of you." Marcos nods, "No, you have to be in the picture. If it wasn't for you, we never would have come here."

While he sets up the shot, he directs us to sit down on the ground. We're all positioned and he moves next to me and extends his arm with the camera. *"Uno, dos, tres, FELIZ!"* [One, two, three, HAPPY!] He yells and we all laugh when he clicks the camera.

He instructs, "Again, in case that one's no good." Now we all yell, "Uno, dos, tres, Feliz!" He takes the photo and I lay back on the ground laughing and when I look up, I see about ten or so butterflies above our heads. I pull Marcos down to me, "Look up!"

The four of us are now resting on the soil taking in the show overhead. Julieta squeals and with her arms stretched out we see two butterflies resting on each of her arms. Marcos snaps pictures of his sister with her blue winged playmates.

Eventually we explore the rest of the garden taking pictures of us in different group formations and return to the first garden so Marcos can take more pictures with the macro setting. While he does that, we all just observe him along with enjoying the sprawling view. Julieta reaches towards me to take my camera, "Let me take one of you two." I hand over my camera to her and I show her how it works. With the roses as our backdrop, she yells, *"Uno, dos, tres."* And Luca and I say, *"Feliz!"* [Happy!]

Luca tells Julieta, "Please take another, just in case." She pulls the camera to her face and looks through the viewfinder and with all seriousness whispers, *"Uno, dos, tres, besos!"* Luca places a gentle kiss on my cheek and I smile sweetly to Julieta and I hear the click. I turn to my love and with his lips still puckered I kiss him on the lips and we hear Julieta chuckling while taking more pictures of us.

On our way back to the car the four of us walk up to the owner's house. Julieta knocks on the front door and we hear footsteps getting closer. When the lady sees us we hear, *"Hola, hola."* [Hello, hello.] She opens the screen door and Julieta thanks her for letting us walk around. She asks me if I liked it as much as the first time I was there. I place my hand over my heart and tell her, *"Me gusto mas, gracias."* [I liked it even more, thank you.] When we say our goodbyes, she reminds us to come back whenever we want and to remember to return at Christmas.

The next few hours we visit two of the three places Teresa suggested and we fit in a quick lunch. Being with the three of them is so entertaining. They have this ease with each other. One starts a story and another finishes it. They eagerly tell one story after the next of their travels here to the house and other activities they've experienced. This gives me a sense that this trio has been doing things for years without their mom in the mix. Even during our drive back to the house, they sing two songs in Spanish that sound like they've been practicing these harmonies for many years.

Looking at the clock on the dashboard I see that it's almost two-thirty. I think to myself, we're not that late. Good thing we're taking the bumpy road to the house.

With the house getting closer into view, it appears that someone is sitting on the porch. During this visit I don't recall anyone sitting out there. As we get nearer Luca says, "Why is Abuelo sitting out there alone?" Julieta laughs, "Maybe it got too loud in the house for him."

Luca parks the car. Julieta and Marcos hop out and run towards Abuelo. They kiss him hello and rush inside leaving the door open. Luca and I walk hand in hand up to Abuelo and I smile at him but his face doesn't seem to change expression. We both lean in and kiss him hello. He grabs hold of our fastened hands and I overhear Julieta exclaim, "Mamá" as Abuelo tells us, *"Violeta esta aqui."* [Violeta is here.]

Chapter 47

STANDING ON THE porch with Abuelo and Luca fearing if I take another step forward, I will fall deeply down a shaft and won't be able to climb out. I knew she was planning to make an appearance, but today of all days. The four of us just had an unforgettable experience together.

Luca brings my hand that he's been holding to his lips and kisses the floral ring he gave to me. "My love, have no worries. Her being here doesn't change a thing. The divorce will soon be final and then our future plans can be made more definite. I love you." I caress his jawline and before kissing him I proclaim, "And I love you."

We glance at Abuelo and he smiles at us both. Luca leads the way into the house and I tug him back and whisper, "Should I stay outside with Abuelo? It might make it easier dealing with her if I wasn't right here." Luca looks into my eyes and says, "Never. I want you at my side. She must see that we are together and she needs to move on." He squeezed my hand and I nod to him while saying, "Let's go."

Entering the kitchen I first see Olivia and Henry sitting at the counter. When they look at us they shake their heads and Olivia looks up to the ceiling. I wave to the both of them. I hear Julieta and Marcos in the living room talking excitedly to their mother. Still with our hands clasped, we step into the archway of the living room and I see Violeta on the couch with her kids sitting on either side of her. Marcos seems to be showing her pictures on his camera. I glance around the rest of the room and find, Frida, Max, Teresa and Rafael sitting at attention on one couch, Rico in the chair near the hearth and Claudia on the same couch as Violeta just on the other side of Julieta.

Luca directs me to the loveseat and we sit while the kids continue with their mother. Not long after we've settled into the cushions, Olivia appears with two glasses of Frida's special juice and gives each of us one. Henry lugs in a chair from the dining room and sits to Luca's left while Olivia squeezes next to me. I whisper, "Thanks, I needed this." Luca looks past me and at Olivia, "Yes me too," and he smiles at us both. We take a much needed swig. Passing my glass back to Olivia she places it on the side table.

While Julieta goes on, Violeta takes a fast glance at us. I remain straight-faced and turn my focus to Julieta. Violeta reaches for a wine glass on the coffee table. She takes a few sips and gushes at Marcos' photos and smiles as Julieta continues to tell her mother about our afternoon. I'm gratified the kids are excited to see her and want to be close to her. There was no way they could be these well-balanced young adults without having some kind of relationship with their mother. Maybe all through the years they've parented separately and this final year when they split didn't seem as much of an adjustment. No sense trying to analyze all this now, I'm sure Luca will explain this to me one day. If not him, my future sisters-in-law will catch me up. I quickly suppress a smile when I think about Olivia and Teresa.

Violeta empties the glass, lifts the bottle and pours herself more wine. It's so odd to be in a room filled with thirteen people and yet only three of them are talking while ten of us just sit by watching. I wonder where the rest of the kids are, maybe they've been told to stay up in the loft. And I was looking forward to playing games with everyone this afternoon. How long is Violeta planning on visiting?

As Julieta slows down her chattering Violeta looks at Luca, smiles at him and says, *"Hola Luca."* Her voice sounds friendly and flirty. Very different from when she approached me in the ladies room on Sunday at the party.

He replies, "Hello Violeta. What brings you here, so far away from home?" Wow his voice is the complete opposite. He's not kidding around and getting straight to the point. That's good, the sooner we know why she's here, the sooner she will leave.

She smiles at him and then at me. She says, *"Vine a ver a mis hijos. Los he perdido los últimos días."* [I came to see my children. I've missed them the last few days.] Olivia translates quietly in my ear.

"But you knew I'll be driving them back tomorrow and then you would have seen them at your home."

"*Bueno, también necesito hablar contigo y con la familia.*" [Well, I also need to talk with you and the family.]

"What is so urgent that you drove all this way when it could have waited until tomorrow? Or you could have called. Incidentally I didn't see your car. How did you get here?"

She chuckles, "*Un amigo me trajo acquí.*" [A friend brought me here.]

Luca remains silent waiting for her to continue but when she doesn't he inquires again, "Please tell us your news." She clears her throat and stares at me. He adds, "Oh and before you continue, please speak in English. I'm sure you don't want to be rude in front of my girlfriend Emelia. I understand you were reacquainted at Frida's party on Sunday."

She glares at him and then again at me and swallows. "*Me sorprende verla aquí, tal vez tú y yo podamos hablar afuera. Lo que tengo que decir es una cuestión de familia privada.*" [I'm surprised to see her here, maybe you and I can talk outside. What I have to say is a private family matter.]

Luca looks at me and replies to her while continuing to face me, "Emelia is part of my family and whatever you need to say to us, you can say in front of her."

Violeta says something to Julieta and her daughter stands, takes the empty wine bottle but before leaving the room asks, "Does anyone else want something to drink?" Julieta looks at me and I say, "Nothing for me but thanks for asking." Everyone else chimes in with a no. She walks away.

With Julieta in the kitchen, we all wait silently for Violeta to tell us her reasons for her visit. Marcos turns off his camera and places it on the side table next to him. He looks over at his father and he shrugs his shoulders. Returning from the kitchen, Julieta brings with her a few empty cups and a pitcher of water. She pours water into two cups, placing one in front of Violeta and she takes the other for herself. Violeta talks with Julieta again and Julieta murmurs something back to her and points to the water. Violeta finishes what's left in the wine glass and rises. Making her way towards us she asks Henry to give up his seat. He cordially does and joins his niece and nephew on the couch.

Violeta brings the chair nearer to Luca and when she sits her knees are almost touching his. His hand that has been grasping mine since we entered the room is now firmly holding on. She reaches for his other hand but he pulls it away from her and gracefully encases my hand with both of his.

Violeta shakes her head and says, *"Luciano, por favor, estoy tratando de mostrarte que podemos arreglar esto."* [Luciano, please, I'm trying to show you we can fix this.] Olivia starts to translate for me and Luca commands, "Violeta if you can't speak with me in English I don't want to hear a word you have to say."

I'm trying not to feel sorry for her, but I can't help but wonder if I was sitting where she is, how I'd feel. Violeta looks at me with disgust and says, "I came here today because I don't want our marriage to end. I want us to be together again, just the four of us. The children are suffering. I know we can put all this behind us and start over. I loved our life before. Being with you, the children and both of our families, we have a history. We can't throw that away. Isn't it worth it to give it another chance? I know we can be happy again. Look at the beautiful family we made together. Tell me how I can make this right again?" She places her hands on his knee and leans in closely to him, "If you go through with the divorce you'll be breaking up our family. Is that what you want to do?"

His hands release mine and he takes Violeta's hands and places them on her lap. Luca picks up his glass and takes a mouthful of juice. He appears to be looking around the room at each of his family members. When he focuses on Marcos he instructs him to check on Abuelo and suggests that he can come back inside if he wants. Marcos leaves the room.

Luca says, "If anyone wants to do something better than listening to all this, please don't feel obligated to stay here." I quickly peruse the room and most everyone remains seated and looking directly at Luca. Frida stands, "Luca, this is up to you, we're here to support you, Jules and Marcos. But we'll understand if you want to talk privately with Violeta."

Luca reaches for my hand and grabs hold. He says, "Frida, thank you for saying that, it means a lot. You see, I'm sitting here surrounded by the people that helped me get through this difficult transition in my life and in my children's lives. We're all here, in a home that we love to be together, a place where we've shared so many precious memories. Like life, we need to take the good with the bad. And today, someone came into our home; a home of love, of joy and most importantly a home where a family knows what it means to be a family. I'm not about to bring even more negativity into this place we love. Violeta, we're at this junction because of the choices we've made during our entire relationship. We've continually gone over this. It's best that we end our marriage and try to make the most of the years we have left. Our children they are not suffering now. They've gotten past the hard part and they along with me are excited to see what happens next in our lives. You can do the same. Because of the two children we parented together, I want you to have the love and happiness you've been looking for. Start a new life. Isn't that what you told me? I did that and now it's your turn."

Violeta shakes her head at him and inhales and exhales loudly. She rises quickly from her seat and with her hands on her hips paces towards the doorway and back to us. "Your family agrees with me, this divorce is wrong. What has come over you? You're not acting like the man I married. In your mind a divorce means failure, you failed as a husband. And I know you never want to fail at anything."

She kneels down to him and says, "I'm begging, don't give up on us." Luca waves his hand at her, "Please Violeta, don't beg, sit back on your chair. We're done."

She huffs at him when she stands, "Don't tell me you're ending all this for her? This romance you have going on is temporary. She's flying home one day and will forget about you. You're willing to put our family on the line for her? You've lost your mind. What is this attraction you have?"

She paces again and then snaps her fingers at us, "I should have guessed. Trust me Luca, I know such things, the sex doesn't last for very long. It might at the beginning be passionate and exciting but you need more than that to make a relationship work. Don't insult this family our family by pushing us aside for some nasty affair with her."

Frida exclaims, "Violeta, please don't make things worse."

Violeta looks over to Frida, "Frida I'm just trying to salvage my marriage. And I have to figure out why my husband doesn't love me anymore."

She sits again beside Luca, "You see with her sitting next to you like that you can't think clearly. Your judgement is weakened by her. I wouldn't have come all this way if I knew she was here. And when she's gone, I know you'll come running back, begging for me."

She's trying to provoke a response from Luca, but he doesn't budge. How can he sit there and let her talk so disrespectfully and without any regard to her children nearby? He has more restraint than I do.

I take a deep breath and on exhale I whisper, "Enough!" My heart is pounding in my chest. I didn't expect to say anything but I just couldn't control what I was thinking. Everyone is looking at me. Luca whispers, "Don't feel you have to say anything, she's confused, hurting and just wants to fight. I'm passed all this and ready to leave it all behind."

I close my eyes and beg to myself, please don't cry, please don't cry. The tears quickly dry up, I motion to Olivia for the glass and I take a drink. Violeta says, "Yes enough of this game, go home and leave us alone."

I give the glass back to Olivia and I turn my attention to Violeta. In a low voice I say, "I don't know what is worse, you coming here begging to rebuild a marriage that was based on lies and manipulation or coming here disrespecting this family who for many years embraced you as one of their own. In your desperate attempt to get your husband back, you never once said you love him. Where is the love? It was all about *YOU* and what YOU want and wondering why he fell out of love with YOU. I doubt anything I say to you will make any sense, for some reason, you find me the enemy in all this. But I suggest you take whatever dignity you have left and apologize to everyone here especially your children and as Luca told you, make a new start and enjoy being a mom to these beautiful children you and Luca brought into this world. Even though your marriage has ended it doesn't mean you can't find happiness once more."

Rafael gets up and strides over to us, "I think we're done here, right brother? Since this is the last day I can be with my whole family, I'd like to get back to our plans. So tell me Violeta where can I drop you off?" Finally, someone else comes forward to end this drama.

Violeta glares at me, "I'm not done here. It's very interesting how you see yourself as the enemy. That's the word I've used all these years Emelia. You've haunted my marriage and because of you Emelia it never had a chance to succeed. So are you proud of yourself and all that you caused? To know these wonderful children you speak of will have to live in a home without both of their parents. Where is your dignity and respect for this family?"

I hide my face in my hands and shake my head. I look at her, "Please stop. Stop hurting these people you love or once loved. I know lashing out at me might make you feel better. But we both know all that you said is not the truth. Just let it go and move on."

Luca rubs and pats my knee and then stands. "Violeta, you've said what you came here to say and so much more. Now I'm asking you to leave. Say goodbye to our children, you will see them again tomorrow and Rafael and I will drive you to your friend's home."

Violeta sits back on her chair and folds her arms, "Well you see I have no place to go but here. I figured after you and I made up I would stay the night. And we'd drive together with our children back to our home tomorrow and restart our lives again. I never thought she would be here and interfere with us."

Luca and Rafael are standing behind Violeta in silence. I understand Luca wants to keep this amicable and calm, but this woman is so hurtful and mean. And she has crossed so many lines with me. I say to Violeta in a low voice, "Wow stop with the lies. Is there nothing you won't do to manipulate this man again? You knew I was here. I saw you yesterday when we were walking in town and you stood across the street watching me. Stop playing these games. These are real people. They are loving and caring people. And if you want to have any tolerable future with them, you will stop this foolishness now."

Julieta approaches her mother, "Mamá is that the truth? Have you been here all along?" Violeta takes her daughter's hand, "It's not what you think. And I only want what's best for you and your brother."

Julieta pulls her hand from her mother's grasp and walks over to Luca, "So, if you want what's best, you need to move on. Marcos and I never want to go back to the way it was the last few years and especially when you were with that other man. I hated you for that and all the pain you put Papá through. I don't know what it's like to be in a relationship, let alone a marriage. I just know I don't want what you two had. And after spending these few days with Papá and Emmy, I can only hope that I'll find someone that loves me as genuinely as they love one another. Coming here to this home has been one of my greatest joys and yet, you came here today to try and taint all that. You're my mother and I will always love you. But for all that you've done and are doing right now I don't like you very much."

Violeta stands and gets in my face and shouts, "I can't believe this you turned my husband against me and now you've succeeded with my daughter. Go home and find another family to steal!"

Luca places a hand on Violeta's shoulder to move her away from me and says, "Violeta! I want you to leave right now. You will never step foot in this home again. Not as long as I'm alive. Wait outside for me and Rafael."

She looks at him with daggers in her eyes walks over to the couch and sits next to Henry. She shouts, "I told you, my plan was to stay here and go home with you tomorrow. You wouldn't kick the mother of your children to the road. I'll just sleep here on the couch. And tomorrow you can drive me home."

Luca begins to laugh, "I won't be kicking you to the road I still show you more respect than you ever have for me. You never wanted to come to this place before and I will certainly not allow you to stay here tonight or any other night. Now get your things and meet me outside."

Claudia marches up to Luca and whispers something to him. From where he's sitting Rico says something to Claudia in a raised but commanding voice. She looks at Rico and continues talking with Luca. Shaking his head, Luca does not say a word to his mother.

I hear the faint sound of luggage being wheeled down the hallway and when the noise gets louder we all look towards the living room archway and see Rafael and Marcos entering with what I presume Violeta's bags. Teresa walks over to Rafael, she tugs on his arm and they slip away towards the kitchen, leaving Marcos standing alone with his mother's things. It's a very sad image. I look to Frida and in a way only true friends can understand. My facial expression communicates my distress for Marcos. Frida promptly gets up and joins him placing her hands on his shoulders. My eyes tear up when we look at one another and she nods to me.

Rafael and Teresa return to the torture room and Rafael informs Luca of something. Luca nods his head and pats his brother's shoulder.

Luca goes over to Violeta, "We can make arrangements for you at a hotel or Rafael and Teresa are offering for you to stay at their home. They will drive you there now. We will figure out your ride home tomorrow unless you can call on your friend to take you back."

Violeta sits wordlessly in defeat. Julieta says, "Mamá, I'll go with you now and get you settled in. Come on." She extends a hand to her mother. Violeta slowly rises and when she walks past Luca turns around and says, "Luciano I will never forget how disgracefully you treated me today. Make the hotel reservation and I expect you to pay. I'll be waiting for you outside." Ominously Violeta pronounced the s sound in Luciano similar to when a snake is moving in on its victim.

Violeta exchanges words with Claudia and they embrace as they say goodbye. Marcos and Julieta walk with Violeta and her luggage through the kitchen and after we hear the door close, everyone that is left in the living room lets out a sigh of relief.

Rafael tells Luca, "I'll just take her to our house she doesn't need to stay at a hotel." Luca replies, "I appreciate you trying to help, but she's still my responsibility and my headache. I do need your assistance, my mind is blanking, I can't think of a hotel nearby. Can you recommend any?" Henry jumps to his feet, "Let me grab my laptop and we'll find one."

Abuelo enters the room as Henry exits. He looks to Rafael for an explanation. Rafael brings Abuelo over to the other couch and when they both sit, I hear Rafael speaking with him. Olivia taps my shoulder and when I turn to look at her, she's holding the glass for me. I smile at her and say, "I'm so tense right now I wish that juice had some rum or vodka in it." Taking it from her I sip the refreshing drink. With a half-smile she says, "I can make that happen very easily."

Henry comes back and with the laptop open is already tapping away on the keypad. Luca sits next to me and says, "Are you doing okay?" I pass the glass back to Olivia and take Luca into my arms, he holds me as securely as I hold him. I whisper, "You ask me how I'm doing. It's you and your kids I'm most concerned about." We stay locked together until Henry announces he found two hotels about thirty minutes away. Luca caresses my face with his hand and says, "I'll be right back." He goes over to Henry and removes his wallet from his pants pocket. "Let me see the hotels you've located."

As they make Violeta's hotel reservation I excuse myself to Olivia to use the bathroom. Before I go down the hall to my room I take a quick glance into the kitchen and I find Claudia standing alone looking out the door. I can't even begin to figure out a way to reach her. More importantly get her to support her son's choices so they can repair their relationship.

After my much needed toilet visit I'm eager to wash away all that just happened in the other room. I brush my teeth and wash my hands and my face. Then I immerse a washcloth in the sink filled with cold water. Wringing it out, I place the cloth on the back of my neck. I just need a few peaceful minutes before going back to everyone. Lying down on my bed for a minute or two with my eyes closed I begin to feel the tension ease from my neck. Luca comes into the room without even knocking and shuts the door gently. Joining me on the bed he cozies himself next to me, resting his head next to mine on the pillow.

"I'm leaving in a few minutes but I want to be alone with you before I go." Turning to face him I notice his blue eyes are missing the zest that was there earlier when the four of us were in the gardens together. Caressing his face he closes his eyes and hums to me. With his eyes still closed he says, "I'm so sorry." I place my finger on his lips, "Luca my love, you didn't do anything wrong, so you should not apologize."

I pause and nervously say, "I should apologize to you and your children." With a confused expression he says, "Why, what for?"

"Luca, I shouldn't have spoken with Violeta. And I certainly should not have said the things I said."

Caressing my face, he replies, "I wish you didn't have to experience any of this. She wasn't very nice to either of us today and it was only natural for you to react that way. Don't be so hard on yourself."

Upsettingly I say, "But Luca, it's not me that I'm worried about. I'm worried about your children." He smirks at me and responds, "They've been around to hear us arguing in the past. Not that it makes it any easier. But like Jules said, she knows that her parents aren't any good together. I doubt whatever you said had any impact on them."

Yet, the heavy weight in my belly tells me something very different. I ask, "So are you saying they know how and why you and their mother got back together and the lies she told to get you back?"

He looks at me blankly and says, "Let's talk about this later. As much as I don't want to leave you, the sooner I take care of this the sooner I return to you."

I nod and before he leaves asks, "Will you stay in here until I get back?"

"Probably not, I just need a few more minutes to calm down and then I'll join them. Unless you think it's best for me to stay away?"

He laughs and nods his head, "No, don't read into that at all. I was just wondering." I wave at him and he's gone.

After lying down on the bed for a while I look at the clock and I'm shocked to see it's almost four-thirty. How long was that awful exchange with Violeta? Timidly I leave my room and venture into the family area. Gratefully my favorite trio welcomes me at the dining table, Frida, Olivia and Teresa. Frida pulls out the chair closest to her and I sit. I ask, "Where's everyone else?"

Olivia says, "The shuttle to the hotel included Rafael, Luca, Marcos, Julieta and their mother. My boys along with Henry, Victor and Max are upstairs and the elders are sitting in the living room." I turn to Teresa, "Are your daughters joining us later?" She smiles and nods, "Yes, they should be here shortly."

After we sit quietly together I say, "I need your advice, this is all new territory for me. Maybe I shouldn't have spoken to Violeta, or said the things I said. It's probably not my place. Should I apologize to everyone especially Luca and the children? Tell me what should I do?"

They all look bemused at each other. And one by one, with Frida leading, they start to giggle. And Frida leans towards me, grasps my shoulder and hugs me. "Oh, Emelia, you don't owe any one of us an apology. Violeta should be asking for forgiveness, for today and so many of her actions."

I inquire, "Do you all feel the same?" And Teresa and Olivia nod in agreement. A wave of relief runs through me.

Claudia treads lightly from the living room to the table and sits near us at the head chair. I don't even know who to make eye contact with so I look at my hands and the inlaid pattern on the table. Until now, I don't think I even noticed the superb woodwork. Clearing her throat Claudia says, "Ladies I'd like to speak with Emelia." They all look to the other and start to get up when Claudia says, "No, you can remain, I just want to talk with her." And I think, I should have taken Luca's comment more seriously and stayed in my room until he got back. But, if this is my future mother-in-law, we need to start building our relationship.

"Tell me, what do you think happened here today?"

As I gather my thoughts I look to the other women and then at Claudia, "I think several things. First, that conversation should not have happened with an audience. Second, I hope Luca talks with Julieta and Marcos. For them to see their mother like that must have been difficult. And third I sensed that Luca gets strength from all of you otherwise I don't think he could have been as composed and direct with her of his wishes. I'm sure when she asked for the divorce initially it rocked his world. But seeing the man he is today, and how he is with all of you, just shows me the love and support you provided him when he needed it most. So, to answer your question about what occurred here today, I can only speak about what I've observed since I arrived last Saturday in order to even interpret what just happened. I think I witnessed another moment of a crumbling marriage. Where one spouse has accepted it's near the end and the other is still in denial."

Claudia stares at me and says, "When do you leave?"

Unsure where she's heading, "My flight is on Saturday."

"How do you plan on dating my son when you live in another country?"

"We haven't charted out the schedule yet, but we anticipate taking turns living in each of our homes while we get to know one another."

"Will this be a healthy situation for my grandchildren after all they've been through, with their father living in two countries? Don't you think maybe you should step aside and see if their parents can repair their marriage? And they can be a happy family again."

"Claudia I have thought about all you just said and I've learned they haven't been a happy family for a while now. But if Luca asks me to give him space, I would oblige him. I even suggested it."

"Well, suggesting it and actually following through are two separate actions. You see, since you're not a mother, you don't understand what it takes to be a wife with children. You'll do whatever you can just to keep your family together no matter what."

"I'm confused Claudia, didn't Violeta ask him for the divorce when she was sleeping with another man? And since you are Luca's mother, why are you siding with the one person in his life that has hurt him the most?"

She sits back and folds her arms, "You just don't understand. Keeping the family together is more important than her past relations with that other man or this fling between you two. It didn't work out years ago and it won't work out now. Just give him up and leave my son alone."

Frida places her hand on mine. "Mamá, YOU don't understand. We are responsible for keeping Luca and Emelia apart all those years ago. You were selfish, thinking you'd lose him and he'd live with her in New York. I was jealous he'd get the chance to live in the city that I had to leave behind. And I was also jealous at how in love they were. I had a love like that before in a place I could have lived the rest of my life. But I ended that because you and Papá insisted I move back home. I don't regret my marriage or the son I have, but there are moments when I wonder how different my life might have been if I stayed in New York. So please, stop interfering and let them finally be together the way they should have been for all these years. You owe it to them. And as his mother, you must see the joy that she brings to Luca. We all see it. Stop denying it. And be part of their happiness." Tears stream down my face as Frida's hand squeezes mine.

And when I close my eyes and wipe my tears I feel two hands on my shoulders and Luca whispers into my ear, "Does my love need a tissue?" Hearing his voice and feeling his touch soothes me and I reply, "Yes desperately." He kisses my temple and gives me the handkerchief with the little blue bird. He says, "I've learned sharing my life with someone with a heart as tender as yours I must always be ready to wipe away your tears." Luca places his arms around me and I squeeze him tightly. He whispers, "Now tell me, what did I just walk in on?"

I busy myself with the delicate square linen in the hopes that someone else might chime in. Rafael's energetic voice startles me, "Have I missed the games? Where are the other kids?" Luca releases me and when I push my chair away to stand Frida rises too. I look to her and we quickly embrace. I whisper, "I never knew how much you were hurting all those years ago. I should have been a better friend to you. Please forgive me."

She tightens her hold on me and replies, "I'm just so thankful to have my best friend back. I hope you can forgive me too." Luca drops a tissue box on the table and through our tears, we laugh. Frida let's go of me to grab tissues for herself.

Luca wraps his arm around my waist, "You'll tell me later?"

I nod, "Yes. How did your transport go?"

He rolls his eyes, "It's a fairly nice hotel. And Marcos offered to keep his mother company. I told him to call me anytime and I'll drive over to bring him back. But he said he'll be fine. He's a better man than me."

I tilt my head at him and say, "Who do you think he is emulating? And she is his mother."

Julieta, Gabriela and Graciela march in from the outside carrying containers and bags of food. Teresa joins them and announces, "With our daughters' quick thinking nobody is cooking tonight."

Chapter 48

THE REST OF the afternoon was just what they promised, filled with family fun. Rafael organized the games in the living room with the help of all the kids. I assisted the ladies in the kitchen and we brought light nibbles and drinks to everyone to hold us over until dinner. After what occurred in this room earlier today, it was good to see the family joking around and smiling again.

We first warmed up with an easy game of charades. It was so funny for me when a player was acting out before their team and the team is yelling to them in Spanish. When my team was up, I tried my best to participate and when I actually figured out one of the charades, Luca was translating my answer as the buzzer sounded. The judges needed to decide if my English answer was acceptable. Luckily the judges were the twins and they sided with me.

When it was my turn I figured I'd require some help translating what was written on the small paper, but much to my surprise I did not. My charade was a movie titled *Magic Mike*. I looked around at the other team to see who put this one in the mix. And I caught Frida giggling in the corner.

I tried to think of the quickest and least suggestive way to act out the title. Frida grabbed the timer and yelled to me, "Are you ready?" I smiled and gave her a thumb-up. "Go!"

After motioning it's a film and with two words, I started to describe the first word, and pretended to be a magician. Henry yells, "Magic!" I nodded yes and hoped some of the ladies on my team would just need that word and solve it. But they were all silent. I go for the second word and act out being a singer and pointed to my imaginary microphone, but maybe they aren't aware of "Mic" being the abbreviation. So in my desperation to get my team a win, I waved my hands to clear their minds and began to respectfully improvise a male stripper. And just when I was about to remove my fake rip away pants, Olivia screamed, "*Magic Mike!*"

Everyone including my love was hysterical and when I took my seat next to Luca he couldn't control his laughter. I spotted Rafael explaining to Abuelo and when I saw the old man's face change from confusion to shock and then amusement I sat back satisfied with my performance.

The next couple of hours were as much fun and quite competitive too. It was a terrific afternoon followed by a delicious dinner with an assortment of dishes from three restaurants. Nobody talked about what took place earlier in the day. And Luca called Marcos during the games and now he just hung up with him.

"He said they just returned from dinner. They met up with a few friends of hers. But now they are back at the hotel watching a movie." Luca places the phone on the kitchen counter takes my hand and we join the rest of the group on the evening stroll to the ridge.

Tonight I am told we have a few newcomers, Olivia, Teresa, Frida and Max have decided to join us. Frida assured Max he'll be fine provided they use a flashlight. I sense a bittersweet energy. After all the happiness we've enjoyed this week knowing tonight is the last night we'll be together at this house along with Marcos' absence.

Reaching the peak the kids are excited to show the first-timers the view. Luca and I stand together with his arm draped over my shoulder, watching everyone as we are surrounded by the starlit sky. My thoughts bounce from my first experience here with only Luca on Christmas Eve, to decades lived without the other, all the events of this week, sitting with Marcos and Julieta the other night talking about the stars and Luca's almost proposal and suddenly the waterworks trickle down my cheeks. Luca kisses my temple and I hear him remove a tissue pack from his pocket. I whisper, "It's almost perfect tonight." We stand together and I say, "Have I thanked you for showing up at my doorstep last Saturday?" He smiles and squeezes me, "Have I thanked you for permitting me inside? I suppose we're even."

With our enlarged group we fit snuggly on the benches. Well, actually just our bench is tight. Frida's trio is sitting with us. So Julieta decides to sit on her dad's lap. Julieta says, "Tía Frida, now with Papá living partly in New York with Emelia, you have to plan many trips to visit me when I'm at school." Frida replies, "Well when they invite me, I will book my flights. Your Tío Max and cousin might want to come along too." Julieta squeals, "Yes absolutely!"

Before we leave the ridge the kids explain the tradition and introduce a new one, they organize us all in one big circle holding hands. Henry begins, *"Para todos los que vienen aquí después de nosotros, les deseo que la risa."* [For all who will come here after us, I wish them laughter.] He raises his hand linked with Benjamin's.

Benjamin says, "I wish them a full stomach."

Olivia adds, "Adventures with loved ones."

Mateo wishes them, "Clean clothes."

Max says, "Good vision."

Victor includes, "Cousins that are like brothers and sisters."

Frida requests, "Honesty."

Julieta wishes they find, "Courage in the face of change."

Luca says, "To never lose hope."

He raises our hands, and with my heart thumping with happiness, I say, "An open heart."

I raise my hand clasped with Teresa and she says, "New beginnings."

Graciela adds, "A safe home."

Gabriela wishes them, "A long life."

And Rafael ends with, *"Amor Eterno."* [Everlasting love]

Since it's the last night we linger back to the house. I wonder when we'll all be together again here at this loving home. As we say our goodbyes to Rafael and his family, he hugs me tightly and whispers, "I better see you before Christmas." I reply, "I hope to see you before then too. But I leave it up to your brother."

Teresa grabs my arms, kisses me and says, "I look forward to being sisters with you." I smile and touch her cheek, "Me too. Thank you for being so kind and honest with me." She replies, "Of course, you're so easy to love. Now go and plan your future together."

When the twins hug me goodbye they call me Tía Emmy. I follow them to their car while Teresa goes on and on about my next visit.

After they drive off I walk towards the rest of the group and I see Frida and Luca talking. When I approach, they suddenly become silent and Frida nods to Luca. Henry asks, "When is everyone leaving tomorrow? And I have room for another in case."

Luca responds, "That's what Frida and I were just discussing. Julieta and I will leave here early and pick up Marcos and Violeta. Since Mamá and Papá rode here with me, I thought they can ride back with either of you."

Henry looks at Olivia and says, "We'll take my parents and the boys can take turns in Frida's car, yes?" Benjamin, Mateo and Victor smile. Until now I hadn't thought about the drive back. All along I thought I'd be with Luca. And didn't he tell Violeta to get a ride back with her friend? Olivia and I make eye contact and remain expressionless. Luca says, "I will say my goodbyes now, in case you're all still sleeping when we leave. But just remember I want you at my home on Friday."

Once inside the house, Luca leads me to my room. "I'll join you after I pack my things, so try not to fall asleep." I smirk, "I'll try my best."

After changing into my pajamas and slipping between the sheets I let out a sigh. Today has been a very long day and I was comforted by Frida telling me we won't be driving back until noon. Maybe I can sleep a bit later. As I begin to doze off I sit up in bed to stay awake. A lot happened here earlier and we need to talk about it tonight. Dragging myself out of bed I sit at the window seat. Looking out into the darkness I begin to hear the terrible things Violeta said to me and Luca. She was determined to get her way, but he wasn't giving into her. Or did he?

Luca enters the room and finds me at the window, "Why are you sitting all the way over there? I thought you'd be in bed."

"I was in bed and I almost fell asleep, so I came over here to stay awake."

He takes my hand, "Ok, I'm here now, come to bed."

I resist, "Don't you think we need to talk?"

Luca sits on the cushion next to me, "Yes, we should talk, but it's late and I have a drive tomorrow that will feel like the longest ride of my life. And

I want us to enjoy our last night together here. Didn't she already ruin our almost perfect day?"

"Yes, she did and she's also ruining our day tomorrow."

"She's ruining my day, not your day."

I grasp his hands with both of mine, "She's getting what she came here for, you. Don't you see; she had a plan and one that always included me being here. So, she has to have a plan B."

"What was I supposed to do, just throw her out, hoping someone would come get her?"

"I don't know, but she did manage to join up with friends tonight at dinner. Why didn't she stay with them and find a ride home herself? She does seem capable, she got herself here."

Not sure if he's clearing his throat or growling at me he gets up and walks around the room and then sits again, "I didn't think of any of that, I just wanted her out of here. And the sooner I get her and the kids back to their home tomorrow, the sooner you and I can be together. I was determined to be with you no matter what."

"Luca, I'm not trying to be difficult you already have enough to manage. I'm just trying to figure out if she's manipulating you again. I realize you're looking out for Julieta and Marcos and you want to treat their mother kindly. But, you made this all too easy for her. Don't you think if I was in the car too with you, she would find another way home?"

He sighs, "I am not driving six hours with the two of you in the same car. Nothing good will come of that."

"You think I want to put any of us through that again? Certainly not, I care too much about you and the kids you're just missing my point. She knew you'd jump in and take care of her. And now, she has a night at a hotel with Marcos and six hours in the car with you and the kids."

"So what are you suggesting?"

I sigh, "Well, I didn't get that far yet. Until an hour ago, I didn't know you'd be driving her home. I thought I was making the ride back with you."

He takes my hand, "I'm so sorry, I didn't forget about you, I was just trying to keep peace. And I figured you wouldn't mind being in Frida's car. I should have discussed this with you. But until last Saturday, I've been making plans without having to consider someone like you in my life. Please accept my apologies. From now on I will talk with you first."

I giggle and he growls again, "What is making you laugh? And it better not spiral into that silly fit like the other night. I'm too stressed."

I giggle again, "It won't and you probably won't see the humor in what I'm about to say, but I'll try my best. When I said I hadn't really had time to think of a plan, because I thought I'd be in your car, I hadn't even thought about you not discussing the change of plans with me. How sad is that? Until last Saturday, I haven't been a girlfriend to someone for years. So, me not being included wasn't the first thing I thought about, I was more focused on her just coming in here and taking advantage of your good nature. My initial reaction is to protect you and the kids from her destructive behavior."

Playfully I add, "Maybe I should feel insulted, huh? Mister, don't ever forget about me again." Pulling him towards me I surprise him with a very passionate kiss. When we part I say, "I hope that's a good enough reminder that I'm in your life now." His laugh comes from deep inside and he scoops me into his arms and carries me to our bed.

"Should I set the alarm for the same time?" He nestles close to me with one arm across my chest and his lips close to my ear, "No, let's change it to seven." I reach my phone and adjust the alarm. "Not that I want you to go, but when are you and Julieta leaving?"

"I told her between eight and eight thirty."

We lie quietly for awhile. He asks, "You're good with the arrangements tomorrow?"

"Yes and no. I would have liked driving back with you, but due to the circumstances, there's no other option."

He cuddles me, "Thanks for being so understanding."

"Plus tomorrow night, we'll make up for being apart all day."

He hums into my neck, "Can I have a sneak preview now?"

I reply, "I thought you'd never ask."

Timidly he says, "Well, I was slightly worried after our discussion and when I noticed you wearing your armor again."

He slips his hand under my top and caresses my skin. I giggle, "I like to keep you guessing. I shouldn't be so easy with you."

Luca says, "Well we have been falling back on our goal. We should start doubling up our efforts or bank a few transactions to stay ahead."

I giggle some more and then he hushes me. While he's removing his shirt replies, "I may be the team captain, but you are a vital part of making this happen too. And you also challenged me that we'd reach that figure in two years. I hope you're not wiggling out of this now."

Flirting, I say, "Oh no captain, I plan to succeed. And with your assistance, you can help me wiggle out of my pajamas." Kissing my neck he whispers, "Ah, my love, I'd be most delighted."

Chapter 49

WAKING BEFORE THE alarm this morning allows me to selfishly enjoy Luca. Careful not to disturb him I gently shift in the bed. When I turn I'm welcomed by my handsome, scruffy, cuddly, kissable and very awake boyfriend. He whispers, "Good morning mi amor. I've been waiting for you." I smile and whisper, "My love, your patience and devotion brought me back to you. I am forever yours."

He kisses my forehead and pulls me into his arms. Tightly we hold one another and savor being together before the chaos of the day begins. "Have you been awake long?"

"No, but it felt like an eternity."

"Just think, tomorrow morning, we'll be alone in your house and won't need to sneak around. Can we spend all morning in bed together? Or have you made plans?"

His melodic kisses begin at my shoulder trail up my neck and along my jawbone. He says, "No plans yet for the morning; just you and me with endless possibilities. How does that sound?"

Humming with delight I say, "Perfect. I think we'll make great travel buddies."

He looks at me strangely and then smiles. I inquire, "What's that look about?" He replies, "What look, I don't have a look."

I smirk, "I meant since we've been getting along easily this week and we like doing the same things, going away on vacation just you and me will be a breeze."

Nodding he says, "Yes, I agree, great travel buddies, but isn't a buddy a friend?"

Understanding his funny look I say, "Oh that's why you looked at me funny." He nodded and shrugged.

"Where are some places you'd like us to vacation?" he asks. Thinking I say, "Well, not in any specific order, Italy, because when I've been there I was a single woman. And now as a woman in love, I'm sure it will be a very different experience. I also can see us away in a snow village, where we spend hours outdoors doing all kinds of sport, freezing our butts off. At night drinking wine and warming up near the fire under blankets with no pajamas. And we both enjoy the beach, so, that's a must go destination."

I continue, "One other place among the long list of places is a city that I hold dear to my heart. I know that I've lived there most of my life and you do business there, but I can't wait to show you my New York."

He smiles at me, "Oh, what would you have us do in your New York?"

I kiss him quickly, "Well, of course I would ask you first what haven't you done, it is your vacation too. But, since you're asking me, I would put on our list, all the romantic activities, like, champagne at The Plaza Hotel, followed by a carriage ride in Central Park, buying each other something at Tiffany's, kissing at the top of the Empire State Building, dinner at some tiny offbeat delicious restaurant where we can canoodle in the corner like teenagers and dance the night away at a hot Latin club, I love when you lead me around the dance floor. And the next day,"

He interrupts, "That was just one day?"

I giggle, "Yes! We'd walk around SoHo and the Village, I'd show you where Frida lived, we'd have brunch, head uptown, find a place to watch the sunset and if the season was right, we'd also catch an outdoor film or concert. Oh and we must go to the opera all dressed up and when we don't have plans, just walk and talk holding hands exploring and people watching."

My eyes tear up just thinking about sharing my life with him. He wipes my face and I ask, "So, do you like any of my ideas? And where do you want us to travel to?"

He responds, "I know you don't like to talk about your first marriage, but, I want to make sure I don't suggest places you've been to with your ex or your droves of other men. Where did you honeymoon? You love Italy so much, you didn't go there together?"

I reply, "Actually we didn't honeymoon anywhere. And all those ideas I just thought about, are things I want to do with you and I never did with anyone else."

He smirks, "We didn't honeymoon either."

I ask, "Really, why?"

"I was not pleasant and made excuses that I couldn't get away because of work. And promised we'd go later on when I had less pressure. That opportunity never presented itself. Why didn't you get away?"

"It was complicated and we had no money. Said we'd wait until our first anniversary and well, we split before then."

We look at each other tenderly, he says, "Let's get back on track here. I like them all. And the only way you'll keep me out in the cold all day, is knowing I'll have you alone naked under the blankets for hours afterwards."

My body trembles and I add, "You know, I should have mentioned, the couples massage and other indulgences. I hope you're a spa guy."

Nodding he says, "I do like being pampered, but I think we should learn the art of massage. Going forward I want to be the only man to put his hands all over you from now on."

"I can understand that, plus I owe you one and I'll include a happy ending."

He closes his eyes and moans, "Can you fit me in tonight, or is that too short notice?"

I grin and say, "Let me check, I think I just had a cancellation."

He grabs me and paddles my bottom and says, "They're all cancelling, you are mine and only mine. I'm tossing out your appointment book." I laugh into his chest.

"Emelia, these moments with you in bed have been very special to me. And I'm not just talking about the sex. Every chance I get to be near you, I feel rejuvenated by your beautiful soul. I thrive on it. That's why when I would come in here to get you and lie with you, it's so my soul can get nourished again. Your smile, your scent, your touch, your voice, your laugh, your kisses, I never want to live another day apart from you."

I lean up and deeply kiss him. While he shuffles out of his pajama bottoms I hear the alarm chimes sounding and I stretch to silence the phone. He swiftly removes my panties. I gasp, "Is there enough time?" Nibbling on my earlobe he says, "I told you before, there's always time. Why else do you think I wake you up so early?"

Chapter 50

"THE CAR IS all packed and I'm leaving in a few minutes." I reply, "I can't believe I fell back to sleep. Are you leaving this soon?"

Looking at his watch Luca says, "It's almost eight-thirty." With my head resting on his chest I say, "I know I said some things last night to you about Violeta. I want you to know that I commend you on the way you spoke with her yesterday. It took a lot of control and focus to not battle with her. You are a very good man Luca and I'm aware this situation is not easy. And if you need me to ride with you today, I'll follow your lead and not engage with her whatsoever."

He chortles, "My love, I wasn't always like that with her. After months of couples therapy or actually uncoupling therapy, I'm handling our confrontations with less emotion and more management. And thank you for offering but, we'll be fine. Julieta and I have always had a unique bond and after this year it's gotten even stronger. Like she said, her parents are not a good fit and she wants this over as much as I do. She'll have my back today."

"I'm relieved to hear that. Now about what I said to Violeta yesterday, you don't seem that concerned, I do and especially after hearing Julieta's wish last night, do you remember?" Luca looks at me thinking and I continue, "She said, courage in the face of change. Please make sure Jules and Marcos are doing okay after all that happened here." He nods, "Yes Emelia, I will talk with them." Softly he kisses me.

"So, I guess I'll see you when I see you. I think we're leaving around noon today. Hopefully that means you'll have a few hours at home before I occupy your space."

He smiles, "Yes, I'll need to prepare for your arrival."

I giggle, "Oh, like clean your mess and restock the fridge."

"Yes, you got me all figured out. And before I forget and this sounds so odd to be asking you just now, you know after all we've been doing." He takes out his phone, "So, I'd like to call you, maybe ask you out on a date, will you give me your phone number?"

I laugh into his chest, "Phew, I was a little nervous wondering what you needed to ask me." He continues, "Actually I meant to ask you on Monday morning before I left, but my mind hasn't been the same since you opened your door to me."

In my best valley girl accent, "So, like, if I give you my number, will you actually call? Or are you just playing games with me?"

With a smirk he says, "What is that voice?" I roll my eyes, "Really, you don't remember the valley girls from the eighties?" He replies, "If I say no, will you never use that voice around me again?" I giggle, "For sure."

He slides his hand down my face to stop me from continuing and covers my mouth. I kiss the hand that's stifling me and he moves it away. I tell him in my regular voice, "So, if you find yourself tense at all during the drive, just think of my valley girl impression and hopefully it'll bring a smile to your face."

He shakes his head, "Oh no, no, no, no. I have a better idea, I will think about you and me swimming together the other day. And all will be good again." I wink at him, "That is a very sweet memory. I'd like to do that again with you." Kissing me tenderly he says, "Your wish is my command. I will make that happen."

When he stands I notice him tapping the screen on his phone, "Do I have to beg for your number?" I grab his phone and see our picture saved on the screen. "Look at you I don't even have one of us on my phone yet." I save my information in his contacts and I call my phone. Grabbing it quickly the number is showing up as private.

"Hey mystery man, what is your phone number?"

He stammers and says, "You know, like I'm not that kind of guy who just gives out his number to any girl that asks. I like to make the first move. Trust me I'll totally call you 'cause you're like totally tubular."

I grab the pillow and scream with laughter. His Latino valley guy impersonation was hilarious. He kneels on the bed pulls the pillow from me and says, "Like you know, my valley boy was more awesome than your valley girl."

I jump up quickly and hug and kiss him, "We're two loonies that are so perfect together."

He swats my bottom, "Ok, I should go. Are you good?"

"Yes, I am good." I kiss him softly, "I love you. And I will miss you more than you know. Be safe."

He smiles, "Te amo, I'll be missing you even more. I'll call you." I point at him, "You better, 'cause I can't call you."

He opens the door to leave, "Oh Luca, will I see Julieta at your house tomorrow?" He nods yes. "Please tell her I said good bye for now." "I will." With a quick wave to me he shuts the door and he's gone.

Left alone in our bed a wave of sadness rushes over me; hurriedly I run into the bathroom, wash my face and brush my teeth. Putting my sweater over my pajamas I slide my sandals on and dash out into the hallway to give Luca another goodbye. Running out the door, I see he's in the car with Julieta and they're still in the driveway.

I wave towards them and I go over to his side of the car, he opens the door and when he gets out I hug him closely. "Oh, Mi Lia, we'll be together soon." I look into his eyes, "I know, I just wanted to give you another hug." He takes my face in his hands, "I was thinking of doing the same." We part and he gets back into the driver's seat. Taking my hand he kisses it tenderly. "I'll see you tonight." I nod, "I can't wait." I tilt my head down and look to Julieta, "Bye Jules see you tomorrow?" She smiles, "Yes, I'll see you tomorrow Emmy." Luca lets me go and I walk over and join Frida, her parents, Abuelo, Henry and Olivia. Frida puts her arm around me and we all wave to Luca and Julieta as their car travels down the bumpy road. I see their hands waving back to us until I don't see the car anymore.

The others go inside and we sit on the porch. "Nice pajamas Emelia," Frida jokes.

"Thanks Frida." I see she too is still in her pajamas, I ask, "Have you been up for long?"

"No, I heard some voices and thought Luca was leaving, and wanted to see him before they left, how about you?"

"No, I woke up when he came into the room a few minutes ago."

She smiles at me, "Are you hungry?" I rub my stomach, "Yes actually. But maybe I should shower first. Are you hungry?"

"I was just remembering that day in my apartment when you had slept over the night before and we spent the entire day in our pajamas and all we did was talk and eat."

I look at her and smile, "Yes that was a very good day."

She adds, "Being with you this week makes me feel like it happened just a short time ago. And the funny thing is I feel like I'm the same age. I can't believe I'm fifty years old."

"Yeah, I can't believe you're that old either." I smile at her and give her a quick hug. "Seriously, you look the same."

"Thanks, you still look good too Emmy."

"That same day in your apartment you showed me pictures of your family that were in a photo album. And when you pointed out Luca, you asked me something like if I was attracted to him or thought he was cute."

She smiles, "I remember, and you said not really but you would have to meet him first to decide or something like that, right?"

"Yeah, without knowing him, the photo didn't convey his personality."

She whispers, "When did you fall for him?"

I smile when I think back on those first days with him. "Well, the night I arrived for your wedding and we went to his place, the spark ignited when we met. And the morning when we were all going to the beach, I first saw him on the terrace and we exchanged words and I felt my heart pounding for him like it was jumping up and down, just to be near him. Every moment that followed, my feelings for him deepened more and more. I wanted to tell you then, but knew it was wrong because he was involved with her. And I wasn't certain of his feelings. The night when most everyone left, he and I went out together and we admitted our feelings to one another."

Frida says, "I meant what I said yesterday. And you can always confide in me, I'm sorry you felt you couldn't. I feel like we could have avoided all this."

I nod to her and say, "Thanks. And I'm done thinking back at woulda-coulda-shouldas, especially when I, WE have so much to look forward to."

And she says, "On that note, let's go inside and see about breakfast."

On our way into the house Frida says, "Oh, remind me tomorrow to get a picture of just the two of us." I smile, "I will, or how about now in our PJs?" She giggles, "We can do that too, but I was thinking about the lovely picture frame you gave me for my birthday."

I nod, "Oh yes, with the photo of us from a million years ago on one side." She puts her arm around my shoulders and says, "Yes, that was a great idea to give me the double frame. With two pictures side by side, then and now, we can see how much we really aged."

The hours after Luca and Julieta left went by very quickly. I showered, packed and helped with stripping the beds and preparing the house for the cleaning service. Thankfully I remembered to preserve some of the flowers Luca gave me. When I put them in my bag, I grab my charged up phone and notice I have a text. It's from my boyfriend and I smile seeing my first ever text from Luca that he sent not long after he left here.

> *Hola, Mi Lia,*
> *So you don't forget me, here's a picture of us.*
> *Con amor, xxx Luca. I will call when I arrive home.*

The picture he sent me is the one he has on his phone. It's of us at dinner the other night, our official first date. Now I have it saved as the wallpaper on my phone. What should I text him?

> *My Luca, you are unforgettable. Thank you for sending the photo. I'm awaiting your charming voice with anticipation. Forever yours, Emelia xxx*

I press send and before putting the phone in my bag, I wait to make sure the text transmits.

Before bringing my bags out I take some last moments in this room that we shared and wonder when we'll be back here again. And what lies ahead for us. Standing in the doorway I whisper, "Goodbye room. Take care of my sweet memories."

Loading up the cars I see the twins have returned to get Abuelo. Olivia and I hurry inside to get the leftover trays of goodies to give to them to bring home. The family extends their goodbyes to Abuelo and when it's my turn he pulls me into his arms and pats my back. As we separate he takes my hand with the ring and he looks at it while rubbing his finger over it. And just like Luca, he places my hand over his heart and taps it gently and smiles at me.

I tell him, "Abuelo, I hold you and your wife close in my heart. Many, many thanks. I look forward to seeing you very soon. Be well." He kisses my cheek gently and as Rico helps him into the front passenger seat he tells Abuelo all that I said.

The house is closed and the cars are fully packed. The first part of the ride, I'm in the backseat with Victor and Benjamin with Max and Frida in the front seat. As I get comfortable I check the clock on my phone and see it's just past noon. In three hours or so, I should hear from Luca and hopefully three hours after that I'll be with him at his home. I make sure the ringer is turned on and I slide the phone into the outside pocket of my bag.

The energy is a bit different from our drive here. Benjamin and Victor are engrossed with some car games, I'm reading a book and Frida and Max exchange light banter. Some moments we all engage in the same topic, but for the most part, I think after the week we've had, we are content with just being quiet together.

Our first rest stop is about two and half hours into the drive. Frida tells me it's a place her father suggested. Entering this little restaurant, I see that the owner knows Rico and they embrace. Rico introduces us to the owner and his wife. When they show us to the table, most of us quickly detour to find the bathrooms leaving Rico, Max and Henry sitting together.

The lunch break took longer than planned, but I didn't mind, the conversation was light and the food was delicious. For this next phase of the trip,

Mateo replaces Benjamin. We're on the road for about fifteen minutes when my phone rings.

"Hello."

"Hola, Emelia, this is Luca."

"Hi, good timing."

"I'm calling to ask you out on our second date."

"Oh really? What do you have in mind?"

"Well, it's for tonight, are you free?"

I giggle, "Yes, I should be free tonight after seven, seven-thirty. Does that work for you?"

"Yes, I can work with that."

We remain quiet for a few seconds, I ask, "Are you okay?"

"Hmm, I'm a little tired but I'm good. I think I'll snooze some after I hang up."

"That's smart of you. I might do the same."

Looking out the window at the passing countryside I listen to Luca moving about his house. "I liked the picture a lot, thank you again."

He yawns, "I can't wait for you to get here."

"Me too. I should let you go."

"Mi Lia, are you trying to get rid of me?"

"Oh no, never...I just thought maybe you wanted to sleep."

"I do, but I want to hear your voice a bit more before we hang up. Tell me about your morning without me."

In a voice just above a whisper I describe to Luca all that I did, my goodbye with Abuelo and our lunch at Rico's friend's place. And during my recap his aha's and uhum's become less and less and I begin to hear his breathing getting heavier and heavier. I say, "Sleep well I'm hanging up now." He replies, "Uh-huh," and sends me a kiss. I do the same and end our call.

Putting the phone back in my bag I see that my seat mates have also fallen to sleep. Using my sweatshirt as a pillow I rest against the door and take a nap.

Our last break was very quick and Mateo remained with us. This final portion of the trip although shorter than the others, feels like it's much longer. I don't recognize any of the streets Max is navigating and I hear Frida tell him to slow down. They exchange words and she laughs. He makes a U-turn and Frida laughs again. She says, "Go two more and you'll see the driveway." I ask, "Are we near?" Frida turns around to me, "Yes, Max always misses the entrance." Placing my bag on my lap, I look to my phone and its seven twenty-five.

The car stops and Max's window opens, he presses a button on the gray metal box. I hear a voice that doesn't sound like Luca's but maybe the intercom distorted it. The gates in front of the car open. Max raises his window and proceeds past the gates. I turn to look out the back window and I don't see Henry's car.

"Where's Henry?"

Frida answers, "He's going directly to my parents' house. After we drop you off he will stop by our house to get Mateo."

My eyes peer through the windshield trying to locate Luca's house, but we seem to be on a dark endless road. Suddenly the road curves and I see a brightly lit house in the near distance.

"Which entrance?" Max asks Frida.

"Go to the front, he said he'll be waiting for her there."

I grab my phone and text Luca.

> *Hi my love, I think I'm just seconds away from seeing you.*

He replies back,

> *My heart beats faster as I watch the car coming closer.*

Max turns into the driveway and I feel the tires riding against the cobblestones. Mateo shouts, "YES! I'm staying at Tío Luca's tonight!"

Frida laughs, "NO. But you'll be visiting tomorrow night."

Max parks the car in the driveway and we get out. With a full body stretch, I feel the effects of the six hour drive. I hope my date will allow me a quick wake me up shower. When I approach the trunk of the car Max is pulling out my bags and I hear Luca's voice nearby. I glance at Max and he looks as drained as I feel. "Thanks for getting me here safely." He nods, "I'll see you tomorrow." I smile, "Yes, see you tomorrow."

I grab my bags and walk to Frida. She and Luca halt their conversation. I place my bags down to say goodbye to the boys and Frida.

Luca and I watch their car disappear down the long driveway. And all of a sudden, I feel nervous to be here alone with Luca. He pulls me into his arms and says, *"Bienvenido a casa, mi reina.* [Welcome home my queen.] I've waited a long time for this moment."

I smile, "Only about four hours."

"Hmm, those four hours seem more like twenty something years."

He finally gives me a much awaited kiss. Takes my hand in his and leads me to the front door. I stop and turn around to get my bags. He pulls me back to him. I say, "What are you doing, I need my bags." Shrugging at me he takes one throws the strap over his shoulder and wheels the other one and takes my hand again. Once inside, he leaves my things in the entryway.

At first glance I can understand why Mateo was so disappointed to be going someplace else tonight. We're standing in a spacious sitting area that opens up to the main level. Light stone floors throughout, honey colored wood slat cathedral high ceilings, windows that I'm sure during the day bring the picturesque outdoors inside. The walls are all unique in themselves, some look like limestone while others are wood panels. Having only visited Luca's apartment I never imagined a home as perfect for his personality as this one. And I'm only seeing a small area of the place so far.

"I will give you the grand tour later, but I think you might want to shower before our date tonight?"

"Yes, I do, thank you."

A man enters the room and Luca nods to him. When he approaches I see he's around our age, average height, olive skin and muscular build with dark curly hair and green eyes with a very gentle smile.

"Tomas, I'd like you to meet mi novia Emelia."

I extend my hand to greet him, "Hello Tomas, nice to meet you." He takes my hand with both of his and firmly welcomes me.

"Tomas and his wife Sofia take remarkable care of me and my home." I smile and say, "Well, from what I've seen so far, this home needs more than just one person to maintain it."

Luca quickly replies, "Yes, you are right especially for a messy slob like me," followed by a wink.

"Tomas, I will bring Emelia to the master suite and then return to go over the plans for later." Tomas nods and takes my bags with him when he leaves. "Emelia, from where you're standing the house appears tremendous, but after you've had a chance to live here, you'll see it's the perfect size."

I smirk and tilt my head, "Perfect size for a family of twenty?" He laughs and looks away from me and then back to me, "That's not what I meant. I just meant, ah, whatever. Let me show you to our room, unless you want to stay in a guest room?"

I close the distance between us and place my hands on his hips. "I only want to stay with you, unless you need some space?"

He nods, "I'm just offering you options."

I whisper, "Well I opt to be as close to you as possible before I leave."

He hugs me tightly and whispers, "Let's not think about that for now. I just want to enjoy being home with you for as long as we can."

Taking my hand Luca leads the way to our bedroom. "Where we just came from is the center of the home. The house is shaped like a semicircle. Over there, is where all the activities happen and the bedrooms are on the far end. Downstairs, is the entertainment area with more guest rooms and this part of the home, our area, is separated and private."

Luca bends down on one knee and removes my sandals one foot at a time. He hands me the sandals by their straps and swoops me up into his arms. He says, "My love, let me bring you into our bedroom." Kissing Luca on his neck, I feel my body tingle with excitement.

The stone floors transition to wood when we enter the corridor leading us to the master wing with pairs of his and her slippers at the doorway. Luca just flips off his shoes and walks barefoot as he carries me to our private area.

Floor to ceiling glass windows continue along the way. I'm welcomed by a cozy den with a fireplace, flat screen television and wood bookcases and cabinets on one wall. The other wall has an oversized sliding glass door. Three pieces of white leather furniture and a metal and glass coffee table sit upon a white shag rug. Spot lights, ceiling border lights and floor lighting along the edges provide a soft glow. Even though the home may look sterile with all the stone and white, the wood textures, wall treatments and furnishings provide a serene and warm atmosphere. The open air ambiance is relaxing and soothing. A very Zen like feeling surrounds me.

From the den, he climbs two or three wide long carpeted steps through a short hallway which opens into the bedroom. This room is decorated simply and with very fine lines. The king size bed is covered in white layers of linens. The bed is against a grey concrete wall with white fabric or leather directly behind the bed and the nightstands with wall sconces give a calming illumination to both sides of the bed. In the corner of the room where the two enormous glass walls meet is a white love seat and ottoman with a glass chandelier above. The upward lights cast a warm glow on the wood ceiling. A limestone wall opposite the bed houses another fireplace and flat screen.

Luca places me down near the bed. He asks, "What do you think so far?"

When I look around the bedroom I search to find the words to perfectly describe how I perceive his home. "I've only really seen this section of your home and the entrance, but being here in this particular area, your area, makes me feel like, if I drifted inside your mind and your soul this is what it would look like. So peaceful...so calm...so open...so hopeful and so natural. And I'm elated knowing you want to share all this with me. It's like a little piece of heaven on earth in here."

He pulls me into his arms and says, "And you haven't seen it during the day, when the panoramic views provide the ever changing natural backdrop. I welcome the chance to share my mind and my soul with you."

"If I was you, I'd never want to leave here."

He laughs, "Somedays I don't, but then I have to, so that when I return I recharge to face the world again. It is a peaceful retreat. And I hope you'll never want to leave here."

We hold one another for a minute or two, "We need to stay on schedule which means let me show you someplace that I know you will be more than excited to see." I giggle, "I think I might know where you're taking me." He pulls me into the hallway behind the bed and through the first door we enter the master bathroom.

The left side has double white sinks sitting on top of a light walnut wood cabinet that's about half the length of the room. On the right is an enormous glass encased shower with a bench matching the grey wall from the bedroom. The wall of the shower that continues towards the two person white stand-alone tub looks like a wall of sand drifts. Some windows in this room are high above the shower and tub and at the far end I see floor to ceiling windows followed by the toilet that's tucked into the corner. There's a vase of white roses sitting between the two sinks.

"This room will probably be in your top five, I do know how you like well-appointed bathrooms. Let me show you to your dressing room." I feel like I'm watching a TV show on the *Home and Garden* network. Back in the hallway, we enter another seating area. I see two full length mirrors on either side of a plush tan couch and two other doorways directly across from each of the mirrors.

"Close your eyes." I giggle and he makes me cover them while directing me into a room, "Now you can open them." I see my bags that Tomas took with him in a closet that is probably the size of my living room. There are wood walls with built in drawers, shelves and clothing bars, an upholstered chaise lounge in the center with a little table and lamp. In the corner there's a dressing table with a three section mirror. I walk up to the table and see a picture frame with flowers along the edges displaying a photograph of the two of us from Christmas in Panama. "Do you like?" he asks.

I wrap my arms around him and squeeze him tight. "This picture, I've never seen this one before. We're so young. Where did you get it?"

"I can't give all my secrets away just yet. I meant do you like your closet?"

"Yes, this is a tremendous and superbly designed closet. It will take years to fill. And it makes me laugh to think of the closet you and I will share in my home."

I hide my head in his chest. He laughs along with me too. With my cheek leaning against him I grab the frame and smile looking at the two of us with such love in our eyes and a lifetime ahead of us. "This is a beautiful surprise Luca." He kisses the top of my head. "Ok, let's keep this moving. You know where your things are and allow me to demonstrate how the shower works and the accoutrement you may need." He looks at his watch and I see that it's almost eight.

We're back in the bathroom and after the quite complicated shower lesson he opens cabinets and drawers, "Just make yourself at home. If you don't see what you need, simply open all the drawers, closets and cabinets. I have nothing to hide. Do you have any questions?" I take him by the hand and ask, "Yes, will you shower with me?" Kissing my hand he says, "As tempting as that offer is Emelia, I need to take care of a few things. But, we can shower together in the morning, yes?" I nod.

"Can you be ready in forty-five minutes?"

"Yes, I think so." He kisses me softly and says, "I will call on my date at eight forty-five."

I reply, "Don't be late."

Chapter 51

WITH A FEW minutes to spare, I relax on the loveseat in the bedroom sipping on a rum cocktail Luca left for me in my dressing room. Unsure what to wear tonight, I unpacked the dresses that I bought with Jenene. And when I placed this one on the hanger, I knew it was perfect for my second date.

It's the one Jenene insisted I get. My favorite slinky halter neckline style always makes my shoulders look inviting and the above knee A-line cut is most flattering and flirty. The provocative front and back keyhole cutouts offer my love a subtle yet sexy peek. An evening breeze or a gentle twirl by my dance partner will have the cream colored layers of chiffon with tiny turquoise flowers delicately flowing around me. In the shop I laughed at Jenene, wondering when I'd even have a chance to wear it during this trip. And after I put it on this evening and looked at myself in the full length mirror I was grateful at her insistence. I don't know if it was the room, the mirror, the dress or how I'm feeling being with Luca, but I must admit, I was captivated by my own reflection.

I hear a faint knock in the distance and I jump up and skip towards the doorway leading to the stairwell into the den. He knocks again and I say, "Hello?" He clears his throat, "Emelia this is Luciano, may I come in?" His manner is so formal. I giggle, "Yes, please do." I move quickly inside the bedroom and wait for him to make an entrance. And when Luca sees me he says, "Ah, there you are my love. And you look stunning."

Kissing me gently on my lips he hums with happiness. He's wearing a light turquoise linen shirt with his sleeves rolled up and cream colored linen trousers. And he smells so delicious. I comment, "You are very handsome Luca. That color enhances your eyes. You shaved, I miss your manly man beard and where did you get ready for our date?" He replies, "Well, for our date, I wanted to look my best and in my dressing room next to yours."

I'm confused, "But when? I didn't see you."

He smiles, "When you were showering I came back to bring you a cocktail and get dressed."

I blush, "Oh, thank you for the drink."

Winking at me he says, "Imagine my surprise when I heard *mi novia* serenading me from the shower. You've been hiding something from me all these years."

My cheeks feel like they're on fire and I close my eyes with embarrassment. "I didn't realize I had an audience."

He caresses my face, "Oh *cariña*, do you know how delightful your voice is? I didn't want to leave and I was so disappointed the door muffled some of the words. I hope you will treat me to an encore later."

I laugh and say, "It will depend on how many of these you give me." Waving the glass at him I take a two shot sip and guzzle it.

Seriously he says, "Don't be like that, I always sing around you and never once have I heard you. And you sing so lovely. I will make sure we change that, because of your singing I fell in love with you even more tonight."

"So, are you taking me on a date or are you planning to hold me captive in your bedroom all night?" He smirks at me and says, "Point taken mi amor." He grabs my hand and before we fly through the hallway I stop and grab my strappy sandals. "So, then you had a preview to what I'd be wearing?" He nods, "Well sort of, I saw three dresses and I hoped you picked this one. And so I dressed accordingly."

When we arrive into the main area of the house, music fills the air and candles of different heights are dispersed around the living room and the kitchen. I notice another picture frame with a red rose lying in front of it. When I get closer I see it's the picture we both have on our phones. As we make our way towards the rest of this part of the house, I find more photos of us with roses next to them. They are from the wedding, the beach in Valencia, Christmas, the one of us with Tía Ada.

"I always wondered about this picture. I was so bummed it was just a Polaroid for I knew I couldn't have a copy. How did you get it?"

He takes the frame in his hand and gazes at it for a moment, "I visited Tía a few months ago just before she died and she gave me an envelope and this photo was inside. And when I took it out and looked at it, she didn't say a word but she smiled at me."

We look at one another and exchange kisses.

Continuing with the abbreviated tour he points to several key areas, including a powder room and before we go outside he gets down on one knee and secures my sandals on my feet. Outside, the large dining table on the veranda has two lanterns lit but the table is not set. Taking my hand he shows me to a pathway leading down to the lighted pool area. It's lined with flaming torches and the music from inside the house follows us all the way. We arrive at the patio adjacent to the pool area. The pool is decorated with flowers and floating candles. There's an intimate table charmingly set for two people surrounded by more candles, lanterns and torches illuminating our private outdoor romantic sanctuary.

Luca grabs the champagne bottle chilling in the silver bucket and within seconds he pops the cork and fills two awaiting flutes and passes me a glass as he takes the other.

"I know we have waited almost a lifetime to get back together and there were moments this week, when I found myself in disbelief that this is finally happening. And even though so many years have separated us, I feel even closer to you now which fools me into thinking almost no time has passed from that moment I held you in my arms on the dance floor in Valencia. I want to toast those two youthful, spirited and fearless romantics for allowing their hearts to secure a bond that would find their way back to one another."

We look into each other's eyes and we tap our glasses and drink to our younger selves. Leaning towards me, Luca kisses me. After our kiss, we sip more champagne and I hear the familiar start of the song we first danced to, Juan Luis Guerra's, "A Pedir Su Mano".

"Would you like to dance with me?" I place my hand in his, "Yes always." And just like our first dance he firmly takes hold of me and leads me with ease. Visions of that night in Valencia fill my mind as our bodies pressed together float gracefully and blissfully around the pool deck. And he's right, even though years have separated us, our hearts and souls have remained connected as if no time has passed. Whirling me around I feel twenty years younger and I'm suddenly dancing on a cloud with him. The song winds down as we dance back towards the table. Luca bows to me and says, "Thank you for letting me relive our first dance."

I start to refill our glasses when I notice food has magically appeared on our plates. I look around and I don't see anyone. Passing Luca his glass, I ask, "Are you a magician?"

He looks at me strangely, "On occasion I may have special powers over you. But no, I'm not a magician, why do you ask?"

I wave my hand over the dishes, "How did this happen?"

He laughs, "Sofia brought them over when we were dancing."

Looking stunned I ask, "Is she hiding around here somewhere?"

"No, she went back up to the house. You didn't see her?"

"I did not I was beguiled by your special powers."

He pulls the chair out for me and when we are both settled we begin to dine on our first course of tomato and mozzarella caprese. Looking around the table I see another photo of us. I place my fork down and bring the frame closer in view. I smile when I recognize it's us at dinner in Valencia before we went out dancing. "I have this one at home too. But I haven't cut out all the other people." He laughs, "Well, I didn't want them in our way tonight." I put the frame back in its place.

I change the subject, "From what I've seen of your home so far Luca, it appears you've done very well for yourself. You should be proud of your hard work."

"Thanks, but what do you really want to say about all this?"

He knows me so well, "From the apartment in Caracas to here, you've had to sacrifice a lot over the years I'm sure, to get where you are today. I hope you had some fun in the process."

After sipping the champagne he says, "When I moved back here and started with that company and my personal life was in disarray I found solace with advancing my career. After the kids were born, a colleague and I formed our own investment firm and our small company grew from five employees to its current prominence. Working was an addiction, I got pleasure from success. And besides my children, nobody else distracted me from my goals. I've been a determined and aggressive businessman over the years and now I'm able to enjoy all this with you and my family."

"I remember you being focused and with a competitive edge, have you ever compromised your values?"

Looking directly at me he replies, "In business no, in my personal life, you know the answer. Gratefully I was enlightened a couple of years ago when I was flying back home from London when I was engrossed in conversation with a fellow passenger. He practiced Buddhism and during the course of the flight, I became a changed man. When I returned, I immersed myself into learning the Buddhist philosophies and began incorporating some of the teachings in my daily life. But felt I was contradictory towards mindfulness existence when I was locked into a loveless marriage. The day she announced her desire to end our relationship, I felt I was free to pursue the balance I yearned for so long."

"Your home reflects some of your new found ideals. It's grand but minimal."

"I lived for a few weeks under the same roof after she asked for the divorce mainly to be there for the kids. But I felt ill most mornings when I would wake up in the guest room of my own house. So, I searched for a new home. I looked at maybe fifteen or more places and I stumbled upon this listing advertised at the meditation center. I honestly thought it was too good to be true but called the number on the posting. Made an appointment to view it the following day and I put an offer on the house after I was given the tour."

"Who owned this house before you?"

Pouring more champagne in my glass he tells me, "An architect and his wife finished building it two years ago hoping their adult children would visit more if they were in a vacation type setting. They gave it a try, but the kids convinced the rest of the family they wanted to see the world together before retiring to a compound like this on a regular basis. So the older couple sold the house to me and now they live in a condo in Florida when they're not exploring the world with their kids and grandchildren."

"Wow, that's quite a story. Do you keep in touch with them?"

He smiles, "Yes, in fact he's invested some of his portfolio in my company. And they plan to visit and stay here in November. You can meet them if you want." My eyes perk up, "Yes, I'm very interested with the man who was inspired to design a home that is perfect for you and for you to share with your family."

Luca looks deeply into my eyes and as if he's envisioned something his expression brightens. Patiently I admire his mind at work and then he nods his head at me.

"Emelia...No...Maybe..." He exhales and closes his eyes. I see his chest rising up and down as he takes longer breaths.

"Luca are you feeling ok?" He replies, "Yes, give me a moment."

He opens his eyes and he stands and begins to pace in front of me. He mumbles, "Could this be possible? Did I make this happen? The timing is..." He sits again and folds his arms on his chest, "Emelia, the other night after we watched the movie at the hotel, you said something that I couldn't agree with. And it has stayed with me since. You said that maybe we just have to believe this was the plan all along. Do you remember?"

I giggle, "Luca we've talked about a lot of things since Sunday." He grimaces. I say, "Give me a second while I try to remember. Had we been discussing the film?" Frustrated he says, "Yes, after the film yes." I try to replay our conversation, "We talked about why we each liked the movie and I said something how after viewing it with you and all that's happened, the time travel aspect affected me because I would have liked the opportunity to go back and relive moments with you or try to correct our past. Oh and yes, then like the movie, if we did, other vital events could change. So therefore, we have to believe this was the plan all along."

He nods his head and looks so focused at me, "Right, but what if I unknowingly did something that altered our paths and led you right to me?" I smirk, "I don't want you to think I'm mocking you, but, inviting me to the party is not some revelation that you've altered our paths."

He shakes his head at me and stands, and begins first in a whisper, "No, Emelia I'm not talking about just that. Before when you asked me about my life and this house, the pieces seem to come together for me. Let me explain."

He sits again across from me. "My marriage for years felt something less gratifying than an arranged union. And I hate to admit this to you, but I experienced a very dark period when I didn't even want to be in the same room as Violeta. This was well before her affair. So, I traveled for work and when I wasn't traveling took the kids to the country home. My life only had meaning when I was being a father or working. And as I previously mentioned, when I met that passenger on the plane his words awakened something inside me. I knew from that point forward I had to build a meaningful life for me. Not just for me, but for my children and the rest of my family. That was two years ago when I began this journey. And two years ago, the architect finished building this home. As if he was actually building it for me. And when I was ready for it, he handed it over to me."

Luca reaches out and takes my hand in his. "So you see when I searched to bring balance into my life it began the transition to bring you back to me. That way I would become the man worthy of being with you. As if I willed it all to happen, including Violeta's affair. By pushing her away from me, I made her seek comfort with another man. That cleared the way for me to be single again. Sadly it also brought distress to my children and my frustrations believing I had been manipulated years ago, when in fact, I was in charge of my destiny all along. By finally letting go the negativity of my life's choices, I began to build a better life for me and my family. During that period, happiness came back into my world. Even when it seemed sadness was around me. I needed to experience the pain and suffering to get me to where I am today as if this was the plan all along."

We sit quietly together considering all that was just revealed. I exhale and say, "Wow Luca. I can't believe you just pieced this all together. What a breakthrough. Certainly this is much to think about."

He smiles, "It is Mi Lia and it helps to free me from the destructive feelings from my past."

I smirk, "Oh Luca, I'm so happy for you. But, I must comment, if this is just our second date, what will you talk about on our third date?" He gives me a hearty laugh, "Emelia you are truly the only woman for me. Now let's finish eating."

With our first course complete, Luca asks me for another dance. It's not to a song from our regular repertoire its Phil Collins' "This Love This Heart." When he holds me tightly in his arms we drift away with the slow melody, he whispers, "I thought maybe we should introduce some new songs into our romance. Plus, I'm reserving the other Guerra song for much later in the evening. I can't risk you ripping off my clothes when Sofia is about to serve our second course." I place butterfly kisses along the edge of his ear as he sings into mine.

Just like before when the song ends we return to the table and Sofia has mysteriously replaced our dishes with our next course of fettuccini primavera. During this part of the meal, we drink, eat, laugh and talk endlessly. And finally Sofia appears and Luca signals to her to come over to meet me. Tomas also comes into view. In the evening glow, as they stand together they look like they could be blood related. Their features are so similar and complimentary. We talk for a while and they leave us to return with dessert.

Alone again Luca reaches across the table and takes my hands in his, "When I hold your hands it always brings me back to our first meeting when you came into my home one night. I looked into your eyes held your hand and love took over me and I've never been the same since. I made mistakes along the way that kept us apart, but I must have done something right, because here you are."

He rises from his chair and kneels down in front of me and places his hands on my knees. "Mi amor, Mi Lia, I promise to devote my life to you. I propose to love you, nurture you, protect you, satisfy you, humor you and provide the best existence we can imagine every day for the rest of our lives. With this ring, I pledge my wish to be your husband. Emelia Caldera, will you marry me?"

"My Luca, you are my joy, my beloved. It would be my greatest honor to be *su esposa*. [your wife] By accepting your pledge, I promise to love you, cherish you, satisfy you, grow with you, inspire you and support you. Yes, yes, yes, Luciano Morales, I will marry you."

He stands and takes me into his arms and we seal our commitments with kisses, hugs and tears. Luca removes the floral band and transfers it to my right hand. He takes a box from his pocket, opens it and when he slides the engagement ring on my left finger, he looks into my eyes and says, "You have been the only one that I have loved and I will love you for eternity."

With each ring secure he kisses both of my hands. I cup his face and say, "You are the one and only man that I have loved and now my heart and soul have found a home with you."

He takes a wine glass from the table and brings it to my lips, I take a sip and he follows. Then he guides me to a double chaise lounge where we lie together entwined under the stars. My head is resting on his shoulder and my hand interlocked with his on his chest. He says, "How did I do? Do you like?"

I sit up and look around and back at him, "Oh Luca, this night has been perfect. I don't even know when you had a chance to plan all of this. Do I like? I've loved every moment. I will never forget your proposal. Thank you for doing all of this for me."

He smiles and takes my hand, "This is my way of showing you how much you mean to me. And actually I was asking you if you like the ring. I know how particular some women are about these things and I wasn't sure of your style, you don't wear much jewelry."

I jump off the chaise and look around the patio and find a lantern and bring it back over to him. He shakes his head at me and laughs. I say, "Well, this is one of the challenges of proposing to a woman in her forties in a dimly lit setting. You could have given me a ring pop and I wouldn't have noticed."

Looking at me confused, I say, "A ring pop, surely you've seen them, they are these plastic rings with a lollipop in the shape of a diamond."

Taking the lantern from me while I join him again on the chaise he holds it up while I use the glow to shine a light on my new ring. The silver or platinum band has round diamonds on both sides of the sizeable center cushion diamond that's almost the width of my finger. "For someone that doesn't wear much jewelry I've collected two rings since I've arrived."

I take the lantern from him and place it on the side table near to me and snuggle close to him again. I raise my hand up to look at the ring and say, "Luca, you know I would have been just as happy wearing the floral band as long as it meant we'd be together. But now after seeing this ring up close, I'm stunned. I've never had something this exquisite and the details are brilliantly timeless. I'm amazed after only being with me a few days you chose a setting that I've often admired."

He holds my hand to his chest, "So you don't want me to return it?" I squeeze his hand, "Oh no, this beauty is not going back. I love it." Snickering at me he says, "I just wanted to know if my love is pleased with my gift to her." I lean up and say before kissing him, "Very, very pleased."

Tomas and Sofia join us again bringing dessert. Luca says, "I made sure I left room tonight for this treat. Come with me *Chica Fresa*." [Strawberry Girl]

We go to the table and I see a double if not triple serving of tiramisu between our place settings and a bowl of strawberries. "I asked Sofia to make this dessert especially for tonight. I'm certain your Italian palate will find it most satisfying."

Looking into his eyes, it suddenly occurs to me our menu tonight is the same as our first dinner with some minor enhancements. "All that I've eaten has been delicious, so I have no doubt that Sofia's tiramisu will be scrumptious."

"Before we get started, I'd like to share our wonderful news. This evening, with the help from the two of you with your superb abilities for putting together a romantic setting and this perfect meal, I asked the most loving and charming woman I have ever known to be my wife and she said yes."

Tomas shakes Luca's hand and hugs him while they exchange words and laughter. Sofia gives me two kisses and says, "When Luca called and asked for our help we couldn't wait to do this for him and be part of this special moment for the both of you. He's been so kind to us and we're so grateful to see him this happy."

Thinking of everything, Sofia quickly snaps some photos of us. And when they are about to leave us alone Luca tells the sweet couple to go home and that we'll take care of the rest. They seem surprised and relieved. Thanking them graciously we wave to them as they walk back to the house.

"Where do they live?"

"Just walking distance from here. The architect's wife is a painter and he had built her a studio down the road. So when Tomas and Sofia started working with me, I had it converted to a home for them."

He dips a fork into the cake and proceeds to feed me. I reciprocate. In between mouthfuls, I say, "I'm impressed you remembered what I ate that night in Valencia."

While serving me again he says, "I mentioned earlier how it just feels like it was yesterday. Don't ask me what I ate last week Chica Fresa. But I remember almost every detail from that night."

Feeding him I say, "And so tonight, not only do you get both desserts you also go home with your strawberry girl."

"Have you been controlling the music tonight or your accomplices?" He reaches behind the flowers on our table and shows me some device, "Do you have a request?"

"Yes, anything to work off this rich dessert and when I'm happy, I love to dance. And tonight, you have made me exceptionally happy."

We samba, merengue and slow dance for the next half hour. Dripping with sweat he picks me up and pretends to throw me in the pool. I hold on to him nervously and he places me on the chair and says, "You know me better, I would never do that to you. Plus I don't want to ruin this dress. I've got an idea."

I look at him and I think I know his idea. He pulls me up and spins me around. "Raise your arms." I turn and look at him over my shoulder, "Luca are we completely alone?"

He whispers in my ear, "Yes, now let me undress you."

I face him and say, "Well you have more clothes on, can I undress you first?"

He tilts his head and raises his eyebrow to me, "Ok, you may start with me."

Kicking off his shoes, I unbutton his shirt and move on to his trousers. Sliding them down to his ankles I take the pants and lay them neatly on a lounge chair leaving him with his open shirt and boxer briefs. When I return to him he says, "Now you." I twirl around and he moves my hair away to unhook the button on my neckline. He bends down and gradually pulls my dress up and over my head. Blissfully he says, "Mm-hmm, you are wearing far less clothes than me."

He lays the dress next to his trousers. On bent knee he begins to remove my sandals while I grasp his shoulder for balance. When he stands back up I remove his shirt. He says, "Now we're even, ladies first."

I look at his watch and then at my new rings. "Maybe we should take good care of these?" Quickly he takes off his watch and I give him both rings and he dashes to the table and places the rings in the box and his watch beside them. When he returns he places kisses along the back of my neck and his hands cup my exposed breasts. His seduction continues down my back and smoothly he slides my lace panties down to my ankles. I turn to do the same to him and before I can he's out of his briefs and lifts me into his arms and carries me into the pool.

"Earlier today you asked if we could swim together again and I told you, your wish is my command."

I kiss him and ask, "Ok what tricks do you have planned for us tonight?"

He snickers, "The list has been slightly revised, since we are all alone." We're in each other's arms and he says, "Have you floated on your back yet?"

I nod, "No."

"Trust me?"

I smile at him and say, "With my life Luca."

He becomes my human raft as he secures one arm under my shoulder blades and the other under my bottom. "I've got you. You will not get hurt. I promise. I am here. Relax. Let go."

His words and movements allow me to drift around the pool with him while my mind clears from all that's happened this week.

After a while he whispers, "I'm right here and I want you to open your eyes and see that you are floating on your own. Remain relaxed and you'll see." Calmly I open my eyes and see his arms are at his sides while I float near him. Within seconds my body begins to sink into the water and he pulls me into his arms and I wrap my legs around his waist.

"Mi Lia, it was inspiring to see you so free and relaxed. Soon I'll have you swimming, really swimming with me." I kiss his neck and his shoulder, "Until you told me to open my eyes, I felt like I was out of my body just floating in the air. It was so tranquil. You have reached into my soul like no one else has, I love you so much Luciano."

He kisses me and when his tongue finds mine our bodies lock together and we are free to finish what we started at the beach just a few days ago. With our desires building he plunges deeper inside of me and whispers, "And now I will take you here under the stars."

Being with him out in the open air after professing our love and our commitment for one another my release feels as powerful as his and I cry out as every part of my body vibrates wildly for him.

When I begin to think consciously again I'm aware that Luca is floating us back towards the shallow end of the pool and places me gently on the lower step. Kissing my forehead he says, "Stay here and I'll get us robes. Are you good?" Finding my balance I say, "Yes, I am more than good."

Luca returns from the pool house wearing a blue striped robe and a matching one tossed over his arm. I step gingerly out of the pool and he helps me with the robe. He says, "Do you want to stay here or go back to the house?"

"Let's continue this back at the house."

He groans loudly into my neck and says, "Your voracious appetite is astounding. It's very high on my, why I can't live without you, list."

I flirt, "Well, another hardship for being with a woman in her forties. I just can't get enough of you."

He moans, "I will gladly relieve you from that hardship every minute of the day."

"Ah ha, well, I fantasized having sex with you in your private sanctuary since you brought me in there. How soon will you be ready to go?"

He picks me up and tosses me onto the chaise. Climbing his way up to me while untying my robe he says, "My dear, we're checking off one of my fantasies first. I hope you'll indulge me."

With my heart racing and my body trembling I say, "Oh yes, yes."

He looks into my eyes and says, "I've been imagining this since our afternoon on the beach, when you said it was like having a bed but with an audience."

As Luca clears away the food and dishes I blow out the candles. We gather our things and he places both rings on my fingers and says, "I may be boasting, but I think you and I know how to make a marriage proposal memorable."

Walking hand in hand towards the house I laugh and think of the night we just experienced. One by one, my fiancé puts out the torches.

"Where do I begin? I would say from the moment I arrived at your home today, you have exceeded any and every expectation I have ever pondered."

He laughs, "I can't wait to hear this, go on."

"Your home, I've only seen a portion and so far, I'm living in paradise. Your proposal arrangements were beyond perfection. Your actual marriage proposal to me, even though this could potentially be your third try, was from your heart and I know now that we're meant to be together for the rest of our lives. The ring, oh my, I can't wait to get inside with even better lighting so that I can appreciate your generosity even more and now to the good stuff."

Snickering he says, "More? Go on."

We get inside and the kitchen is spotless, the candles have been extinguished and the photos with their roses remain. Still clutching the picture frame from the pool, I plan to place it on my nightstand in our bedroom.

He says, "I'm waiting."

"Let's go to the bedroom and I'll tell you the rest there."

Holding me in place, "It's just you and me; nobody else will hear you."

I look around the kitchen and all of a sudden I find myself embarrassed. "I'm thirsty can I have some water please?"

He smiles and serves me. I take a long sip and he patiently waits for me to continue. After licking my lips I confess, "Until tonight, I never skinny dipped, I never floated on my back, I never had sex in a pool, nor anywhere near a pool or outside of the normal settings. And you, my very considerate and skilled lover, because of you, tonight I experienced my very first multiples."

He's silent. I continue, "I know, shocking right? I've read about women having them, never actually talked with women about them, so I never believed it could happen."

His silence bothers me, "Say something."

Looking at me seriously he says, "You were right, you should have waited to tell me all this, until we were alone in the bedroom."

And then he laughs and tries to grab me but I run from him. I look for the hallway to the bedroom and suddenly I come upon two doorways and with him fast approaching he's laughing and yells, "Go left, Go left!"

I tear down the left hallway and see our awaiting slippers and am comforted knowing he correctly directed me. He swats my bottom passing me and runs ahead to the bedroom laughing the entire way.

I get to the bedroom and I don't see him. When I walk by the bathroom to my dressing room, he's not there, so I guess he's in his dressing room. Although I'm only here for another day, I should make use of this incredible closet. Hanging my dress near the others and placing my sandals on the shoe shelves I wonder what it will be like to live here someday. Quickly rummaging through my luggage I locate my pajamas. Placing the robe on the hook I slip on my slinky bed wear. When I turn around to leave I see Luca watching me from the doorway.

"I looked for you. Were you hiding?"

"No, I was in the bathroom."

I tilt my head, "But I looked in the bathroom, ah, that sneaky little corner there."

He hums, "Yes, now you know one of my hiding places." He touches the fabric, "Oh I'm so thankful you're wearing this and not the armor."

I smirk, "Imagine the looks I would have gotten this morning if I was wearing this under my sweater when I ran out to say goodbye to you?"

"Ready for bed?" he asks.

"In a minute or so, I have a couple of things to do." I give him the picture frame from the pool, "Can you put this on my side of the bed?"

He looks at it, "And what side is that?"

"I guess any side."

"Maybe we don't have to pick sides just yet."

"Ok, we'll just lie in the middle on top of each other."

With a naughty expression he replies, "Well, that's how I intend to start off. Don't be too long, I'll be waiting. And we have to talk about the good stuff again." Giving him a sendoff kiss I push him out of the room and into the hallway.

Finished with my nightly routine, I enter the bedroom and see he's lit a fire. I crawl under the sheet and snuggle close to him.

I ask, "No alarm for the morning?"

"Mm-hmm, no alarm. We wake up when we wake up." He shifts in the bed and faces me, "So about all these new experiences this evening. I'm impressed you allowed yourself to be uninhibited and let go and I'm not just talking about the multiples. How do you feel?"

"Ha, about all of it, I feel so alive with you. You make me feel like I can do anything. With you I want to do EVERYTHING."

"Emelia, you can do anything with or without me. I'm just thrilled to be included in all this with you."

Smiling I say, "Well there are multiple things you had a major role in making happen. So don't be quick to say I can do those things without you. What actually happened there at the end? And why did you wait until tonight to do that?"

With a mischievous grin he says, "Tonight was a special night for you and me, I couldn't just do that on any night. So you like?"

Feeling a slight tremble course through me, "Oh Luca, yes. And will we have to wait for another special night for you to do that again?"

He laughs. "You surprised me with all that you revealed to me, I sensed your level of intimacy with me has escalated as mine has for you. We should continue to find more ways."

He kisses me and I smile, "I agree, I've never felt this trusting and connected with another man. And I'm open to experimenting more ways with you."

Kissing my neck and then my shoulder he whispers, "But now before we go to sleep, I want to slowly and tenderly make love to my future wife in our bed."

Chapter 53

⸻

FLOATING ON WATER, floating on a cloud and floating in my dreams; waking up to a new day my surroundings gradually become familiar. Warm breezes, soft sheets, weightless in our bed, I feel so rested, so calm and so loved snug in Luca's haven. Opening my eyes to search for him I find myself alone. My mind awakens from sleep when I recall him whispering something about going to the gym. How long ago was that?

After my full body stretch I stand and saunter over to the windows. And in my head I hear his voice telling me, "The panoramic views provide the ever changing natural backdrop," as I observe the vistas from this room, he was so right. When I'm not focused on the blue sky, or the white puffy clouds I see trees, grass, a lake and mountains in the distance, paradise. And he wakes up to this view almost every day.

After freshening up I put on the blue stripe robe and set out to explore hoping to find Luca along the way. Now that it's daylight some of the rooms I've been to have a new appeal and I can appreciate the scenery from the tremendous windows. Finding my way to the kitchen I see a note and some yummy edibles.

Mi Corazon,

Reading this note means you haven't gotten lost in your new home. Have a nibble or two but not too much, I want to enjoy breakfast with you. Come look for me, I'm not that far away. Love, Your Future Husband

I smile and kiss the note. Snacking on a few pieces of honeydew I look at the ring he gave me last night. With the sun streaming into the windows near the sitting area I walk over to allow the sunrays to shine on the ring. The diamonds are magnificent, in fact jaw-dropping with the colors bouncing off the sunlight. Over the years jewelry of this worth has not been that important to me or attainable. But looking at this piece of art so delicate, I feel like I want to protect and admire it. Not just for its beauty but for its meaning. I can't believe he bought this on Monday. He was so sure of his feelings then? I guess it's conceivable, I've always been sure of my love for him. And he did say this was his way to convince me that when I leave here tomorrow, that it would be different from my previous departures.

Grabbing another piece of fruit I hear voices coming from somewhere. Going towards the opposite direction from the master suite, I venture into unknown territory. He did tell me to go find him. Passing the formal dining room I enter a hallway with several doors and a staircase leading to the lower level. But I don't hear the voices all the way over here. I return to the kitchen and the voices are back. But surely I would have seen him on the way from our bedroom. Maybe I should check the other hallway that confused me last night. This one is very short and has a bathroom, laundry room and several doors that when opened are filled with kitchen supplies. Now I know where to go when I need a snack. He must be somewhere near the bedroom. I guess there's a room in that area that I missed.

Luca's voice gets louder and he's laughing. Oh, sounds like he's on speaker phone, or has a guest. Now there are two voices plus Luca's. They're all men speaking Spanish and from what I can tell, very enthusiastic. The closer I get, the clearer the conversation becomes. I hear one of the men say my name. Luca replies. I wait unseen near the doorway and listen for the appropriate moment to interrupt. Smiling when I hear his laugh, I adore his laugh and the other guys are laughing too. The exchange continues and it's like three best friends joking around when one says something the other makes a snide remark, one laughs and the other insults the one that made the joke.

My name is said again and the dialogue shifts. Luca's replies are easily understood but the others get cut off when one talks over the other. So, I'm only catching snippets of what they're saying, but what I'm grasping is baffling and troubling. Turning my head to listen better the engagement ring catches my eye and the words naturalization, resident, New York office are tossed around. The other guys laugh again and Luca replies, "I would have done this months ago had I known it would have been this easy." One mumbles something while the other says, "Have a safe trip, make us lots of money," and something about being free in three to five years. When I think I've heard enough Luca tells them, "I've sacrificed so much more for the company, five more years will be painless."

In a daze I walk cautiously back to the bedroom and once there I sit on the edge of the bed but end up sliding to the floor and all that I just heard keeps echoing in my head. I must be wrong they must be talking about something else. But they said my name. I feel nauseous. Have I been a fool? Blinded by the romance I didn't see what was really happening. It all makes sense. Everything has been so rushed. Even Henry advised him to lock it in. I can't believe this has been all an act. All he said, all that I said, his feelings felt so real for me, mine have been real for him. I tug a pillow off the bed and curl up with it as I lie still on the rug. His phone call keeps repeating in my head.

What do I say? I have to ask him. I know I shouldn't have been listening but that's nothing compared to this. If I'm wrong then we'll have a good laugh and I'll die of embarrassment. But if I'm right, I'd want to know, I have to know. Lying there almost paralyzed tears stream down onto the pillow and I hear footsteps. My heart is racing. Luca hums as he approaches the bedroom. I'm hidden by the bed and he calls out my name as he goes towards the bathroom and dressing rooms. He says my name again. He walks to the sliding doors to check the back deck and when he turns he sees me on the floor.

He falls to his knees touches my arm and says, "Did you hurt yourself? What's wrong?" I'm so afraid to talk because I don't want to ask him. And when I do ask him, I won't like the answer and all of this will be over. He rubs my shoulder, "Can you hear me? You're frightening me. Talk to me." Maybe I shouldn't ask him. I'm leaving tomorrow anyway. I could just pretend and once I'm gone, I won't ever see him again.

I make eye contact with him and whisper, "I'm all right." He exhales, "Oh my love, you had me so worried. Tell me what's going on?" I just nod my head.

He lies down next to me and caresses my face, "It can't be the bed it's very comfortable. Why are you on the floor? Did you drop something?"

I take his hand from my face and place it between us and I sit up and lean against the bed still clutching the pillow. He also sits up and watches me, "Did you have a bad dream?"

In a low voice I answer, "No, I didn't have a bad dream. I woke up and you were gone."

He nods, "Yeah, I told you I was going to the gym. It's just downstairs. You said something to me and fell back to sleep."

"I remembered that and I brushed my teeth, washed my face, saw my scary hair and then I went to look for you."

He smiles, "Your hair is not scary it's just wild this morning. Did you find the kitchen?"

"I did."

"Did you see my note?"

"I did. That's when I heard your voice and so I went to find you."

"Yes, after the gym I went to my office and made a few calls while I waited for you to wake up."

Here goes, at least I'll walk away from this being the honest one. "When I got to the door I heard you laughing and also other voices so I didn't want to interrupt. But I also didn't mean to spy on you. You sounded so happy and the others were playful. I didn't want to ruin your fun."

Grinning he says, "I had a call with my partner and then he connected our attorney, our in-house lawyer, we're all friends. You'll meet them and see that we're juvenile when we're not talking about work. So, why are you on the floor?"

"Well, I also overheard." I stop and look into his eyes and I put my head down on the pillow. He slides closer to me and grasps my arms, "What did you overhear? Did they say something insulting?"

Into the pillow I say, "I know about your plan."

He yanks at the pillow, "What? Did you say plan?"

I lower the pillow and look at him, "I know my Spanish isn't that great, but I was there when you were all joking about your plan. So I know Luca."

415

He clears his throat, "I'm still not following, please explain."

In a slightly raised and forceful tone I say, "Five year plan, citizenship, marrying me to benefit the company. You know *THAT* plan."

He looks at me shocked, "What are you talking about? Oh no..." Nodding his head he pauses then continues, "Please don't be angry when I tell you this, but your Spanish comprehension is terrible. And I'm arranging a private tutor in New York and here for you."

Appalled I stand and toss the pillow on the bed. "I'm not in the mood for your jokes Luca. That's what I heard and I also heard you say, you would have done this months ago had you known it would have been this easy. And before I left, you said you've sacrificed so much more for the company and that this would be painless for you. So, tell me now Mister Obnoxious, isn't that what was said? Certainly I understood that correctly."

He stands and comes over to me, "Emelia, what you heard was completely out of context. I wish you would have walked into the room."

Hurt and frustrated I say, "Out of context? So in what context would this all be okay?" I shake my head and continue, "I've been such a fool. Until today, it never occurred to me that all that was happening around me was part of some bigger plan."

Annoyed he says, "Emelia, stop it, let me explain."

"So crazy to believe that you'd fall in love with me and propose to me in just five days of reuniting... But I believed it because I have always loved you. I guess that's why I was such easy prey. It's not the first time you married someone to further your career."

He grabs me, "Just listen! Give me a chance to explain."

I smirk, "The part that I don't understand is who else was involved in this game? Your brothers most likely, the women, I doubt it." And I look to my hands and see the floral band. "Oh Luca, Abuelo, how can you do this to him? Maybe this was your original plan, right, but at some point, you actually started having feelings for me. Tell me, be honest, I need to know the truth. You owe me the truth."

He moves me to the loveseat and he sits on the ottoman across from me. "Will you stop so that I can explain?"

I nod, "Yes. But I don't know what good will come of it."

He smiles at me, "One day, I promise you, we will laugh about this."

I begin to say something and he puts his finger over my lips, "Hush now, before you take this too far. I will start from the beginning."

Looking directly at me he says, "I called my partner Dario to tell him we're engaged. And he was so thrilled that he wanted to get Rojelio, our attorney and friend, on the phone. I think they had some bet about me asking you to marry me that I don't believe you had heard. So we were joking like men joke about getting married and stuff, I guess. And Rojelio was talking business and how marrying you would benefit the expansion of the New York office. They've been urging me to spend more time there, but I've been hesitating. We joked some more and Dario the hopeless romantic said something about how he knew one day I would fall in love and want to marry again. That's probably when I said the part about it being so easy and I would have done it months ago had I known. So you see it's been a big misunderstanding."

"What about the five years, the painless sacrifice?"

He places his hand against my cheek, "Oh my sweet, it was my way to tell those two clowns that being away from them and living in New York with you would be a joy and that I welcome the sacrifice. Now do you understand? We were just caught up in the excitement and one silly comment lead to another. There is no devious plan. I want to marry you because I love you and can't be apart from you. Not to become a U.S. citizen."

Trying to put all the pieces together I ask, "What did he mean when he said have a nice trip? Where are you going?"

His face turns serious and he covers his eyes with his hands and inhales and then exhales, "On a business trip."

Sneering I state, "No, I don't believe you. That was too vague."

He grins at me, "What day is today?"

I answer, "Friday."

"And what is tomorrow?"

Rolling my eyes I say, "Saturday."

"What happens tomorrow?"

I swallow and say, "I leave tomorrow."

"That's right, you leave tomorrow. What is your biggest fear when you leave tomorrow?"

Sadly I reply, "That when we're apart all of this will come to an end."

He nods, "And what did I promise you?"

Looking down at my hands, "You promised it would be different and that you would make sure when I got on the plane I wouldn't have those fears or doubts."

He raises my chin to look at him and says, "That's right, that's what I promised you. And so far, have I come through? What's different now?"

I look away from him to think about the differences. And after a moment or two I reply, "Your family knows we're together, you proposed and gave me this gigantic ring."

He smiles and replies, "Yeah, it is different, but I sense you still fear our separation. Am I right?"

Still feeling anxious I reply, "You're changing the subject I'm still confused about the phone call. And now you're distracting me."

He continues, "You asked me about a trip and I'm trying to explain to you."

I gaze into his eyes and they seem to appear sparkling or playful and as we sit there quietly, I begin to figure out all that we've been saying to one another.

And all at once I grasp what he's been alluding to and my heart skips a beat. I immediately jump into his lap and he smiles at me and I say, "Are you telling me what I think you're telling me?"

He laughs, "Oh Emelia, haven't we had enough misunderstandings this morning? Tell me what you think I'm telling you."

I don't know if it's due to the phone call and all that I heard and how I thought all this would be lost but I suddenly start weeping into his chest and he rubs my back. He whispers, "Oh come on my love, say it."

Wiping my face I smile at him and say, "Are you telling me we're flying together tomorrow?"

He nods and squeezes me tight, "Yes, how else would you be sure that I'm committed to you? I'm crazy in love with you Emelia and can't live without you. Of course I'll be on the plane with you tomorrow."

I blanket his face with hundreds of kisses and he hoots and hollers. He dips me in his arms and my head feels just inches from the floor and says, "You know how much I love surprising you and now you have ruined it."

I giggle while he tickles me with kisses on my neck. I screech, "I'm still surprised, it's not ruined."

He pulls me back up, "I remembered how much you hate goodbyes and I wanted to completely shock you at the airport tomorrow. You have to make up for this."

I giggle nervously, "What do you mean? What do I need to do?"

He glances away and then his eyes light up, "Let's go."

We get up and I ask, "Where are we going?"

Running his hands through my hair, "Come on wild one, let's shower and you can make this up to me in there."

Looking at him seductively he grabs my hand and hurries us into the bathroom.

Once we're stripped down and the dual shower heads are spraying, he pulls me under the water and kisses me. My hands explore his body and when I endeavor to give him a special treat he says, "Oh not just yet my love. My request is something very charming and dear to my heart."

I look into his eyes and when he caresses my jawline says, "Please sing to me the song you sang in here last night."

In total embarrassment I hide my face into his chest. "I'm not even liquored up."

He laughs, "You weren't liquored up last night when you were singing." I look in his eyes.

Sweetly he says, "How about you just go under the shower and pretend I'm not here. I'll be washing myself while you do the same."

He gently pushes me to the other side and I seek refuge under the warm cascading water. And he begins to rub the soap on his body and turns his back to me. He knows so well, how much I love seeing those sweet dimples. I rinse down my body, wet my hair and grab a shampoo bottle. Just when I begin to lather the shampoo, I clear my throat and nervously begin to sing for someone other than me, the Billy Joel song, "You're My Home".

Chapter 54

FOLLOWING LUCA'S EXCLUSIVE shower concert we blissfully prepared breakfast together and are dining on the massive deck outside the kitchen. Now with bellies full, my handsome guide gives me the complete tour of his home. With three additional bedrooms on this level, he informs me they are for Julieta, Marcos and Abuelo. This floor includes the kitchen, dining room, two seating areas, the bedrooms and the master suite quarters.

Taking the steps down to the lower level I comment on the art work and he tells me several pieces are Frida's originals, Marco's photographs and others are from local artists. Reaching the bottom step the room opens into another seating area with a television, a game room follows with a bar area, tables for billiards and ping pong, and an area for console games that seats about four. One side of the basement has a couple of guest rooms, bathrooms for each and a home theatre.

Entering this very impressive theatre Luca puts his arm around me and says, "This room makes it into your top five?"

I smile, "I'll tell you at the end of the tour Mr. Morales."

"What was the name of the movie we watched together?"

I reply, "The movie I couldn't understand, or the one from the other night?"

He quietly laughs, "The other night."

"*About Time*, why?"

"We should add that one to our collection and watch it here."

I nod, "Yes, I agree. That will be one of my house warming gifts to you."

"House warming? I can think of other ways you can warm my house with me." Luca pulls me closer and kisses me and his hands begin to explore.

When we take a break from kissing I ask, "Hey, do you have *The Big Blue* in your collection?"

He shakes his head, "My sweet you are so cruel to me."

My mouth pops open, "How so Luca?"

While he kisses my neck he whispers, "Since I was a teenage boy I've always wanted to, you know, at the movies with some hot girl. But I never did for lack of nerve and opportunity. And now, I'm at the movies with a hot woman, and her mind is somewhere else."

I gaze at my always alluring love and say, "I think this hot woman might allow this very patient teenage boy to live out his fantasy. Provided we set the mood. I wouldn't want him to be disappointed after he's waited, so, very, long."

Luca kisses me quickly and dashes off to what I think must be the controls closet.

While I wait for the projectionist to start the film, I get comfortable in the first row seat made for two. I look around and just like the rest of his home the theatre is simply designed yet fully equipped for a very comfortable viewing experience. Some seats are recliners where others have ottomans. I overhear Luca talking to himself. A minute or so passes and he sits next to me with an expression of disappointment. I try not to laugh so I observe him with the most supportive look I can muster.

He shakes his head, "I have forgotten how to play a movie in my own theatre. My son usually takes care of this for me."

I take his hand and say, "Well, we have three options."

He glares at me, "Three?"

"Probably more, but do you want to hear them?"

"Go on."

"First, maybe you and I can figure it out together." He shakes his head.

"Second, call your son." He ponders that idea.

"Third, continue with the tour and leave this for another day."

Luca raises my hand to his lips and after leaving a few kisses says, "Your optimism is inspiring, but sadly I lost my enthusiasm. Let's keep the tour moving along." I giggle.

He stands and pulls me up to his side, I say, "I'm sort of glad you couldn't figure out the system."

Walking out of the theatre Luca switches off the lights, "Why?"

"Well, so that when we eventually do see a movie, this moment you've been waiting for, will happen more spontaneously. Like last night at the pool."

"Yeah I get what you're saying. But, I think my enthusiasm will return very soon."

The other side of the basement has a gym, guest room and bathroom. A meditation yoga room with a hot tub tucked in the corner surrounded with glass windows bringing nature inside. Arm in arm we stand together in this peaceful room and look out in the distance.

I ask, "How much time must you devote in New York?"

Kissing my temple he says, "You want to stay here?"

I nod, "Your home is more than just a home Luca it feels like a place you come to when you need to restore balance. I can't keep you away from here for too long."

He hums, "My sweet, don't worry, you won't. Our plan, which means you and me, is whatever we want it to be. I would suggest in the beginning we spend two weeks in New York and the rest of the month here. But we can go month to month and decide. What do you think?"

I reply, "I think my home is anywhere you are. We can figure it all out as we go along. But I've seen what brings you joy, being with your family and this place and the country house."

Luca holds me in his arms and says, "You bring me the most joy. And now that you're in my life I want to be anywhere you are, so let's keep this simple and not make any formal arrangements. Plus, I'm looking forward to experiencing your New York."

Now sitting on the steps on the deck outside the kitchen looking out to the mountains I take his hand in mine and say, "I want to apologize for this morning." He says, "Don't worry, it's almost forgotten."

"Let me finish. First, it was very mean of me to say what I said about you marrying to further your career. I truly am sorry for saying that to you."

He nods at me and says, "Emelia, I hurt you a very long time ago and you believed I was hurting you again. I understand."

I continue, "And second it's been years since I shared my life with another man and when I did, it always ended with disappointment. I don't mean to bring all that baggage into our relationship, but there were moments I couldn't help but think this too will come to an excruciating end. And when I heard the call today, that part of me clouded my judgement and made me believe you were just like all the others."

I pause, "But you know the odd thing about all this, none of the others ever measured up to you. You were always the one that I wanted and none of them came even close. And so I've known from the start, you are a man of integrity and who I am meant to be with, for you'll be just as good to me as I will be to you. This all came to light this morning. As if the confusion had to happen in order for me to let go of the past and trust you and trust us, because suddenly I feel as if this weight has been lifted and I can be with you looking ahead and not looking behind."

He says, "Don't you think it helped knowing I'm travelling with you tomorrow?"

"Yes, absolutely...when did you decide to fly back with me?"

He smiles, "Promise you won't be mad at me?"

I grin, "I promise."

Luca replies, "On Monday morning."

I giggle, "Since Monday?"

"Yes, when you were in the living room and I was packing, I snooped through your bags to find one of your rings and while I was looking I came upon your flight information."

I ask again, "Monday?"

He insists, "Yes, Monday. If you really want to know, I knew on Saturday night that I never want to be without you ever again."

Leaning to him I kiss him softly. We part and he says, "Can I ask you something?"

"Yes, anything."

"When did you know you were in love with me?"

Caressing his face I look into his eyes, "I knew my love was still strong for you when you told me about your past decisions, your life and your marriage ending. And when we got back from the beach and spent the afternoon loving one another, I knew and remember at the house when you were talking with me and the ladies and I was in a daze, I was so taken by you and just wanted to grab you and tell you that then. Each moment we spent together this week, my love kept growing more and more for you. So if I was to specify exactly when, it would take away something from all those other moments."

He kisses me, moves me closer to him and holds me in his arms. For a while we sit together quietly just being in the moment.

"Emelia."

"Yes Luca."

"A few days ago I asked you something about your first marriage and you asked if we could discuss it later on. And just now you commented on previous relationships. Do you feel comfortable now telling me what happened?"

I close my eyes to think about how best to describe or inform Luca of one of my greatest failures or mistakes.

He adds, "If it's too painful to explain, I will understand."

Opening my eyes I look at Luca and say, "It's more like, I haven't had to talk about that part of my life for a long while. And even though it is a memory, years have passed leaving my feelings numbed somewhat and it almost feels like it never happened. You'll see what I mean after you're divorced for several years."

"What can you tell me about it?"

"Maybe I should ask you, what is it that you want to know."

"Well, first and foremost, why did it end?"

I smirk, "Are you sure you don't want to ask me again if I learned how to swim?"

He nods and says, "Ah, no."

"After years of trying to figure out why it ended, I think I actually wasn't the person he was supposed to love forever. Nor was he my forever person. And we had conflicting interpretations regarding forsaking all others."

"Did he find his forever person?" he asks.

"Well, he's still with the same woman he married shortly after we split. So far their marriage seems to be working out. Maybe he never loved me, or maybe fell out of love for me."

"Did he physically hurt you?"

"No, he did not."

"Do you ever hear from him?"

I reply, "Maybe once a year."

He asks, "How do you feel when he contacts you?"

"Mostly I'm content knowing he's doing okay. Other times I feel hurt that he made more effort for her than me. And almost every time, I find it brings those old feelings of mistrust, disappointment and resentment back to the surface."

"Have you told him that? And asked him never to contact you again?"

"No, I've never told him that. And no matter how or why our marriage ended, I remember we once shared a life together. I can't bring myself to turn my back on that person. That doesn't mean I love him. It just means that I'm showing respect for the love that was once there."

He looks into my eyes, "Would you ever go back to him?"

"No. And I say this with confidence. I know that I've changed, from the woman that I was when I was with him. And I never loved him as I love you."

We sit quietly again for almost a minute. I ask, "Do you want to know more?" He replies "I'm good for now. Plus we have a lifetime to discuss all of our past." I rest my head on Luca's shoulder.

"Between your revelation last night and mine today, I think we both have experienced some profound changes since last Saturday." He smiles, "Yes Emelia, we have and I can't wait to walk hand in hand with you for the rest of my life."

"I know you showed me most or your house today, but I haven't walked around the property with you. So I wonder, is there a hammock anywhere nearby?"

He shakes his head, "Why do you ask?"

"I remember you had one on your terrace the first night I met you. And on our last night we snuggled in it together. So I figured you must have one or two here."

"Emelia, you know me so well. There's one just outside the master bedroom, I'm surprised you didn't see it. And I have two others near the trees in the pool area. But when not in use they are rolled up in the pool house."

He says, "I forgot to tell you, we're having a little party tonight." I bump up against him and laugh. "I know your family is coming over. When you say party, what do you exactly mean?"

"Very casual, my family, soon to be your family, some friends and your two favorite guys from the phone call this morning."

"Now I know the guest list. Can you tell me more, like when this is happening and are we making dinner or just serving drinks and nibbles?"

"Everything has been organized. And they will arrive about five."

"Oh, that's in a few hours. Will Tomas and Sofia be around?"

He answers, "Actually yes, but as our guests tonight."

I comment, "I would suggest, for this to work, you know, *US*, you should probably give me more than five hours' notice for a party in the future."

"Oh my love, I will note that. But be assured tonight's party is fully catered with a bartender and servers."

I respond, "Mmm, sounds like a special occasion, what are we celebrating?"

Leaning close to me he whispers, "US," and kisses my ear.

"Tell me, was this party planned last Monday?"

He bursts out laughing, "No, actually it all came together this morning."

I inquire, "When did you wake up?"

He says, "I don't even remember. Waking up with you next to me in my home now your home too, felt like Christmas morning. I couldn't wait to be lazy with you in bed all morning."

"Ah, I forgot about that. I guess all the early starts this week caught up to me. Oh Luca you should have woken me."

Snickering he says, "I tried."

My turn to burst out laughing, "I'm sorry. I bet I'll be that way on Sunday when you're waking up in my home, now your home too."

He announces, "A man can only dream."

"I haven't asked again but how did your drive back yesterday go?"

426

He says, "It started off a bit tense, someone wanted to sit up front, but Julieta and I teamed up and we won that battle. After an hour into the drive, everyone settled in. My focus was on the road and counting down the hours until I would see you again."

"Do the kids know about our engagement?"

"I discussed it with Julieta yesterday and I called Marcos this morning."

"What were their reactions?"

"Jules didn't seem surprised. And asked where we'd live. When I explained, she seemed fine and pleased. Marcos was neutral and asked if he'd have to move out. I told him certainly not, but we might have to shift the weeks around when he stays here. He was the one who suggested the two week plan."

"Luca you know, your children are the way they are because of your relationship with them. I don't want to cause any stress or put a wedge between you and them. So, we should work together on this."

He nods, "Yes, I agree."

"Did you talk with them about Violeta's unplanned visit to the house and our confrontation?"

He sighs, "No, I forgot, but I'm sure they're fine. I will talk with them before we go to New York if that eases your mind."

"Luca, you know your children better than me. But yes, it would ease my mind."

Rising he extends his hand to me, I grasp it and we walk inside the house. I ask, "What do you want to do now?"

He replies, "I did get up awfully early this morning. Since we have a few hours before our party I thought maybe you'd like to be lazy with me this afternoon and snuggle in our hammock."

I smile, "Sounds delightful."

Chapter 55

THE LAZY AFTERNOON with Luca was the best therapy after our on the go and roller coaster week of emotions. Getting ready for our guests, my handsome man-in-waiting zippers my dress and we admire together our reflections in the full length mirror.

I remark, "Another one for the list."

Kissing my bare shoulder, he says, "Tell me."

I flirt, "Having you around to dress me."

Moving my hair off my neck he says while kissing and nibbling me, "I've started my own list."

"Have you now? What kind of list?"

He whispers, "I should wait to tell you when we're alone in the bedroom."

I giggle and whisper, "Don't be afraid, nobody else is here, you can tell me."

He looks around takes my arm and places kisses starting from my wrist all the way up my arm and says, "Mi amor, my list will make you blush."

Slipping his hand into my dress he touches my breast, "My list will make your heart race."

I close my eyes and squeal. His other hand travels under my dress caresses my thigh while pressing me against him. "My list will make you moan."

With his hand holding me in place, I feel his hips rock against me and his fingers venturing inside my panties, "My list will make you quiver."

And on command my body trembles, "Oh Luca. Do we have time?"

He whispers in my ear, "I told you, we always have time. Plus they're not arriving until six."

I moan, "Tell me more about your list."

Chapter 56

―――――⌒―――――

RECOVERING FROM OUR impromptu pre-party pleasures Luca's mobile phone rings. Swiftly he grabs his trousers from the floor and takes his phone out of a pocket. Ending his call he quickly dresses.

"Who was that?"

Fixing his hair hurriedly in the mirror he says, "The caterers and they've been at the front gate for ten minutes ringing the bell."

Amused I say, "Oops, so much for that extra playtime."

He looks at his watch, kisses me on the lips and says, "Once I let them in and show them around, we still have forty-five minutes." He winks at me and rushes out of the dressing area.

Resting on the couch I smile thinking about his liveliness, his caring nature, his infinite love for me and find myself addicted to Luca. How can it be possible that I arrived here just a week ago with such apprehension and tonight I'm in Luca's home preparing to see his family and friends to celebrate our engagement? Life is full of surprises. And before my irresistible love returns I better start getting ready again for this evening.

Applying some finishing touches I hear someone or something knocking. Checking, I leave my dressing room and I see Frida walking towards me from the bedroom. Grateful that I wasn't waiting for Luca in my previous state of undress, I smile at her and say, "Hi Frida."

She gives me a big hug and says, "We couldn't wait any longer. I hope you don't mind that we arrived a bit early."

I reply "No, I'm always thrilled to see you."

When we part she takes my left hand and says, "Now let me check out my brother's idea of an engagement ring."

With her shocked expression, I can't imagine what will be her response. "Emelia, he's ridiculously in love with you. I've never seen diamonds like these."

I blush and say, "Neither have I."

Holding my hands Frida says, "Besides when his children were born, I haven't seen my brother this excited about someone in so very long. You are responsible for bringing love back into his heart."

We embrace again and I add, "Well, you're part of why we're together in the first place and why I'm here again."

She says, "Thanks for not saying any more."

"Frida, I am so grateful that we're finally together that I can't look back at all that happened. We're at this place, at this time for reasons we can't explain. And I've learned to welcome every day that I live with Luca at my side, as a gift, a gift of time. Sure we'll have our challenges and we'll face them together along with all the happy occasions. That's what living is all about. And now I'm given the chance to live my life with him. So let's all keep enjoying the present and work on our futures as one big mostly happy family."

Frida smiles and says, "I think we're almost there."

I nod, "Your mom will come around at some point. She can't be angry with us forever."

Frida replies, "It might seem like forever. To be honest, I don't think she loves any of her sons' wives. But what mother does? She just tolerates them."

I giggle and smile, "Does she like your husband?"

"Yes, she does. Mainly because he keeps me here and she knows he's a very good man. All I'm trying to say is don't worry too much about trying to please my mother or this family. You and my brother need to focus on making a life for yourselves and his kids. That's your first priority."

Luca walks into the room humming a song. He says, "Hey, look who's here."

Frida laughs, "Yes, I snuck away to visit with my friend. Remember she was my friend before becoming your friend."

He wraps his arms around me and says, "Yes, I do remember and I will respect your friendship, for I never would have met the love of my love. But once your friend is my wife, you'll need to step aside." He says jokingly while waving my left hand at her.

"I'm so glad my friend changed *mi hermano serio* [my serious brother] back to my funny brother. I like that brother so much more." Luca pushes me with him towards Frida and we have a group hug.

"Frida my dear sister, I need a few minutes alone with my fiancée, if you don't mind."

Nodding her head, "Oh, my dear brother, I get the hint. I will see you both at the party. And by the way, congratulations Luciano, I'm glad she said yes."

Giggling on her way out Frida waves back to us and then she's gone.

Spinning me around Luca kisses me softly and hugs me tightly. "Was Frida in on the proposal or aware of your plans?"

"Yes. Why?"

I smile and say, "Just wondering."

"I had to tell her why I needed you to arrive later last evening. You know, in order for me to get things ready."

I ask, "How would it have worked if I travelled back with you as originally planned?"

"That was easy, the first plan had me going to the office for a fake emergency and you would have stayed at Frida's for a few hours while I took care of the arrangements here."

I reply, "Huh, so maybe Violeta did you a favor."

He simply states, "No." And sternly he continues, "And I'd like this rule put in place from now on, that when we're in this part of the house, her name is never mentioned."

Trying to change the subject I say, "Oh, rules. Aren't they like lists? You never actually got to tell me what's on your list."

Kissing me again he says, "I love how your mind works. But now we must focus on the party and not our desires. It will make me want you more when we're alone again."

I flirt and say, "Easy for you, the more I have you, the more I want you." Kissing him passionately I look at him and say, "How do we improve perfection?" I spin him around to take a more thorough inspection of my fiancé.

A few minutes of primping and we walk hand in hand from the bedroom. Approaching the hallway between the master suite and the rest of the house Luca stops us and says, "Thank you for saying yes to me."

I reply, "Thank you for asking me."

We hold each other close and I breathe in his fragrance. I'm not sure how the next few hours will play out but knowing we'll be back here in our bedroom later provides me with some level of serenity.

Chapter 57

ENTERING THE MAIN section of the house I'm stunned at the transformation. The catering team has waved a few magic wands in just under an hour. Floral bouquets of different heights are scattered around, as well as candles and balloons. I never thought of Luca as a balloon kind of guy. The aroma of food being prepared stirs my appetite and waiters are loading their trays with drinks and appetizers. I hear music playing in the background and see guests mingling all throughout.

Benjamin and Mateo approach us immediately and Mateo says, "Tío, can we go to the game room?"

Luca replies, "After you tell me why you're here tonight."

The boys look at each other and Benjamin's eyes widen, "We're here because you got married?"

Luca puts a gentle hand around both of their necks. "Gentlemen, last night, I asked this very loveable woman if she will be my wife. And she said yes. That's what we call a marriage proposal. We are now engaged to be married. Tonight you are here to celebrate our engagement. Now do you understand?"

They smile and nod. Mateo replies, "Does everyone first get engaged? Or only when you're waiting to be divorced?"

Olivia gasps, "MATEO, you didn't just ask your Tío that question!"

I cover my mouth to conceal my laughter. Luca replies, "It's fine, my nephew is just clarifying the process. Mateo, most couples whether it's their first marriage or next ones, get engaged and then plan their wedding."

Mateo responds to his uncle, "So, since this is not your wedding, you won't mind if we go downstairs and play?"

I look to Olivia and she's shaking her head, "My son, my son, my son."

Luca replies, "Mateo, we won't mind, but maybe you and your brother have something to say about this fantastic news?"

Benjamin answers, "Yes, we're happy that you are engaged to Emelia. Now we will visit you both in New York and you will visit us in Arizona."

Mateo looks stressed, "You're not moving from here are you?"

Luca replies, "No, we are not. And you still can visit and stay with us, whenever you are here."

Looking relieved Mateo announces, "Great, good luck with your engagement. Can we go downstairs now?"

Olivia whispers something to the boys and they extend their hands to me and say, "Welcome to the family Tía Emelia."

I crouch down to the boys, "Thank you. I am most honored to be your Tía." And I kiss them each on their cheeks and hug them. Benjamin seemed okay with my kiss and Mateo was like most little boys, a bit shy and grossed out.

Luca tells them, "Now, you can go and have your fun. Don't break anything." They hug their Tío and dash to the lower level.

Henry joins us and pulls his brother into his arms and they exchange a few words. Olivia does the same with me. And we switch hugging partners.

"Let me look at it." Olivia asks while tugging at my hand. "Frida was right. Luca I must commend you on the ring, good job."

While we're talking I notice Rico and Claudia arriving with Julieta and Marcos. Luca moves closer to me and places his arm around my waist. It's like he sensed my anxiety. Shortly after, his parents with his children join us. The greetings go smoothly and there's no mention of our engagement. Luca takes me around to meet the other guests.

Coming upon two couples Luca starts to introduce me when one of the men about our age with salt and pepper curly hair wearing a very loud print button down shirt over a pair of equally loud orange trousers with navy blue shoes interrupts him. He says to me, "This must be the brave woman giving up her freedom for this ugly greedy lout."

I look to Luca and back at the man and say, "This must be Rojelio." Luca laughs and shakes his head, "My love you are correct."

Rojelio extends his hand to me and when I grasp it I say, "Luca and I talked about you today, but I'm sure you must know that." I turn and leer at Luca and he says, "No, I did not. I want to live at least another day with you."

The other man, a little younger than us, with touchable sandy blonde hair, kind blue eyes and neatly dressed with a tan linen blazer over a white shirt and navy slacks. He looks like he's just off a fashion runway. If he wasn't standing next to an equally beautiful woman, I might consider setting him up one day with my friend Jenene.

"Emelia, first let me introduce you to Dario. He is one of my dearest friends and business partner."

Dario takes my hand and holds it tenderly in his, "I am so happy to finally meet you Emelia. Thank you for giving my friend another chance. Take it from me, he won't disappoint you. And you are all he's talked about since they started planning his sister's party. And now I know why."

Letting go of me Dario says, "I'd like you to meet my wife, Vittoria."

Not long after we greet one another Rojelio jumps back into the conversation. "I don't need any introduction, but I'd like you to meet my date, Regina." She's a tall slim much younger woman with black hair in a pixie cut and wearing a skin tight black dress.

Having heard these men this morning on the phone makes me slightly hesitant to like them right away. But it's hard not to see the exceptional camaraderie between Luca and Dario. As for Rojelio, he's a character that will require me to have an open mind and patience. Looking around I see all the people that Luca shares his life with and suddenly I realize along with loving him, they too will be in my life. My single girl's world unexpectedly has changed almost overnight. With that change my circle now includes my fiancé, his children, his family and his friends. And one day very soon, he will be experiencing the same with all the people in my life.

"Emelia, would you like something to drink?" Luca asks. He's holding two rock glasses and I take one from his hand.

"Thank you Luca."

He inquires, "You seemed distracted."

Smiling at him, "I was a bit, just taking all this in. You're quite the party planner. I think you missed your calling." He smiles at me. Taking a sip my tongue relishes the smooth rum taste as the cool liquid glides slowly down the back of my throat.

Tomas and Sofia approach us with big smiles and in Tomas' arms I see a handsome little boy with his arms and legs flailing with excitement. Luca hands me his glass and quickly the boy jumps from Tomas' grasp and into Luca's arms. They both squeal with delight.

Luca says while the little guy is kissing him, "Emelia, this is Eduardo, Tomas and Sofia's son."

I pat Eduardo's tiny little hand and say, "Hola Eduardo."

His mostly all gums smile is friendly and slightly shy and he quickly replies, "Tí Luca." Eduardo and Luca play around and soon they are all giggles.

"Sofia, how old is Eduardo?"

"He just turned one last month."

"My goodness, he's a beautiful and happy boy."

Sofia replies, "Thank you. He generally is very content. And when he sees Luca he bursts with joy. You might have some competition tonight."

"I won't mind a bit. Plus, their energy is contagious."

Luca and Eduardo are now babbling words more like sounds at each other while Eduardo touches Luca's face and giggles. Sofia adds, "Don't worry, Eduardo also likes playing with Jules and Marcos. When you want Luca back to yourself, we'll call them over."

I reply, "I'm having fun just watching them. How often do they see each other?"

Sofia says, "Usually about once or twice a week. And the last few months, their special bond became even stronger when Luca started teaching Eduardo how to swim."

Marcos comes over to us and within seconds Eduardo's arms extend out to him and the little boy's enthusiasm passes on to the next eager volunteer. Marcos gets the approval from Eduardo's parents to take him downstairs to the playroom. After this exchange I excuse myself and quickly go to the master suite to use the bathroom.

Glancing at the mirror in the dressing room I apply a fresh dab of lip gloss. Now wandering into the den with thoughts of our flight to New York tomorrow I focus on the hallway leading towards the party. I'm startled by a subtle movement near the couch. It's Claudia and she's resting in a chair in the master den.

With her eyes closed, I'm not certain if I should disturb her or not. Standing still I pause and watch for a moment. Then I whisper, "Claudia." I wait a second or two and I whisper again, "Claudia, are you alright?" If she doesn't reply, I'll leave her alone and ask Luca or Frida to check in on her.

Just when I was about to get one of her children I hear, "Emelia."

I turn and Claudia's eyes are open and she's watching me. "Hi, want me to leave you alone to rest? Do you need anything?"

She nods her head, "Would you mind sitting with me for a bit?" she asks.

"I don't mind at all, would you like a drink or something first?"

She replies, "No, unless you want one."

I sit on the couch next to Claudia's chair. She says, "We've had such a full week. I bet you're anxious to go home tomorrow."

Hoping this is not a repeat of the chat she had with me at the other house, I try to keep this calm and friendly. "Yes and no. I would like the chance to stay put somewhere for more than just a few days, whether here or back at my home. It's been really nice reconnecting with all of you. I'm sad to be leaving here tomorrow, I feel like we only just got started. But I'm looking forward to coming back."

"When do you think you'll return?"

"I'm not sure exactly when, but Luca thinks we'll be back in a couple of weeks maybe."

Her eyes widen, "Luca is going with you tomorrow?"

Oh no. Should I have let Luca tell his mother about his travel arrangements? I reply softly, "Yes, that's the plan."

She folds her arms across her chest, "I didn't realize he was leaving too."

I inquire, "Did he forget something? Do you need him to stay back a day or so? We can adjust our flights."

Claudia inhales deeply and then replies, "No not really. I'm surprised he's proceeding so quickly."

I want to smile as I think about the humor in her statement. Yes, we're moving quickly and aren't we all here tonight to celebrate our engagement. Not sure why she's surprised at all by the pace. Hasn't that been Luca's speed all week?

"Well, I think the New York office situation has a lot to do with his trip."

Her eyes squint just like her son's, "I'm sure that's part of the reason. What are his children doing while he's gone?"

I nod, "I don't know, you'll have to ask Luca."

She responds, "I'm not trying to be difficult. I just want what's best for my son and his family."

"Neither am I, but I don't know what Jules and Marcos are doing while Luca's in New York. He must have made some preparations with their mother."

Claudia immediately replies, "That's not what I meant."

With furrowed brow I ask, "What are you trying to tell me then?"

"Emelia the other day at the house when I was talking with you about your relationship with Luca, I didn't mean to be difficult."

Slightly shocked, I wait silently to allow her to continue. "You may not know this or feel it, but I do like you. I've always liked you. Especially for all you did for Frida. It's true, when I noticed the bond developing between you and Luca many years ago, I was not pleased. As a mother, first I want my children near to me in case they need me and then I focus on what makes them happy. But over the years, I've had to push my first objective aside and be thankful that they are happy wherever they decide to live."

"Claudia, thank you for sharing this with me, I've always liked you too. And I never wanted to hurt you or your family."

"You haven't hurt us. In fact, we should be apologizing to you. Emelia I'm a very traditional woman with traditional values for myself and my family. As I've been told, I need to change with the times. But I don't think that advice is fairly accurate. What I see, is a society of people that want to have relationships, but don't want to do the work. Not too long ago the marriage vows were respected and seldom broken. I understand you were married before."

"Yes, I was."

"Did you like being married?"

"I liked sharing my life with someone."

"Did you have many struggles?"

"We weren't married for that long to experience many struggles."

"But if it ended, surely you had some struggles."

"Yes, we did."

"Emelia, I'm not judging you on your past marriage. I'm just trying to find out if you have the potential to maintain a long happy marriage."

I reply, "And I don't think knowing all about my previous relationship will give you the answer you're looking for, because the people are different and so are the situations."

Claudia leans close to me, "Luca is very important to us and it's been painful for me to watch him during the last few years of his marriage. We are grateful he is where he is today. And we never expected to see the vibrant, passionate and humorous sides of him return after all he's endured. Part of me wants to see the two of them try to fix their marriage. Yet another part of me knows, they never had the love or the joy, I see between you and my son. I wish we could turn the clock back but we can't."

She sits back in her seat and continues, "When I said earlier that marriages take work, Luca and Violeta worked at their marriage but didn't have the love to support it. So I say to you with much reluctance and gratitude I'm trying my best to embrace this new relationship. And as Luca's mother, I must thank you for giving him another chance. I know he made mistakes and we did too. I pray you both succeed in this union that was taken from you."

I reach out to hold Claudia's hand and she nervously offers it to me. "Claudia I know it's not easy talking with me about all this. I admire you for being honest with me. And so I want to be honest with you. You are right that marriages require work to succeed. And both in my failed marriage and Luca's they were missing some of the key elements, respect, trust, honor and love. We have those elements and many more which provides a strong foundation for us to work together building our future. One of the many reasons why I love your son is his devotion to his children, his siblings, their spouses, his nieces and nephews, Abuelo and you and Rico. I hope you can share with Luca all that you shared with me. I know he misses the relationship you once had together."

Claudia's eyes fill with tears and she places another hand over mine. She says, "I miss my son too. Do you think he will ever forgive me?"

"Hello ladies, there's a party happening in this house. Why are you two hiding in here?" Luca eagerly inquires. He walks over to where we're sitting and sees us holding hands. I squeeze Claudia's hands and release them when I stand. Before going to Luca, I grab a tissue from the side table and pass it along to Claudia.

Standing before him I look into his eyes and say, "Spend a few minutes with your mom, I'll meet you both at the party."

His expression becomes very serious. I whisper, "We're getting there, you'll see." I smile at him, kiss him softly on his cheek as I leave a mother and son alone with the hopes they find some resolution.

Chapter 58

Upon my return to the party, Frida joins me in the kitchen. "Did you see Luca? He was looking for you."

"Yes, he found me."

Frida asks, "Is everything good?"

Ambiguously I respond, "More or less. This has been quite a week."

She smiles, "Yes, a memorable one. We haven't had this much excitement since, well, for a while."

I smirk, "I bet I know where you were going with that. Thanks for holding back."

"Emmy you fly out tomorrow, when will you be coming back?"

"I'm not sure, maybe in two weeks. Luca and I haven't decided yet. We just want to take this day by day."

"Luca mentioned he's joining you. Just want you to know, I told him he can rely on me to help out with Jules and Marcos."

"That's very kind of you Frida. How did he respond?"

"He was appreciative and somewhat relieved. I'm thrilled for you that he's making the trip. Now you two can experience life as a couple."

"Yes, Luca and Emelia as a couple living in the real world, is very different than our vacation fantasy world. I'm thrilled too. We'll finally be graduating to the next phase."

"Emmy, even though you've been on a holiday this week together, you have to admit, you've survived a few real events. You will succeed."

Luca and Claudia rejoin the party and Frida looks questionably at me. She asks, "I wonder how that came about?" I reply, "Frida, life is full of surprises." We smile at one another and Luca walks pensively over to us.

He kisses my temple and places his arm around my shoulders. Grasping his hip I hold him snugly. I'm too nervous to inquire how it went with Claudia. I ask, "Have all the guests arrived Luca?" He inhales deeply and upon exhale says, "I think so."

Luca follows with, "Frida has Jules spoken with you at all today?"

Frida looks at her brother, "Just here at the party when I said hello to her. Why?"

"Did she say anything that I should be aware of?"

"Luca, we only exchanged greetings and I haven't seen her much. Figured she was downstairs with the cousins. What's going on?"

Luca tightens his hold on me while I glance around the room to see if his daughter is near but I don't see her. The rest of the guests seem to be enjoying themselves and unaware of the family matters.

Luca continues, "From what I understand, she had a rough day with her mother. Frida, I know she confides in you and I'm thankful that you have that kind of relationship. I don't want you to break that trust. But if you know something about what happened today, it would help me when I talk with Jules."

Frida looks directly at Luca, "I'm telling you the truth. Here at your home tonight was our first encounter since we said goodbye yesterday morning. And she only said hello. Who did you hear this from?"

His mouth forms a tense line and he replies, "Mamá."

Not knowing what is really going on I offer Luca some support, "Luca, we can change our flight to another day if you're needed here. Or better yet tell the kids they can come with us."

He kisses my forehead and whispers, "Oh, Mi Lia, your compassion eases my mind. But like you suggested the other night, I should not allow her to manipulate me anymore."

I'm guessing he's now talking about Violeta. I reply in a low voice, "Yes, but when her games upset your children they'll need your involvement, right?"

He looks into my eyes and says to Frida and me, "Why can't we just have fun at our engagement party? I went looking for you earlier to get everyone together for a toast. And then we were sidetracked." He growls. "I'm going to find Julieta. If you see her before I do, ask her to meet me in my office." He kisses me quickly on the lips and before he leaves us Frida says, "I'm here Luca if you want me to talk with her."

My heart is racing; I don't know exactly what is happening. I can just believe, Violeta was upset all day about our engagement and Julieta was stuck listening to her and possibly consoling her.

"Frida, I'm at a loss, I'm not certain what I should be privy to just yet. And I don't want you to feel pressured to give me all the details. But if there's something you think I should know, please tell me."

She grimaces at me, "First I should give you back your own advice, this is yours and Luca's party and we should be celebrating. And second, you and I are friends ask me whatever you want to ask me. If I don't know the answer or feel I'm violating someone's trust I will tell you."

"Well, is this fairly common with Violeta, you know, her putting the weight of her own world on the children's shoulders?"

She nods, "More with Jules less with Marcos."

"How has it been for Jules so far?"

"Most times she's been strong and unmoved. Other times, she's had to ask me or Luca to step in."

Frustrated and concerned I ask, "Besides being a shoulder to cry on, how is their relationship? Before all this happened, did they get along? And now since their separation, how do they get along?"

Frida confides, "Well, I think before her parents split up, they were a typical mother-daughter. They did things together, mainly shopping, had their mother-teenage daughter moments. And now, they still get along, but when Violeta gets annoyed with Luca she airs her grievances to Jules thus putting her in the middle. That's why we're so thrilled she's going away to college."

"Do you think the kids still need Luca here? And he shouldn't be going to New York?"

Frida nods, "Emelia he goes on business trips fairly regularly for a week or two weeks. So whether he's in New York or elsewhere they're used to it."

I say, "I hope Jules is alright. It's a lot for a teenager to manage. I'm glad she knows you and Luca are there to support her."

Julieta enters the kitchen and goes directly to the fridge. "Emmy, please excuse me." Frida whispers and leaves to talk with her niece.

Not sure what I should be doing I turn my body away from them to provide privacy. Seconds pass and I feel a breeze across my back and when I look up I see Julieta marching towards the master wing. With a tap on my shoulder, "Please tell Luca I'm with Jules in his office. We'll be waiting for him." I nod to Frida and she quickly follows Julieta.

Glancing around the main floor I don't see Luca. I set out to find him downstairs. Approaching the stairwell, I see him just getting to the top step.

"Have you seen Jules?"

I nod, "Yes, I was just coming to get you. She and Frida just went to your office."

He grabs my hand and fortunately our path to the office is free of the party guests.

Before crossing the threshold to the master wing I ask, "Luca, are you sure you want me there? This is a family matter."

"You are family now. Yes, I want you there."

"What about Jules? Think about what she may want."

He looks at his watch. "I'll go first and then you come back for us in ten minutes." He lets go of my hand and we go our separate ways.

Feeling unsure whether to rejoin the party or just wait it out in the private den, I return to the living room. When Olivia spots me she promptly comes over. She smiles, "How's my future sister-in-law doing?"

I smirk, "Have you heard the phrase, two steps forward and one step back or is it one step forward and two steps back?"

She nods, "Yes, what's going on?"

"Well, earlier Claudia confronted me and I thought we made some progress. And when Luca found us talking, I suggested they spend a few minutes together."

"That's good, right Emmy?"

"Yes, I think so. However Claudia informed Luca to speak with Jules."

Olivia takes my hand, "Oh Emmy, I'm sure it's a teenager thing. She's probably feeling some anxiety about making her big move for college."

Not exactly knowing what is going on I simply reply, "Yeah, maybe you're right. Luca said for me to get them in a few minutes. So most likely it'll be worked out by then."

Henry joins us, "Do you know where Frida and Luca are? Raffy and Nicolás want to group chat with us at the party, when Luca makes his toast." Glancing at Olivia and then back to Henry, I say, "I'll go find them."

Chapter 59

WORRIEDLY I AMBLE down the private hallway towards the master wing, thinking was it only twenty-four hours ago I first entered Luca's home? Having now just lived here almost an entire day it feels as if so much has taken place. My thoughts are interrupted by voices coming from Luca's office.

Just steps away from the entrance I hear Julieta's voice and realize her volume is much louder than the others. As they try to talk over her I can't understand what's being said. I learned my lesson the hard-way earlier and taking a deep breath I enter the room.

Having not officially visited his office previously I'm taken aback by the décor. It's spacious like all the other rooms, with high ceilings, floor to ceiling windows but the furnishings are warmer with more vibrant colors. Julieta and Frida are sitting on a midnight blue canvas upholstered couch adorned with Panamanian Indian print accent pillows and a burnt red chenille blanket rests over one end. Luca is sitting inches across from Julieta in a dark tan leather swivel chair. A distressed wood coffee table is positioned in the center. While Luca continues talking with Julieta, I quietly take my seat in a matching swivel chair opposite from Luca.

Neither of the ladies takes notice of me as they are concentrating on Luca's words. I try to understand what is being said. And just when I look towards Luca something on the table grabs my attention.

It's a small book with a colorful jacket and it reminds me of something I've seen before or have at home. Luca begins to talk in English and they turn to look at me.

Not sure what to say as it seems they are still discussing whatever issue. Luca says, "Julieta, please, if you don't believe what I'm saying to you is the truth, ask Emelia."

Julieta glares at me with tear filled eyes. "Papá no, you probably told her what to say to me."

Luca replies, "Jules, you know me better. Until a few minutes ago, I had no idea why you're upset. How could I have told Emelia what to say to you? I've been here with you."

Julieta takes the book and slides it over to me. I grab it before it falls to the floor. When I take the book in my hands I slowly examine it and realize it's the book I gave to Luca for Christmas. I smile and rub my hand gently along the front cover.

"Oh, I kept meaning to ask you if you still had this." I look to Luca and smile at him, "So long ago Luca." I flip through the pages and ask, "Jules have you read it yet? It's a great story." She doesn't say a word.

I ask, "So, what do you want to ask me?" Tears trickle down her face and she rests her head against Frida's shoulder. "Jules, I'm sorry, did I say something wrong?" I ask. Frida gives her niece a tissue and I hear Julieta clear her throat.

"When did you give my Papá that book?"

That was an easy question, I quickly answer, "My first Christmas with your family. I wrote an inscription, I'm sure I wrote the date." I flip the pages to locate my note to Luca. While I turn each page slowly Julieta says, "Were you and my father together all these years?"

I reply, "The last time I saw Luca was during that trip and then last Saturday when he surprised me at the hotel." I glance at Luca and he nods his head. I continue, "What else do you want to know?"

"My Mamá said the other day you were the reason Papá couldn't love her. How could he love you if he didn't see you?"

I think how best to answer her question, "Jules your father and I have not been in contact all these years. No phone calls, no letters, no emails, no secret meetings. There are people that you will have in your life that you love and even though you don't see them, your heart still cares for them. So that when you next meet, the love is still there. Like when you go off to college. Your family will be here, and you will be there. Just because you don't see them, doesn't mean you don't love them. Years ago your father and I loved one another. But we both made life choices that kept us apart. I can't speak for your father about this, but I know, that no matter how many years passed, I never stopped loving him."

She looks at me wide eyed and with very little expression, "You told Mamá their marriage was started with lies and not real. Is that true?"

Hesitantly I respond, "Oh. That day at the house, in the heat of the moment I said some things that shouldn't have been said. I wasn't here when your parents got married. I have no way of knowing why they got married. I just know what your father told me last Saturday, that he cared for your mother and found love in his life with the people he shared it with. And said he couldn't imagine life without you and Marcos." We sit silently looking at each other.

Not sure what to say, I inquire, "Jules, what is this all about? If I hurt you please tell me so I can make things right again. I never wanted to cause you this sadness."

Frida whispers to Julieta and she nods at her aunt. Clearing her throat Frida says, "Violeta was very upset today when she learned from Marcos that you and Luca are engaged. And Jules thought after all that Violeta was rambling about, that Luca never really wanted his children because he wasn't in love with their mother. Thus making Jules feel like she and her brother were mistakes."

I glance at Luca and nod my head as my eyes begin to water thinking about how hurtful Violeta was to her own daughter to say such things. And yet, I can understand after all that's been said these last few days about how much her father loves me and loved me, why Julieta might feel this way.

Taking a deep breath I respond, "Jules I don't know exactly what your mother has said to you in the past and earlier today. I wasn't here to see your parents as a married couple. So, I can't speak about any of that. All I can say is what I've observed this week. And whatever the circumstance as to why or how you and your brother came into this world, came into this family, to me seems irrelevant, however, very significant to you. These days and nights I've spent with you, Marcos and your Papá, have shown me you share this special bond. A bond like this can only come from love. He's your father and he loves you. You are his daughter and you love him. You know that, right?"

"I don't know what to think right now. Why would Mamá say those things to me?"

"I don't know why she would, has she ever said that to you before?"

"No."

"How about when she was with her boyfriend did she say harsh things to you then?"

"She said some mean things but nothing like this before."

I add, "Well, your Papá told me the other day, before I said harsh things, that your Mamá is hurting, confused and just wants to fight. In no way am I giving her permission to act this way, but if she's going through a rough stage, she's just lashing out to those that are near to her and saying things that don't make much sense. Although you feel hurt, try not to take them personally."

She nods at me. I continue, "I know, easier said than done."

Luca says, "Julieta, as I've told you, all that is going on between me and Mamá has nothing to do with you and your brother. Sadly you both are caught in the middle. From the moment you were born I fell in love with you and the same for Marcos. Emelia wasn't lying; I told her I can't imagine my life without you. I know you don't believe that you were a mistake. Your Mamá and I wanted to have a family, if we didn't, neither of you would be here. Mi niña, tell me how can I help you? Do you think living here full time at our house until you leave for college will make this easier for you?"

Luca moves over to the couch and sits next to Julieta and places his arm around her, "Jules, I have and always will be your Papá, I love you. Tell me what you need." She rests her head on her father's chest.

Julieta says, "Maybe Mamá was just having a bad day. I can stay with her until you come back from your trip."

Frida says, "My sweet Jules, you know when your Papá is not here, you can come to me. Or we can all stay here when he goes to New York."

With tears streaming down her face, Julieta adds, "I just feel bad leaving Mamá alone, now especially."

Luca caresses his daughter's head, "I can understand. But promise me, if she gets this way again and I'm not here, just call Tía and she will get you and bring you back to our house. We'll take care of the rest. Yes?"

Julieta nods her head, "Yes, I promise."

Luca straightens his back, "Now, what about your brother? Was he around for this conversation? Do I need to sit with him also?"

Julieta replies, "No, he was out at a friend's house today when I was home with Mamá."

"Did you tell Abuela all this?" Luca inquires to his daughter.

She looks up to her father and says, "No, why?"

"Well she was the one that told me you had a difficult day with Mamá. I don't mind if you said something to her. I just wondered how she knew."

Julieta shakes her head, "Maybe Mamá told her."

Luca kisses Julieta on her forehead and continues to hold her close, "Tell me, what else is on your mind?"

She glances at me and then looks up to Luca. "Maybe I shouldn't ask or maybe I'm not supposed to know. But Papá, if you and Emelia loved each other, why didn't you marry her back then? What happened?"

"Oh mi niña, I've asked myself that same question. And after reuniting with Emelia, I've discovered I can't spend the rest of my life questioning what happened between then and now, for I can't change a single thing. So for me to love and live life fully, I must be grateful that somehow we found our way back to each other. And we have to believe this was the plan all along."

"Papá, I am happy, truly happy for you and Emelia. It's just so much has changed in the last year. And now I'll be going away to school. The life we once had all living at the same house is completely over and as much as I want to grow up and be an adult, part of me is sad to leave all that behind. Seems like time is passing so fast now and I just want to slow it down." She places her head against Luca's chest. And he holds her tightly.

In her youthful observation Julieta has described so tenderly and so eloquently, how most of us feel about life. And the four of us sit quietly together reflecting on all she has shared and not one of us has a dry eye.

Frida passes tissues to all including Luca and when I reach for one, Frida motions for me to join her on the couch. I nestle close to her. Luca gazes at each of us and says, "Julieta, my loving and wise daughter, I'm sorry you're feeling the anxiety and sadness of growing up. But if it helps you get through it any easier, know we all experience this, even when we're all grown up."

She looks up to her dad, "You do? How do you get through it?"

With all eyes on Luca he continues, "Well, it's taken me years to learn this; first, when I look to my future, I realize sometimes you need to leave things in the past. And I reflect on those memories and the people that I shared them with and tell myself how lucky I was to have those experiences. Second, when I'm about to make a big change in my life, I must think it through and be confident this is the right path, even if it turns out to be the wrong one. That way I'm certain all will happen as it should. And finally, this one is the hardest, for all the moments we spend looking back and looking towards the future, you must never forget to give the most attention, to what's happening here and now."

Suddenly Henry rushes into Luca's office, "I thought you should know your guests are growing tired waiting for you." His expression changes from playful to serious when he sees us. "Oh, no, what's happened? I can tell them all to go home."

Julieta hugs her father and when they separate she says, "No, Tío don't let them leave. Tonight, we're here to celebrate Papá and Emmy's engagement."

We all rise from the couch and I glance to Luca. He says, "Henry, Emelia and I will join the party in a few minutes." Henry nods to his brother as the three of them leave Luca's office and close the door behind them.

Luca says, "I know, you were right, I should have talked with my kids about what happened the other day. I didn't make it a priority or I was avoiding the topic. So let me have it. And then I will call Violeta and we can go back to the party."

Before I sit on the couch I take the book from the coffee table. Once I'm seated I flip through the beginning pages to find my inscription. And there it is after all these years.

Feliz Navidad Luciano,

 This story made me think of us. My Christmas Wish for you,
May the love and encouragement from those around you continue
to fuel your kindhearted soul.
 Love always, Emelia

Luca sits beside me and says, "Mi Lia, what are you doing?"

I place the book between us so he can read the inscription too. I reply, "I wanted to spend a moment with my younger self by reading the words I wrote to you." He glances over them.

"Luca, I'm not the type of person to let you have it. And your call with Violeta maybe you should wait a while. Anyway ... Jules was very honest with us. We should think about all she said especially the part about slowing things down."

He looks at me with confusion, "You want to call off our engagement?"

I reply, "No, that's not what I was thinking. Do you?"

He nods, "No, so what are you saying?"

"Well, during this last year, your children had to face their parents' separation and had to endure their mother's new relationship with another man. They've had to live in two different homes. Do you think they're ready for you to be married to someone so soon that they barely even know?" He sits looking at me.

I continue, "What I'm saying is, let's all just settle into this and then we can plan accordingly. I love you. And I want to marry you. But, I also want us to enjoy this getting to know you stage, the dating, the romance, the good surprises all that we missed out on years ago. What do you think?"

He holds my hand in his, "When you put it that way, it does make sense. I have been fast tracking us all week. But I won't agree to postpone our nuptials for years."

I smile at him, "I don't want a long engagement either." He kisses me and we leave his office to join our guests.

Before we enter the party area he whispers, "Plus, if we want to make a couple of babies of our own we can't wait too long." Kissing my temple we stroll hand in hand into the kitchen.

I smile, thinking from this point forward that my life with Luca is going to be unpredictable, and I love it.

Chapter 60

AS WE ENTER the kitchen I see the waiters loading up their trays with champagne glasses. Luca smiles at me and whispers, "I guess they're ready for us."

He leads me into the larger living room and we find our guests scattered around either sitting or standing. The fireplace is lit, music surrounds us and the waiters are passing out the champagne. Henry approaches us, "If you wait a minute, I'll get the kids up here." Luca nods to his brother as Henry hands Luca some device. Henry instructs, "Hold this and say hello to everyone before Abuelo falls asleep again."

Luca raises the screen and we see Raffy, Abuelo and the rest of his family at home. Abuelo does look sleepy in his pajamas and robe. They're all smiling at us. And with the guests chattering and the music playing I can't hear them. So I do the typical wave and smile back. Luca says, *"Hola, Buena noches."* [Hello, good evening.]

They too return the wave and Teresa motions for me to show her the ring. I laugh and present both my hands and kiss each of the ringed fingers before showing her. That way Abuelo can see the other ring too. I look to Luca and I surprise him with a gentle kiss on his cheek. He laughs. And with his hands holding the device, I wrap my arms around him.

Luca taps on the screen and suddenly Nicolás and his wife are on view too. They wave at us and Luca whispers, "Emelia, this is Carla, Nicky's wife." I wave to both of them and Carla signals for me to display my ring. After I flaunt it I gesture something to her. Carla laughs and stands to show Luca and me her very pregnant belly. We blow them kisses and Nicolás bestows a kiss on the enormous baby bump.

Henry returns with a parade of children following him and he grabs the device from Luca. One of the waiters comes to us and Luca takes both glasses from the tray and gives me one. He asks the waiter to lower the volume of the music.

While we wait for everyone to receive a glass and the music to be silenced Luca and I approach the middle of the room and he asks for Julieta and Marcos to stand near to us.

Julieta and I make eye contact and she gives me a sweet smile and I smile and nod back to her. With Henry off to the side I can still see Luca's family on the screen with all the others standing near to us.

Luca begins, "Good evening everyone, I am, ah, WE are." He smiles at me and I hear some giggles. "We are so fortunate to be surrounded by our loving family and friends this evening. Last night, as you all know, I proposed to Emelia and when she said yes all the pieces in my life finally fit together. Our journey began long ago when my sister Frida introduced me to Emelia on one ordinary night. And upon meeting this beautiful woman, I learned immediately that evening was going to be far from ordinary." He pauses, looks into my eyes and kisses my hand.

"Emelia was visiting to attend Frida and Max's wedding. Lucky for me she spent a week with us. I got to know her and get close to her and our friendship developed. Since my sister was busy getting married, I nobly volunteered to take care of Emelia." He smiles as the group laughs.

"We were thrown together and after the week was over, we realized more than a friendship had transpired. But, we, or I was a fool and allowed for life to get in the way. The next year, Emelia thankfully, joined us again for Christmas and allowed this fool, to win her heart again."

He clears his throat and continues, "After that Christmas I was supposed to arrange my life to include Emelia. But fate had other plans for me, for us. I stand here with my family and my friends, many of whom I would never have met, had I traveled down a different path. I am grateful to have you all in my life. You know that I love you. Well, most of you." He looks over to Rojelio and they smirk at each other.

"Destiny, destiny; this word that has been on my mind since Emelia opened the hotel room door to me last Saturday; when she actually was expecting my little brother Henry." Luca looks to Henry and they share smiles.

"Every second, every minute, every hour and every day, that I have spent with Emelia this week has been extraordinary. It reminds me of those first hours, days and years when Jules and Marcos came into my life."

He looks to them, "I'd watch you breathe and sleep. I couldn't wait to be with you. Even if all you were going to do was sleep. And Marcos slept a lot. And your first smiles, your first giggles and your first words, I was and always am amazed that you are a part of me and grateful that we'll be connected for the rest of our lives. Our love our bond is so strong. I knew that all these years, but during this past year, it has helped us get to the other side of this." Luca walks over to his kids and kisses them.

"Emelia and I are here with all of you, looking towards our futures together. Thank you for walking beside me on this road that has led me back to Emelia. We invite you all to continue this journey with us. Let's raise our glasses for the love of family, the love of friends and for the love of my life Emelia. Salud!"

With tear filled eyes, Luca kisses me and when we part we tap our glasses together and sip champagne while looking at one another. I say, "My heart forever belongs to you." He responds, "And my heart is forever yours to keep."

Luca's family and friends come near to us and we all tap our glasses. And each and every one exchanges hugs and kisses. Once again, Luca hands me his glass as little Eduardo leaps into Luca's arms. Seeing the joy between Luca and this little boy makes me think of my love's unexpected suggestion of us adding to this family.

Frida hugs me and says, "After all this we will finally be sisters."

I reply, "The love in my heart for you and your family is overflowing. And knowing we'll be part of each other's lives again is beyond any words I can describe. I love you my sister friend, I love you." We hug again.

Henry comes to us with the family on video chat and Luca and I raise our glasses to them. They in turn show us a variety of mugs, cups and glasses toasting us.

With everyone dancing, singing and devouring Sofia's delicious tiramisu, our engagement gathering even with all the bumps and turns has a glorious finale.

Chapter 61

⎯⎯⎯⎯⎯⎯⎯⎯⎯⎯

THE CATERING TEAM is packing up their trucks after leaving the kitchen and party rooms neat and tidy. Luca and I wave goodbye to our last guests. And when we get inside, I notice most of the flowers and all the balloons went home with our family and friends.

Suddenly I'm feeling anxious about leaving tomorrow. So I head back to the bedroom to pack, as Luca wraps things up with the caterers.

With almost all my clothes away, I hang up my outfit for the morning. Just as I'm about to brush my teeth, Luca enters my dressing room holding two glasses of water. I take one from him and smile, "Thank you."

While I take a sip, Luca says, "This house is too big when it's just you and me."

I inquire, "Should we ask some of your family to come back? I know Mateo won't be hard to convince."

He laughs, "No that's not what I meant. After the caterers left I looked around for you and didn't see you. And I had to come all the way back here to find you and be near to you."

I move towards Luca and he takes me in his arms and I wrap mine around his waist. With my face pressed against his chest, I purr and say, "Honestly, I was sort of hiding from you."

He asks, "Why?"

"I started thinking about tomorrow and was feeling slightly nervous."

He caresses my back, "Why? Are you nervous about me going home with you?"

I look into his eyes, "We've never gotten past this point. You know, this is a big step for you and me. After all these years we're finally doing this and I almost can't believe this is happening."

Rubbing my face he says, "Do you want to get settled alone at your home first and I join you later this week?"

I nod, "No, that's not what I was thinking. Do you?"

He nods, "Me neither, I just want you to be happy. But if I'm making you nervous, I was offering to do whatever it takes, for you to feel more at ease."

I smile and kiss him tenderly on his lips. "Luca, what I'm feeling is a good nervous. Like, how you feel before a first kiss, or when you're on a roller-coaster and those brief moments before you take that first dip or on Christmas morning when you first see all those gifts under the tree. You know something good is about to happen, but it hasn't happened yet."

Relieved he says, "Oh Emelia, I thought maybe you were experiencing some hesitations for us living together. You know, you've lived a single life for many years and maybe this is all too much and too soon for you. I get that."

I nod and with a smile I say, "I can't wait to cohabitate with you. I just hope you adjust as smoothly at my homes as I have in your homes."

Confused he says, "Homes? You have more than one home?"

I giggle, "I can't believe this never came up. And I guess until about twelve hours ago, I was flying home solo. Yes, I have two homes. Well, now three if I'm counting this one."

I wink at him, "I've hit the jackpot. In just one week, I now have three homes, two rings, another family and the most handsome loving fiancé. This has to be the best vacation EVER!"

He laughs, "Oh Mi Lia, you are too much. I'm going to pack a bag. And then you can tell me about your other homes."

Excitedly I say, "Good. While you do that, I need to prepare for your surprise. How much time do you need?"

With his eyes lit up, "Surprise?"

I nod, "Yes, a surprise for you."

Luca dashes into his dressing room yelling, "Just fifteen minutes."

Chapter 62

GRABBING THE CANDLES and flowers I put aside earlier, I run back to our bedroom from the kitchen with the hopes of creating a tranquil and sensual ambiance for the love of my life. Now if I could just figure out how to work this music device and the fireplace.

Luca knocks on the door to announce he's ready to join me. I open the door slowly and move quickly to the other side, trying to keep him from seeing what I'm doing. He smiles at me.

I say, "You can't possibly be finished packing. You do remember we plan to be away for two weeks."

He nods, "Oh, yes, I did remember that and I also remembered what you do for a living."

I tilt my head and smirk, "And what does that mean?"

"It means I don't need to bring that many clothes, you and I will go shopping for the rest of my wardrobe. Can you take on another client?"

I nod, "Yes, I think you might be an easy client to shop for. Now, I need your help, but don't ask any questions."

He grins at me, "Go on."

I show him the music device I've been hiding behind me, "Can you please set this thing, to play in the bedroom?"

Luca kisses me gently, "Yes of course. What type of music?"

I reply, "Either instrumental or easy listening love songs."

While he taps away on the screen I ask, "Can you also tell me how to light the fire?" After telling me where the switch is, I give him specific instructions and leave him alone while I head to the bedroom.

Everything is all set and the music is perfect. He's chosen a mix of Eddie Vedder's *Ukulele Songs*. I join him again on the other side of the door. I ask, "Are you ready for your appointment Mr. Morales?"

He closes his eyes and he lets out a tender moan. "Yes, I am ready, I think." I giggle and take his hand in mine, "Please follow me."

When we enter the bedroom Luca looks around and says, "Nicely done." I point to the bed with scattered red rose petals, "I will leave you now so you can get comfortable for your very special massage."

Before disappearing I treat him to several luscious kisses and say, "I expect to find you completely undressed when I return." His eyebrows rise as well as his grin and he says, "Of course, I will do as you command." I pat his bottom on the way to my dressing room.

Giving him a minute or so, I take off my robe and with very little props to work with I decide to just wing it and go topless. Feeling slightly shy, I dash to his closet and grab one of his dress shirts. Still rolling up the sleeves when I enter the bedroom, Luca is resting on his stomach across the bed with his feet dangling off one side.

Taking his tossed robe from the bed I hold it in my arms as I offer him a glass of water. He takes a sip and settles back down with his head resting on his arms. Standing near to his feet I ask, "Are you comfy? Do you need anything?"

"Yes, I am comfy. And all I need is right here." I feel his ankle brush up against my thigh.

I reach for the long stem rose from the night stand and begin to gently move the top of the flower against his skin starting from his right heel past his muscular calf, behind his knee, moving up his thigh to his sweet dimples. I bring the rose back to the starting point and do the same with his left leg. When the flower arrives again at the dimples I rest it across his bare back.

Pouring body lotion on my hands I massage his feet one by one. I always admired his pleasingly pedicured feet but never realized until now how smooth they really are. Getting the sense my love is not as patient as I was I decide to massage his legs simultaneously.

Crawling beside him on the bed, I prepare to tend to his upper body. Removing the rose from his back, I straddle his thighs. I lay a tender kiss on each dimple and I hear him release a moan. Leaning down I place light kisses on his back. The loose material from the shirt I'm wearing lingers on his skin and I feel his body flinch from the sensations. I remove the shirt and leave it by the edge of the bed.

I squeeze lotion into my hands and begin to work his back. I start with the lower region and when I reach up to his shoulders I press my body against his. I feel his body tremble beneath me and he whispers, "Mi Lia." Sensing, my treatment is working, I continue this method over and over again. And every time his body responds pleasurably.

When I finish with some deep tissue kneading around his shoulder blades and neck I slide over to his side and whisper, "Mr. Morales, please turn over so I may continue."

He does a full body stretch before rolling over. As he begins to position himself he quickly rises up and pulls my face towards him and thrusts his tongue into my mouth and passionately kisses me.

Luca's hands travel to my breasts and I feel him begin to move his body towards mine. I pull away from him and end our kisses. "Mr. Morales, I'm not finished with your massage yet. I believe you requested the exclusive experience."

He falls back onto the bed and says, "Emelia, I don't think I can hold off much longer. I want to be inside you right now."

Standing on the bed, securing my feet between his legs I say, "Don't worry my love your wish is my command."

He watches me while I slowly and seductively slide my panties down my thighs, past my knees and to my ankles. Tossing them to the floor, I straddle his legs while taking his hands in mine.

Luca sits up again and holds my arms behind my back. His mouth tantalizes my breasts while one of his hands finds its way between my legs. Arching my back I whisper, "But you've stopped me before the finale, the happy ending."

Releasing my hands Luca grabs my hips and lowers me down onto him. When our bodies join in the natural pace of our rhythm Luca says, "Emelia, waking up next to you every morning and sleeping beside you ever night is my happy ending. And so far, everything else in between is beyond my wildest dreams. *Quiero hacerte el amor.*" [I want to make love to you.]

Chapter 63

"Luca, how early do we need to wake up tomorrow?" He smiles, "Oh, I forgot to tell you, I switched our morning flight to the afternoon, I hope you don't mind." While gathering the rose petals from our bed I nod to him, "No, I don't mind." Luca blows out the candles as I walk away to get ready for bed.

When I return, he is adjusting the bedding and the pillows. And I sigh thinking how perfect we are together. I ask, "Have you decided yet, which side of the bed you prefer?"

He replies, "No, I haven't. Have you?"

"Before I came here, what side did you favor?"

"Emelia, that's a good question, this side, closest to the door I guess. But usually by morning I was either in the middle or the other side."

"Well then, if we start with you sleeping on your regular side of the bed, naturally you'll move towards me. I worry that if you flip sides now, you might just roll off the bed."

He looks at me with furrowed brows, "Are you trying to say, I'm too old to change my ways?"

I giggle, "Certainly not. I just thought, while we're adjusting to living together, I shouldn't come in here and push you out of your comfy spot."

Luca takes my hand and walks with me to the other side of the bed. "Mi Lia, thank you for considering my well-being, but, I'm easy going when it comes to such things. If it doesn't make much difference to you, let's start you off on this side of the bed tonight. And when we come back in a couple of weeks, we can take turns and decide then where we are most comfortable. Yes?" I sit on the bed and say, "Yes. Good plan."

After switching off the fire, Luca slides onto his side of the bed and I snuggle into his awaiting arms. "Luca, have I ever told you how much I like listening to your toasts?" He hums, "No, not that I recall. But usually I can tell by your smile and your eyes that you liked what I said."

"That first night at your apartment in Caracas, on the terrace, you made a toast to me and we drank rum together. Each toast thereafter your ease, your honesty and your powerful words have moved me. I wish I could find the nerve to speak like that in front of a roomful of people and so eloquently. I admire you for that."

Luca leans down and kisses my forehead. "Thank you Emelia. You see, when I was growing up, I learned this tradition from Abuelo and my father. No matter what was going on in our lives, good or bad, they'd always share their thoughts, their wisdom with the family. Some occasions it was a way for us to get reconnected. And it was a way for them to tell the family and friends they cared about how much they loved and appreciated them."

I sit up in bed next to Luca and say, "Well, after the very thoughtful toast you gave tonight, I've been thinking about something to say to you." Luca sits up and positions himself against the headboard, "Ok, I'm listening."

My stomach does a flip and I feel my heart racing. "Gosh, you make this seem so easy."

He laughs, "Oh Mi Lia, it's just me and you alone together in our bed. Just tell me what your heart wants to say to me." I lean to him and kiss him softly.

"It was only last Saturday, when you found the courage to come to me and tell me why we couldn't be together all those years ago. That must not have been easy for you. Nor the years we've been apart. But even so, you have been a loving father, a generous son and brother, a supportive grandson and nephew, a loyal husband, a kind friend and a successful businessman. I'm so proud of you Luca and all that you've achieved. You are a strong man with conviction. And you are a man with a tremendous heart. This heart, that still loves me. Still beats strongly for me. I want to thank you for making me feel so loved again, so cherished, so desired and so needed. After all these years, I never thought I'd find love again. I feel so fortunate that the earth, the moon and the stars aligned for us perfectly to give us this opportunity once more.

I don't know what life has in store for us over the next few days, months and years. I do know this, a life shared with you is better than a life apart from you. And each and every night when I rest my head upon your chest, just before I fall asleep, I lie silent until I hear the rhythm of your tender heart and soon its sweet song lulls me to sleep."

Luca leans towards me with tears in his eyes and caresses my face. "That was so lovely Emelia. You're a natural. Soon you'll be swimming and giving toasts in front of a roomful of people."

I smile and say, "Slow it down, Luca. Thankfully for the next few weeks, neither of my homes has a pool. Now let's go to sleep before you get any ideas to get me out swimming."

He laughs as we both slide back down into the bed and snuggle together. "That's right Emelia you're supposed to tell me about your homes. Where do you live and where will you be taking me tomorrow?"

"Ah, good question Luca. Well, a few years ago, I bought a farmhouse in Connecticut that needed some renovations. And I rent a little apartment in a client's brownstone in Manhattan."

He clears his throat, "How little?"

I giggle, "Well, it's a one bedroom apartment on the third floor about the size of the master den and bedroom here, but with only a few closets and not the size of these."

He laughs, "And the house, how far have you gotten on the renovations?"

"I would say the house is half done. But the rooms that haven't been worked on yet, are not in bad condition. They just need updating. You'll see. I don't want to tell you too much. I think it's best for you to just experience it first without knowing more."

He asks, "Are we going to the house tomorrow or the apartment?"

I reply, "I thought, of course depending on your work schedule, we'd first go to the house. And either Sunday or Monday we go to the apartment and stay there the rest of the week. What do you think?"

I feel him nodding his head. "I don't have any meetings on schedule until Tuesday. And I can work from home in either place on Monday. So, let's plan on staying at the house until Monday night."

I nod, "See, I told you we'll make good travel buddies."

He laughs, "Emelia, when you said that to me the other morning, I thought you found out about me flying back with you."

I look at him, "Oh, that's why you made that funny face at me." I give Luca a quick peck. And rest my head against his chest.

"Luca before we fall asleep, can I ask you something? And if you don't want to talk about it now, I'll understand."

"Ok, what do you want to know?"

"How did your conversation with your mother go?"

He sighs, "I'll go into more detail tomorrow with you. But it was more pleasant and more encouraging than I thought it would be. I think you were right when you said we're getting there."

"That's good to hear Luca. I'd hate for us to fly off tomorrow with you and your mom still at odds."

With my hand resting on his chest, I say, "Good night Luciano my love." He purrs, "Good night Mi Lia, mi amor."

Chapter 64

EVERYTHING IS DIFFERENT today on my flight back home. Sitting next to the window not on the aisle I watch the airport crew finish loading up the belly of the plane. Glancing further in the distance I see the clear blue sky ahead while I stretch my legs in my First Class seat, another change of plans today and a very welcome perk. As the plane reverses back from the gate I sit and wonder as I stare out the window what today would feel like if it all remained the same as I planned three months ago when I purchased my tickets.

I would be sitting on the aisle in coach class. I would be listening to *My Brothers* playlist either seeking solace or getting lost in my thoughts from the week I just had with my friend and her family.

Now as the plane taxis to the runway I turn away from the window and look around the cabin. I notice the seats ahead and the closed cockpit door. And as I shift my gaze to the left my heart races when I take in my most beloved and treasured view of all, my travel mate.

I was most thrilled and elated when I entered the airport today and went through the lines of check in and security not alone but with the love of my life. For most of the way we walked hand in hand.

After we boarded the plane and took our seats, the flight attendant brought us two glasses of champagne. Looking into each other's eyes, Luca said, "I haven't felt this excited about a trip in a very long time. I want to commemorate our first flight together. The funny thing is I have no idea what awaits me when we reach our destination. But I don't have any worries, as long as I am with you; I know I will love each and every part of this extraordinary journey."

Secured in my window seat with Luca next to me on the aisle a position I gladly gave up for him today and for all our future travels. The plane rushes for takeoff as we hold hands and lock eyes.

Today I'm not counting the seconds after the plane lifts off I'm not even peering out the window. When I booked these tickets I would never have predicted my return flight home would have me holding hands with my fiancé as we embark on our next phase of melding our lives together.

Promises that were made so many years ago that for reasons I cannot question nor despise were pushed to another chapter in our lives. Luca's promises to me just last Saturday have been kept. He promised everything would be different when I travelled back home today and even with all his assurances I could never have prepared for this moment.

The nose of the plane is powerfully moving skyward as we still gaze at one other. Luca takes his free hand and brushes it against my cheek. He asks, "Mi Lia, are you happy?"

I giggle and my eyes water slightly. I take his hand and press it against my chest. "Oh Luca, am I happy? My heart is jumping up and down with excitement."

His eyes glisten and he takes my other hand, gives it a tender kiss and holds it over his heart. I smile when I feel his heart pounding as vigorously as mine. I whisper, *Te amo con todo mi alma.* He replies, "And I love you with all my soul."

Author Biography

Marcella Vineis grew up in New York City in an Italian American home. Her passion for writing began in her younger years exchanging letters with pen pals who have become life-long friends.

Vineis considers herself a true romantic, and that comes through in her debut novel, *At This Place, At This Time*. Now residing in Connecticut, she enjoys spending time with her family and friends, traveling, and going to sporting events, concerts, films, and plays.